WILD HORSE MESA

WILD HORSE MESA

ZANE GREY

Thorndike Press • Thorndike, Maine

Thorndike Large Print ® Western Series.

Published in 1993 by arrangement with Golden West
Literary Agency.

The tree indicium is a trademark of Thorndike Press.

The text of this Large Print edition is unabridged.
Other aspects of the book may vary from the original.

Set in 16 pt. News Plantin by Juanita Macdonald.

Printed in the United States on acid-free, high opacity paper. ∞

Library of Congress Cataloging in Publication Data

Grey, Zane, 1872–1939.
    Wild Horse Mesa / Zane Grey.
      p.   cm.
    ISBN 0-7862-0075-8 (alk. paper : lg. print)
    1. Large type books. I. Title.
    [PS3513.R6545W5 1993]
    813'.52—dc20   93-35503

WILD HORSE MESA

Chapter 1

The mystery and insurmountable nature of Wild Horse Mesa had usurped many a thoughtful hour of Chane Weymer's lonely desert life in Utah. Every wandering rider had a strange story to tell about this vast tableland. But Chane had never before seen it from so lofty and commanding a height as this to which Toddy Nokin, the Piute, had led him; nor had there ever before been so impelling a fascination as that engendered by the Indian.

For the Piute claimed that it was the last refuge of the great wild stallion, Panquitch, and his band.

Panquitch! He had been chased out of Nevada by wild-horse wranglers, of whom Chane was not the last; Mormons had driven the stallion across Utah, where in the canyoned fastnesses south of the Henry Mountains he had disappeared.

Chane's gaze left the mesa to fall upon the swarthy lineaments of his companion. Could he place credence in Toddy Nokin? The Piutes loved fine horses and were not given to confiding in white hunters. It occurred to Chane, however, that he had befriended this Indian.

"Toddy — you sure Panquitch — on Wild Horse Mesa?" queried Chane, in his labored mixture of Piute and Navajo.

The Indian had the solemn look of one whose confidence had not been well received.

"How you know?" went on Chane, eagerly.

Toddy Nokin made a slow, sweeping gesture toward the far northern end of Wild Horse Mesa, almost lost in dim purple distance. The motion of arm and hand had a singular character, never seen in gesture save that of an Indian. It suggested deviations of trail, deep canyons to cross, long distance to cover. Then Toddy Nokin spoke in his own tongue, with the simplicity of a chief whose word was beyond doubt. Chane's interpretation might not have been wholly correct, but it made the blood dance in his veins. Panquitch had been seen to lead his band up over the barren trailless rock benches that led to the towering wall of the unscalable mesa. These wild horses left no tracks. They had not returned. Keen-eyed Piutes had watched the only possible descents over the red benches. Panquitch was on top of the mesa, free with the bighorn sheep and the eagles. The fact wrung profound respect and admiration from Chane Weymer, yet fired

8

him with passionate resolve. For a long time that wild mesa had haunted him. The reason for it, the alluring call of the wandering lofty wall, now seemed easily understood.

"Panquitch, I've got track of you at last!" he exclaimed, exultantly.

There awoke in Chane then something of abandon to what he had always longed for — a wild freedom without work or restraint or will other than his own wandering fancies. Indeed, his range life had been rough and hard enough, but up until the last year he had been under obligation to his father and other employers, and always there had been a powerful sense of duty and a love for his younger brother, Chess. These had acted as barriers to his natural instincts. Chess was eighteen now and considered himself very much of a man, so much so that he resented Chane's guardianship.

"Boy Blue doesn't need his big brother any more," soliloquized Chane, half sadly, remembering Chess's impatience at being watched over. Time, indeed, had passed swiftly. Chess was almost a man. It seemed only a short while since he had been a baby boy, back there in Colorado, where he had been born. Chane reflected on his own age — thirty-four, and on those past years when this beloved brother had been a little child.

Those early days in Colorado had been happy ones. The Weymers were a family of close ties. Chane's father had been a ranchman, cattleman, and horse dealer. It had been on the prairie slopes of Colorado, under the eastern shadows of the Rockies, that Chane had learned what was now his calling — the hunting of wild horses. In time he sought wilder country — Nevada, Utah — and his brother Chess, true to childish worship, had followed him. There had been a couple of years in which the boy had been amenable; then had come the inevitable breaking out. Not that Chess had been bad, Chane reflected, but just that he wanted to be his own boss. Chane had left him, several weeks ago, back across the rivers and the stony brakes of that Utah wilderness, in the little Mormon town of St. George. Chess had begged to go on this expedition to the Piute country, where Chane had come to buy a bunch of Indian mustangs. Here Chane's musings and reflections were interrupted by Toddy Nokin, who said he would go down to his camp.

"No want leave daughter alone," he added, significantly. Chane was reminded that one of the horse-wranglers who had fallen in with him — Manerube by name — was not a man he would care to trust.

The Indian's moccasined feet padded softly

on the rocks. Presently Chane was left to himself, and his gaze and mind returned to the object that had caused him to scale the heights — Wild Horse Mesa.

This early September day had been one of storm, clearing toward late afternoon, leaving cloud pageants in the sky to west and north. At the moment there seemed no promise of color — something which Chane always looked for in the sky. All the northland was obscured in paling clouds, leaden in hue.

Chane was at loss to understand the spell which had fascinated him since his first sight of Wild Horse Mesa. It was as if he had been arrested by a prophetic voice that bade him give heed. He could not grasp the vague intimation as a warning; it was rather a call which urged him to come, to seek, to labor, to find. Chane thought of the wild stallion, Panquitch, and though he thrilled, he could not satisfy himself that pursuit of the great horse wholly accounted for this strange beckoning.

A broken mass of gray storm clouds had lodged against the west end of the mesa, where the precipitous red wall towered above the waved area of wind-worn rock. Apparently the cloud hung there, as if against an obstruction, yet it appeared to change form. Chane gazed as he had a thousand times, in idle or

11

wondering moments, yet there was a subtle difference now, either in the aspect of this mesa or in himself. That made him keen-eyed as an Indian and unusually thoughtful.

But it seemed only a vast landscape, grand because of outline and distance, yet at the moment dull and somber. Still, was it not hiding something? The lower edge of the broken mass of cloud extended far down the wall; in some places the top of the mesa was obscured. Above the cloud and all to the west was clear. The sun had gone under the huge dark slope that climbed from the undulating canyon country to the mountain.

The cloud above Wild Horse Mesa broke in the center and spread slowly, while the gray color almost imperceptibly changed. Between the mesa and the mountain slope sank a vast deep notch, through which V-shaped portal the ends of the earth seemed visible. Low down the distant rock surfaces were gold; above them the belt of sky was yellow. Canopying this band of pale sky stretched a roof of cloud, an extension of that canopy enshrouding the mesa, and it had begun to be affected by the sinking sun. At first the influence was gradual; then suddenly occurred swift changes, beautiful and evanescent — white clouds turning to rose, with centers of opal, like a coral shell.

The moment came when Chane saw the west wall of Wild Horse Mesa veiled in lilac haze. He was watching a phenomenon of nature that uplifted him, that indefinably troubled him. The flat roof of the cloud took on a fiery vermilion; the west end of the shroud became a flame, and mesa, sky, mountain slope, and canyon depths seemed transfigured with a glory that was not of earth. It held Chane through its stages of infinite beauty — only a few moments of evanescent power — and then the burning fire changed to the afterglow tones of gold, silver, violet. Last came a single instant when the whole world of rock lay under a mantle of purple. When that faded, there spread the encroaching of the shades of twilight.

Chane left his lofty perch and descended rapidly over the smooth rock benches, zigzagging the curved slopes, and at last the cedared ridge above Beaver Canyon. Twilight yielded to night; the babble of the brook broke the desert stillness. Then a bright camp fire shining through darkness changed the vague spell that had come to him upon the heights.

The camp fire lighted up the weird cedar trees and the dark forms of men standing in a half-circle. The scene was natural, one Chane had long been accustomed to, yet just now it struck him singularly. He halted out there in the darkness. One of the men was talking but, owing to the rush of the brook, Chane could not distinguish any words. Several Piutes stood grouped near the fire, wild, picturesque figures, lean, ragged, dishevelled, with their high-crowned sombreros.

Chane moved on again, not intentionally walking stealthily, yet approaching quite closely to the camp fire before his boot crunched on a stone. He saw Manerube start and cease his earnest talk to the three men who had been listening intently. They too relaxed their attention. It struck Chane that his abrupt arrival had interrupted a colloquy not intended for his sharing. If he had not been deliberately watching the group he would not have observed how obvious this was. But he had marked the quick change and it roused his suspicions. What were these men up to?

They had all been strangers to him before this visit to the Piute country. Three of them had ridden into his camp one night a few weeks before. They claimed to be wild-horse wranglers on the way across the rivers, and offered their services in exchange for camp rations, of which they were short. Chane had been glad to have them help him collect and run the mustangs he was buying to sell to the Mormons, and he could not find any fault with them. Manerube, however, who had joined

14

them recently, was not a man to inspire Chane's liking. He had been loud in acclaiming himself the best wild-horse wrangler in Utah; he was overbearing in manner and he was brutal to horses, and lastly he had made trouble with the Piutes.

Chane strode into the camp-fire circle with the thought in mind that he might be moody and unreasonable, but he would keep a sharper eye on these unsolicited comrades.

Manerube had his back to the camp fire. He had a rider's figure, long, lithe, round of limb. As Chane came up Manerube turned to disclose the sunburnt face of a man under thirty, bold, striking, sardonic. It bore lines not easy to read, and its gleaming light eyes and curling blond mustache seemed to hide much. Manerube claimed to be Mormon. Chane had rather doubted this, though the fellow was well educated and had a peculiar dominating manner.

"Well, how was the little squaw sweetheart tonight?" he drawled at Chane. One of the other men snickered.

Chane had good-naturedly stood a considerable amount of this scarcely veiled badinage. He had not been above being friendly and pleasant to Toddy Nokin's dusky-eyed daughter — a friendliness Manerube had misconstrued.

"See here, Manerube," replied Chane, at last out of patience, "Sosie is not my sweetheart."

Manerube laughed derisively and seemed more than usually antagonistic.

"Bah! You can't fool a Mormon when it comes to women, white or red," he said.

"I've lived a good deal among Mormons," returned Chane. "I never noticed they talked insultingly about women."

Manerube's eyes wavered for a second, yet something was added to their pale gleam.

"Insult a squaw!" he ejaculated, coarsely. "Say, your bluff don't work."

"It's no bluff. I don't make bluffs," replied Chane, deliberately. "Sosie's nothing to me. And I'm telling you not to hint otherwise."

"Weymer, I don't believe you," returned Manerube.

Chane took a quick long stride toward the other. He rather welcomed this turn to the situation.

"Do you call me a liar?" he demanded.

There was a moment's silence. The Piutes took note of Chane's sharp voice. Manerube's comrades backed away slowly. He made a quick angry gesture that was wholly instinctive. Then he controlled his natural feeling. His face showed sudden restraint, though it remained just as bold.

"If Sosie's nothing to you, why'd you tell her father to keep her away from me?" demanded Manerube, avoiding Chane's direct question. "She's only a squaw, and one white man's the same as another to her."

"Sosie likes white men. So do all these Indian girls," said Chane. "They're simple, primitive children of the desert. That's why so many of them are degraded by such men as you, Manerube."

Manerube evidently held himself under strong control because of some feeling other than fear. The red faded out of his face and his eyes glared in the camp-fire light.

"Chane, I heard about you over in Bluff," he burst out, in scorn. "And now I'm not wondering whether it's true or not."

"What'd you hear?" queried Chane, calmly.

"That you'd been a Navajo squaw man."

Chane laughed at the absurdity of that and replied: "No, I never married a Navajo. But I'll tell you what. I'd sooner marry a girl like Sosie and be decent to her, than treat her as you would."

Manerube eyed Chane guardedly and studiously.

"Well," he said, finally, "I'll treat Sosie as I like."

"Not while you're in my camp," flashed Chane. "I didn't ask your help or your company. I don't like either. You take your horses and pack, and get out, pronto."

"I'll think it over tonight," replied Manerube.

His impudent assurance irritated Chane more than his insults. Moreover, the intent faces of the three comrades were not lost upon Chane. These men had laughed and joked on a former occasion when Chane had voiced his objection to Manerube's actions. They were different now. There was something wrong here. It did not need to be voiced aloud that these four men understood one another. At the same time he grasped the subtle fact that they were not unaware of his reputation. Chane's lone-wolf ways and his championship of Indian maidens, his hard fist and swift gun, forced a respect on the wild-horse ranges of Utah and Nevada.

"Manerube, I reckon you don't want any advice from me," declared Chane. "But I'll tell you — don't let me run into you with Sosie."

Chane looked into Manerube's eyes with the same deliberate intent that had characterized his speech. It was the moment which fixed hatred between him and this self-called Mormon. Chane wanted to read what he had to expect from the man. And his first impression had been right — Manerube was not what he pretended to be and he was dangerous.

Sooner or later the issue would be forced. Chane did not care how soon that would come. He had lived a good many years among hard men of the open ranges, and it was not likely that he would be surprised. Nevertheless, as he turned away from the group he watched them out of the tail of his eye. He carried his roll of bedding away from the camp, out under a thick cedar tree, where the night shadow was deep.

Snug in his blankets, he stretched his long limbs and felt grateful that slumber would soon come. But he was too sanguine, for sleep held aloof. Somehow the day had been different from others. It had left him full of resentment toward Manerube and his associates, worried despite his fearlessness. Most significant of all, however, was a sense of dissatisfaction with his life.

If Manerube stayed longer at this camp and persisted in his attentions to the little Piute girl — which things he would almost certainly do — there was going to be trouble. Chane had settled this in his mind before he gave Manerube to understand what would happen. But as a matter of fact Chane did not know exactly what would happen. He had concluded that the man was dangerous, but not out in the open face to face; and Chane decided to force a fight at the slightest opportunity and let Manerube's response settle how serious it would be.

Then Chane pondered over the other men who had attached themselves to him. Day by day, and especially since the arrival of Manerube, they had grown less welcome in his camp. They called themselves Jim Horn, Hod Slack, and Bud McPherson — names that in this wilderness did not mean anything. Chane was not well acquainted on the south side of the San Juan River, having been there only once before. During that time he had hunted horses among the Navajos. The Piutes did not know these men well, and that in itself was thought-provoking. Horn and Slack had not appeared to exhibit any force of character, but McPherson had showed himself to be a man of tremendous energy and spirit. If he had not been so closed-mouthed about himself, so watchful, and manifestly burdened with secret ponderings, Chane would have liked him. Chane brought all his observation and deduction to bear on the quartet, and came to the conclusion that the most definite thing he could grasp was their attitude of watchful waiting. Waiting for what! It could only be for him to get together all the horses he meant to buy from the Piutes. There was nothing else for them to wait for. Wild-horse hunting had not developed into a profitable business, yet it had sustained a few straggling bands of horse thieves. Chane almost convinced himself that these unwelcome wranglers in his camp belonged to such evil fraternity, and that aroused his resentment to anger. But he must be cautious. He was alone and could not expect help from the few Piutes in the vicinity. It seemed wisest to delay completing his horse deal with the Indians.

"Pretty mess I'm in," he muttered to himself, disparagingly. "This horse-hunting is no good." And he reflected that years of it had made him what he was — only a wild-horse wrangler, poor and with no prospects of any profit. Long he had dreamed of a ranch where he could breed great horses, of a home and perhaps a family. Vain, idle dreams! The romance, the thrilling adventure, the constant change of scene and action, characteristic of the hard life of a wild-horse hunter, had called to him in his youth and fastened upon him in his manhood. What else could he do now? He had become a lone hunter, a wanderer of the wild range, and it was not likely that he could settle down to the humdrum toil of a farmer or cattleman.

"I might — if — if —" he whispered, and looked up through the dark foliage of the cedar to the white blinking stars. In the shadow, and in the pale starlight, there seemed to hover a vague sweet face that sometimes haunted his inner vision. Bitterly he shut his eyes. It was a delusion. He was no longer a boy. The best in his life seemed past, gone, useless. What folly to dream of a woman! And suddenly into his mind flashed Manerube's scathing repetition of gossip spoken in Bluff. Squaw man!

"All because I befriended a Navajo girl — as I've done here for Sosie!" he muttered. It galled Chane. Suppose that rumor got to the ears of his father and mother, still living at the old home in Colorado! What would his little brother Chess think? Chane still cherished the family pride. If he had not made anything of his life it had not been because he was not well born, or had lacked home influences and schooling. It shocked him to realize how far he had gone. Few people in that wild country would rightly interpret attention or succor to an Indian girl. Chane had never cared in the least what had been said about him or his ways. He had been blunt in speech and forceful in action toward those brutes who betrayed the simple-hearted, primitive Indian maidens. And these cowards had retaliated by spreading poisonous rumor. What little justice there was in it! He knew deep in his soul how honest and fair he had been. But he had befriended more than one

22

little Indian girl like Sosie, and ridden with them and talked with them, interested, amused, and sometimes in his lonely moods grateful even for their feminine company. Chane could not see how that had been wrong. Yet these Indian girls were only too quick to care for a white man — good or bad. They were little savages of the desert. Chane realized where he had given a wrong impression of himself, perhaps to them, certainly to the white men who had run across him among the Indians.

Chane endured a bitter hour of reflection and self-analysis. A morbid resignation seemed about to fix its dark lichen upon his heart. What folly these dreams! How futile to love a horse! Was even the grand Panquitch on Wild Horse Mesa worth the time and toil and pang that it would take to capture him, if such were possible? What hope lay in the future? Why not forget his absurd dreams, his strange belief in the romance that would come to him, his parents and the little brother? Why not drift as the tumbleweed of the desert, where the wind listed? Why not find some solace in little Sosie's dusky eyes?

But with that thought a revolt stirred in Chane, a fight against the insidious weakness which would make him ashamed of himself. Whatever he had done and however he had failed of the thing people called success, he had remained a man. He clung to the idea. Evil tongues could not hurt him. His life, profitless as it was, still had wonderful charm. He was free, healthy, active, he found that the wild desert meant infinitely more to him than he had known; he had loved a horse, and he could love another. There was always his brother to return to. What did anything else matter? Thus the dark mood was beaten down and conquered.

The cool wind had died away, except for low intermittent moans through the cedars, and the lonely desert silence settled down. The brook murmured faintly and the insects sang their melancholy notes, but these only accentuated the vast dead stillness of the solitude. Chane fell asleep.

He awoke at dawn, when the dark luminous light was changing to gray. The September air held a nipping edge of frost. Chane found that something new, a spirit of strength, had seemed to awaken with him. Not resignation nor bitter dissatisfaction with his lot, but stranger, stronger faith! His life must be what he felt, not the material gain he had once wanted. He lay there until he heard the men round the camp fire and the crack of unshod hoofs on the stones. Then he arose, and pulling on his boots, and taking up his coat, he strode toward the camp. His saddle and packs lay under a cedar. From a pack he lifted his gun belt, containing a Colt and shells, which he buckled round his waist. This he had not been in the habit of wearing.

Two Piutes had ridden in and sat on their mustangs, waiting to be invited to eat. Three of the men were busy — Slack rolling biscuit dough, Horn coming up with water, and Mc-Pherson cutting slices from a haunch of sheep meat. Chane's quick eye caught sight of Manerube washing down at the brook.

"Say, Weymer, your Injun pards hev rustled in for chineago, as usual," remarked Slack, dryly.

"So I see. Seems a habit of riders — rustling in on my camp to eat," replied Chane.

"Wal, them Piutes are pretty white. They'd never let any fellar go hungry," said Horn.

McPherson looked up at Chane with a curious little gleam in his sharp eyes. He was not so young as his comrades. His face showed experience of wild life in all its phases, and the bronzed lean cheeks, the hard jaw, the lined brow seemed parts of a mask which hid his thought.

"Ahuh! Packin' your hardware," he said, with a glance at Chane's gun.

"Yep. These September days are getting chilly," replied Chane, with animation.

Slack burst into a loud guffaw and Horn's dark, still visage wrinkled with a grin.

"What's eatin' you, pards?" queried McPherson, with asperity, as he shifted his penetrating gaze to his comrades. "It shore ain't funny — Weymer struttin' out hyar, waggin' a gun."

"Wal, it was what he said that hit my funny bone," returned Horn.

"Weymer," went on McPherson, slowly, "I reckon you ain't feelin' none too friendly toward Manerube. An' I'm sayin' as I don't blame you. What he said last night wasn't easy to swaller. I told him so. He didn't show up much of a gentleman, seein' he's been eatin' at your camp fire. Wal, I reckon he's sorry an' ain't achin' to start trouble with you."

One casual glance at McPherson's calm face was enough to convince Chane that the man was as deep as the sea. His appearance bore out too well the content of his words. A less keen observer than Chane would have been won to charitableness. But Chane had felt too poignantly and thought too deeply to be deceived by anyone. These men did not mean well by him.

"McPherson, I never look for trouble — except in front of me, and especially behind," replied Chane, sarcastically. "I just woke up feeling uncomfortable without my gun."

"Ahuh!" ejaculated the other, soberly, and bent to his task.

Chane reasoned that he had not the slightest fear of these men and wanted them to know it. As long as he kept them face to face they could not shoot him in the back; and if the issue came to an open fight at close range they would suffer as much as he. Men were not quick to draw under such circumstances. As for a fight at long range, Chane would have all the best of that, for he possessed a rifle, which he meant to hide when he did not have it in his hands.

Presently Manerube came up the slope from the brook, wiping his clean-shaven face with a scarf. Chane conceded that the man was a handsome devil, calculated to stir the pulse of a white woman, let alone an Indian girl.

"Good morning, Weymer," he said, not without effort. "Hope you'll overlook the way I shot off my mouth last night. I was sore."

"Sure. Glad to forget it," replied Chane, cheerfully. Manifestly Manerube had been talked to.

At this juncture Slack called out, "Come an' git it."

Whereupon the five men attended to the business of breakfast, a matter of cardinal importance in the desert. They ate in silence until all the food and drink had been consumed.

"Bud, what're you doing today?" inquired Manerube, as he rose, wiping his mouth.

"Wal, thet depends on the boss of this hyar outfit," answered Mcpherson, slowly, and he stared hard at Manerube. But this worthy did not take the hint, if there really was one.

"Weymer, you said once you'd be hitting the trail for the Hole in the Wall," went on Manerube, "soon as the Piutes rounded up the rest of the mustangs you bought."

"Why, yes. What's it to you?" asked Chane, easily.

"You're going to sell in Wund, so you said. Well, that's where we're bound for, and we'll help you drive through. But let's rustle along. It's been raining up at the head of the San Juan. There'll be high water."

"The San Juan is up now, so Toddy told me yesterday. I reckon I'll wait for it to go down," replied Chane.

"But that might take weeks," declared Manerube.

"I don't care how long it takes," retorted Chane. "You fellows don't need to wait for me. I'll take some Piutes. I'd rather have them, anyhow."

"The hell you say!" burst out Manerube, suddenly flaming.

At that McPherson violently struck Manerube in the chest and thrust him backward.

"See hyar, Bent Manerube," he said, in voice contrasting with his action, "we ain't goin' to have you talk for *us*. Me an' Jim an' Hod are shore glad to wait on Weymer. We're out of grub, an' we don't aim to let you make him sore on us."

The sullen amazement with which Manerube took this action and speech convinced Chane that he had no authority over these three men, and a break was imminent.

Chapter 2

Chane abruptly left the camp-fire circle, not averse to the possibility of argument and action that might leave him less to contend with. Loud angry voices attested to a quarrel among the men. He made significant note of the fact that he did not distinguish McPherson's voice.

"Cool sort of chap," soliloquized Chane. "If Manerube has any sense he'll not rile that man. But I hope he does."

Chane possessed himself of his rifle, which during his daily rides he had left in camp. For a wild-horse hunter a rifle was a nuisance and a burden on a saddle. But he had reflected that such a long-range weapon might do more than even up the advantage Manerube and his associates had in numbers, for they carried only the short Colt gun common to riders of the range. In the future he would pack the rifle on his saddle, whether it was cumbersome or not.

With this in hand, and his bridle, Chane

left camp to hunt for his horses. Glancing back from the edge of the slope, he was pleased to observe that the four unwelcome guests were engaged in a hot argument.

"I'd sure like to know just what and who they are," muttered Chane. "I'll bet they're going to steal my mustangs. Well, that'd be no great loss. But they've all taken a shine to Brutus. I don't like that. They'll have to take him over my dead body."

Brutus was Chane's new horse, an acquisition of this last trip through the Mormon country. Chane had not ridden him and had not yet seen him go through any kind of test. Two years earlier, Chane had lost a beloved horse and since then had been indifferent to all horses except the great and almost mythical Panquitch. The loss had hurt Chane so deeply that he dreaded to find another animal he might love. Brutus, however, had been gradually growing on him, especially since the arrival of the four self-styled horse-wranglers. Horn had tried to beg Brutus of Chane, Slack wanted to borrow him, Manerube offered to buy him, and McPherson jocularly declared that he intended to steal him.

"Funny how men will take to a certain horse," thought Chane as he swung down the slope. "Now Brutus filled my eye first time I saw him, but I'd never have bought him if he hadn't been such a bargain. Reckon I was wrong."

And Chane tried to recall the remarkable eulogy given the horse by the Mormons. Brutus had come from the finest strain of Colorado-bred stock. His sire was a stallion that had been born wild; his dam had come from a long line of blooded horses. He was six years old. All his life he had run over the rockiest, brushiest country in western Colorado. His equal as a cow horse had never been seen there. And as he had not been ridden by cowboys, his fine disposition had not been ruined. He had never been known to fall, or pitch, or balk at anything. He was fast and no rider yet had ever tired him. So much Chane remembered, and he was surprised at himself that he had not taken credence of it long ago. He understood his reluctance, however, for the very thought of Brutus or even Panquitch taking the vacant place in his heart gave him a pang.

Chane left the trail where it crossed Beaver Brook, and followed the watercourse up the canyon, through willow and cedar thickets, under a looming yellow wall of stone. Chane had three pack horses, and two saddle horses besides Brutus; these had been herded by Toddy Nokin up Beaver Canyon. The brush was still wet from the rain yesterday and the water of the brook was not so clear and amber-colored as usual. Bits of brush and dead leaves floated on the swift current. Blue jays screeched from the piñons; canyon swifts twittered and glinted in the sunlight. Indian sheep were bleating somewhere in the distance.

Presently the canyon opened into a narrow park, purple with sage, dotted by red rocks, and bordered by a wandering line of green where grass and willows lined the brook. Here Chane found his horses. He had been riding a white animal called Andy, which, according to the wranglers, was known at St. George as a one-man horse. Chane, more out of vanity to show he could manage Andy than for any other reason, had given him precedence over Brutus. Andy was white, except for a few black markings, lean, rangy, tough, and of nervous disposition. Chane had found him good in every kind of going except sand. Andy did not know sand.

Chane approached the horses with the usual caution of a wrangler, and all of them, except Brutus, moved out of his reach. Brutus gave his superb head a quick uplift and regarded Chane with keen, distrustful eyes.

"Brutus, I reckon we've got horse thieves in camp, so I'm going to look you over," said Chane. He had a habit of talking to horses, perhaps owing to the fact that he was so much alone.

33

Whereupon he walked round Brutus as if he had never seen him before. He made the discovery that he had never really looked at Brutus. Reluctantly Chane had to confess the horse was magnificent. And he suffered a twinge of conscience that he could ever be so far faithless to the memory of the beloved horse of the past. That confession and remorse changed the status of Brutus.

"Well, you and I must get acquainted," Chane decided.

Brutus was not exactly a giant of a horse, though he was much higher and heavier than the average. His muscular development made him appear unusual; indeed, a little more muscle would have deformed him. His chest was massive, broad, deep, a wonderful storehouse of energy. Such powerful, perfectly proportioned, and sound legs Chane had seldom seen, and his great hoofs matched them. His body was large, round, smooth, showing no bones. He had a broad arched neck and a fine head, which he held high as he looked directly at Chane. There was an oval white spot on his face, just below the wide space between his eyes. His color was a dark mottled brown, almost black, and his coat glistened in the sunlight.

At the last Chane always judged horses as he judged men — by the look in their eyes.

34

Horses had as much character as men, and similar emotions and instincts. Chane had a theory, not shared by many wranglers, that kindness brought out the best in any horse. If a horse was mean it did not always follow that he had been born so.

Brutus had large dark eyes, soft yet full of spirit, just now questioning and uncertain. They showed his intelligence. Chane made sure that the horse had not been spurred and jerked and jammed around as had most horses six years old. He had not been hurt. The way he threw up his head appealed strongly to Chane. There was pride and fire in his look. It seemed he questioned Chane — what have you to say for yourself?

"Brutus, I had — a horse once," said Chane, faltering a little, "and I haven't cared for one since . . . but you and I are going to be friends."

With the words, Chane's old gentle and confident way of handling horses came back to him. He approached Brutus, placing a slow, sure, strong hand on the glossy neck. Brutus quivered, but did not jerk away. He snorted, and turned his head to look at Chane. It pleased Chane to find that he did not need a rope or halter. Brutus stood to be bridled, not altogether satisfied about it, not liking the rifle Chane held under his arm, but he took the bit easily and began to champ it. Then he followed Chane willingly. He had a long stride and his nose soon came abreast of Chane's shoulder. Before Chane reached camp he decided that Brutus had missed the attention and company of a rider.

Chane discovered McPherson and his two comrades in camp, but Manerube was not in sight. While Chane saddled the horse McPherson strode up. His face seemed the same rough bronze mask, his eyes told nothing, yet there were traces about his person of recent spent passion.

"Wal, Manerube helped hisself to your grub, packed, an' rode off," announced McPherson.

"He's welcome," declared Chane, heartily.

"Me an' him had some hard words, but he wouldn't throw a gun, so nothin' come of it."

"Where'd he head for?" queried Chane.

"He said Bluff, but I reckon thet's a bluff, all right," returned the other. "He took the main trail out of Beaver. I climbed the stone over thar an' watched him. I seen him turn off the trail in the cedars."

McPherson pointed with sturdy hand across the canyon toward the foot of a cedared ridge. A trail branched off there, leading to the camp of the Piutes.

"I savvy, Bud," rejoined Chane, laconically. "You're giving me a hunch."

"Man, shore as you're a hoss-wrangler he'll rustle off with your little Piute squaw."

Chane's good humor gave place to irritation. He eyed McPherson with plain disfavor.

"She's not my squaw," he said, sharply.

"Wal, I meant no offense. But she belongs to somebody. Toddy Nokin shore. An' I'm sayin' thet if Toddy or you hit Manerube's trail —"

"I'll beat him to Toddy's hogan," interrupted Chane, leaping on Brutus.

"Hey!" yelled McPherson, hastily. "Don't git the idee because Manerube didn't draw on me thet he won't on you. Me an' you might be different propositions."

"Much obliged," Chane called back. "If Manerube beats me to a gun you're welcome to my grub."

McPherson yelled another parting sally, which Chane could not distinguish, owing to the sudden pounding of hoofs. Brutus had not needed spur or word; his answer to the touch of bridle was something that thrilled Chane.

"Say, old boy, you're there!" he called.

But only a few rods away was the edge of a rocky slope, where Chane had to rein Brutus in. It was not necessary to haul on the bridle and hold hard as in the case of Andy and most spirited horses Chane had ridden. Brutus pounded down the rock-strewn trail and splashed across the brook. His hoofs rang hollow on the stone bench where the water rushed. Chane rode at a gallop up the canyon, through the sage flat, and on to a low cedared break in the wall. There was a trail leading over this, down upon the sage upland beyond, where the Indians pastured their horses and sheep. By the time Chane surmounted this ragged rocky eminence he was aware that he bestrode one horse in a million. His heart warmed to Brutus. Apparently he climbed with no more effort than that required on a level. Once on top, he gave a great heave of his bellows-like chest, and that was the only sign of exertion he manifested.

"Look here, Brutus, I reckon I overlooked you, but you needn't rub it in," remarked Chane.

It was an easy ride down the long gradual slope. The fragrant breath of the sage came strong on the breeze. Away rolled the heaving purple upland, with its clumps of green cedar, its groups of yellow rocks, its long level lines of canyon rims, red in the morning sun. Herds of mustangs colored the soft gray and purple of the sage flats; a flock of sheep moved like a wide white-and-black patch out on the desert. A sage prairie it seemed, almost endless to the eastward; but in the north interrupted lines and notches betrayed the break-off down into the wilderness world of wind-worn rock.

Toddy Nokin's hogan, and that of his relatives, stood at the base of the slope, on the edge of the bare upland. These mounds of earth plastered over framework of cedar were no different from the Navajo structures. The one door faced the east. Door as well as hogan invited the sun. Temporary as were these homes of the Piutes, they yet had the appearance of service. Blue smoke curled from the circular holes in the roofs; white and black puppies played with half naked, dusky-skinned children. Mustangs with crude Indian saddles and blankets of bright colors stood, bridles down; in a round corral, made of cedar branches planted in the ground, a flock of sheep and goats baa-baaed at Chane's approach, and the shepherd dogs barked viciously.

As Chane rode down to the first hogan, the Indian children disappeared as if by magic, and one of Toddy Nokin's squaws came out. Inquiry for Toddy elicited the information that he was out hunting horses. An old brave, gray and wrinkled, appeared at the hogan door, to bend a dark skinny hand in direction too complicated for Chane's deduction. Then he asked for Sosie, assured that, if Manerube really had designs upon her, there was time to outwit him. The squaw pointed toward a clump of cedars on the rise of slope just beyond the corral.

Chane rode thither, to find Sosie in the shade of the trees, beside an older squaw who was weaving a blanket. Chane dismounted and, approaching them, he bent a more than usually interested gaze upon Sosie. His greeting was answered in good English. The Indian maiden, though only sixteen years old, had spent the latter nine of these in the government school. She was very pretty, compared with the older Indian women, as she had retained the cleanly and tidy habits fostered upon her at the school. She was slight in build, with a small oval face, a golden-bronze complexion, and hair black as the wing of a raven. Her eyes were too large for her face, but they were beautiful. She wore a dark velveteen blouse and necklaces of silver, and her skirt was long, full, and of a bright color. Her little feet were encased in silver-buttoned moccasins.

Her somber face changed at Chane's arrival. He was used to finding her moody, and thought that indeed she had reason to be. Sosie talked well, and had told Chane more about the Indians, and the tragedy of educated girls like herself, than he could otherwise have learned. It appeared that this morning she had another grievance. Her father, Toddy Nokin, wanted her to marry a young Piute who already had a wife, and he could not understand her objection. Chane sympathized with her and advised her not to marry any Indian she could not love.

"I couldn't love an Indian," replied Sosie, in disgust.

"Why not?" queried Chane.

"Because Indian boys who are educated go back to the dirty habits of their people. We girls learn the white people's way of living. We learn to like clean bodies, clean clothes, clean food. When we try to correct our mothers and fathers we're accused of being too good for our own people. My father says to me: 'You're my blood. Why aren't my ways right for you?' Then when I tell him, he can't understand."

"Why don't you leave them and live among white people?" asked Chane.

"I'd have to be a servant. Only a few Indian girls find good places."

"Well, Sosie, it doesn't look as if education for Indian girls was right," said Chane, soberly.

"I don't say it's wrong, but it's hard. If I could help my family I'd be glad. But I can't. And when I look at a white man they are angry."

"Sosie, most white men — out here, anyway — are not fit for you to look at," replied

Chane, earnestly.

"Why? I like them better than Indians," she said, bluntly.

Chane found his mission rather embarrassing, as it had not occurred to him that Sosie would prefer the company of a bad white man to the best Indian her father could present. After deliberating a moment, he talked to her as plainly and kindly as if she had been his sister, explaining why Manerube or one of his class meant nothing but evil toward her. Chane exhausted his argument, at the conclusion of which Sosie said: "You preach like our missionary at school. I'd rather be made love to."

"But, Sosie," exclaimed Chane, aghast at her simplicity, "I never made love to you!"

"No. You're different from other white men out here," she replied, in a tone that did not indicate that she respected him for it.

"If I made love to you I'd ask you to marry me," continued Chane, at a loss what to say to this misguided child.

Her reception of this was a shy surprise, a hint of coquetry and response singularly appealing. It made Chane pity her. At the same time he divined that other white men, in their attention to her, had never touched the chord of fineness and sweetness that lay deep in her. Suddenly he realized the fatality of her po-

42

sition, and it distressed him. He did not love her, but almost he wished he did. In his anxious perturbation he launched into an emphatic declaration against Manerube. Sosie listened intently. It was evidently an exciting hour for her.

"But Manerube says he will take me away," she replied when Chane had concluded his tirade.

Chane was shocked. "Surely he will. But you mustn't let him."

"I'll run off with him," the girl replied, with something inevitable about her.

"No, you won't, Sosie," declared Chane. "I'll stop you. I told Manerube he'd better not let me see him with you again."

"What would you do, Mr. Chane?" she asked, a curious dark flash in her eyes.

"Well — that depends on what *he* did," rejoined Chane, somewhat taken aback. "I'd beat him good and hard, at least."

"I thought you said you weren't in love with me," cried Sosie, in a sort of wild gladness.

Chane threw up his hands. It was impossible to hear her talk and remember she was Indian, yet the content of what she said forcibly struck home the proof that she was not white. Chane had a momentary desire to tell her he did care for her and thus save her from Manerube; but he reconsidered the hasty thought because,

43

once acted upon, that would involve a greater sacrifice than he could offer.

"Sosie, can't you understand?" asked Chane, striving for patience. "I don't love you as a man of my kind must love a girl to want her — to marry her, you know. But I like you. I'm sorry for you. I think you're a bright, fine little girl. I want to help you. Manerube means bad by you. I know. I've heard him say as much to his pards. He'll destroy your soul. Promise me you'll not see him again."

"Yes, I promise — if you'll come sometimes," she replied, won by his spirit. There were tears in her big dusky eyes. She was a simple, impulsive child, honest at heart, with the hot blood of her race.

"Of course I'll come — as long —" he said, breaking off suddenly. He had meant to say he would come as long as he stayed in camp there, but he thought it best to hide from her that he was leaving soon. "I'll be back in an hour. You stay here."

"*Adios*, señor," she murmured, gladly, speaking the Spanish he had told her pleased him.

Chane rode back to the hogan, hoping to find Toddy Nokin or one of the Indian men. He thought it best to tell someone to keep an eye on Sosie. He was not sure he could trust her. But he did not find anyone, and turned Brutus for the open sage. As he rode, perplexed by the unsolvable problem of this little Indian girl, he became conscious that now, although he pitied her, somehow his sympathy was different from what it had been. He had rather idealized Sosie. It affronted and alienated him to learn she was quite willing to run off with such a man as Manerube.

Chane rode across the rolling upland, keeping sharp lookout along the ridge that Manerube would cross if he had ventured toward the Indian camp. There was, however, no sign of horses in that direction.

"Reckon it was a bluff," declared Chane, with relief. In spite of McPherson's hint, he did not entertain a very high regard for Manerube's courage.

Circling to the south, Chane at length reached the rise of ground running along a shallow league-wide valley, gray and purple with sage, spotted with rocks and cedars, and animated by moving horses. Toddy Nokin and his braves were driving in the last of the mustangs Chane had bargained for. This pleased Chane, for some of these had been ranging Piute Canyon, a deep long gorge, accessible by but few trails.

Brutus saw the moving dots below and lifted his head high, his ears erect. Then Chane put him to a lope down the gradual descent. It soon became evident to Chane that this horse did not need to be guided, except possibly in exceedingly bad ground. The sagebrush did not bother Brutus any more than if it had not been there. He crashed through it; and the little washes and ruts in the red earth, that sometimes tripped an ordinary horse, apparently were the same to Brutus as level ground. His hoofs were so big, his legs so strong, his dexterity and judgment so good, that it seemed safe to ride him anywhere a horse could run.

Down in the center of this oval bowl lay a natural corral, a long narrow space of the best pasture land, barred on two sides by low stone walls that came to an apex at the head of the depression, and shut off at its mouth and widest part by a cedar fence. Even at dry seasons there was always water in the deep hole in the rocks where the walls met; and at this time there was a running stream. Chane arrived as Toddy Nokin and his Indians were driving a bunch of mustangs into this corral.

Chane rode inside to take a look at these mustangs. There were nine of them, and the best of the lot he had seen. A blue roan stood out conspicuously among the tan-colored, black-maned buckskins. They were young horses, fat and sleek, and, unlike most Indian ponies, not at all wild. The Piutes handled

46

horses better than the Navajos. The latter were nomads of the desert, and seldom took time to break and train a horse properly. Most Navajo mustangs were head shy, which was a trait Chane did not like. They had been beaten about the head, or broken with cruel hackamores, or in some way hurt so that they never recovered.

Toddy Nokin rode into the corral, and his braves, who were his sons, put up the poles that formed a gate. He held up his hands to Chane and counted with fingers to the number of twenty-six, and informed Chane he would not sell more. Chane had hoped to buy a larger number, but knew it was useless to try to change Toddy's mind.

He motioned to Toddy to dismount, and, getting off himself, he went among the mustangs. They would not allow him to get close enough to put a hand on them, until Toddy's sons drove them back into a bunch. Then Chane, following a habit that was pleasure to him as well as business, leisurely examined them one by one. He just naturally loved horses, and if he had been rich he would have owned a thousand. The blue roan at once took his eye.

"Blue, reckon I'll keep you," he said.

Presently he had looked them over to his satisfaction, and repaired to the shade of a cedar, where Toddy squatted, making a flat wisp of a cigarette.

"Toddy, they're worth more than I offered and you agreed to take," said Chane, frankly.

The Piute made a gesture that signified a bargain was a bargain. Then he asked, "How much Mormons pay you?"

"Twenty-five dollars for most of them and more for the best," replied Chane.

Toddy nodded his grizzled old head as if that was something to consider.

"Why good horse trade now?" he asked.

Chane explained to him that a St. Louis horse-dealing company had recently stimulated the wild-horse hunting in Nevada and Utah, which business had stirred the Mormons to more activity.

"Ugh!" grunted Toddy, and then he told Chane he would round up more mustangs of his own, and buy from the Navajos, and drive them across the rivers next moon.

"Next moon," repeated Chane. "That'll be after the middle of October. Fine. Will you sell to me or the Mormons?"

"Sell Mormons," replied Toddy, shrewdly, adding he would pay Chane for finding purchasers.

"Maybe I can get a better price from the wranglers," replied Chane. "Now, Toddy, where will we meet?"

Whereupon the Piute brushed clear a place in the dust, and taking up a bit of stick he began to draw a map. This sort of thing always interested Chane. The Indians were natural artists, and they held in their minds a wonderful knowledge of the country. Toddy Nokin drew lines to represent the San Juan and Colorado rivers; he made a dot to mark the Hole in the Wall, an outlet from the canyoned wilderness made notorious by outlaws a few years before. He drew the Henry Mountains to the right and Wild Horse Mesa to the left, and between these he laid down a trail he would follow. Somewhere beyond Wild Horse Mesa, at a place he called Nightwatch Spring, he would hold the mustangs to fatten up after that long hard journey over the barren rocks.

"Nightwatch Spring," said Chane. "I've heard of that place from someone — maybe a wrangler . . . Toddy, mark out where this water lies."

Toddy showed Chane where to branch off the main Piute trail, north and west of the low end of Wild Horse Mesa, and he gave Chane the impression that this spring had never been known by whites and lay in a beautiful wide canyon where grass was abundant.

"You want have horse ranch sometime," concluded Toddy, nodding with great vehemence. "Toddy show you place."

So much from this old Piute thrilled Chane with its possibilities. How well it paid to be kindly and helpful toward the Indians! No Piute had ever left a debt unpaid to him.

"Toddy Nokin, you're a good fellow," said Chane as he took out his worn wallet and opened it. "Here's your money for twenty-six horses." He counted it out, bill after bill, and placed the sum in Toddy's wrinkled hand. The Indian did not recount it, and slowly rolling it up he put it in an inside pocket of his coat, after the manner of a white man.

"Grass gone here," he said, waving his hand to indicate the long pasture-corral. "You go now."

To leave at once with his newly purchased mustangs, which Toddy manifestly advised, had scarcely been in Chane's calculations. But a moment's study told him how necessary that was. If the mustangs were turned loose again to feed they would wander in one night back to their regular haunts. It had taken two weeks to collect the band. Chane saw it the same as Toddy — the mustangs should be driven at once on the way across the rivers, and herded at night or hobbled on the best available grass. It had been his intention to postpone leaving the Piute range, owing to his distrust of McPherson, but this now was obviously impractical. If he ran any risk from McPherson and his comrades it could hardly be any greater now than it might be next week. Chane decided to break camp that very day, and he told Toddy Nokin so. Whereupon the Piute said he and his sons would ride with him a couple of days, until the mustangs were off their range.

Leaving his sons to follow with the mustangs, Toddy accompanied Chane up the sage slope toward the mounds and knolls of yellow rock that marked the canyon country. Toddy's hogans lay somewhat south and west of this sage valley where the mustangs had been kept. So that upon his return Chane rode in a direction which would cross Manerube's trail, if this worthy had approached Toddy's camp. The fact of such possibility reminded Chane of his promise to Sosie. He would see her, to bid her good-bye, and then he must hurry to his camp. From that moment McPherson, Horn, and Slack occupied Chane's thoughts. The situation was not to his liking, yet there had not occurred to him an alternative.

Riding along at a brisk trot, Chane, with Toddy Nokin loping behind on his shaggy little mustang, approached a zone of gray and yellow wind-worn rocks, as high as hills, and with both sloping and abrupt walls. Cedars grew thickly around them and in the winding lanes that separated them.

Turning a corner of wall, Chane's quick eye sighted a packhorse trotting toward him, and then part of another horse, mostly concealed by an intervening cedar. They were in line with Chane. Quick as a flash he leaped off, and motioning Toddy Nokin to do likewise, he led Brutus behind a thick, low-branched cedar. Toddy slipped close behind him, stooping to peer through the branches.

"Ugh!" he grunted.

Chane saw Manerube ride into sight, coming at a good trot and leading a packhorse. Behind Manerube bobbed a black head, now in view, then disappearing. Presently Chane got a better look at it.

"Sosie! Well, I'm a son-of-a-gun!" he ejaculated, in amazement and dismay.

The Indian girl was riding behind Manerube, and she had both arms round him. At the moment her gold-bronze face flashed in the sunlight. Chane watched intently, standing motionless until Manerube had ridden within one hundred feet of the cedar that concealed Chane and Toddy. Sosie's face bobbed out to the side of Manerube's shoulder. Most assuredly it was not the face of an unwillingly abducted girl. It wore a smile. The wide dark eyes gleamed. Her white teeth showed.

Chane's rush of anger was almost as much against her as Manerube. Jerking his rifle from its saddle sheath, he cocked it and stepped out to level it at Manerube.

"Stop! Quick! Hands up!" he ordered.

The approaching horse snorted and jumped. Manerube hauled it to a halt. Then as his hands shot aloft his ruddy face paled.

"Up they are!" he said, hoarsely, in rage and discomfiture.

Chane strode forward, and he heard the padding of Toddy's moccasined feet close behind him.

"Sosie — get off that horse," called Chane, sharply.

The Indian girl almost fell off in the hurry that actuated her. There was no radiance now on her face, nor any of the stoical Indian courage which should have been a heritage. Her big eyes were distended.

"Manerube, I've a mind to shoot you," declared Chane, with the rifle steadily leveled.

"What for? I've not done you any dirt," replied the other, thickly. "You've no call to kill me on this little hussy's account."

"I'm not so sure. You've made her run off with you," retorted Chane.

"Made nothing. She wants to go."

Toddy Nokin shuffled round to the side of Chane and approached his daughter. He

53

swung his quirt. Chane saw Sosie shrink and her eyes dilate.

"Hold on, Toddy!" called Chane, and then, stepping aside so that he had the girl in line with Manerube, he addressed her: "Sosie, were you willing to go with him?"

"Yes," she answered, sullenly. "But it was because he says he'll marry me."

"Manerube, you hear what Sosie said. Is it true? You're talking to a white man now."

"No, you damn fool!" shouted Manerube. "I wouldn't marry a squaw."

Chane eyed Manerube in silence for a moment. The man had no sense of guilt, and he was not afraid to tell the truth.

"Well, I reckon you'd better sit tight and keep your hands high," went on Chane. "Toddy, you take his gun."

The Piute advanced upon Manerube, and quickly jerking his gun from its holster, he stepped back. Then Chane strode round Manerube to see if he had another weapon.

"Get off your horse," ordered Chane, and handed both his rifle and his short gun to the Indian.

Manerube stared, without complying. At the outset of this encounter he had showed fear, but now, as there seemed no certainty of a fatal issue for him, the color was returning to his face.

Chane wasted no more words. Laying a powerful hold on Manerube, he jerked him from the saddle to the ground, where he sprawled hard.

"Get up, before I kick you!" went on Chane, yielding to an anger that grew hot.

Manerube got to his feet, with astonishment giving way to fury. Chane rushed him and knocked him flat. He raised on his elbow, then on his hand, while he extended the other, now shaking with passion. A reddening lump appeared on his face.

"I'll kill you!" he hissed.

"Aw, get up and fight!" retorted Chane, derisively, and he kicked Manerube, not with violence, but hard enough to elicit a solid thump. It served to make Manerube leap erect and plunge at Chane. They fought all over the place, dealing each other blow for blow. Manerube was no match for Chane at that game, and manifestly saw it, for he tried to close in. Failing that, he maneuvered until he was near enough Toddy to snatch at one of the guns Toddy held. The Indian showed surprising agility in leaping aside.

"Manerube — you're just — what I said — you were," panted Chane, hoarsely. Rushing at Manerube and battering him down, Chane did not let him rise, but beat him soundly until he was most thoroughly whipped. Then Chane got up, to wipe sweat and blood and dust from his face.

"Take your gun — and your horses — and rustle," ordered Chane, jerking the weapons from Toddy. He threw Manerube's gun at his feet. Then with rifle leveled low Chane watched the man sit up, draw the gun to him by the barrel, and rise with his back to Chane. He shoved the gun into its holster, and strode, staggering a little, toward where his horses had moved. Chane kept close watch on him, ready for another show of treachery. But Manerube mounted and took up the halter of the pack animal, not looking back until he had started to ride off. Then his pallid discolored face expressed a passion that boded ill to Chane. He rode out of sight among the cedars. Chane turned to the Indians. Toddy Nokin had in no wise lost anything of his dignity, at least in his attitude toward Chane. He returned the small gun Chane had handed him. Sosie had quite recovered from what fright she had sustained, and was now regarding her champion with dusky eyes alight. Not before had the fragility of her, nor the prettiness, and something half tame, half wild, struck Chane so forcibly. But his sympathy and her appeal both went down before his anger.

"Sosie, you're not good," he declared.

Instantly she grew sullen, defiant.

"I'm what white men have made me," she responded.

Chane had not adequate reply for that, and indeed felt helpless.

Toddy Nokin yelled something in Piute at his wayward daughter, and as she whirled he aimed a swing of the quirt and likewise a kick at her, both of which fell short. Like a flash the supple figure moved out of reach. She screeched back at them. Chane could not decide whether it was the wild-cat cry of an Indian squaw or the passionate expression of her white learning. Perhaps it was both.

Chapter 3

Sue Melberne's father would never have allowed her to come on this wild-horse hunting expedition if he had not calculated on finding a new country where he could homestead. Back there at St. George she had heard her father say to Loughbridge, his partner in this venture, "You know, Jim, I've shore got to take root in new soil."

This significant remark had remained in Sue's mind, like others that had struck her strangely since her return from school in Silver City. Her father was always looking for someone to come unexpectedly, so it seemed. There had been some reason for him to leave the south, then Silver City, then Vegas, and lastly St. George. Sue did not want to dwell on the meaning of this. She had been born in Texas and she had lived long enough in the West to know Westerners.

The pursuit of wild horses had a remarkable fascination for Sue, but she hated the brutality. She loved to see and watch wild horses, not to capture them. Then the camp life, the riding and packing from place to place, the days in the open country — Utah in its beautiful, wild, carved-stone majesty — coming after her four years at school in a bustling town, had irresistible appeal for her.

There had been a chance for her to remain at St. George, teaching a school where most of the children were Mormons. She did not dislike Mormons particularly, but she had no wish to live alone among them. On the other hand, the prospect held out by her father had not at first struck Sue as alluring. It would be, sooner or later, no less than hard pioneer life. But she had decided to try it, to be with her father and younger brother. Sue's mother was dead, and her father had married again while she was attending school, a circumstance she had not hailed with joy. It had turned out, however, that her stepmother was a clever and lovable woman, who had certainly been good for her father.

Therefore, Sue, who had undertaken the trip out of love for father and brother, and a longing for experience in the desert, found in a few weeks that she was fitting admirably and happily into this nomad life of wild-horse wrangling. She was young, healthy, strong; she could ride a horse and cook a meal over a camp fire. She found in herself a surprising response to all that was characteristic of primitive life in the open. Still she held most tenaciously to her few worldly possessions — dresses, pictures, books — things that had been a part of her development at school. Many a time, on the journey east from St. George, she had ridden on the wagon-seat with Jake, just to keep him from driving recklessly over some of the fearful places along the road. She did not want to see that wagon wrecked, with her precious chest of belongings.

Melberne's outfit was not a large one, as wild-horse-hunting outfits were considered, but as he and his partner, Loughbridge, had brought their womenfolk and the necessary teamsters, wagons, camp equipment, supplies, all together they made quite a party. If a desirable country were found, with abundant grass and water, Loughbridge would be willing to homestead a ranch, along with Melberne. Their main idea, then, was really not alone the capturing and marketing of wild horses. In the interest, however, of that pursuit it was necessary to keep within one day's travel of the railroad. Melberne was shipping carloads of unbroken horses to St. Louis. In considerable numbers, at thirteen dollars a head, he could make money. But he was not striking any country rich in ranching possibilities.

It was on an afternoon of September that the Melberne outfit halted at the head of Stark Valley, which was thirty miles from the railroad.

Sue had heard the men talking about this valley, and all the ride down from the divide to the welcome grove of cottonwood trees below she had gazed and gazed. Utah had been strikingly beautiful with its pink cliffs, wide plains of white sage, rugged black mountains, and then the colorful stone-monumented desert. She had marked that as they traveled eastward the scale and ruggedness and wild beauty had appeared to magnify. This valley was something to make her catch her breath.

She had grown capable of judging the colorful distances, the deceiving purple shadows, the long sweeping lines of the desert. Here she saw a valley which she estimated to be twenty miles wide and eighty long. Really it seemed small, set down in a vast panorama, with a ragged black range of mountains on one side, an endless waving green rise of land sweeping to a horizon on the other. Far beyond the long length of this valley stood what appeared a flat mountain, very lofty, with red walls now sunlit, and a level black top. It was so different from any landmark Sue had ever seen that she was forcibly struck with it. How far away! How isolated! It had a strange, impelling beauty.

"Dad, what's that mountain?" asked Sue, pointing.

Her father, a stalwart bearded man, turned from his task of unhitching a team, to answer Sue. He had gray, penetrating, tired eyes that held a smile for her.

"Shore I don't know," he replied as he glanced in the direction Sue was pointing. "Wal, no wonder it caught your eye! See heah, Alonzo, what's that flat mountain yonder?"

Alonzo was a half-breed Mexican *vaquero,* guide to the outfit, and reputed to be the best wrangler in Utah. He was a slim, lithe rider, very light of build yet muscular, and he had a sharp, smooth, dark face, and eyes of piercing black. He gazed a moment down the valley.

"Wild Horse Mesa," he replied, briefly.

"Reckon I ought to have known, considerin' all I've heard," said Melberne. "Sue, that's not a mountain, but a mesa. Biggest mesa in Utah. It's a refuge for wild horses, so the Mormons say, an' no white men have set foot on it."

"Wild Horse Mesa!" exclaimed Sue. "How beautiful — and wild! So far away . . . it's good there's a place where horses are safe."

"Wal, lass, there'll shore be a lot of wild horses safe for a long time," said her father as he surveyed the valley. "This country is full of them. Look! I see hundreds of wild horses now."

Sue focused her dreamy gaze, and was surprised and thrilled to see bands of horses dotting the valley. They appeared to be of all colors, and grew in numbers until they faded in the gray haze.

"They'll shore be the devil to catch," continued Melberne as his keen eye swept the valley. It was a vast green hollow, treeless, stoneless, with its monotony broken only by the bands of horses and pale gleams of winding streams.

"Dad, we're to make permanent camp here, didn't you say?" asked Sue.

"Yep, an' right glad I am," he rejoined, heartily. "We've shore been on the go, with no chance to make you womenfolk comfortable. Heah we can make a fine camp. Plenty of grass, water, wood, an' meat. This grove is in a protected place, too. We'll be heah days, an' maybe weeks. I'm shore goin' to trap a great bunch of wild horses."

"Dad, you mean trap them at one time?"

"That's my idea. Jim doesn't agree, but he'll come to my way of thinkin'."

"If you'd only keep the wild horses you do catch and tame them!" protested Sue.

"Tame wild horses at thirteen dollars a

head!" ejaculated her father, with a laugh. "Child, it can't be done."

"Some of the horses I've seen, if properly broken, would be worth hundreds of dollars," replied Sue.

Melberne scratched his grizzled face and pondered thoughtfully; then he shook his head as if the problem was beyond him, and returned to his task.

Many experienced hands made short work of pitching camp. Before the sun set, tents were up, fires were blazing, blue smoke was curling upward through the golden-green leaves of the cottonwoods; the fragrant steam of hot biscuits, venison and coffee permeated the cool air.

"I refuse to call out that cowboy slogan," announced Mrs. Melberne, cheerfully, "but I say come to supper."

She was a short, stout, pleasant-faced little woman, just now ruddy from the fire heat. Her helper, Mrs. Loughbridge, afforded a marked contrast, in both appearance and manner.

Young Chess Weymer, who was always offering gallant little courtesies to Sue and Ora Loughbridge, lifted a seat from one of the wagons and placed it conveniently out of line of the blowing camp-fire smoke.

"There, girls, have a seat," he said, in his rich bass voice.

Sue complied with a nod of thanks, and seated herself with burdened tin plate in one hand and a cup in the other. But Ora did not get up from where she squatted on the ground. She was a dark-eyed handsome girl, and just now rather sullen of face.

"Come have a seat, Ora," called Chess.

She flashed him an illuminating look. "Chess, I wouldn't deprive you of such a chance," she said, with sarcasm.

"Oh, well, if you won't, I will," replied Chess, and seated himself beside Sue.

Sue rather enjoyed the situation. Ora had been plainly captivated by this good-looking boy, who showed a preference for Sue's society. He was a clean-cut lad of eighteen, brown of face and eye, and possessed of a fine frank countenance, singularly winning. At St. George, where he had joined the caravan, he had appeared to be a wild, happy youngster, not above drinking and fighting, and utterly unable to resist the girls. Sue liked his company so long as he did not grow over-sentimental. She was two years older than Chess, and in her mind vastly more mature. She had condescended to regard him with sisterly favor until the Loughbridges joined the party, when Ora had taken most of the pleasure, as well as Chess's society.

Everybody was hungry after the long ride,

and ate without conversing. Sue's appetite was as healthy as any. It took considerably less time to dispose of the supper than it had required to prepare it. This meal hour, and the camp-fire hour afterward, were about the only opportunities Sue had to observe the men all together, and she made the most of them.

The wranglers of the outfit were a continual source of delight to her. There were six of these employed by her father, and they worked in every capacity that such travel and strenuous activity demanded.

Alonzo, the half-breed, was the most fascinating, by reason of the knowledge he could impart. Utah, a wild-horse wrangler, was probably a Mormon, though he never admitted that — a sharp-featured, stone-faced young man, long, slim, bow-legged, hard as rock, and awkward on his feet. He somehow resembled the desert. Tway Miller appeared to be a cowboy who had abandoned cattle riding because he hated wire fences. He complained that there were no great ranges left, and when taken to task about this, he showed his idea of a range to be the whole southwest. Tway was a tough, wiry little rider, dusty always, ragged and shiny, and he had a face like the bark of a tree. He got his name Tway from a habit he had of stuttering, something his comrades took fiendish glee in making him do. Bonny was a stalwart Irishman, sandy bearded and haired, freckle-faced, and he possessed a wonderful deep bass voice, the solemnity of which suited his big light-blue eyes. His age was about thirty, and he had been ten years in America. His one dislike, it appeared, was anything in the shape of a town. Jake, a man of years and experience, possessed a heavy square frame that had begun to show the wear of time. He was bald. His round brown face was a wrinkled record of all the vicissitudes of life, not one of which had embittered him. Everything ill had happened to Jake. He had once had wife, children, home, prosperity, position, all of which had gone with the years. Yet he was the most cheerful and unselfish and helpful of men. If anyone wanted a service he ran to Jake. And Jake would say: "Why, sure! I'll be glad to do it." Jake had been engaged, as had the others, to chase wild horses, and betweentimes help at all jobs. But it turned out that his active riding days were past. It tortured him, racked his bones, to ride all day even on a trotting horse. As teamster, however, cook, and handyman around camp he was incomparable. The last of this sextet so interesting to Sue was a tenderfoot they had named Captain Bunk. The sea to him had been what the desert was to the riders. Somehow he had drifted to Utah.

His talk about boats, engines, ships, his bunk-mates, had earned him the sobriquet of Captain Bunk. He had a face as large as a ham, bright red, an enormous nose that never got over sunburn, and eyes and lips that always showed the effect of the dry winds of the desert.

Supper had long passed and the sun was setting when the chores of these men had been completed for the day. Sue stopped a moment, on her way out to find some quiet outlook, there to watch and dream as was her habit, and listened to the camp-fire conversation.

"How many wild horses in the valley?" inquired her father, eagerly.

"Reckon I seen five thousand," replied Loughbridge, holding up his field glasses.

"Shore you're jokin'," ejaculated Melberne.

"No. These glasses don't lie."

"By thunder! That's great news," declared Melberne, clapping his hands. "Now to plan some kind of a trap to catch five hundred — a thousand — at one clip!"

"Reckon you're locoed, Mel," declared his partner. "If we could ketch a hundred at once I'd be satisfied. What's the use ketchin' so many when we can only drive a few to the railroad?"

"Wal, that's so. But we've got to learn a way to catch a bunch, an' drive them, too.

Alonzo says he has seen that done, but it kills a lot of horses. An' he won't tell me."

Like a majority of the real wild-horse wranglers, Alonzo had a love for all horses. Melberne was not a hard man, but he was keen to acquire money. Loughbridge would have been glad to sacrifice any number of horses, just so long as he saved enough to make a rich stake. He argued with the reticent Mexican, but to no avail. Alonzo would not reveal the secret of how to capture and drive large numbers of wild horses. Sue liked him for that, as much as she disliked Loughbridge. Her father, she knew, was earnest, strong, but easily led, especially in the direction of profits. Presently he and Loughbridge strolled off into the grove, evidently to talk alone. Whereupon the conversation grew loquacious and general.

"Bonny, how do you like this country?" inquired Captain Bunk, with a defiant note of curiosity.

"My Gawd, Captain, it's shure gr-r-rand!" replied Bonny, his deep voice ringing solemnly.

"Blow me if it ain't a hell of a place — this Utah," exploded Bunk, disgustedly. "There ain't any water. Why, you couldn't float a skiff in the whole of this desert!"

"Shure this is land, mon, an' dom' foine land," expostulated Bonny. "All we need is water enough to drink."

"I-t-t-t-twa-tway-tway-" began Tway Miller.

"Aw, hev a cigarette," interrupted Utah, handing Miller his pouch. "Listen to our Irish pard an' this seafarin' man."

"T-t-t-t-t-ttt-tway-d-d-da-dam' it! I can talk if I w-w-want to," shouted Tway.

"Talk! Say, *hombre,* you've never showed me any sign of talkin' yet," drawled Utah.

"Bonny, you wouldn't live out here among all these headlands?" queried Captain Bunk, hot for argument.

"Live here? Shure I'm goin' to. It's gr-r-rand country. I'll marry one of them squaw Injuns phwat owns a lot of land. Mebbe they'll be gold or oil. An' afther I'm rich I'll git rid of her."

Some of his listeners howled with glee, while Captain Bunk ejaculated in amazement: "Get rid of your squaw! How?"

"Shure there'd be ways. Knock her on the head, or somethin' loike," replied Bonny, earnestly.

"You're a bloody pirate!" declared Captain Bunk.

"Aw, Bonny's just talkin'," put in Jake, in his easy, friendly voice. "He wouldn't hurt a flea. I think he's stringin' you boys."

"Wal, my Irish lad, if you'll take a hunch from me, shut up on thet squaw talk," advised

70

Utah, forcibly. "Squaw men ain't liked in this country."

"P-p-p-p-per-perfectly natu-ral," interposed Tway Miller. "You Mormons want all the w-w-w-wim-wim-men, red skins an' white."

"Tway, if you make a crack like thet in St. George, you'd sure get cured," replied Utah.

"C-c-c-cured of w-w-what?" demanded Tway.

"Talkin'!" retorted Utah, his lean face lighting with a smile.

At this sally all the men, except Tway, roared with mirth. Even the half-breed laughed at Tway's discomfiture.

Sue lingered near until her presence became rather obvious to the bantering riders; then she strolled farther on, to the edge of the cottonwood grove, where she found a seat on a log.

The sun had set. The valley was full of purple shadows, and far beyond them rose the dim strange bulk of Wild Horse Mesa. How vast and open this Utah wilderness! Reluctantly she confessed its beauty, its appeal to the depths of her, its all-satisfying, inexplicable charm. She heard the fluttering of cottonwood leaves; she smelled fragrant wood smoke, and saw the dim bands of wild horses down on the level floor of the valley. Something took hold of her soul, and the nearest she could come to interpreting its meaning was in her vague glad sense that this experience of hers had just begun and would last long. It seemed connected with dreams of childhood, far off, sweetly remembered things, yet too deep, too mysterious to recall.

A footfall on the leaves roused Sue. Turning, she saw Chess coming, a smile on his frank face.

"Sue, may I sit with you?" he asked.

"Yes — if you'll be a good boy and fetch my coat. It's on the wagon tongue."

"Sue, I'd get anything for you," he said, and turned away.

Presently he returned with it and held it for her. Chess had thoughtful, courteous little ways that pleased Sue. They spoke well for what he had been to his mother and sister, and for the home where he had learned them.

"Sue, you take me for such a boy!" he expostulated as he flopped down before her and sat Indian fashion with his legs crossed. He was bareheaded and his curly brown locks had a glint of gold.

"Of course I do. You're only eighteen," replied Sue.

"Sure. But I'm a man. I had *that* out with my brother Chane. I feel old as the hills. And,

Sue, you'll be only twenty next month. You're no Methuselum, or whatever they called him."

"How did you learn my age?" she inquired.

"I asked your dad."

"Well, suppose I am only twenty. That is very much older than you."

"Sue, I can't see it . . . I'm sure old enough to — to be in love with you," he rejoined, his voice lowering at the last.

She regarded him disapprovingly, not quite sure that there was not more earnestness or something different about him today. She had always disarmed his sentiment by taking it lightly, and she now decided on the same tactics.

"Chess, when did you say the same thing to Ora?" queried Sue.

"I — I never said it," he denied, stoutly, but a flush tinged his healthy cheek.

"Don't fib. You know you did," retorted Sue, shaking her finger at him. "You've made love to Ora."

"Yes, I did, at first — same as I have to all the girls. I reckon I just couldn't help that. I always liked girls. . . . Ora, now, she's pretty and clever, but she — I — I don't like to say anything about a girl, but, Sue, she's catty."

Sue merely looked at Chess, trying to hide

the fact that she knew this well enough. Chess was laboring under some stress.

"Ora's catty. She's spiteful. She says things about you I don't like, Sue. That's about settled her with me."

"Any jealous girl is that way, you know. Jealousy is the hatefulest feeling. Don't be hard on Ora. She —"

"Ahuh! All right, but she can't talk to me about you," he declared. "And you didn't let me say what — what I wanted to."

"No? Well, get it over, then, if it will relieve you."

"I can prove I wasn't in earnest with Ora — and all the girls you hint of," he said, manfully, gazing straight at her.

"Oh, you can!" murmured Sue, wanting to laugh.

"I never asked Ora — or *any* of them — to marry me," he declared, in solemn triumph.

This liberated Sue's laugh, but it was not hearty. His earnestness touched her.

"You never asked *me*, either," she retorted, and then could have bitten her tongue.

"No, but I'm asking you now," he flashed back at her.

"Chess!" exclaimed Sue, aghast.

"You needn't be so surprised. I mean it. I'm old enough to love you — and big enough to work for you. I've thought it all out. You're too wonderful a girl to mind my being poor; you're . . ."

"My dear boy, don't say any more," interrupted Sue, forced to gravity. His clean brown face had turned white. "I'm sorry I teased you — didn't take you seriously. But — Chess, I feel like — like a mother to you. I can't marry you, boy."

"Why — not?" he asked, swallowing hard.

"Because I don't love you," replied Sue, earnestly.

"I knew that, but I — I hoped you might come to it," he said, bravely struggling with his emotions.

Sue watched him, rather dubiously inquiring into her memory. Had she been unduly friendly to this impulsive lad? But, though she felt a kind of remorse, she did not have a guilty conscience. She saw Chess fight down his cherished dream. Then it seemed he turned to her with a stranger earnestness, with more eloquent eyes and eager lips.

"All right, Sue. I'll take my medicine," he said, hurriedly. "But I want to ask you something just as important."

"What is it?" she asked, curiously.

"If you won't marry me, will you wait for my brother Chane? You can't help but love *him!*"

"Why, Chess . . . !" murmured Sue, and

then she halted. She had never been quite so astounded in her life. There had come a sudden change in the boy's voice — in his big dark eyes — so eloquent and beautiful that it was impossible to consider his request as ridiculous. Sue did not know how to answer him.

"Chane had gone to the Indian reservation — over the canyons," went on Chess. "He went to buy horses to sell to the Mormons. I wanted to go, but he wouldn't let me. He tried to make me stay at my job in St. George. But I saw you — and I asked your dad for work so I could be near you. . . . Now Chane, as soon as he gets rid of those horses, he'll be hitting my trail. He always hunts me up. He thinks I'm still a boy. He still calls me Boy Blue. He's afraid I'm going to the bad. . . . Well, when he finds me he'll see you, and he'll fall in love with you. Chane never fell in love with a girl, to my knowledge. But you're the sweetest, wonderfulest girl in the world. He just can't help himself . . . and then I could have you for a sister."

The swift words rushed out in a torrent, and the simplicity of them touched Sue to the heart. Indeed, she had not known Chess Weymer. Less than boy — he was a child! But now she understood better why she had liked him.

"I-I'll be your sister, anyhow," said Sue, trying to think of something to say that would not hurt him. She sensed a singular relation between him and this older brother who called him Boy Blue. It thrilled Sue. There must be a wonderful love between them. It made her curious to hear more about this brother, yet, in view of Chess's proposal, she did not quite like to ask. Perhaps that would not be necessary, so she waited.

"Sue, you just can't help but love Chane," began Chess, his face lighting. "I've watched you. I've studied you. I know what you care about. But any girl would love Chane. I've never been anywhere with him where there was a girl — that she didn't fall in love with him. Without his even looking at her!"

"Indeed! Well, this brother of yours must be a — quite a fellow," replied Sue. "What's he like?"

"Oh, Chane's grand," burst out Chess, thus encouraged. "He's like my father, only he's got mother in him, too, which makes him finer. He's tall and dark, and, say! he looks right through you. Chane's got the sweetest, gentlest disposition. But he's a fighter. It's because of his kindness that he's always getting into fights. He's had some worse than fistfights, I'm sorry to say. He's ridden all over and has been in many outfits. He hates cattle

77

and loves horses. I guess the Weymers were all horse lovers. My father was born in Kentucky. Chane never settles down. He goes more and more to the wild places. He's a lonely sort of fellow — gets restless where there's lots of people. Somebody will get into trouble and then Chane takes up that trouble. He'd never have any trouble if he'd keep away from people — and *me*. I give him most trouble. I'm always in hot water; then, sooner or later Chane rides up and gets me out of it."

"No wonder he calls you Boy Blue!" said Sue, impulsively.

"He doesn't any more, to my face. I hate it," declared Chess, darkly.

"Is this brother a wild-horse hunter?" asked Sue.

"Chane's been everything, but he loves horses best. They don't have to be wild. They just have to be *horses*, tame or wild, good or bad, young or old. But I reckon lately the wild-horse wrangling has gotten more into Chane. It's been sort of a fever across Nevada and Utah, you know. Two years ago he saw that great wild stallion, Panquitch. You've heard of him. Well, Chane was actually dotty over that wild horse."

"I can understand the thrill of chasing wild horses. I've felt that when I've ridden out to watch you riders. But I can't bear to see horses hurt, whether wild or tame."

"Chane's the same way, Sue," rejoined Chess. "Oh, you and he are a lot alike. Just wait 'til you meet him. Just wait 'til you see *him* handle horses."

"Very well, Chess, I'll try to possess my soul in peace — until Chane trails you up," replied Sue, laughing gayly. "Good night now. I'm sorry if I hurt you — yet, I'm glad you told me about yourself — and Chane."

Sue left him sitting there in the dusk and returned camp-fireward. But she did not tarry in the ruddy circle where the men were talking and laughing, nor did she go to her tent. She went off alone into the deep shadow of the cottonwoods. The air was crisp and cold, sweet with its wild tang, white stars were burning in the deep-blue vault above, the leaves were rustling in the night breeze, the late crickets were chirping with a melancholy note of coming frost. Far out in the lonely darkness coyotes were howling.

"So I must wait for this wonderful brother Chane who calls him Boy Blue," murmured Sue, dreamily.

She had been strangely, profoundly stirred, and could not grasp just why. She reasoned at first that it was because this boy Chess had paid her the highest honor possible, and then because she felt sorry for him, and then, at the revelation of such a beautiful attachment between brothers. These, however, were not conclusive. Chess's words had struck at a hitherto untouched chord in her heart — the romance, the glory and dream of some love to come, vague, deep, latent, mysterious. Absurd indeed was the boy's hope and assurance that she could not help but love Chane. What an odd name! She had never heard it before. In spite of her common sense, and her appreciation of Chess's boyish sentiment, there had come into her mind a sudden strange establishment between her vague dream hero and this lonely desert rider, this horse lover so eloquently portrayed by his adoring brother. Sue scouted the inception. But it was there.

"Oh, it was so silly — his talk," she whispered. "Who ever could guess what was in that wild boy?"

Sue at last turned away from the lonely night and the speaking stars, and repaired to her little tent. She went to bed not quite mistress of her vagrant fancies, not wholly sure of herself. Night always had that effect upon her; on the morrow she knew she would be her old, practical, sensible self. But the hour at hand, when sleep did not come readily, held her at the mercy of the unknown, the calling voices, the dim awakenings of instinct.

Chapter 4

The settling of Melberne's outfit into permanent camp at Stark Valley was characterized by the advent of perfect weather, a welcome change from the storms and winds of the past weeks. The rainy season had lingered late. It was most beneficial to the desert, but hard on wild-horse wranglers and others exposed to the elements. But the very day after Melberne pitched camp in the cottonwood grove it seemed the wonderful Indian summer of Utah smiled its golden purple-hazed welcome. It made camp life a joy, whether there was work or not, especially if some of the time could be idled away. Sue heard Loughbridge say that they might expect such weather to last for a month and possibly longer.

Melberne was not an experienced wild-horse hunter. This game was comparatively new to him. But he had great force and energy and he could handle men. Whatever his weakness, which perhaps was mostly a susceptibility to suggestion, he was just and fair in his dealings. The riders would not take orders from Loughbridge.

"Wal, men, we're heah," announced Melberne, cheerfully, after breakfast that first morning at Stark Valley. "An' now let's rustle. I'm not goin' to drive this valley till I've a plan mapped out. Some way to trap a lot of horses. I'll ride with Alonzo an' Jim down into the valley an' get the lay of the land. Reckon I can give you all plenty to do . . . Jake, you keep charge of camp an' help the womenfolks. Build a stone oven, make a stand for the big kettle, pack water, an' whatever offers. . . . Captain, saddle your horse an' snake in a lot of dead hardwood. My boy Tommy will help you saw it. He just loves the end of a crosscut saw. Ha! Ha! An', Miller, you an' Utah ride up into some of them canyons that open into the valley. Take stock of any place where there's sign of wild horses. Chess, you like to hunt. Now we're out of meat an' I look to you as provider. Don't hunt alone. That's bad business. Take Bonny with you. There shore ought to be lots of game heah."

"In a pinch we can eat wild-hoss meat," observed Utah, with a drawl. "It shore ain't bad."

"Dad, you wouldn't kill a beautiful wild horse to *eat!*" exclaimed Sue, in horror.

82

"Wal, lass, I never did," he replied. "Fact is I never tasted horse flesh. Is it good, Alonzo?"

"Señor, I don't know," answered the Mexican *vaquero*, almost curtly. Manifestly the suggestion was not to his liking.

"I'd starve first," added Sue, spiritedly.

Her father laughed good-naturedly and gave order for the saddle-horses to be brought in. Chess went whistling his pleasure at the duty assigned him, and taking his bridle up he halted before Sue.

"Little Girl Gold," he said, gayly, "do you want your pony fetched in?"

"No, thanks, Chess. I've a heap of mending — washing to do. And why did you call me that? I'm not little. I weigh — or did — a hundred and thirty. My hair is chestnut, not gold."

"It had nothing to do with looks," replied Chess, mysteriously.

"Oh, very well, little Boy Blue," returned Sue, lightly.

"Say, I can stand that from *you*," flashed Chess, "but don't say it before anybody."

"You'll see. Wait till your brother Chane rides in on your trail," said Sue, teasingly.

"I wish I hadn't told you," he replied, with regret. "Because if you do I'm going to get mad."

"Chess, you have called me a number of names, and none of them suited me."

"Mrs. Chess Weymer would suit fine, but you're hard to please," he retorted, with a laugh. Then he went whistling on his way, leaving behind him a pleasant sense of something fine and gay and irresponsible in him. Sue reflected that it was rather inconsistent of her to note he apparently had not been cast down by her rejection. Sometimes she regarded some of her thoughts and feelings quite dubiously.

She set about her own necessary duties, which, however, were all personal. She was not often called upon to help in the general camp chores. First she got Jake and Bonny to lift her chest out of the wagon and place it in the back of her tent.

"Now, Sue, I'll bet you've got some pretty dresses in here," ventured Jake, his tanned face wrinkling. He had big brown eyes, full of the kindliest expression.

"A few, Jake. And all the other possessions I have in the world," she replied.

"No wonder you were afraid I'd drive the wagon over a bank," responded Jake, with tremendous interest. "Some day you'll dress up for us, won't you? I'd like awful well to see you. My little girl, if she'd lived, would be about your age now."

"Yes, Jake, I will if it would please you," said Sue.

"Please me! Well now, listen to her! Bonny, wouldn't you like to see Sue all dressed up?"

"Shure, Miss Sue, it'd be g-g-grand," replied the Irishman, with the most intense gravity. "I'd like to see you knock out the black-eyed wench."

Jake and Bonny stooped out under the tent flaps, leaving Sue on her knees beside her precious chest. "These men . . . it's funny how they give Ora a little dig now and then. She's pretty. But, no, I guess it's not funny."

Sue dragged her tarpaulin and roll of blankets, and her chaps, spurs, gloves, gun, slicker, coat — all her belongings except the big chest, out into the sunlight. She spread the blankets in the sun.

"Jake," she called, "I want you to help me some more."

She dispatched the genial Jake to fetch a tarpaulinful of cedar and piñon boughs; and on second thought, finding she had no task at hand while she waited for him, she followed him up the slope and helped him gather the boughs and drag the loaded tarpaulin back to her tent. Jake was the best of company, and, moreover, he had a way of making one feel more thoughtful and tolerant of others. "I'll tell you, Sue," he said, very confidentially, "don't let Bonny or anybody put you against Ora. She's a nice girl, if you just like her. She's been spoiled. It's plain she was sweet on young Chess, and everybody saw Chess favored you. That's a hard place for a girl. It brings out feelings we all have."

"Jake, I liked Ora, but lately she's different," protested Sue, and she tried to explain to the earnest old fellow how hard it was to be always sweetly disposed toward Ora.

"Yes, I know. But you'd feel better if you never had hard feelings," replied Jake.

With Jake's help, Sue laid a mattress of fragrant boughs, a foot deep, along one side of her tent, holding them in place with a small log, cut to fit snugly against the canvas at each end. Upon this she spread the tarpaulin, made her bed of blankets upon it, and pulling the long end of the tarpaulin up, she tucked it in all around. That done, she and Jake covered the rest of the floor space in the tent with the remaining boughs. Upon this springy carpet she spread the few Indian blankets she had. Jake fashioned a crude little rack to hold whatever she chose to hang upon it. Her duffle bag she placed in a corner. Then upon the chest, which could serve as a table, she placed her little mirror and the other toilet articles she possessed, her sewing kit, and a bag of sundry materials. Whereupon she surveyed the interior of her canvas home with a great deal of satisfaction, and sat down to consider which of her other numerous tasks she would begin first.

The hours sped apace. It was Melberne's way in camp to have only two meals, breakfast and supper, and the latter usually came around sunset. Sue heard the men ride in, at different times, and she knew the afternoon was waning. But she kept at her mending until Mrs. Melberne called that supper was ready.

"Sue, you should have been with me," shouted Chess, the instant she appeared. And with a biscuit in one hand and a cup in the other he burst into the narrative of his adventures. She caught more of his thrilling enthusiasm and excitement than of his story. He was radiant. He had shot his first deer — a buck so big that Bonny had to help him pack it to camp.

The Irishman was evidently an inexperienced hunter. He had wasted a good deal of ammunition on deer, without success.

"Shure, I follered them," said Bonny, "an' loike as not I'd soon have hit one. But I saw a bear! He walked roight out of a thicket — a gray furry brute, big as a steer — an' thot's all I rimimber."

"Say, mate, didn't you heave a shot at him?" queried Captain Bunk.

"My horse run, an' I thot I'd better run after him," replied Bonny, seriously.

"Haw! Haw!" roared the seafaring man.

Sue's father rode in just before dark, dusty and weary, but so elated over his day's experience that, like Chess, he had to talk before he could eat. He had seen thousands of wild horses that apparently had never been chased, so tame were they.

"If there were only trees or brush down in the valley, we could cut them and drag them into long fences leading to a trap!" he ejaculated. "What a haul we'd make! But there's not a tree in this heah valley, so far as we rode . . . Sue, I saw a sorrel today — the finest piece of horseflesh I ever beheld. He was light color, not red or brown, but something between. A stallion with mane and tail that almost swept the ground. He had a whole bunch of bays and blacks. As we rode toward them he drove them on. They shore wasn't bad scared. He whistled like a bugle note."

"Dad, you may give him to me," replied Sue, thrilled by his excitement.

Utah's report appeared equally interesting to the men. Some ten miles or more down the slope of the valley he had come upon a canyon which he thought it well to explore. At the head of this he encountered a wild, broken-up section of ridges, all sloping down from two converging walls that met above. He discovered fine grass and water, and a drove of wild mules. They were in a natural trap, and it was Utah's opinion they could be caught in one day.

"Wal, shore that's fine," declared Melberne. "We're going to be busy round heah."

Miller was the last to come in, and he had his supper by the light of the camp fire. Manifestly he had unusual and good reports to make, but, unfortunately, it happened to be a time when his fatal stuttering affected him most. Once he nearly got launched into clear speech, but Utah, who seemed peculiarly irritated by his rider comrade's failing, yelled out, "Whistle it, you Chinese poll-parrot!"

That was too much for the exhausted wrangler; casting a baleful glance at Utah he subsided into silence.

Long and earnestly the other wild-horse hunters talked. It was an interesting evening round the camp fire. Sue, inspired by Jake's kind words, deliberately sought out Ora Loughbridge and persistently made herself agreeable. At first Ora was stiff and what Chess had called snippy. But she was not proof against Sue's kindliness, and gradually she thawed. Somehow during that hour Sue got an impression of Ora's really deep attachment to Chess. She was about Chess's age, and a romantic girl of strong emotions. Sue noted that Ora could scarcely keep her eyes from wandering in his direction, yet at the same time she was trying to hide her secret. Her state of mind seemed no longer trivial and amusing; indeed, Sue found that by exerting herself to be kind she had roused her own sympathy for the girl.

Sue divided the mornings between her own tasks and helping her stepmother; in the afternoons she was free to idle or ride or read. The men had not yet completed their reconnaissance of the surrounding country, nor had her father hit upon a satisfactory plan to trap a large number of wild horses.

The first frosts had begun to tint the foliage of the deciduous trees, and this added fresher beauty and contrast to the evergreens. The cottonwood grove was half gold, half green; the oak brush of the canyons began to take on a bronze and russet hue. The vines overgrowing the ledges of rock back of camp showed red against the gray; and up in the canyons, bright spots of scarlet stood out strikingly.

Sue liked colors. Blue was most becoming to her fair complexion and chestnut hair, but she was not partial to it. Red caught her eye, held her, thrilled her with something nameless, but it was purple which she loved. And it appeared that on the Indian summer afternoons the whole sweep of valley and stone barriers beyond slumbered under a haze of purple, ethereal and mysterious close at hand, dark and heavy and enveloping in the distance.

The autumn season had halted for the present and all nature seemed to slumber. Even the birds showed the spell, banding in flocks, seldom taking wing, twittering plaintively. Down on the valley floor, the wild horses moved almost imperceptibly.

Sue rode far and high one afternoon, accompanied by Ora and Chess, who, however, were more concerned with other things than scenery or Indian summer. Chess had been complimented on his successful hunting and was eager to win more commendation. Ora was mostly concerned with Chess, and liked the hunting only because it furnished means to ride with him. They left Sue on a high open point, back of which was a big country of ridges and ravines, all thickly covered with brush and trees. Here the young hunters disappeared.

Dismounting to await their return, Sue found a comfortable seat and gave herself up to the solitude and loneliness of the surrounding hills, and the wonder of the purple open beneath her. The cottonwood grove which hid the camp appeared a golden patch on the edge of the green valley; the wild horses were but dim specks. The valley itself was only an oval basin lost in a country as wide as the horizons.

What lay and upreared and hid beyond that level rangeland was the thing which drew and chained Sue's gaze. It was the canyon country of Utah. Long had she heard of it, and now it seemed to spread out before her, a vast shadowy region of rock — domes, spurs, peaks, bluffs, reaching escarpments, lines of cleavage, endless scalloped marching rocks, and rising grandly out of that chaos of colored rock the red-walled, black-tipped, flat-topped mountain that was Wild Horse Mesa. Here Sue could see a magnificent panorama of the canyon country, above which the great mesa towered a sentinel. If it had earned Sue's interest from the valley far below, it now fascinated her. Indeed, the rock wilderness emphasized by this isolated tableland called forth feelings which were strange and unintelligible to Sue. Was it just the beauty, the loneliness, and the majesty of nature that had come to arrest her thought and trouble her soul? What was she going to meet out here in wild Utah? Of late her working hours, her idle hours, even her dreams, her walks and rides and rests, had been vaguely haunted by the shadow of a mood that did not wholly break upon her consciousness.

"Something's wrong," sighed Sue, and her practical common sense did not drive away the conception. It was in the very solitude of her surroundings, and she could not grasp its meaning. But she divined that much as this new life in the open had come to mean, color and landscape and action, the fun afforded by the riders, and the interest of Ora's love affair — these were not the secret of her subjection.

At last Sue confessed to her heart that she must be in love. It was one of the most secret of confessions, one of dreams almost, unaccepted by intelligence. But as the vague idea grew it developed out of that deep unconscious sphere where she had hidden her girlish fancies and ideals. It became a thought, amazing, ridiculous, inconceivable. It could not be supported by any facts. With whom could she be in love? Not Chess or Utah or any of the riders! Could it be with herself or life or this magnificent wilderness, or the nature that brooded there so solemnly? Sue tried to recall the dream hero, knight, lover that had been an evolution of her fairy-tale days, but he did not suit her new and masterful image. The new one seemed like this country, hard, rough, wild, untamed, exacting, dominating.

"But it's only an idea!" burst out Sue, ashamed, astounded. Her cheeks were hot. Her blood ran strong from her heart. She felt it beat, beat, beat. Then there flashed into her mind what the boy Chess Weymer had said about his brother Chane: "You can't help but love *him!*"

Sue at once laughed away the absurdity of any connection between the boy's loyal worship of his brother and her own undivined yearnings. Yet there was something, and to strike a compromise with herself she acknowledged that any girl would have an interest in this wild-horse hunter who had such a great love for his brother and called him Boy Blue. There was enough romance in any girl for that, and if not romance, then a mother feeling.

"I've no work," soliloquized Sue. "It's this wandering, idle life, like an Indian's. I think too much. But — there's the other side to it. How beautiful the earth! I've learned to know the sunset, night, the stars, the moon, the sunrise, day — storm and cloud and rain, and now this purple summer. The birds, the animals — horses I love. I love the smell of the cedars, the pines, the earth, the grass. I love the feel of the rocks . . . oh, something has come into my life. There's a step on my trail!"

Sue waited long for Ora and Chess, and at length they appeared riding under the trees, close together, without any game. Sue had a suspicion that they were holding hands just as they rode out of the timber, but she could not be certain. A further glance told her that they were no longer quarreling, which had been decidedly the case on the way up. Sue mounted her pony and started down the winding descent of the ridge.

About halfway down to camp, Ora and Chess caught up with her, and both appeared to overdo their excuses for such long absence.

"Were you gone long?" inquired Sue. "I hadn't noticed that."

Chess's account of their hunt did not ring like those of former occasions, when he had found game. This time there was not a deer on the mountainside.

"My brave hunter boy, I'm sure you found one *dear*," said Sue, tantalizingly. She felt a tiny feminine twinge of pique. Chess had not long resisted the propinquity of the other girl.

"Aw, Sue, I reckon you are a lot older and wiser than me. There's no fooling you," declared Chess, half in regret and half resignedly.

This allusion to her proudly maintained maturity did not please Sue. It was all right for her to think it, but for Chess to accept it all of a sudden somehow irritated Sue. But she reflected that she was in a strange mood and not so kindly disposed as usual. She decided to let them do the talking.

Ora was overdoing it more than Chess. She was enthusiastic about the ride, and the canyon up there, and about a great deal in general, and nothing in particular. Ora's big dark eyes were unusually bright, her cheeks were redder than seemed natural for slow riding, and her hair was disheveled. There was a singular radiance, a glow in her face, that contrasted markedly with the sullen shade which had characterized it recently. Sue concluded that this rascal Chess had really been making love to Ora.

"Sue, isn't it just perfectly gorgeous?" murmured Ora, dreamily.

"What?" asked Sue, rather bluntly.

"Oh, everything — the bright colors, the sweet, sleepy something, the horses, riding out this way, this camp life," babbled Ora.

"I think I know what you're raving about, Ora," replied Sue. "I'm glad you've come to feel it. Not long ago you were disgusted with the desert, Utah, wild horses, wranglers, and yourself."

"Yes, I know, Sue," said Ora, somewhat dampened, "but I — I'm not now."

There appeared to be a humility in Ora, at this moment, that Sue had never observed before. It strengthened Sue's conviction as to the cause. Then Chess, who was riding half a horse's length behind Ora, caught Sue's eye and winked mysteriously, with a hint of deviltry. Almost it seemed that he was telling Sue that if he could not have her he could have Ora. Sue flashed him a very scornful and accusing glance, and did not deign to notice him again. A little later, however, she could have laughed. She was beginning to understand why this boy's brother believed he needed looking after.

"Some stranger in camp," spoke up Chess, quickly, as they rode into the back of the cottonwood grove. Whereupon he trotted on ahead of Sue and Ora. Sue sustained a little shock of excitement that made her conscious of her own interest in a strange rider. What if it might be Chane Weymer! She saw a muddy, weary pack horse sagging under a bedraggled pack. But trees obstructed her view of the rider.

Ora headed her horse for the quarters of the Loughbridges and Sue turned for her tent. When she dismounted, Chess rode up at a lope and leaped off. One glance at his face told

Sue that the newcomer was not Chane. Sue felt a sudden relief and vague disappointment! This annoyed her and made her resentful toward Chess.

"Doggone — it! I thought maybe Chane had come and I'd get even with you," said Chess as he began to unsaddle her horse.

"Get even with me! What for?" queried Sue, exasperated.

"Well, I reckon I'd call it lack of reci-pro-city," declared Chess, cheerfully.

"Chess, you're not very witty . . . and please explain how the possible arrival of your brother would enable you to get even with me, as you call it."

"You're sure likely to fall in love head over heels, and you *might* get the cold shoulder, as I got it."

"Chess, you're adding rudeness to your many other faults," retorted Sue, haughtily.

"Aw, Sue, I beg pardon," said Chess, contritely, as he slid her saddle and blankets to the ground. "I'm only sore. But I'll get over it . . . and listen. Chane'd never give you a cold shoulder. Now remember what I tell you. He'll fall terribly in love with you."

Suddenly a hot blush burned Sue's neck and face. Ashamed, furious with her ungovernable and conflicting emotions, she turned away from Chess.

"Don't talk — non-nonsense," she replied, hastily. "Who is the stranger?"

"When I saw he wasn't Chane I just rode back," returned Chess. "But soon as I 'tend to the horses I'll find out for you."

Chess mounted and went off whistling, leading Sue's mount toward Ora's tent. Sue kicked off her spurs and chaps and went inside her tent to change her masculine garb. It might have been that she paid the least bit more attention than usual to her appearance. Still, though she liked the more serviceable and comfortable garb of men for riding or roughing it, she had always, when possible, given preference to feminine dress. Sue sat down to await the supper call, quite aware of an eager appetite, which, however, did not prevent her from reflection. Presently there came a rustling footfall outside.

"Sue, I yelled once supper is ready," called Chess. "I'll bet my horse to your spurs that you've been doing the same as Ora."

"What's that?" asked Sue, as she spread the flaps of her tent and came forth.

"Aw, Sue!" he ejaculated, staring at her. His handsome boyish face expressed both delight and regret. "I never saw you — so — so sweet . . . all for the benefit of the stranger! Ora primped up, too. Sue, you women are all alike."

"Why, of course! Aren't men all alike?" returned Sue, archly.

"Not by a darn sight," he denied, "and you'll find out some day."

"Well, who's the stranger?" demanded Sue, with undue interest, just to torment Chess.

"Ahuh! Well, his name's Manerube — Bent Manerube. How's that for a handle? He's a horse-wrangler from Nevada. Husky, good-looking chap. He's just in from the Piute country, across the canyons. Sure looked like he'd been riding rough."

"That's the country I saw today from up high. Wild Horse Mesa! He can tell us about it, can't he?"

"I reckon. But see here, Sue," went on Chess, and as he faced about to walk with her toward the camp fire he took her arm gently and firmly. "Don't forget you're to be Chane's sweetheart — and my sister."

"Little Boy Blue, I'll not be won by proxy," rejoined Sue.

Whereupon he let go her arm and maintained a rather lofty silence. Sue stole a glance at him out of the tail of her eye. His face seemed different, somehow. Then they reached the camp fire and the supper table. Manifestly the men were all waiting.

"Hello, lass!" called her father. "Shore you an' Ora have held up the festal board. Sue,

meet Mr. Benton Manerube of Nevada. —
This's my daughter. Now, everybody, let's eat."

Sue saw a tall man standing beside her father
and she bowed in acknowledgment of the
introduction. He had gleaming eyes that
seemed to leap at sight of her and absorb her.
Sue dropped her own. Chess, as usual, was
promptly on hand with a seat for her and Ora;
and in a moment they were supplied with
bountifully laden plates.

"Sue, isn't he handsome?" whispered Ora.

"Who?" queried Sue.

"Mr. Manerube, of course. Did you think
I meant Chess?"

"Why, I hadn't noticed."

"Well, he's noticed *you*, and I'm jealous,"
declared Ora.

"Yes, you acted like it on the ride back to
camp . . . but I'm hungry."

Some moments later Sue covertly stole a
glance at the newcomer, who sat opposite, between her father and Loughbridge. Ora had
not been mistaken about the man's looks, despite a discolored bruise on his face. His hair
glinted in the sunset glow, and his complexion,
though browned by exposure, was still so fair
that it made the other riders look like Indians.

Sue, perhaps following Ora's example,
rather prolonged the eating of her supper. One

by one the riders got up from round the tarpaulin tablecloth and clinked away to the tasks necessary before dark. Chess remained sitting cross-legged beside Ora, while Jake, always helpful, began to gather up the plates and cups. Sue's father, having finished his supper, rose to his feet and threw some wood on the fire. Loughbridge got up and said something in a low tone to Melberne. They were both interested in the newcomer. Naturally this quickened Sue's perceptions. Finally Manerube stood up, showing the superb figure of a rider and the worn, soiled garb of one who had surely been in contact with hard country. He wore a belt which swung low on his right hip with the weight of a gun. His blouse was a heavy checkered woolen garment, made by the Mormons, Sue thought, and as he wore no coat or vest, his broad shoulders and deep chest showed strikingly. His unshaven beard, of days' growth, was so fair that it did not detract from the fresh ruddy virility of his face.

"I sure was starved," he remarked, in a deep voice with a pleasant ring. "No grub for a week, except with Indians. Reckon I could bless your womenfolk, Melberne."

"Shore, I've been hungry," replied Melberne, heartily. "You looked fagged. An' Alonzo said your horses were ready to drop.

Where you bound?"

"Well, nowhere in particular," replied Manerube, slowly. "I was disappointed in my errand across the rivers. Fellow got ahead of me, buying horses from the Piutes. Reckon I'll tie up with the first wrangler outfit in need of a good rider."

"Ahuh! Do you know this wild-horse game?" asked Melberne, quickly.

Manerube uttered a short laugh. "Do I? Well, Melberne, I reckon so."

At this juncture Sue noted how Chess sat up, after the manner of a listening jackrabbit. Sue appreciated her own little thrill of interest. What assurance this rider had!

"Have you ever caught wild horses in large numbers, so they could be shipped unbroken?" went on Melberne.

"I'm the man who started that game," replied Manerube. "Shipped three thousand for Saunders last year."

"Saunders? Do you mean the Mormon cattleman?" asked Loughbridge.

"Jim Saunders of Salt Lake. He brought me over from Nevada. I was with his Kanab outfit."

"Mel, I'm thinkin' Manerube is the wrangler we're after," added Loughbridge, turning to his partner. "Let's give him charge of our outfit."

"Shore," rejoined Melberne, quick to respond. "Manerube, if you'll hang up heah we'll pay you top wages, with a percent of our profits."

"Glad to help you out," said Manerube, with a wave of his hand, as if success was assured. "Who're your riders?"

Melberne enumerated and named them, as he knew them, by their first names.

"You're forgettin' Alonzo," interposed Loughbridge.

"Alonzo. Is he a Mexican, a half-breed *vaquero*, catches wild horses alone?" asked Manerube, quickly.

"Yes, we have him," replied Melberne.

"Know of him. Great wrangler, they say," returned Manerube, thoughtfully. "But I reckon I never saw him. Well, you've hardly got enough good riders to handle big bunches of horses. Perhaps the young ladies could help?"

Manerube, while talking, had not been unaware of the presence of Sue and Ora, and now he launched this query at them as well as their fathers.

"Oh, you're not serious?" exclaimed Ora.

"Never more serious in my life," replied Manerube, with a winning smile. "Can you ride? I don't mean like a cowboy, but well enough to ride fast and hard."

"Shore they can," declared Melberne, speaking for the girls. "You're sworn in as wild-horse wranglers."

"Dad, I'm not so sure I want to be one," said Sue, shaking her head.

"Why, are you afraid?" queried Manerube. "I can see Miss Loughbridge likes the idea."

"It'll be gorgeous," burst out Ora.

Sue looked at the new rider and did not like the something in his eyes any better than his intimation of her cowardice.

"No, I'm not afraid," she said.

"Say, Sue's got more nerve than a man," interposed Chess, with spirit. "But she hates to see horses hurt."

"Wal, we won't argue aboot it," replied Melberne, genially. "Sue can do as she likes. Manerube, you come across the valley. Did you see many wild horses?"

"Thousands every day. All the way from Wild Horse Mesa. That's what the Mormons call the last stand of the wild horses. I saw the finest stock in all this country. It'd pay you, Melberne, after you catch and ship all horses possible near the railroad, to go after the fine stock."

"But shore we can't drive over thirty miles," protested Melberne.

"No. I meant to take time — catch the best wild horses and break them."

"Wal, shore heah's a new idea, Jim," declared Melberne. "I like it. What kind of range land over there?"

"Finest grass and water in Utah," replied Manerube.

"I heah there are horse thieves in the canyon country," said Melberne, dubiously.

"Reckon some outfits hold up over there. But you're just as liable to run across them here. Fact is I run into some Mormon outlaws over across the San Juan. Stayed with them a few days. Not bad fellows to meet, though."

"Who were they?" asked Loughbridge.

"Bud McPherson and two of his pards, Horn and Slack."

"Bud McPherson's pretty well known over St. George way," declared Loughbridge. "You've heard of him, Mel?"

"Shore, I've heard of a lot of these horse thieves," replied Melberne. "They're not worrying me. I've had to do with that brand down in Texas."

"Say, Manerube, how'd you come to camp with McPherson?" inquired Loughbridge, curiously.

It struck Sue that Manerube was not averse to talking about himself. She was interested, naturally, in so forceful a character, and there seemed something compelling about the man, but all at once she found she did not like him.

Ora, however, appeared completely fascinated, a fact that Manerube had manifestly grasped. Chess, too, had, if anything, grown more attentive.

"I was hunting for some Piutes, and run right into Bud and his pards," began Manerube, taking a seat on a log before the camp fire, somewhat closer to the girls. "It really wasn't their camp, as I learned afterward. It belonged to the wrangler who beat me getting to the Piutes. You know I told you I went to buy horses for the Mormons. This wrangler got there first. Lucky for me, because Mc-Pherson was only hanging round to steal horses. It rather tickles me, for I had a little set-to with that wrangler. He gave me this black eye. But you should have seen him!"

Manerube put his hand to the discolored blotch on his face, and his last remark was addressed to the girls.

Sue became suddenly very attentive, not because of Manerube's words, but because she saw that Chess was reacting strangely to this rider's story. He half rose and leaned to listen. His slender body quivered. Through Sue flashed a sudden intimation.

"You had a fight?" queried Melberne, much interested, and he crossed over nearer to Manerube.

Jake likewise had caught the drift of the

story, and he stood still, staring at the back of the rider's head.

"Reckon so. He didn't seem eager to throw his gun, and I had to beat him."

"Wall, you don't say!" ejaculated Melberne, now as interested as any boy at the recital of a fight. "But shore you must have had cause?"

"Yes, I reckon I'd have been justified in shooting the wrangler. But as I said, he wouldn't draw. It was all on account of a pretty little Piute girl named Sosie. She'd been to the government school, talked English well, and was crazy about white men. The wrangler had been a squaw man among the Navajos, so I'd heard. Well, he was after Sosie pretty hard. Toddy Nokin, the old Piute father, told him to stay away from her. But he wouldn't. Finally I felt sorry for Sosie. She was being fooled, poor kid. So I just picked a fight with that wrangler and pounded him as he deserved."

Manerube ended his story with a casual nonchalance and a deprecatory gesture, as if he rather disliked his personal contact in the affair.

Sue was more than thrilled to see Chess rise with the guarded movement of a cat, sustaining and banding strength, as if for a leap.

"Ahuh!" ejaculated Loughbridge, with

gravity. "Did you catch that wrangler's name?"

"Why, yes, come to think of that," replied Manerube, blandly. "It was Weymer — Chane Weymer."

Loughbridge uttered an exclamation, either of surprise or dismay. And Chess leaped wildly to confront Manerube.

"You damned liar!" he burst out, in ringing passionate fury.

Manerube was certainly astounded. "What?" he ejaculated, blankly, and stared.

Chess's face was white, his big eyes burned, his jaw quivered. He seemed strung like a whipcord.

"Chane Weymer's my brother!" he cried, and his quivering hand reached to his hip for a gun that was not there. Then, quick as a flash, he struck Manerube violently in the face, a sudden blow that almost toppled the man over. Righting himself, he sprang up with a curse. Rushing at Chess, he lunged out and beat the boy down. Chess fell into Jake's arms, and Loughbridge sprang before Manerube.

"That's enough. He's only a boy," ordered Loughbridge, hurriedly, and he pushed the other back.

"Boy or not, I'll — I'll —" panted Manerube, hoarsely, with his hand on his face.

"No, you won't do anythin'," said Loughbridge, forcibly, and he pushed Manerube to a seat on the log. "Reckon you was provoked, but cool down now."

Jake was having trouble holding Chess, who wrenched and lunged to get free.

"Easy now, Chess," said Jake, persuasively. "I'm not going to let you go. Why, boy, you're just mad. You want to look out for that temper. I had one once. I know. Now you just hold on."

Melberne came to Jake's assistance, and then the two men, one on each side of Chess, held him firmly until he stopped wrestling. There was blood on his ashen face, and a piercing passion in his eyes. Sue read in them a terrible intent that horrified while it shook her heart. Chess fixed his gaze on Manerube.

"If I'd had my gun I'd have — shot you," he panted, thickly. "You dirty liar! . . . I'll bet *you're* what — you made out my brother to be."

Then Chess turned to Melberne. "Let me go. I'll — I'll behave. But I want you to know my brother's — the soul of honor. If you'd known my mother you couldn't believe this skunk. Chane wouldn't lie — he couldn't hurt a girl, white or red. If he went out of his way for an Indian girl — it was to befriend her . . . he's big enough. He could marry a squaw, but it'd be out of the kindness of his heart."

Sue was aware that Ora was clutching at her with nervous hands. Chess, just then, seemed magnificent in defense of his brother. Without another word he wheeled away, his white face flashed in the firelight, and then he was gone.

"Manerube, shore you might have kept Weymer's name to yourself," said Melberne, with asperity.

"How'd I know he had a brother here?" demanded the other, wrathfully. "He hit me — right where his brother hit me . . . and he'd better keep out of my road."

"Reckon I'll see that he does," returned Melberne. "And you'll oblige me by not making trouble, if you want to stay with us."

Ora began to cry and ran off in the darkness. Sue sought her own tent, considerably upset by the incident. Sitting down upon her bed in the dark, she went over the whole situation. After all, as far as Chess was concerned, it had only been another fight. It was not the first. This one, however, was serious. Chess had looked dangerous. He had been like a lion. Sue thrilled anew as she recalled the blaze of his eyes, the ring of his voice. Manerube did not show admirably. Sue had not been favorably impressed by his narrative; besides, he was too big a man to beat a boy that way. True, Chess had given great provocation. Sue was thinking back to the real cause of the trouble when she was interrupted by her father outside.

"Sue, are you in bed?" he asked.

"No, dad."

He opened the flaps of the tent, letting in a ray of firelight. Then he entered, to take a seat on the bed beside Sue.

"Lass, reckon I'd like your angle on the little fracas between Chess and this Manerube," said her father as he took her hand in his.

Sue told him briefly and candidly what she thought about it.

"Wal, wal, I reckon I think aboot as you," he replied, ponderingly. "It looks like this heah to me. Manerube wanted to cut a dash before you girls . . . chesty sort of rider. But I've met lots like him. Only not so well spoken. Either he's not what he pretends or he's been something different from what he is now."

"I felt sorry for Chess," murmured Sue.

"Poor boy! But shore I can't see as he needed sympathy. He said what he thought, like a man, an' he banged Manerube hard . . . Sue, if Chess had been packing a gun — there'd have been blood spilled."

"Oh, dad!"

"Wal, I reckon I can control the youngster. Sue, he shore must love that brother Chane."

"Dad, I happen to know he worships him."

"More's the pity. I'm afraid Manerube was telling the truth."

"Ah!" exclaimed Sue. "How — why — ?"

"Wal, Loughbridge told me he had heard a lot aboot this Chane Weymer. Wonderful man with horses! He's been in some shooting scrapes. Lonely sort of chap. But, shore, that's all to his credit. It was the rumor aboot Indian squaws . . . Loughbridge heard talk in Bluff. Shore, it was Mormon talk. I don't know. I'd like to believe Chess — he was so damn fine. Somehow he just made me jump. But I reckon the boy's wrong an' Manerube's right. Loughbridge thinks so. Wal, wal, I'm sorry. Good night, lass."

Sue went to bed without lighting her candle. She felt a little shaken, and slipped under the blankets more quickly than usual. Then she lay wide awake in the darkness. She heard the low voices of men talking by the camp fire. The wind mourned through the cottonwoods. The night seemed sad. Poor devoted Boy Blue, with his wonderful love for the wonderful brother! It was well that the boy's mother was far away in Colorado, far from the gossip that would wound a loving heart. Chane Weymer! The vague, strange shadow of an ideal faded. Sue experienced a slight sinking sensation, almost a sickness, and following that a little heat at her vagrant and unfounded fancies. She whispered to herself: "Poor boy! He said, 'You couldn't help but love my brother Chane!'"

Chapter 5

To Chane Weymer's surprise, Toddy Nokin did not drive the mustangs toward the left on the Beaver Canyon trail, but in the direction of the great green bowl of shelving land that led down into the rock country. The long string of bobbing mustangs stretched out, with Toddy's sons riding in the rear. At the junction of the two trails the old Piute waited for Chane, and motioned for him to dismount. Toddy's demeanor was in no wise different from usual, yet Chane felt a quickening of his pulse.

Toddy Nokin made one of his slow gestures toward Chane's camp.

"No want white men," he said, significantly.

Chane regarded his Indian friend with surprise and dawning comprehension. Toddy had reasons for signifying that Chane should dispense with Bud McPherson and his cronies.

"All right, Toddy. If you say so. I sure don't want them," he declared, with finality, and waited for the Piute to speak further. Manifestly Toddy was pondering deeply. At last he said, speaking in his own tongue, that Chane would be wise to leave his camp and supplies, without telling McPherson of his intention to drive the mustangs across the rivers. He could say he was going to ride across country to see a relative of Toddy Nokin's about purchasing more horses, and this would give Chane opportunity to drive his mustangs across the San Juan before McPherson became aware of the ruse. Toddy did not give any reason for this. But the mere suggestion was enough. Bud McPherson was undoubtedly a horse thief. Chane had vague recollection of the name, somehow connected with shady horse deals.

"But, Toddy, what'll I do for grub and blankets?" queried Chane, reluctant to surrender his outfit. "And there're my packhorses."

The Piute said he would get the horses, and without further comment he mounted his mustang and rode down the trail after his sons.

Chane did not have any choice, it seemed, yet he deliberated before getting on his horse. It galled him to sacrifice his outfit to three outlaws. Still, there was nothing of any value, except the food. Perhaps this was the wisest course to get rid of the men, but he could not satisfy himself wholly with it. Would Bud

116

McPherson be so easily fooled? Chane's hostility had roused with the certainty that these men had imposed upon him and were not what they claimed to be. Why not ride into camp with a drawn gun, fight it out with them, or, better, take possession of their weapons, so they could not ambush his trail?

"Reckon Toddy knows best," he soliloquized, finally. "There's less risk in his plan — maybe. I don't know . . . but I'd like to have it out with Bud McPherson."

Chane did not find it easy to abandon that last idea. He had fought the same thing before more than once, and every time it had been harder. He did not like violent issues, but as he had grown older among the rough men of this desert, he had not seen any advantage in turning his other cheek to those who struck him. That stone country taught stern measures.

Mounting Brutus, he headed west on the Beaver Creek trail, reached the great corner of yellow cliff, and rode round under its looming wall, down the rock ledges to the stream, and up the other slope to camp. The cedars were thick, and through them he thought he saw an object move. Then a jackrabbit loped off through the sage. It might have been what he had seen. Chane rode to the cedar where he kept his bed and one of his packs, and

117

here he dismounted. It was some distance from the main camp. There did not appear to be any of the men in sight. This relieved Chane. He strode over to the camp. A fire of cedar boughs was still smoldering, and a pot of beans was smoking. The camp-fire duffle appeared as usual. McPherson and his men had ridden off somewhere. Chane returned to his pack, and rummaged round until he found his little notebook and lead pencil. On a leaf of this he wrote that he was going off toward the Navajo country to buy more mustangs. This he tore out of the book, and going back to the camp fire he placed it in a conspicuous place, with a little stone to weigh it down. Upon the return it occurred to him that as the camp was deserted he might take what he wanted. But he must exercise care not to pick up anything McPherson might miss.

When he reached the cedar he found Brutus stamping, either excited about something or impatient to be off. Chane had not known the horse long enough to understand him.

"What's the matter, old boy?" queried Chane.

Brutus snorted and tossed his head. His ears were up and he had fire in his eyes. Whatever the cause, Brutus's actions made Chane wary, and he peered around uneasily. No man or Indian or beast appeared in sight. Chane procured a box of rifle shells from his pack, a small leather case, and a bag of parched and salted corn, which he kept for emergency travel. These he folded in his coat and tied on the back of the saddle. As he finished this his quick eye, accustomed to running over horse and saddle, suddenly fell upon his rifle sheath. It was empty.

Annoyance succeeded to dismay. Chane swore, and then thought swiftly to ascertain when last he had surely seen the rifle. It must have joggled out of the sheath, and by retracing his steps he would find it. That often happened to a rider.

"No. It was there — when I got off Brutus," he said, suddenly. He remembered. He never made mistakes about things like that. Chane peered all around, then down upon the ground. In a bare dusty spot he espied a moccasin track. Fresh! It gave him a start. He recognized it as belonging to a crippled Piute who had often been in camp. Chane had not trusted him. Toddy Nokin said he was a bad Indian. There was no mistaking that malformed moccasin imprint.

"Now, the thing to decide is, is he just a sneak Indian thief, or did McPherson put him up to stealing my rifle?" pondered Chane. It might be either, but Chane leaned to the opinion that McPherson had had a hand in it. If this surmise was correct, then the present locality might not be healthy for Chane. The Piute was somewhere close, in possession of the rifle, and possibly with the hidden outlaws. Chane leaped upon Brutus and for the first time spurred him. The result was grimly thrilling to Chane. Brutus left that spot like an arrow shot from a bow. Chane fully expected to hear the report of his rifle. It would take an unerring marksman to hit Brutus at that speed; and as far as pursuit was concerned, that would be useless.

Chane headed west, directly opposite from what McPherson would have calculated upon, if he were waiting in ambush. The open cedar ridge slanted away for a couple of miles, and Brutus covered it at a pace that positively amazed Chane.

"By golly! I begin to believe what they said about this horse," he muttered.

The wind whipped his face, blurring his eyes. But dim as his sight was, he made certain there were no riders in pursuit. Therefore checking Brutus, he rode down round the brow of the cedar ridge to the rim of Beaver Canyon. Here it had begun to box into walls, but he was sure he could find a place to cross before it grew deep. Half a mile farther on he encountered a trail used by horses going down for water, and here he reached the canyon floor. It was a shallow canyon, but showed signs of growing ruggedness. Chane had never been down it, and could not risk the easy travel over sand. He took the first possible ascent, a small side ravine sloping out, and soon found himself on the green level above. Here he headed east, putting Brutus to his long easy lope. The horse had as smooth action as one of the light Indian mustangs.

"You never can tell about a horse — what he is — until you know," mused Chane. "But I'll have to give McPherson credit for sizing up Brutus. He knew, all right. And he was sure crazy to get Brutus. Meant to steal him! Well, Bud, I think we'll fool you."

Chane kept sharp lookout for sight of Toddy Nokin and the string of mustangs. This league-wide basin appeared deceptively level, but there was a decided pitch down toward the yellow rounded rocks, and shallow washes deepened and narrowed in that direction. The gray sage prevailed here, and it was growing stunted. Grass and weed were abundant, and a few cacti. No animal or bird life crossed Chane's roving gaze. Often he looked back, up at the brow of the purple-sage upland, marked now by the sharp outline of cedar against the sky. He was traveling fast down toward the weird canyon country; still, all around him was open and beautiful, sunny and fragrant.

Chane began to quarter more to the northeast, and soon turned into the trail Toddy Nokin had taken. The dust was cut with fresh hoof tracks. Brutus swung into this winding trail, heading north and sloping perceptibly. As the miles swiftly passed by, Chane saw the great round yellow rocks come closer on each side, and gradually encompass him. They at first stood isolated, like huge mountainous beasts, then gradually they grew closer together until they coalesced into the waved wall, so strange to see from the upland country. A mile-wide space appeared to open into this wilderness of rock, and it sloped from each wall down to the beginning of a canyon.

Chane had not come in this way, but farther to the eastward, by a trail crossing the San Juan east of Piute Canyon. Toddy Nokin was leading toward the little-known trail called the Hole in the Wall, long a rendezvous of outlaws. Presently Chane rode to the rim of a canyon that headed abruptly there. It had sloping bare stone walls, and soon yawned deep and rugged, an irregular vent that wandered down to the chaos of red and yellow rock. Across this canyon Toddy Nokin and his sons appeared, driving the string of mustangs. Chane rode down and climbed out, soon catching up with his Indian friend.

He was quick to observe that the trail here was very old and dim, in places scarcely perceptible. It had been little traveled. Evidently the trail that he had just left was the one mostly used on the way to the Piute ford of the San Juan. Chane lost no time telling Toddy Nokin about the loss of his rifle and the moccasin track of the clubfooted Piute.

"Ugh!" grunted Toddy, and his accent was not reassuring. Halting his mustang, he looked back toward the uplands. It was the gaze of a desert falcon. Chane trusted to it, and was relieved that Toddy turned away without comment. But he urged the mustangs to a little faster trot.

They headed narrow, deep, intersecting canyons, which necessitated a good deal of travel without marking any considerable progress in a straight line. At length the Indians came out on flat hard ground, a bench under a lofty crackling wall, and verging precipitously upon the canyon they were following. The bench was marked strikingly by immense boulders that had broken from the cliffs above and had lodged along the brink of the abyss. Some were ready to topple over. Their prodigious size, from fifty to a hundred feet high, and almost as thick, and the marvelous balancing on the rim, made them objects of awe and speculation.

At length the Piutes started down over the rim, at a place apparently perpendicular, a succession of rocky zigzag steps rather than a trail.

Chane dismounted at the rim and watched the file of mustangs clatter down, sending the rocks rolling to gather in momentum and volume, until there was an avalanche roaring down into this red chasm of ruined stone. Chane had his doubts about Brutus getting down that slope of solid corners and loose footing. He was too big a horse to be nimble enough to turn at the sharp zigzags. But Chane had no choice. He took a last long look up the gradually ascending desert gateway through which they had entered this maze of rock. Nothing moved except the heat veils rising from the stony floor. If McPherson had discovered Toddy Nokin's ruse to elude pursuit, there was not yet any sign of it.

"Well, Brutus, if you can get down here I'll be ready to believe you can fly," said Chane. Heretofore, in climbing or descending bad places, Chane had held the bridle and led Brutus. It occurred to him here to trust the horse, making travel easier for both of them, provided Brutus was clever and supple enough to go it alone. So he tied a knot in the end of the reins and hung the loop over the pommel. Then starting down, he called Brutus to follow. For some rods the descent was not so very bad, and Brutus rolled the rocks without paying any heed to travel. He was just walking down, and looking for a tuft of grass here and there. Presently, however, the long zigzags gave place to short ones, narrow, crowded with boulders, winding under projecting walls, and broken by many abrupt steps, some of them four feet straight down. Chane soon realized the fact that this trail, if it were a trail, was never used except in descent.

To Chane's utter astonishment and delight, Brutus followed him absolutely without nervousness or hesitation. On the short turns he was as quick and supple as a jackrabbit. His big bulk did not hinder him; he had the feet and legs of a mountain goat. When he came to the high steps he would halt and look down at Chane as if for instruction. Chane would call out, "Come on, Brutus." The horse would look at Chane and snort, then lift both great hoofs evenly, and plunge down, landing them squarely. He would slide. His hind hoofs would follow, to thump down. Then the rocks would roar and scatter. The dust would rise. Chane had to leap and run to keep from being hurt. If Brutus had not met often with the abrupt steps, where he halted until called, Chane would have found it difficult to keep ahead of him.

Down and down horse and man worked, until the ragged red wall loomed terrifically above and the hazy depths began to grow clear, and the opposite wall of the canyon rose higher and higher, to blot out part of the glaring sky. Chane could not see either mustangs or Indians below, but he heard the crack and rattle of rocks and the shrill cries of the drivers.

About halfway down, and perhaps a thousand feet from the bottom of the chasm, this tortuous passage wound out upon a narrow cape that looked down sheer into the depths. It was a place to make a man go cautiously, with tense muscle and clear eye. Chane passed it, drew a breath of relief, and stifled a vacillating consideration for Brutus. The horse must not be stopped now. Chane called him. But Brutus did not wholly obey. He pounded down readily, and stamped out on the narrow projection, where, instead of turning, he espied a tiny tuft of grass on the extreme edge. He took two steps, reached for it, plucked it, and then stood on the very edge of the tremendous abyss, gazing down.

Chane's heart leaped to his throat. The front hoofs of Brutus lapped the edge. If the ground crumbled! If he made a slip! Chane was afraid to trust his voice. Then Brutus turned on the apex of that small point as nimbly as a burro, and came on.

"Hey! I give up!" exclaimed Chane as the horse reached him. And he meant that in more ways than one. He put a hand on the soft warm muzzle and looked into the big dark eyes. It seemed to him those eyes were intensely alive. Brutus understood him. Was it possible for him to understand Brutus?

Chane clambered down, no longer worried about his horse. The canyon wall began to slant more easily toward the bottom; the abrupt places disappeared, the zigzags grew longer, winding through monumental debris from the cliffs above. Soon the mustangs and Indians below became visible, and at length they stretched out on the narrow floor.

When Chane walked out on the level, Brutus was right behind him. So Chane got into the saddle again and soon caught up with the Piutes.

This narrow red gulch, with its lofty overhanging walls, opened into a wider canyon, where color and ruggedness and ruin appeared to keep pace with the increased dimensions. When Chane turned the corner of wall he came upon a wonderful garden spot of green cottonwood and grass, perhaps ten acres in extent, set down like a gem amid the brazen iron devastation. A stream of water, shining like silver in the sunlight, passed through this oasis. A long wide canyon yawned to the west, and at the extreme end, where it notched, the golden sun hung, perceptibly dimming. From the direction of this canyon and the stream that wound through it, Chane decided it must be Beaver Canyon. Upon inquiring of Toddy Nokin, he found that his surmise was correct. Beyond the verdant spot the great walls appeared to have collapsed, to choke the canyon mouth and bar egress to the river. Somewhere in the red and russet jumble of rock the stream disappeared.

Toddy Nokin and his sons drove the mustangs into the oasis and let that be the end of the day's journey. It was obvious that the mustangs would not stray from that luxuriant place. Birds, rabbits, squirrels gave life and color to this beautiful fresh oval of green.

Chane took the saddle and bridle off Brutus, and watched him roll, four times over one way, three times back. He had to confess again that the horse possessed extraordinary powers.

Toddy Nokin said this was the safest place he knew to stop for the night, and the only one where there was plenty of grass. Chane was surprised not to find any indication of Indian camps or travel. Not a hoof track showed along the sand of the stream. It was one of the lonely places seldom frequented by Indians, perhaps never by white men. Chane lost some of his apprehension about McPherson. There did not seem to be probability of the horse thieves surprising him here. The danger, perhaps, was farther on, at or near the ford of the San Juan. Chane did not, however, cease to be worried about the loss of his rifle. If he had that he could afford to laugh at McPherson and his allies.

Chane sought a sandy seat under a cottonwood. He was tired and the heat still hung heavily in the canyon. Bees were humming around the clusters of yellow flowers that gave the oasis a gleam of gold. While he rested, the Indians started a fire and began preparations for a meal. Chane saw Toddy's younger son stalking rabbits with a bow and arrow, a weapon still much used by the Piute boys.

The shadows grew. Slowly the dull iron red of the walls changed to blue. Low down a purple veil obscured distant objects. When the bees ceased to hum there was left only the murmur of the stream. Tiny bats darted through and above the cottonwood oasis.

Chane partook of the meager Indian supper with relish enough. Many a time he had lived on less. Dusky smoky sunset quickly succeeded to twilight, and at that depth under the canyon walls, twilight reigned only a moment before yielding to night.

The Indians did not talk. Toddy Nokin was more than usually reticent and somber. Chane grasped anew the risk in this venture for him. Tomorrow would tell the tale. Chane made a bed of his saddle blankets, on soft warm sand, and lay down to sleep. But the solemnity of this solitude and the encroaching of the weird canyon influence kept him awake for a while. He was in the gateway to the labyrinthine network of canyons unfamiliar even to the Piutes. It weighed upon him. What would happen? Could he ford the rivers? There seemed to hover over him a shadow of calamity which had not clouded his mind in the light of day.

At last he was succumbing to drowsiness when he was startled and thrilled by a crash of thunder. It filled the canyons — a great volume of sound. But the stars were bright in the heavens. There was no storm. The thunder and bellow came from a section of cliff breaking away and plunging down the rock-strewn slope. It gathered volume until Chane seemed to be deafened. Then it ended, and the weird echoes boomed from cliff to cliff, and rolled away, thundering, rumbling, dying. After that the silence seemed unreal. Chane had a strange sense of his loneliness and helplessness. At last he dropped off to sleep.

★ ★ ★

Chane awakened toward dawn and found he was cold. From that time he slept no more, and in the gray wan light he was glad to see a fire kindled by the Indians. He got up, cramped and stiff, and moved about until something of warmth began to creep along his veins. The Indians were cooking sheep meat. Chane ate his scant breakfast before daylight. Toddy Nokin's sons glided away to drive in the mustangs. Chane stood back to the fire, his hands spread to the heat, his gaze fixed on the wonderful white morning star. It hung over a notch of the canyon rim like a radiant beacon.

"Ugh!" grunted Toddy Nokin, presently attracting Chane's attention. The Indian had cut strips of the cooked meat, which he had spread on a stone near the fire. He indicated that these were for Chane, and he should salt them or not, as he chose, and take them with him. Chane gathered them up, not forgetting to thank Toddy for his thoughtfulness, and carrying them to his saddle he stowed them away in the bag that contained the parched corn. He would fare poorly until he got among the Mormons.

At daylight Brutus came trotting into camp. He had found good grazing, to judge from his sleek full sides. Yet he nosed around the saddle and blankets, as if hunting for grain. Chane saddled him, and waited for the Piutes to come with the mustangs.

The morning was exquisite, clear, cool, bright, with a sweet tang in the air. Above the eastern rim flared a pale rose glow, herald of the sunrise. The birds had begun to sing all over the oasis, a welcome breaking of the melancholy canyon silence.

Presently Toddy Nokin's sons rode in with the mustangs, and in a few moments the day's journey began. Chane faced it with a grim eagerness. They climbed out of the oasis on the eastern side, and threaded an uphill course through sections of broken wall. They came to a level rise of ground upon which the rocks stood scattered like the tents of an army. Some of these boulders had oxidized surfaces, almost black, upon which Indians had inscribed their crude signs.

The sun rose dazzlingly bright above the eastern rock that waved along the horizon. This wall Chane knew to be across the San Juan, but he had not gotten far enough up to see below the waving hummocky crest. The day bade fair to be hot down there.

Chane rode up out of that maze of scattered blocks of sandstone, out upon a height from which he could gaze down into the canyon of the San Juan River. The Indians kept on driving the mustangs down, but Chane halted Brutus and gazed spellbound at the awful scene. Three times before he had crossed the San Juan, far above this point, and at places where desert ruggedness was not wanting. But this was different.

A terrible red gulf wound from east to west, a broad, winding iron-walled canyon, at the bottom of which gleamed and glinted a chocolate-hued river in flood, its dull roar striking ominously upon Chane's ear. Miles to the east it came rushing out of a narrow split in the sinister walls, to wind like a serpent toward the west, pushing its muddy current into another river that swept on between majestic towering walls. This was Chane's first sight of the Grand Canyon of the Colorado. He had crossed this larger river above where the great walls boxed.

It held him mute, this scene of the grandeur of rocks, the desolation of the denuded surfaces, the manifestation of the ruin and decay of millions of years. He did not see a patch of green in all that area of barrenness. There was no life. But there seemed to be an infernal beauty. High above the canyon wall of red and bronze, rose the waving rounded horizon line of yellow stone, the wind-carved surfaces Chane had seen from the sage upland. There appeared to be no break in that opposite wall.

It bulged and towered out over the river. On the side from which Chane gazed there were canyon mouths yawning everywhere. The descent from this side down to the river was gradual, and of such a rough nature that travel seemed impossible. Yet Chane saw the Indians and mustangs winding down. Far below the vast rock slides were ridges of colored earth, mostly red, but some of gray, and below these stretched sandy levels parallel with the river.

Brutus did not wait for word from Chane. He started down, and soon Chane felt lost in a world of crumbled cliffs. From time to time he would come out where he could see the river and the lifting walls beyond, but for the most part he was hidden among the broken rocks. The trail here, however, was neither steep nor difficult. Brutus soon was upon the heels of the Piute's mustangs.

Chane did not fail to note how Toddy Nokin's falcon gaze often studied the vast slope to the right, and especially a rugged corner of canyon. Chane strained his eyes, but he could not discern anything more. All was red glaring rock, reflecting the sunlight. It took a long hot dusty hour to descend to the ridges of red and gray earth, a welcome change of travel. Here the mustangs resumed the leisurely trot that covered distance rapidly. From the ridges the Indians rode down upon a gravel level, almost wholly bare of vegetation. A weed that grew there was as gray as the ground.

The red slope that Toddy Nokin watched now slanted and heaved upward, a steep mile of jagged rocks, to end in a seamed wall which touched the sky. It broke abruptly into a notched mouth of canyon that cut clear down to the level where Chane rode. No doubt out of this canyon came the trail from which Toddy had switched yesterday, and from which he felt apprehension today. No living creature gave contrast to the appalling desolation of that red abyss. The river roared sullenly, low, deep, strange, not at all like a natural water in swift current.

The strip of gravel level, that had appeared narrow from far above, now proved to be wide and spacious. The time came when Toddy pointed to a break in the opposite wall, at the bottom of which shone a dense patch of green growth. Also a line of willows began to appear on this side of the river. Here was the place where the Piutes forded the river, to climb out on the yellow rock above.

To Chane the San Juan looked impossible to cross.

"Can I get over?" he asked, voicing his anxiety.

The Piute answered that he had crossed at

135

worse stages of flood than this one, and he pointed ahead to the ford. They rode on, and had passed the mouth of the intersecting canyon when Toddy Nokin suddenly exclaimed, "Ugh!"

His gesture made Chane's heart sink. Low down over the rocks beyond the sand showed moving clouds of dust.

Chapter 6

Those dust clouds had been kicked aloft by moving horses. Toddy Nokin called to his sons, one of whom was far ahead with the mustangs.

"Toddy! Who's raising that dust?" flashed Chane. "Indians?"

"Ugh!" ejaculated the Piute. His dark gaze was fixed on the isolated boulders that had rolled out upon the level.

As Chane shifted his roving eyes to find what attracted Toddy, he suddenly espied a white man rising from behind one of the foremost rocks. Chane recognized Jim Horn. On the moment he was leveling a gun, resting his elbow on the rock. He was perhaps fifty paces from Toddy's older son, who was at the head of the string of mustangs.

"Horn! Don't shoot!" yelled Chane, at the top of his lungs. "These mustangs aren't worth bloodshed."

But Horn paid no heed to this call. He shot once — twice at the nearest Piute, who was knocked off his pony, but got up and ran back. Horn now directed his fire at Toddy's younger son, a mere lad, who uttered a yell and wheeled his horse. The string of mustangs, frightened by the shots and yells, stampeded and turned away with pounding hoofs, raising a cloud of dust.

Chane reached for his rifle. Gone! A swift fierce fury possessed him. How he had been tricked! Toddy Nokin's dark hand shot out toward the rocks to the right and back. Even as Horn fired again, this time at Chane or Toddy, for the bullet whistled close enough to make Brutus jump, Chane saw Hod Slack riding forward, gun in hand, and directly behind, Bud McPherson appeared, goading his white horse and waving his rifle.

"Run, Toddy!" yelled Chane. "Run for the canyon!"

Brutus was plunging to be off, so that Chane had difficulty in holding him. Perhaps his movement was fortunate for Chane, as another bullet from Horn whizzed uncomfortably close over his head.

In a second more Chane saw his only chance was to outrun McPherson with the rifle, and take to the ford. The Piutes were gone like rabbits in the rocks. The mustangs had run wild, back over the trail by which they had come. Two of the outlaws, one armed with a rifle, blocked escape in that direction. Chane saw if he followed in Toddy Nokin's steps he would soon have to abandon Brutus. That thought did not hold in his mind.

"Hyar!" yelled McPherson, in voice coming clear. "Git off thet hoss!"

It was Brutus the thief wanted. Chane saw him level the rifle. That was a signal for Chane to spur Brutus and yell at once. The horse leaped into action, head pointed up the river. Chane drew his gun and shot at Horn. That individual was frantically trying to reload. He ducked back behind the rock and returned Chane's fire. This time his heavy bullet tugged at Chane's shoulder. The touch of lead infuriated the rider and, suddenly reckless, he swerved Brutus directly at the rock behind which Horn was hidden. The thief broke cover and darted for other rocks. Chane could have shot him in the back, but he held his fire.

"Run him down, Brutus!" called Chane, and goaded the horse.

He saw Horn fumbling at his gun as he dodged away. He dropped shells on the ground, stumbled and fell, sprang up and lunged on. His heavy weight made quick action a thing of extreme violence. The horse bore down upon him like a whirlwind of dust. Chane yelled. Brutus hurdled a rock. Then Horn, frantic in his terror, tried to elude the horse that was thundering down on him. As he whirled and lifted his gun Brutus ran into him. Chane saw a red flame and smoke, but did not hear the shot nor feel the bullet. Horn's distorted face, livid and savage, gleamed under the horse. Then came a shock, light and sharp, that did not even check Brutus. Horn was thrown as if from a catapult. But he had not been killed. He got up, staggered on, waving his arms, and fell again.

Brutus stretched out in his stride, headed for the curve of the river. Then Chane gave heed to McPherson. That worthy was behind him, between him and the river, and at the instant there flashed a white puff of smoke from the rifle. Chane experienced the bitter impotent rage of a man who heard the hiss of a bullet from his own rifle. But rage could not help Chane. He was in a precarious situation. McPherson had a good horse and possession of the gun. Again a puff of white smoke! Chane saw the whip of sand where the bullet struck far ahead. McPherson was shooting high, evidently careful not to hit this horse he coveted.

"Now, Brutus, make good all that wrangler brag about your speed," shouted Chane, and he urged the horse to his utmost.

The ground was level hard gravel, and there was a mile of it between him and the bend of river where Toddy had pointed out the ford. Chane did not look back. He gave every sense to his riding of the horse in that critical race. He heard the bullets sing above him and saw them strike ahead. Then, in a moment more, when Brutus settled into the terrible strain of a horse running to save the life of his master, it seemed to Chane that he was sailing through the air. The wind tore at him. The ground became a sheeted dim expanse, sliding under him. Rocks and walls blurred on either side. Never in his life had he bestridden a horse as fleet, as powerful as Brutus. He ran away from McPherson's white horse.

At the turn of the river Chane looked back. McPherson and Slack were far behind, but they were urging their horses, evidently still sure of their quarry.

Beyond the bend of the river the huge walls of shattered rock encroached upon the banks. Chane saw that he could not ride farther up the river. His one chance was to cross the ford before McPherson could reach him with the rifle.

Chane pulled Brutus out of that dead run. The river widened at this bend. At a glance Chane saw the ford was a shallow rapid half a mile long and perhaps a quarter in width. From the ripples close to shore and out to the middle Chane could tell that the stream bed was rocky. He rode to the upper end of this rift and then sent Brutus plunging into the muddy water. Manifestly, water had no terrors for the horse, any more than steep rocky trails. Brutus ran through water a foot deep, heading across and downstream. His iron-shod hoofs clanged on rocks like submerged bells. Chane had ridden round the bend of the river and so had lost sight of his pursuers. But they could not be far.

Chane directed Brutus toward the green break in the red wall opposite. It was a peculiar formation, evidently of steps worn by water flowing from above. An oval thicket of green willows choked the lower level. Chane discerned where the trail climbed the ledges, and knew if he could cross he would be safe.

Brutus had reached the middle of the river when McPherson and Slack appeared half a mile down the gravelly beach. They were punishing their horses. Chane gave them one dark glance. If he ever got out of this alive he would remember them!

The horse, aided by swift water now reaching to the stirrups, kept quartering toward the shore. Chane directed anxious gaze toward the point he wished to make, and he discovered that the rocky stream bed did not extend all the way across. The character of the surface water proved that; it changed from choppy little ripples to long, smooth, gently swelling waves. Under them was quicksand! Chane studied the lay of the water straight across from his position. It was better than below, but if he put Brutus to bucking the current, instead of having it aid progress, he would waste time and let McPherson get in range with the rifle. All the time Brutus was magnificently plunging on, going fast, keeping his foothold, snorting his excitement. The water grew deeper. Chane lifted his feet out of the stirrups and held them up. Soon Brutus reached the line where the swift current verged on the stiller smoother water. Chane felt the horse catch in the sand and labor to extricate himself. As the water was not deep enough for Brutus to swim in, Chane dared not risk going into the sand. So he turned Brutus straight down with the current toward the rapids. Chane saw where he might make a rocky point that marked the extreme limit he dared not pass. He would have to work out above or at that point, or be lost. If he went through the rapid alive he would drift into the narrow stretch below, where McPherson could stand on the bank and easily reach him with a rifle bullet.

The swift water almost swept Brutus off his balance. An ordinary horse would have been swamped here. If Brutus slipped he lunged powerfully and kept his head. The waves grew higher, the current swifter. Chane saw yellow-white froth rushing round the black noses of rocks. He felt Brutus strike with shoulder and leg, but always he was able to guide the horse on the right side of these obstructions, keeping in line with the ledge he must gain.

In a moment more Brutus had the whole force of the current behind him. It swept him along, the waves washing over his haunches, splashing all over Chane. Here was depth of four to five feet. Brutus no longer walked. He was carried, and when his hoofs struck he plunged with tremendous strength.

The heavy roar of the rapids filled Chane's ears. He all but gave up. He could do no more, yet he still called to Brutus, as if in that din of waters the horse might hear him. Chane's distended sight fixed on a smooth rushing channel that now lay between him and the ledge of rock. It looked too heavy, too deep, too swift for Brutus to stem. It ran like a mill race, yellow, hideous, seething, and it poured down a slant into the turbulent rapids. This channel ran at right angles with Brutus, coming from the back eddy of smooth water that swung in toward the break in the wall. Just before entering this mill race Brutus was carried against a rock and the weight of the water held him there. Chane crouched in the saddle, and leaping ahead of the horse, floundered and lunged with all his might. His almost super-human efforts, aided by the swift current, carried him within reach of the ledge. He crawled out.

Brutus, free of his weight, plunged into the swift place. The water rushed round him, splashed over the saddle, but it did not over-power him. He stemmed that current, passed the danger line, reached shallower water, whence he waded. Chane led him to the rocky shore. And it was then he remembered Mc-Pherson.

Gazing across the river, he saw McPherson gallop down the sandy bar and leap off, rifle in hand. But he had been distanced. Too late! Even as he shot, Chane drew Brutus behind the protecting corner of wall.

"Bru—tus!" gasped Chane, and reached for the horse, to stand clasping his neck. Brutus was heaving like a huge bellows. The breath whistled from his nostrils. Chane heard the great heart pound. And in that moment such love as he had never given a horse stirred in him.

Presently Chane left Brutus to recover and took care to look about him. This green patch of willows hid a little cove, upon the opposite side of which the trail rose to the first curved ledge. By keeping behind the willows, along the base of the wall, Chane could reach the point where the trail started up. From here he would be out of range from across the river. Returning to Brutus, he found him about recovered from his tremendous exertions. Certainly his excitement was past. Brutus raised his noble head with the old inimitable lift of pride, curiosity, alertness. He whinnied at Chane.

"Well, Brutus —" began Chane, with impulse to burst out in gratitude and love. But they were too deep. He did not even lay a caressing hand on the tangled wet black mane. But he was thinking hard. He had no possession save this horse. Again he was a poor wrangler. Yet was he not rich? Chane's one thought of regret concerned the wounding of Toddy Nokin's son.

Brutus had a bloody welt across the side of his broad breast.

"Horn's shot — that last one," concluded Chane, angrily. Removing the saddle, he wrung out the wet blankets and replaced them. His coat and bag of food had remained intact, though somewhat the worse for muddy water. Chane led Brutus along the base of the cove, round to the far side where the trail started up. He climbed to the first step, a half circle of stone, worn smooth by water. From here he looked across the river.

Slack had joined McPherson, and sat astride his horse, while the latter stamped up and down the beach. Then Slack, espying Chane, drew McPherson's attention. The horse thief stood like a statue, gazing across the river; and it seemed to Chane that the gaze was one of baffled longing for Brutus. Chane shook a menacing fist at McPherson and called aloud, as if the man could hear above that roaring water, "Bud, we may meet again!"

With that Chane turned to the ascent and straightaway forgot his enemies and his loss. He was far from being safe. He had crossed the San Juan, but the Colorado ran between him and the security beyond. If the Colorado, too, was in flood, Chane felt there would be grave risk. He did not know whether or not a trail led from this ford up the river to Bluff. His food supply was too short for anything except straight travel toward the Mormon country, and even then he was going to experience hunger.

The trail wound across the first circular ledge, zigzagged up smooth rock to the next ledge, back across that to the opposite side of this strange break in the cliff, and so on by a succession of steps to the top of the red wall that had appeared insurmountable to Chane.

He found himself among the yellow wind-worn hills of stone that he had seen for days. The trail led through winding defiles and at last up over the smooth soft sandstone. Like a yellow swelling sea the rock waved away toward the north. Chane rode Brutus at a swift walk up and down these slopes and across the rounded summits, and at last down into a narrow break that grew in all dimensions as he descended. All indeed was stone, except for the narrow strip of blue sky above, but this canyon had little in common with the ones Chane had lately traversed. There were no great slopes of talus, no splintered heaps of ruined cliff, no toppling rim walls, ready to crash down. It was a smooth, clear-cut, well-defined canyon, growing to noble proportions. So deep it went down that the light of day became gloom, almost of dusk.

At length this somber shade brightened and Chane rode round a corner of wall, suddenly to be confronted by open space and sunshine, the silent swift roll of the Colorado River, and the stupendous walls of the Grand Canyon. Across this sullen red river opened the Hole in the Wall, and to Chane it did not belie its reputation.

The river was scarcely any wider than the ford of the San Juan, but it ran deep, swift, strange, somehow tremendous and terrific in flood. But Chane was not daunted. He knew

Brutus could swim that tide. What concerned Chane was to what distance the current would carry the horse downstream. It was not possible to get Brutus very far along the bank up this side; otherwise Chane would have had little concern about the crossing. On the other side, however, the break in the great wall was considerable. Brutus might drift a goodly way downstream and still come out within reach of the Hole in the Wall. Far down other breaks showed, canyon mouths, and dark clefts, just mere shadowy lines.

"Brutus, I reckon we don't want to hang around long," muttered Chane as he dismounted. "We've got to cross."

Then leading the horse upstream as far as the rugged bank permitted, he looped the bridle over the pommel.

"Go on, boy," he called, with deep expulsion of breath; and as Brutus plunged into the water Chane grasped his tail and held on. A few steps took Brutus over his depth and compelled him to swim. Chane merely held on to his tail.

It developed that Brutus was as powerful at swimming as he was in other kinds of action. He headed straight across for fifty yards before the current made any perceptible change in his course. Gradually after that he drifted downstream. Chane realized that the current had more weight and volume than had been apparent. No man or beast could have resisted it. But as the river was not very wide and Brutus swam rapidly, Chane did not despair of reaching the break in the canyon wall.

The river made no noise. Brutus seemed to be swimming in oil. The water felt cool, thick, weighted. Chane realized that he could not have held up very long in it. The next time he raised his head to look, Brutus had drifted past the center of the Hole in the Wall, and as he was not yet halfway across, there seemed little hope of his making the mark. Indeed, the current grew swifter. Before Brutus had achieved two-thirds of the distance, he had drifted beyond the line where he could climb out. Chane had difficulty in keeping his hold. He appeared a leaden weight, at which the water tugged.

When Brutus saw that he was going to run into the frowning blank wall he grew frightened, and tried to turn round to swim back. But Chane, letting go his tail, in several strong strokes reached the bridle. He headed the horse downstream and quartering across, talked to him. Brutus allowed himself to be led, and as in the other river, helped by the current, he made better time. Chane let go of the bridle and dropped back to catch the floating tail. He missed it. Then with a second lunge he secured it, and held on grimly.

Thus horse and man drifted rapidly down the river while slowly making for the opposite wall. Brutus was in no distress. And Chane saw that the cleft he had aimed for was enlarging into a canyon mouth, and that Brutus would make it with room to spare. But when they reached the rocky bank it was too steep and slippery for Brutus to climb out. He lunged again and again, wasting his energy. The current here swirled and chafed at the shore. Above loomed the dark towering walls, split by the sinister canyon. Chane got hold of the bridle and made the shore. But he could not help Brutus. It was impossible to get him up that steep bank. He floundered along, hanging to the bridle, calling to encourage the horse. They passed down yard after yard and the bank appeared to grow steeper.

Chane resolved to go on down the river with Brutus if he could not get him out here. But that moment was a desperate one. The silent river had a horrible repellant force; the walls of rock seemed barriers lifted against him.

They reached the extreme end of that canyon break in the wall. Chane leaped over a jutting point of bank to keep even with Brutus, and was about to plunge back into the water when he saw the horse find bottom. Brutus had fastened those powerful hoofs on solid foundation. He snorted and blew spray all over Chane. He lunged to get hold with his hind feet. Another lunge brought him half out of the water. Then with a magnificent leap, crashing out, he landed on the slippery ledge. Chane had to be quick to get out of his way. Brutus was off his balance. He was quivering when Chane dragged hard on the bridle, helping him to make the step that meant safety.

Brutus blew a great blast of a snort that appeared to get rid of both his fright and the dirty sandy water. As for Chane, he fell in his tracks and lay still a few moments.

"We're across," he said, presently, as if that fact ended the hazard. But this canyon mouth was far below the Hole in the Wall. It might have no outlet; it might end in boxed walls. Urged by these considerations, he got up and led Brutus away from the river.

The canyon presented no difficulties of travel that Chane could see. The ascent was gradual, the floor for the most part covered with boulders. The walls were so high and so close that he could scarcely see the sky. The gloom down there was almost dark as night.

Gradually the canyon widened and lightened. Chane mounted Brutus and rode on at a trot wherever possible, impatient to see if he were trapped. But as he progressed, the nature of the canyon appeared to favor his ultimate escape from its confines. The hoofs of Brutus rang off the boulders and struck hollow on the black ledges. Some narrow places required slowing up, but for the most part Brutus had no difficulty. The walls began to shade from red to gray. Water appeared running over gravelly beds; grass and vines and flowers made color on the ledges.

Chane rode on for what he considered several miles, always gradually uphill, and meeting with no insurmountable obstacles. This canyon ran north, which was the general direction favorable to him. If he had not been greatly concerned about the possibility of being trapped he would have enjoyed this changing canyon. It narrowed and widened by turns; its walls had an endless variety of blank spaces, caves, bulges, slopes. But, in vast contrast to San Juan Canyon, it had no jumbled heaps of rock. All the debris along that winding lane had been washed down with water at flood time.

Presently Chane rode round into a long wide stretch that permitted him to see afar, both north and south. And he was amazed and thrilled to discover far above and back of his position the unmistakable southern end of Wild Horse Mesa. He could not mistake that majestic fluted wall of gold and red, with the black line of timber fringing the level rim. Like a grand bold-faced mountain, it towered above him. This canyon that had engulfed him apparently ran along the eastern base of the mesa. Chane, studying all he could see of the lofty cape, concluded that Wild Horse Mesa sheered down perpendicularly, then spread out great flanges of surrounding escarpment that in turn sheered down to lend its base to winding canyons.

Chane rode on. The hot sun soon dried his clothes. He began to feel the pangs of hunger, but desisted from breaking in upon his slender store of food. The farther up this strange canyon he traveled the more he became prey to apprehension. At any moment he might turn a bend and face an insurmountable wall. Chane could stand to go long on scant ration, but Brutus had to have grass. Therefore Chane lost no time working toward the head of this canyon.

The first sight of cottonwood trees, still beautifully green, cheered him to hopefulness. Brutus could browse on cottonwood leaves if no better offered. Other trees met his trail, and then a grassy bench, a strip of willow bank. It was still summer down here, dreamy, lulled to repose, free from frost and wind, the very heart of the deep canyons.

Again the walls converged and there followed a long stretch bare of green growth or glint of water. At the end of this lane, insulated by its gray walls, Chane saw a sunlit space, and he gave a sudden start, believing that the canyon headed out there into open country. But an instant's thought scouted this idea. He was still in the depths of the rocky fastnesses. Nevertheless, he quickened to the beautiful vista ahead.

All at once Brutus halted. His long ears shot up. He had seen or scented something that was alive.

"What's up, old boy?" queried Chane, patting him and peering keenly ahead. He had no fear of what lay before him in the shape of living creature. His enemies were behind. Still, he was intensely curious. Urging Brutus on, Chane kept a sharp outlook.

To his amazement, the canyon aisle led into the most wonderful place Chane had ever beheld. It was an enlargement of the canyon, green and gold and silvery, fragrant and sweet, walled on his right by a cliff that reached to the skies, and on the left by a strange slanting area, a falling of the wall, to a gradual slope of bare yellow stone, dotted by cedar trees growing out of niches in the rock.

Chane's swift gaze had just time to take this all in when Brutus jumped to a halt and whistled an alarm.

Following that came the swift padding of hoofs on soft ground. Chane had heard that sound too often ever to mistake it.

"Wild horses, by gum!" he ejaculated, with the old thrill of his boyhood.

Then out of the cottonwoods trooped a band of wild horses, bays and blacks, sleek, shiny, with hanging manes and switching tails and keen wild heads erect. They faced Chane.

Brutus neighed now, more with welcome than affright. These were creatures of his kind. His neigh was answered by a piercing whistle that rang like a bugle down the canyon.

"Say, that's a stallion!" exclaimed Chane.

Then out of the green pranced the most beautiful and wildest horse Chane had ever seen. He recognized him, though he had only sighted him once, and that afar.

"Panquitch!" gasped Chane, in bewildered ecstasy. His heart leaped to his throat and he shook in the saddle.

The king of wild stallions was the color of a lion except for black mane and tail. This quivering mane seemed to stand erect like an arched wave, and fall almost to the sand. He had the points of a racehorse, with the weight and muscle gained from wild life on the desert. But his symmetry and grace, his remarkable beauty, were dwarfed by his spirit. His

156

black eyes shot fire. His nostrils dilated to send forth another piercing blast. Wild, proud, fierce, he was a creature to stop the heart of a wild-horse hunter.

Then with a backward spring, like that of a deer, he wheeled to race into the green. He disappeared, and his band of bays and blacks raced after him. Chane thought they would run up the canyon. No! The sharp click, click, click of bone hoofs on rock told him they had taken to the slope. Above the green of cottonwoods they appeared, Panquitch leading on a run uphill. What a torturing thrill the sight gave Chane! For his first instinct had been one to capture.

Panquitch slowed to a trot, and led his band up and down the waves of slope until Chane lost sight of them. He sat there astride Brutus and marveled. Then he galloped Brutus through the open, and the grove, to the slope. Here he dismounted and took to climbing. As he got up his range of vision widened. Climbing until he was breathless, he halted to look.

He could see north over the waving slope, to the far height where the spreading flange of Wild Horse Mesa met this rising plane of yellow rock. But there was no sign of the wild horses. Thereupon Chane climbed less violently, until he had passed the zone of straggling cedars growing out of the bare rock, and mounted high enough to command the prospect. A canyon split the escarpment to the north. Panquitch could not cross there, nor climb to the towering rim of Wild Horse Mesa from that side.

Chane waited. At last, far above, he espied the tawny stallion now driving his band ahead of him. Manes and tails tossed wildly on the summit of a yellow ridge, and vanished. Then Panquitch stood silhouetted against the red of the mesa wall, far beyond. His mane waved in the wind. Every line of his magnificent frame seemed imbued with freedom. There was something about him that made Chane ache. Wild and grand he stood outlined there on the height. Then he vanished.

Chane looked long at the place where he had disappeared. Not easy was it to resist following. But as he was not equipped to chase wild horses, he gave up. Then he studied every line of the heights above, thrilling under the favorable position that had fallen to him through sheer luck.

"Toddy Nokin had it figured wrong," decided Chane, at length. "Panquitch gets on top the mesa round this end and not to the north. He comes down this canyon to climb up here. Somewhere above he has found a trail to the rim. But — if he comes down this canyon, why hasn't he been trailed? I'll find out."

Chane descended to Brutus and rode on out of the beautiful colored oval. As he had expected, he found fresh horse tracks in the sand, headed toward him. Keen on the trail, he kept on and did not look up until the perceptible darkening of the light demanded his attention.

The canyon had narrowed to a V-shaped cleft, with gleaming walls slanting almost straight up to the sky. How weird and strange! This pass of gleams narrowed and widened as Chane traveled on.

He came to pools of water over beds of gravel, then boulders almost blocking passage. But the trail of the wild horses led Chane on. He heard the gurgle of running water and saw where a stream disappeared under the cliff. He came to a pool that Brutus waded, clean, clear, beautiful green water. Beyond this was bare stone which showed no hoof marks. Then came sand again and the telltale tracks.

Looking ahead, Chane was utterly astounded to see the cliffs come closer and closer together. This cleft grew gloomy and somber. Chane kept on. He was sure of exit now. The wild horses had come down here, and his escape was certain. Besides, he would learn how Panquitch eluded his trailers.

Boulders had to be clambered over, and more pools traversed. The water now was running swift and deep in places. Brutus had trouble keeping his footing. The converging walls took on a darker, weirder gleam. Chane could touch both walls at the same time. The floor of this strange canyon was bare solid rock, with the stream covering most of it.

Chane came to a pool that was twenty feet deep. Brutus swam it. No horse tracks showed now on the granite floor. Even the iron hoofs of Brutus left no trace. The sand was gone.

Pool after pool of deep water Chane had to drive Brutus to swim. And the last was a hundred yards long. Chane could see the green depths under him. Beyond that the canyon widened and the stream rushed shallowly over a granite bed. No intersecting canyons broke these tremendous walls. The trail of the wild horses had come down that stone-floored stream.

Chane remembered the canyon he had marked bisecting the eastern flange of the mesa. Soon he must come to where that opened into this one, unless both were one and the same. He traveled a tortuous mile or more before he reached it. But one glance was sufficient to prove to him that Panquitch had never come down there. It was impassable. Chane kept to the winding lane of denuded rock until at last it opened out into bright space. A stone slope that dwarfed the one below greeted Chane's expectant gaze. The canyon pierced it and ended in a cleft.

Brutus carried Chane up that long slope and out on a wide desert bench which fell away from the mesa and merged on the seamed and cracked canyon country below. The bench with its scant bits of green appeared rock as far as the eye could see. Everywhere along its rim slanted rugged bare declivities of stone, any one of which might lead into a canyon. Chane had marked the place where he had climbed out. He meant to come back. Panquitch's access to Wild Horse Mesa was no longer a mystery to Chane. He could trap that great stallion.

But what a baffling country was that eastern lower escarpment of the mesa. It appeared endless. To the right stretched the sea of carved rock, lined by its canyon rims, and ending only in the dim rise of purple upland. All on the other side of Chane, the towering fluted wall of red wandered northward. Chane's sense of appreciation had been overwhelmed, yet he gazed on and on with tired eyes.

Fifty miles and more, Wild Horse Mesa stretched its level, black-fringed horizon line toward the Henry Mountains. Chane rode until sunset without seeing another horse track or a living creature of any species.

Darkness overtook him and he decided to rest for the night.

"Brutus, there's no grass for you, so I'll go hungry myself," he said. "Tomorrow we'll have better luck."

He made his bed in the lee of a rock, and tying Brutus with his lasso, he lay down. What amazing good fortune had been his! He thought of the horse thieves and of his miraculous escape. The cold night wind swept mournfully down this bench; the colossal black wall loomed back of him and white stars burned through the blue sky. Wild-horse hunter though he was, and with the secret of Panquitch revealed, Chane thought last of Brutus, and prayed he could get him safely across the barren land.

Chapter 7

Sue Melberne missed Chess so much that she was surprised, and compelled to admit appreciation of the lad's many little acts of thoughtfulness and service, not to mention the interest aroused by his personality. She missed the pleasing sight of him, his cheery voice, his whistling, and the fun it created for her to watch him with Ora.

Chess and Jake had taken the big wagon, drawn by two teams, and had driven off to the railroad to fetch back a load of barbed wire. Sue had overheard Manerube's talk with her father about how easily a trap to catch wild horses could be constructed in the valley; and despite her own pleadings not to use so cruel a method, and Alonzo's disapproval, and Utah's silence, he had listened to Manerube, who was strongly backed by Loughbridge. Therefore he had dispatched Jake and Chess to fetch the wire.

This incident had marked in Sue a definite attitude of mind toward Manerube. Her first impressions had not been favorable, yet these had not kept her from feeling an inexplicable fascination when the man was in her presence. Sue had experienced it when near Mormons she had met in St. George, though not so powerfully. Moreover, she never felt it except when she could see or hear Manerube. But after he had successfully put through a plan to catch wild horses with barbed wire, Sue thought she despised him. Nevertheless, she was inconsistent about it, for only when alone was she conscious of active dislike. The fact seemed that Manerube's coming had precipitated a strange sort of crisis in Sue's life, and she could not understand it any more than welcome it. But she grew convinced that it was owing to her loneliness and to the vague gathering forces of her heart. Once she found herself wishing she could love Chess. This not only amazed her, but made her angry. Moreover, it focused her mind on a bewildering possibility, and that was that her mental unrest had something to do with love.

Three days after Chess had left, Manerube had apparently ousted him from his place in Ora's fickle affections. Ora certainly was not proof against the virile fascination Manerube seemed to exert. She babbled to Sue about Manerube, utterly forgetting that she had babbled almost as fervently about Chess.

"Ora, listen," said Sue, finally driven to irritation. "I feel bound to tell you Benton Manerube has tried the same kind of talk on me."

"Wha-at! Why, Sue?" faltered Ora, suddenly confronted with realities.

"Yes, I mean what I say. It's not nice to tell things, but if you're going to be a little fool . . . to be blunt about it, he has tried to make love to me."

"What did he say?" asked Ora, with curiosity that approached jealousy.

"Oh, I — I don't remember," replied Sue, blushing. "But soft flattery, you know. About my pretty face — how sweet I am — that he never saw anyone like me. Then he makes eyes . . . and more than once he has got hold of my hand. Does that sound familiar, Ora?"

"Yes, it does," she replied, solemnly and ashamed. "But, Sue — he has kissed me!"

"Ora!" cried Sue, aghast.

"I — I couldn't help it," hastily added Ora, greatly troubled. "We were out under the cottonwoods, last night. He just grabbed me . . . he's like a bear. I boxed his ears, but he just laughed. Then I ran off."

"Ora, I'm surprised," returned Sue, much concerned. "Chess is a boy — nice, you know, and maybe harmless. But Manerube is a man, and likely a Mormon who has power over women. I've heard of that. He is queer —

sort of dominating. But I never felt he had any reverence for women. Ora, I think you had better keep away from him. At least don't be alone with him."

"Leave him all for you, I suppose?" queried Ora, sarcastically. "I'll play hob doing that."

Sue steadily regarded the girl for a long moment. "Ora, I believe Chess was right — you are catty. Now stop coming to me with your confidences — about Manerube or anybody." With that Sue turned her back and went to her tent, tingling with anger. She resolved to pay no more attention to Ora and to avoid Manerube.

This latter decision was not easy to uphold. Melberne's outfit ate and talked and worked as one big family. The geniality of the leader was reflected in all his party. Moreover, Manerube had evidently struck Melberne with unusual favor. During the early hours, and especially at supper time and afterward, Sue could not keep out of Manerube's way. He watched her across the spread tarpaulin around which they ate, and across the camp fire, and when Sue slipped away to watch the sunset Manerube followed her and stood by the log where she sat. He did not ask for privileges, as was Chess's way.

"Ora says you told her to keep away from me," he began, quite pleasantly.

"Did she?" replied Sue.

"Yes. What made you say that?"

"Why don't you ask her?"

"I will. Say, is Ora Chess's girl?"

"She was."

"Humph! Well, Miss Melberne, I'm sorry you think I ought to be avoided. I can't see that Ora ran away from me." He laughed, not exactly with conceit, but certainly with a pleasing assurance. "Girls are different. I've been weeks alone riding the desert — lonely, hungry for the look and voice of a woman. Would you expect me to avoid one? Ora is full of fun. She's like a kitten. She'll purr and scratch. And if I'm fond of being with her, teasing her, how do you think I feel about being with you?"

"I never thought about it," replied Sue, shortly.

"All right. Think of it now. I'm settled in this horse deal with your father and am likely to go in the ranch business with him later. We're talking of it. So you're going to see a good deal of me. And I tell you it's a different thing from seeing Ora. You're a woman, a beautiful young woman. If you'd rather I stopped tormenting you, trying to make you like me — I'll do it. But then I'll get serious, and when I'm serious I'm dangerous."

"Mr. Manerube, you seem to take a good

deal for granted — about yourself," retorted Sue.

Manerube was not to be offended, rebuffed, or alienated. Sue let him talk and she listened. He grew rather more forceful in his arguments and statements, and as he waxed more eloquent and personal he drew closer to Sue until he sat beside her. His proximity seemed more compelling than his speech. Sue felt that. She knew she was levelheaded and had contempt for this man's estimate of himself. The more he talked the less she liked him, yet she was conscious of some singular attraction about him. When at last the sun sank and the purple shadows of twilight fell like a mantle over the valley, Sue decided it was time to return to camp. So she slipped down off the big log.

"It's chilly. I'm going back to camp," she said.

Manerube grasped her hand and tried to draw her closer. It took no small effort on Sue's part to get away from him.

"Keep your hands off me," she said, with a heat she could not restrain. "Didn't I tell you before?"

"Sue, I reckon I'm in love with you," he replied.

Without replying, Sue fled and went to her tent. She was furious. Her cheeks were hot. She felt them with her cool hands. Not until she was snug and cozy under her blankets did she find composure. Then she thought out her estimate of Manerube. He might have had some education, some advantages beyond those of a range rider, but he was not a gentleman. Sue intuitively grasped that Manerube was not influenced in the least by her objection to being courted. He was not a man to care what a woman thought or said or did. He had no sense of shame, or perhaps of honor. He would work his will with a woman one way or another.

But as for his effect upon her — that was a matter very much more difficult of analysis. Sue was honest, most of all with herself. She had an honesty of soul and she was not afraid to tell herself what she found out. In this case she seemed baffled. If Manerube did not cease his importunities she was going to hate him, that much was certain, but it did not imply she did not feel some strange power in him. And she pondered over that. It could not be because he was a big bold-looking rider and handsome. She acknowledged that he was that, though she preferred dark men. There must be something which came to her in his presence that thrilled her, yet did not belong to him. Being masculine, virile, strong, he must represent something to her. Then she happened to think of Chess and the singular emotion his simple avowal of love had stirred in her heart. Strange to recall, Manerube's had likewise quickened her pulse, though she scorned it. This vague power, then, had to do with love. Before that word love, she trembled like a guilty creature surprised. It was an Open Sesame. Any man, did he choose to employ it, could make a woman's heart quiver, if she happened to be in Sue's peculiar state of unrest, of longing, of fancy-freedom.

Next morning Sue was awakened by her father's cheery call.

"Up with you, lass, if you're goin' to be a wild-horse wrangler."

Sue sat up in bed with a start. It was dark and the air felt cold.

"But, dad — it's still night," complained Sue, reluctantly.

"Fine mawnin', Sue," he replied. "Heah's breakfast ready. Crawl out. We're shore goin' to chase wild mules."

"Mules? Oh, I forgot," said Sue, with a reviving thrill. "All right, dad. I'm a-rarin' to go."

Sue got up, not without feminine qualms and shivers, despite her enthusiasm, and nimbly put on her riding clothes and boots in the dark. Then she rushed out to get to the fire. Her hands were tingling with the cold. Hot water was a boon that morning. She brushed her hair by the light of the blaze, and quickly braided the long mass. Manerube, at her elbow, disconcerted her with a remark that she should be more careful of such beautiful hair.

"If I have to ride any more through the brush I'll cut it short," retorted Sue.

"Shore you will not," replied her father. "Not until you get some boss besides your dad."

Sue ate her breakfast in a wonderful dark morning twilight. In the east, low over the black waving range, hung the morning star, radiant, blue-white, blinking, a beacon that heralded the dawn. A grayness was imperceptibly stealing over the sky. The other stars looked pale, spectral. Down in the valley the shadows seemed lifting, changing, drifting.

The horses were in, and stamping the ground or champing their bits. When the riders, spurred and chapped, came trooping to the camp fire, Melberne called out:

"Wal, we're off. Jim, shore somebody has to stay in camp with the women."

"I reckon so. But we're short of riders now, Manerube says," replied his partner.

"Bonny, you an' Captain Bunk toss up for who goes an' who stays heah."

"I'll stay, boss," spoke up Tway Miller,

with astounding fluency.

"Say, Miller, is this heah stutterin' of yourn all put on?" demanded Utah. "Playin' to the porch, huh?"

"T-t-t-t-t-ta-ta-tain't so!" retorted Miller, hotly, all of a sudden victim to his weakness.

"Aw, now yore naturool ag'in," replied Utah, dryly.

Bonny won the choice of the toss and graciously waived it in Captain Bunk's favor, who manifestly was eager to ride out on the mule chase.

"Shure you can go, Cap," he said. "I was kicked by a mule once."

"Thanks, mate. I'll take my chances navigatin' mules," replied Bunk, animatedly.

Sue rode beside her father out into the crisp frosty morning. Once beyond the fire she realized how really cold it was. Yet how exhilarating! They rode at a brisk trot, with backs to the lightening east, toward the long wandering dim line of the western wall of the valley. Utah and Alonzo were in the lead; Manerube rode on the other side of her father. Loughbridge with Ora and the two remaining riders brought up the rear.

The exercise soon sent the warm blood dancing all over Sue. How wonderful it was to ride out on an autumn morning like this! The wild quest would not wholly be resisted.

She did not want to see a mule hurt any more than another creature, but the adventure appealed to her. Utah and Alonzo rode there ahead, lithe, erect, yet easy, somehow as wild and picturesque as their calling. Then as the morning grayness brightened to full daylight, Sue looked to the horizon line with a swelling heart. It was something original, big, splendid to ride along, and gaze at the purple changing to rose, to feel the loneliness and solitude of that vast land. She realized how subtly and surely the charm of this wilderness had enfolded her. Yet she struggled against that which implied surrender.

Jackrabbits and coyotes trotted before the band of riders. A gray wolf watched them from a ridge top. Wild horses kept moving away continually, not allowing near approach. They would stand like statues, erect, sharply defined, resembling the wolf in their wildness; then they would race down the valley, swift as the wind, presently to halt and look again.

Sue heard Manerube propounding with great vehemence his plan for capturing a thousand wild horses, all at one drive. She felt her father's intense interest, and somehow it filled her with sorrow.

Wild Horse Mesa caught Sue's eye and held it. Far away, yet how clear-cut and lofty, an endless black-fringed rosy-walled tableland, rising out of purple chaos! It did not seem real. It reached the soft, creamy, fleecy canopy of clouds that was turning pink. Then the sun burst over the obstructing range. All that rolling valley and waving rock line changed so suddenly and wondrously as to bewilder the vision. Wild Horse Mesa became a horizon of fire.

Presently Alonzo and Utah led off the valley slope into the mouth of a canyon, wide, low, gray-saged, and ribbed with outcroppings of ledges. No water showed in the sandy stream bed. As they rode up the level meadow-like canyon floor, the walls gradually grew more rugged, and the breaks fewer. Thickets of oak with gold and russet leaves livened the gray. Deer bounded up the slopes; birds flew in flocks from the acorn copses.

After several miles of travel, mostly over even and scarcely perceptible rising ground, the canyon walls came together, forming a narrow gate. These rugged walls did not rise far without a breaking and falling back to ragged and crumbling steps.

This rock-walled lane opened into a long oval valley, sloping gently on each side up to rugged rims, colorful with dark green of cedars and a few straggling pines. The notches at the heads of the ravines were choked with oak thickets, lending an autumn touch of gold to the scene.

Straight ahead, however, the valley changed, showing lines of cottonwoods along a rock-strewn brook, and a number of remarkable ridges that ran up toward the head of the canyon like the ribs of a fan. It was a big country, this oval boxed end of the canyon, and beautiful enough to bring loud acclaim from Melberne.

"Shore this heah's a place for a ranch!" he ejaculated, slapping his leg. "What do you say, Jim?"

"If we don't find better we'll homestead here," declared Loughbridge, with enthusiasm.

"Pretty enough. Good water and grass," agreed Manerube. "But it's nothing to some of the box heads of canyons west."

Sue was asked for her opinion, which she did not give in words. She just gazed as if spellbound. Manerube saw her rapt attention and asked her if she could be happy living there in a log cabin. The half-curious, half-ironic query gave Sue a remarkable thrill. It was one of deep emotion and it seemed to fling at her mind the truth that she could live happily in such a place — with the man of her dreams.

"Wal, boss," said Utah, "you all wait an' I'll ride up a ways an' see if the mules are here yet."

While Sue sat on her horse, looking to all points of this shut-in park, her father and the other men discussed animatedly the wonderful natural trap this canyon afforded. Manerube rather dominated the council. Presently Utah rode back to the group.

"They're shore here," he said. "Seen mebbe a hundred. An' 'pears to me the boss of the bunch is a gray old cuss thet's been branded. I didn't see him the other day. Shore he wasn't born wild. An old mule who has run away makes the wildest kind of a beast. He'll take a lot of ketchin'."

Manerube, with the common consent of Melberne and Loughbridge, began enlarging upon plans for the drive. Utah, who had found the band of mules and manifestly had plans of his own, did not take kindly to being disregarded by a stranger. But Manerube was indifferent to Utah's suggestions. He ordered cedars cut and dragged to block the far end of the narrow defile through which the party had entered the park.

"We'll trap the whole bunch," he concluded, with great gusto.

"Ahuh! Mebbe we will," declared Utah, sourly, and the look he gave Manerube was expressive. Tway Miller rode off with Utah and his stuttering speech floated back.

"W-w-w-w-why in t-t-t-the h-h-h-hell

didn't you kick? These are y-y-y-yore mules."

Manerube at last turned to the girls.

"You can help without hard riding," he said. "When we get ready to drive the canyon you ride up on top that first ridge. Watch the mules, and when they run into the trap here wave your scarfs, so we can all see."

"I thought I was to chase mules," pouted Ora, with a reproachful look at Manerube.

"Chase them all you like when they run down this way," replied Manerube.

The men then set to work cutting and dragging cedars. Sue dismounted and let her horse graze, while she sat under a cottonwood. Ora very manifestly avoided her. As always when resting or waiting, Sue passed the time in dreams. And those several hours were short.

It occurred to Sue that it was not necessary for Manerube to escort her and Ora to the station he had assigned them on the ridge, but he did so, giving his attention solely to Ora. This brought Ora out of her sulky mood, and if the truth had been known, pleased Sue as well. She scorned an incipient idea that she had begun to be afraid of this man.

From the ridge top Sue saw the band of mules perhaps a quarter of a mile up the canyon and now below her position. They were out in the open. Some of them were grazing, but most were facing down the canyon, as stiff and erect as any wild horses. Several white ones showed conspicuously. There were also some tans. Most of them were brown. They looked shaggier than any mules Sue had seen before. Finally her glance fell upon the one gray mule in the band. He was large and there was something distinctive about him. Presently the riders appeared below, rounding the corners of the ridge. The big gray mule was the first to move. He headed up the canyon and his band fell in behind him. They were soon out of sight.

At the head of the grassy park the horsemen separated into pairs and rode on, spreading out, until they too disappeared around slopes and into the brushy thickets. That end of the canyon formed a kind of amphitheater with the ridges wide apart at the base and sloping up toward the wall, growing closer as they ascended. The ravines between these ridges were green and gold with oak thickets; the ridges were treeless, some gray with sage, some touched with patches of green grass, some yellow with exposed earth.

Sue was thrilled to see the mules, led by the gray chief, appear in a compact band on the center ridge and move quite swiftly up toward the wall. Puffs of dust rose and, forming clouds like yellow smoke, blew away on the wind.

This ridge was long, still Sue could see the mules plainly. By the time they had reached the base of the wall four of Melberne's riders were climbing. The old gray mule watched them, with his band huddled behind him. There seemed something incongruous about this watching-and-waiting process. These mules did not appear wild.

Presently the gray leader wheeled away, to trot along the base of the wall. His band followed. They passed the heads of several of the ridges, until they came to the last rib of the fan-shaped slope. Here they halted.

Meanwhile, two other riders appeared climbing another ridge. Sue recognized Manerube and Loughbridge. One of them yelled. At this signal Melberne and his men broke into a gallop along the base of the wall in the direction of the mules. Sue began to get excited.

"Ora! Look!" she cried to her companion, some paces distant. "These horse-hunters of ours won't have such a picnic as Mr. Manerube thought."

The girl responded with the glare of one whose idol had been insulted.

Then the gray mule tore down the far slope, with his band at his heels. They were lost in clouds of dust. Both groups of riders rode down their particular ridges. Evidently the descent was rather steep. Utah was the only one who maintained a gallop. Both riders and mules disappeared, but the trampling of their hoofs proved they were still moving.

In a few moments Sue saw the band of mules appear from behind the far slope on her side of the canyon. They were running. Sue thought they would come down the valley. But the wary old leader never even headed down that way; he ran across the wide part of the park and took to another slope.

"I'm going to enjoy this," declared Sue, in delight.

"Don't you want them to catch the mules?" snapped Ora.

"I sure don't. Do you?"

Ora did not deign to reply to that.

Alonzo was the first of the riders to come again into view. He had lassoed a mule and was running with it out into the open. Sue had forgotten the vaquero. He bestrode a racy black horse, without saddle or bridle. There appeared to be a broad strap round his horse. He had hold of the lasso and was handling the mule roughly. Presently he hauled it to a stop and cautiously closed in on it. Suddenly the mule wheeled swiftly, to kick with a violence and viciousness that made Sue gasp. Then she heard the half-breed yell, evidently for help. Manerube hove in sight next, waving his arms.

"What — we — want — one mule? Let go! Help us drive!" came in a faint roar to Sue's ears.

"Aha!" chuckled Sue. "Ora, your great horse-wrangler is not happy."

All the riders came into sight and clustered round Manerube. The Mexican somehow dexterously released the mule he had captured, yet restrained the lasso. Manerube waved his arms, manifestly to emphasize the harangue he was giving the riders. There were other waving arms, that attested to a loss of temper, if nothing more. Then Manerube led three riders down to the base of the slope up which the mules had gone. Melberne took the remaining men up the central slope. When both groups had climbed about halfway up their respective ridges, the wise old mule led his band along the wall, and taking to a slope between those being ascended by his pursuers he ran down to the level again. The riders halted, manifestly bewildered.

Sue let out a peal of laughter that was most offensive to the sentimental Ora.

"They'll never catch those mules — not while that old fellow leads," declared Sue. "Oh, what fun! I wouldn't miss this for worlds."

Ora rode down the slope and out into the park. Sue had a desire to follow, but she did not want to lose any of the ridiculous chase. So she stood her ground and watched.

Plain it was that Manerube's plan had been to get behind the band of mules and drive them down the canyon into the trap. Easy to plan but vain to achieve, was Sue's contention. Three times as many riders would have been necessary to accomplish this. But the chasers kept on chasing, and grew more violent as the game progressed. Always the gray mule led down an unguarded ridge to run up another. Fast and furious grew the riding of Manerube. He did not spare his horse. It seemed to Sue that Utah and Alonzo did not here live up to their reputations as great riders. Sue did not blame them. Here were a lot of fools chasing a wise old mule.

Once several of the riders got quite close to the mules along the base of the wall. It happened that when the mules charged down a ridge Captain Bunk on his white horse appeared ascending that ridge. For some reason, perhaps the steepness of the slope, he did not see them until they were right upon him. Above the trample of hoofs Sue heard his yell. His horse wheeled in fright and plunged down. Despite her concern for his safety Sue suffered a spasm of glee. The tenderfoot seafaring man made a grotesque figure trying to hang on to his horse. Twice he was unseated, but lurched back into the saddle. The mules caught up with him, and no doubt the roar of their hoofs, their snorts and whistles, increased his terror to the extent that he swerved his horse away from them, over the steep bank, and went sliding down into the brush out of sight.

The running up and down these ridges apparently left the mules as fresh as ever, but such hard work began to tell on the horses. Manerube's last effort was to collect all the riders in one group and run the mules without trying to head them. This worked well so far as it went. The horses, even though tired, soon overtook the mules on the level run beneath the wall, and also on the open ground at the foot of the ridges. But the mules could not be headed or turned; they ran right back up one of the slopes.

At last Sue saw the riders give up. Whereupon she rode down from her station and up the canyon. When she turned the curve of the canyon she espied the men in the narrow level where the brook ran. They had halted, manifestly in hot argument. Ora had already joined them. Sue loped her horse the remaining distance, keen to hear and see what was going on. The horses were heaving, and wet with sweat.

Alonzo grinned at her as she rode up, showing his white teeth. Utah sat on his horse solemn as a judge. Manerube was raving in a rage. His tawny hair stood up, his face was hot and sweaty; his eyes glared. At the moment they happened to be fixed upon Captain Bunk. The sailor was a spectacle to excite both mirth and sympathy. His clothes had been torn to shreds; his face was scratched and bloody.

"Why didn't you turn them back?" shouted Manerube, angrily. "That was our one chance."

"Mate, I took this berth to hunt wild horses, not to be run down by a wild ass," declared Bunk, with most peculiar significance.

But Manerube was obviously too thick or too chagrined to catch the covert slur flung at him. Sue did not miss it. And as she met her father's twinkling eyes she was delighted to see that neither Bunk's wit nor the general humor of the whole chase had been lost upon him. He winked at Sue. Loughbridge, however, was inclined to be sour-faced. Then as Manerube directed his tirade upon Tway Miller, that worthy burst into an astonishing sputter, the meaning of which did not require correctly enunciated speech.

"That damned gray mule made fools of us," fumed Manerube as he dismounted.

"Wal, he shore did," agreed Melberne.

"I'll fix him," declared the rider, and

snatching a rifle from Utah's saddle sheath he faced the slope. Perhaps five hundred yards up, right out in the open, stood the gray leader in front of his band.

"Kill him, Manerube," shouted Lough-bridge.

"I should smile I will," announced Manerube as he looked at the mechanism of the rifle, then threw a shell into the chamber.

Sue had stiffened on her horse. Surely Manerube would not murder this wise old guardian of the band. But as the rider leveled the rifle Sue saw the dark grim passion on his face and in that moment she likewise saw the nature of the man.

"Dad!" she cried, poignantly. "Don't let him shoot! Oh! don't!"

With a sweep of his long arm her father struck up the leveled rifle just as it was discharged.

"What the hell!" ejaculated Manerube, harshly, whirling to face Melberne.

In that instant Melberne's humor left him. Sue sustained another kind of thrill, one that struck a chill on her heart.

"Manerube, let the old mule go," said Melberne, tersely. "He shore outwitted us, an' I won't see him shot."

But Manerube's fury had not yet cooled. Jerking away, he again looked up to locate the mules. They had disappeared.

"Say, man, who's runnin' this heah outfit?" demanded Melberne, with voice still calm, yet edged as by ice. He took the rifle away from Manerube. "I'm allowin' for temper, because that old gray devil was shore exasperatin'. But cool off now, if you want to get along with me. Jim, I reckon we might as well rustle for camp."

"But, Mel, if we killed thet gray leader we'd trap the rest," complained Loughbridge.

"Mebbe we would, as Utah said. I've dealt with mules all my life an' I'm tellin' you we cain't catch this bunch. We haven't enough riders. I shore knew that first off."

They rode back to camp with the westering sun behind them. Sue felt particularly pleased with the day. What a splendid man her father was! In times of stress he seemed so different, such an anchor, more a Texan then. She shivered a little as she recalled things she had been told about him long ago. She felt gratified at Manerube's discomfiture, and not a little pleased at Ora's peevishness. Both Utah and Alonzo had let Sue know, without a word, that Manerube's methods had not inspired them.

The horses, campward bound, were full of spirit and eagerness. They made short work of the miles. Sue rode the whole distance at a swinging lope. When they reached camp the sun had just set. The camp fire was smoking. Sue rode to her tent, and quickly turned her pony loose. Kicking off spurs and chaps, she wiped the dust from her face and brushed back her disheveled hair. Then she hurried out with a ravenous appetite.

Manerube passed her without even seeing her. His face seemed strangely pale. How different he looked from the rider ranting in temper about the failure to capture the mules! It stuck Sue so forcibly that she turned instinctively to gaze after him. Manerube appeared to be striding aimlessly away from the camp fire.

Then Sue espied a wonderful shiny horse, almost black, standing with head down. Her father had just helped a rider to get out of the saddle. Sue halted with a start.

Melberne half supported a tall lithe man whose back was toward Sue. His garb showed rough travel. He could not walk without support. Loughbridge was talking somewhat excitedly as he walked beside Melberne. Utah strode on the other side. The others present appeared much concerned.

Sue ran forward, and reached her father just as he carefully let the stranger down under a cottonwood.

"Never — mind — me," said the man, in

187

a husky whisper. "Look after — Brutus — my horse!"

"Wal, stranger, we'll shore have a care for you both," replied her father, in his hearty way.

Utah folded a blanket to slip under the man's head, raising it. Sue saw piercing dark eyes, and a black ragged beard of many days' growth. Something seemed to stop her heart. But it was not the pain in those eyes or the pallid lined brow. Sue recognized a man she had never before seen.

Chapter 8

Melberne drew up the blanket that Utah had spread over the stranger.

"Reckon you're Chane Weymer," he affirmed, rather than asked.

Sue did not need to see the man nod affirmation of his identity. Yet the weary action seemed to set a ringing in her ears. Venturing closer, she dropped upon one knee beside her father.

"Are you hurt anywheres?" went on Melberne, solicitously, with his big hands passing gently over Weymer.

"No — just starved — worn out," came the whispered reply.

"Ahuh. So I reckoned," said Melberne, and looked up to tell one of the riders to fetch Mrs. Melberne.

"Wal, I shore knew you was Chess Weymer's brother the minute I laid eyes on you. Didn't you reckon that way, Sue?"

Chane Weymer gave a slight start and would have sat up but for Melberne's restraining

hand. The weariness seemed momentarily gal-
vanized out of him.

"Chess! Do you — know him?" he asked,
huskily.

"Shore do. He's in my employ, an' a fine
lad. Isn't he, Sue?"

It was then the piercing eyes flashed upon
Sue and seemed to be penetrating to her very
heart.

"Yes — dad," she replied.

"Where — is he?" queried Weymer, his
searching gaze going back to Melberne.

"Wal, he was heah. But I sent him to the
railroad with the wagon. He'll be back aboot
tomorrow."

The weary face of Weymer underwent a
singular transfiguration. Those falcon eyes,
dark as an Indian's, shone with a beautiful
light. They met Sue's, and a smile seemed to
open them, showing the man's soul. Then they
closed, and he whispered something inau-
dibly that Sue interpreted as, "Little Boy
Blue!"

At that moment Mrs. Melberne came bustling into the group, her comely face wearing
an expression of concern.

"Is — he hurt?" she inquired, breathlessly.

"No, Mary. He's starved. Now I reckon he
ought not eat much of anythin' heavy. A little
warm milk with bread, or some soup."

"Seems like he has some fever," replied Mrs. Melberne, with her hand on Weymer's face. "An' see how he's twitching . . . make a bed for him — right here — an' put him in it. I'll look after him."

"Shore that's good," responded Melberne, heartily, as if both glad and relieved. "I'll fetch blankets. An' say, Utah, will you take charge of Weymer's horse? Feed him a little grain — very little — an' mix it in some warm water."

They left Sue kneeling there, uncertain what to do, strangely influenced by something that was not all sympathy. Chess Weymer's brother had come. It seemed a simple, natural, anticipated event, yet its culmination held a significance which was not made clear by his presence. Suddenly Sue felt a thrill of gladness for Chess. Then, on the instant, Chane Weymer's eyes opened to meet hers.

"Can I do anything for you?" she asked, a little hurriedly.

"Who are — you?" he returned, curiously, his voice again a husky whisper.

"Sue Melberne. He was my father," replied Sue, with a motion of her hand toward the camp fire.

"Do you — know Chess?"

"Indeed I do. We're great friends," she said, feeling a warmth steal to her cheeks.

"Well!" The single whispered word was expressive enough to cause Sue to drop her eyes and be relieved that her father returned with his arms full of blankets.

"Shore we'll have a bed in a jiffy," he said. "Sue, help me fold them. Reckon there ought to be three doubled to go under him. He's been sleepin' on the hard ground, if he's slept at all."

Sue helped her father make the bed.

"Now, Weymer, let me lift you over," he said.

"I'm not — quite helpless," was the reply. And Weymer edged himself over into the bed, where Melberne covered him.

"Shore you're not. But you're tuckered out. Sue, stay with him until mother comes. I've got work to do before dark."

Again Sue found herself alone with this brother of Chess Weymer's. The fact was disturbing. She did not feel natural. She had an unaccountable shyness, almost embarrassment.

"You're kind people," whispered Weymer. "My bad luck — seems broken . . . a fellow can never — tell."

"Tell what?" asked Sue.

"When there's — no hope left. Maybe there's always hope."

"You mean hope of life — during such terrible experience as you must have had?"

"Yes — of life — and happiness," he whispered, dreamily. "Always, both have seemed just beyond the horizon — for me . . . I'll never be hopeless again."

"Your strength left you," said Sue, earnestly. "But of course there's always hope for any man — if he . . . but here comes mother with something for you to eat."

It fell fatefully to Sue's lot to help Mrs. Melberne feed this newcomer, who was so weak he could not sit up without support. The practical motherly woman bade Sue hold him while she lifted spoon and cup to his lips. Thus Sue found herself kneeling beside Chess Weymer's brother, with her arms round his shoulders. Pity and kindliness actuated her, the same as these feelings prompted Mrs. Melberne in her gentle motherly way, but there was something else. Chane Weymer's shoulder touched Sue's heaving breast as she knelt beside him. Of all the moments of Sue's life, these endless few were the most astounding and inexplicable.

Weymer might have been nearly starved, but the fact was he could not swallow much, though he tried hard. Soon he lay back on the folded pillow, with whispered thanks, and closed his eyes.

"It's sleep he needs now more than food,"

declared Mrs. Melberne as she rose from her knees. "Sue, stay beside him a little till he falls off. If he doesn't sleep, then I'll sit up with him. He might need medicine. But if he sleeps he'll be better tomorrow an' can eat."

Then for the third time Sue found herself alone with the man who called his brother Little Boy Blue. In a few moments indeed he was fast asleep. Then Sue's stultified emotions seemed to be released.

Dusk stole softly down through the rustling cottonwoods. She heard the clink of riders' spurs and the thud of hoofs. A mournful coyote barked out in the valley. The sweet fragrance of burning wood blew over her. And the moon, topping the mountain, cast a pale glow down upon the encampment. It lightened the face of the sleeping man. Sue did not want to gaze at him, yet she was powerless to resist it. The dark disheveled head, the ragged black beard, gave something of wildness to this stranger's presence. He was breathing deeply, as one in heavy slumber.

Sue peered round about her. Darkness had set in; the camp fire blazed, casting a circle of light, through which the riders passed to and fro on their errands. Her position was in the shadow of the cottonwoods. Someone was singing a song. She heard her father's deep voice. Sue edged noiselessly closer to her charge, so that she could see him better. She suffered a sense of something akin to shame, yet she bent to look at him closely.

In the moon-balanced shadow his face lay upturned, and it seemed to have a sad cast, a level noble brow burdened with pain, dark hollows where the eyelids shut, blank spaces, yet how compelling, and stern lines that faded in the ragged beard. Sue drew back, strangely relieved, though why she could not tell. But that face held something which did not mock her interest in the wild rider who called his brother Little Boy Blue.

A sound of wagon wheels rolling down the hard slope back of camp disturbed Sue's reverie. It did not occur to her, in her thoughtful state, what that sound signified, until she heard someone yell out that Jake and Chess were back.

"Oh, I'm glad!" murmured Sue, with a quick glance at the still face of the sleeper. Chess's return afforded her some unexplained relief, while at the same time it stirred in her as vague a reluctance to have him find her watching over his brother. Sue could not see that there was any more needful to do; and therefore she rose hastily and went to her tent, intending to go to bed. Once in the dark confines of her tent, however, she sat motionless, lost in thought.

★ ★ ★

Some time later, how soon she had no idea, she heard quick footsteps rustling the dry leaves outside, and then an eager voice calling her name.

"Hello, Chess! You back? I'm sure glad," she replied.

"Oh, Sue! — Chane has come!" he went on, his low voice betraying deep feeling.

"Yes, I know," replied Sue.

"Are you in bed?" he queried.

"No. But I was just going."

"Please come out. I want to tell you something," he begged.

Sue had no wish to resist that earnest appeal; indeed, her pulse was far from being calm. Rising, she slipped out between the flaps of her tent. Chess stood close, a tall dark figure, his face indistinguishable against the background of shadow. He made a dive to secure her hand, and, bending, he kissed her cheek.

"Why — Chess!" exclaimed Sue. Amazement was succeeding to anger when she felt the shaking of his hands, and then, as she peered up, she made out his face. He was greatly excited. Evidently he had no consciousness of a bold action. He was not thinking about her.

"Chane is asleep," whispered Chess, hoarsely. "I went close — to look at him. Say,

196

it was hard not to wake him. But I was glad, for it gives me time."

"Time? For what, Chess? Why, boy, you're all upset!" replied Sue.

"Upset! Huh! You'd be upset, too — if you knew Chane," went on Chess, hurriedly. "If he finds out Manerube knocked me down — and what for — my God! Sue, he'll kill him!"

Sue felt a cold tightening prickle of her skin, and her thoughts raced.

"You must keep him from finding out," she said.

"Sure. I'm going to. When I found out Chane was here I asked your father if anyone had told about my fight with Manerube. He said he'd forgotten that. Then I begged him not to tell Chane. He said I had the right idea. He went with me to fix it with Jake and the other fellows who saw the fight. They were all darn nice about it."

Sue warmed to the boy as breathlessly he talked, leaning over her, holding her hands in a grip that proved his agitation.

"Then, Sue — what do you think?" he went on, almost pantingly.

"Go on, Chess. Tell me. How can I think, when I don't know?" rejoined Sue, in haste.

"We looked for Manerube," whispered Chess, tensely. "No one had seen him since

Chane rode into camp. Your dad said that 'shore was damn strange.' But I didn't think so . . . maybe Manerube knows Chane. Anyway, we hunted all around camp, and at last we found him sitting back on a log away from the camp fire. He was thinking deep and our coming startled him. I pitched right in to tell him I — we didn't want Chane to know about the fight . . . I reckon that surprised Manerube. He looked like it. And he got a little chesty, right off. You know how he is. Well, I made my part of it strong. I *crawled*. Think of me begging that liar's pardon, just to prevent a fight here!"

"But, Chess, you hardly needed to humiliate yourself so," responded Sue. "Manerube would not have told Chane you struck him, that's certain."

"Darn my thick head!" ejaculated Chess, in exasperation "Sure he wouldn't. I could just feel how relieved he was . . . well, I did it, and I reckon I'm not sorry. It was for Chane's sake."

"Chess, it was manly of you," said Sue, earnestly. "Never mind what Manerube thinks. But, Chess, in your excitement because of your brother's return, haven't you exaggerated any danger of his — of any —"

"Sue," interrupted Chess, "I'm not exaggerating anything. Chane might overlook insults — such talk as that squaw-man stuff, or the vile hint about the little Piute girl. It'd be just like Chane to pass all that by, at least in a camp where there were womenfolks. But if he learned Manerube had struck me — beat me in the face for defending his honor — why, so help me Heaven — he'd *kill* him!"

"Then, boy — you've done right," faltered Sue, unnerved by Chess's passion.

"Don't misunderstand me, Sue," went on Chess, as if suddenly he had been stuck by an idea. "I haven't any fears for Chane's life. Did you think that? Say — wait till you know this brother of mine! But it's that I'd hate to have him shed blood on my account . . . he's done it, Sue. He shot a rowdy who mistreated me — in a saloon where I was drinking. Thank God, he didn't kill him. But that was only luck. Sue, I ask you to help me be a better man, so Chane will never fight on my account again."

"Chess — you're confessing now? You've been bad," whispered Sue.

He dropped his head and let go of her hands.

"Don't be afraid to tell me. I'm no fair-weather friend," continued Sue.

"Bad! I should smile," he replied, with a lift of his head. Then he looked down squarely into her face. "Sue, I was only a wild youngster. You've helped me. And I'm getting older . . . seems to me. Chane coming at this time — just makes me think. I don't want him to fight for his sake, more than for mine. And for *yours,* Sue!"

"Mine!" murmured Sue, suddenly shocked out of her warm solicitude. "I — why — what concern is it of mine?"

"Didn't I say if I couldn't have you for a wife I'd sure have you for a sister?" he queried, forcefully.

"Yes, you did, and it was very foolish talk," responded Sue.

"Just you wait! But never mind about that. All this talk of mine means only one thing. I'm scared stiff for fear Chane will fight again. He was terrible the last time. Now, Sue, Chane will get a job riding for your father. He'll be with us. I knew that was coming. I'm glad, if only he never finds out about Manerube. If only I can be half a man!"

"Chess, I think you're pretty much of a man right now," declared Sue.

"You mean it, Sue, honest?" he asked, eagerly.

"Yes, judging from all you've said here. If you stick to that I'll be proud to help you."

"You could do anything with a fellow."

"Very well, flatterer," returned Sue, trying to be light and gay, but failing. "I'll put my remarkable powers to a test. Make me one promise?"

"Yes. What is it?" demanded Chess.

"Don't drink any more. I know these men have liquor in camp."

"Have you heard anything of my drinking? I haven't lately," he said, simply. "But you've hit my weakness."

"Well, then, good night, Little Boy Blue," she said, with a laugh.

The pitchy blackness of Sue's tent, the heavy protecting feel of her blankets, had never before been so welcome as on this night. She was too thoughtful to sleep, at least for long. A kind of shame assailed her, that she could have appeared calm, even patronizing to Chess, where the truth was that she verged on tumult. The cause of such possible agitation forced itself upon her consciousness. She made denials to her accusing self. They were of no avail. The brother Chess had eulogized, the man who had been forced into her inmost thoughts, the wild rider of many adventures and whose name bore a stigma, lay out under the cottonwoods, his stern sad face blanched in the moonlight. He was there. She could not forget his face. These facts had an importance before which all her arguments failed. A restless impatient wonder at herself

201

led at length to rebellion. She called herself a sentimental fool. This desert adventure, throwing her in contact with men of the open, with the primitive life of wild-horse wranglers and the loneliness of that vast land, had warped her for the time out of her sensible and practical habits of mind and action.

"But — how do I know this strong new self is not more truly me than the other?" she whispered to herself. "I always used to hold myself in. Maybe I wasn't natural."

So she pondered until she seemed lost in a sea of imaginings. What good did it do to think, considering that her feelings were not dependent upon her thought or governed by it? And as far as understanding what she regarded as queer reactions to a situation in which a strange rider seemed paramount, she arrived nowhere.

But when she remembered Chess and Manerube, then she was not in the least bewildered. Chess loved his brother Chane with a great boyish worship. Manifestly he had been a trouble to that brother. No doubt he was guilty of some act through which the loyal Chane had suffered. At any rate, Chess showed the pangs of remorse, likewise the noble longings to redeem himself. In the few moments of his eloquent talk with Sue he had risen immeasurably in her regard.

As for Manerube — that man had been frightened by the arrival of Chane Weymer. Sue's observation and intuition met perfectly on this plane. She had clearly seen his pale face, his somber, amazed, sullen look, his preoccupation, his hurry. He had rubbed against her in passing, yet had never seen her. Only one reason for this occurred to Sue — he was afraid to meet Weymer.

"Why, I wonder," she pondered. "Did he truly whip Chane Weymer, as he bragged he did? He feared Chess would tell Chane about the fight. That he had beaten Chess — been the cause of those dark-blue splotches which still showed on Chess's face."

Whatever else there might be behind Manerube's behavior, the main cause was that he was a coward. Sue had not liked the man, though she admitted his compelling personality, but this development damned him forever. Sue experienced a lifting sense of vague freedom; she had not been certain about Benton Manerube. She realized now where she stood in regard to him. Then, with the inconsistency of sex, which she admitted, Sue's mind lingered on another phase of the situation; and it was a speculation as to what would actually happen if Chane Weymer were told the truth.

"Chess never asked *me* not to tell," she

whispered. "Of course I never will — yet, I didn't promise not to. . . . What am I thinking? I believe I'd like to see Manerube beaten as he would have beaten Chess!"

Sue could scarcely have believed that, had she not heard her own voice, in low thrilling whisper. It absolutely destroyed what poise she had attained. Rolling over to bury her face in her pillow, Sue gave up to the climax of nervous excitement and cried herself to sleep.

Sue awoke early enough, but she did not answer Mrs. Melberne's call, or Chess's; and not until her father slapped on the tent and in hearty stentorian voice ordered her out, did she make any effort to get up. A lassitude seemed to hang on her, and a reluctance to face the clear open day.

When she presented herself for breakfast she found she was the last one. Mrs. Melberne's eyes twinkled as she observed Sue's carefully brushed hair, and clean white blouse with bright tie, and a soft woolen skirt, and beaded moccasins.

"Daughter, I thought yesterday's ride must have been too much for you, seein' you didn't bounce out as usual," she said, drily. "But I reckon you're well enough. You sure look pretty. Ora tidied up a bit, too, but you needn't let it worry you."

204

"Mother!" exclaimed Sue, with a hot blush. Seldom indeed did she call Mrs. Melberne mother. "Do you mean to insinuate I — you —"

"My dear, don't mind me," interposed Mrs. Melberne, suddenly warmed and won out of her teasing by that word mother.

Then her father came striding up, and he too was quick to notice Sue did not have on her usual rough and comfortable garb.

"Wal, girls will be girls," he said, mischievously. "Sue, I reckon you don't ride with me today."

"Why, sure, dad! Where are you going?" rejoined Sue, with a tremendous effort not to appear to have caught his inference.

"Ha! Ha! You shore fooled me, lass," he replied. "Fact is we're restin' today an' drawin' plans for the great barbed-wire trap to catch wild horses."

"Dad, are you really going to use barbed wire?"

"Wal, I reckon so. Shore I'm not keen about it. But we use wire or nothin'. The trap will take miles of fence. We cain't use wood. We'll have hard enough work cuttin' an' draggin' enough wood for posts."

"Dad, I'm surprised, that's all," returned Sue, coldly, and bent to her breakfast.

Melberne showed that his daughter's disapproval cut him to the quick. He argued and explained, but as Sue did not look up again or speak, he finally dropped his head and strode off, grumbling to himself. From this Sue divined that she had more influence with her father than she had supposed; and it convinced her that if the barbed-wire trap turned out to be actually brutal she might persuade him to abandon such means.

Before finishing her breakfast, Sue discovered with a little shock of dismay that she was vastly curious about Ora this particular morning. Mrs. Melberne's hint had helped along a feminine interest which had until today fallen to low ebb. She looked everywhere round camp to locate the girl, and the last place was the cottonwood tree where she and her father had made the bed for Chane. It annoyed her, too, to note that she had begun to call him Chane in her thoughts. The bed had been removed and Ora was not in sight. Thereupon Sue insisted upon helping Mrs. Melberne wash and wipe the breakfast utensils, an act which, under the particular circumstances, evidently mystified the good woman.

Jake happened along, his arms full of bundles brought from the wagon; and at sight of Sue his brown seamed face wrinkled into a shiny mass.

"Now, Miss Sue, if you don't just look good

for sore eyes!" he ejaculated. "Is there anything going on today?"

"Not that I know of," replied Sue, with a smile.

"We're a lucky lot of bushwhackers, to have two such lasses as you and Ora to remind us of home. Now I intended to fetch you a box of candy, but the old fellow in the store near dropped dead when I asked him for it."

"Thanks all the same, Jake."

Jake stepped closer to Sue and spoke in lower tone: "You know about Chess's brother being here?"

"Yes, I saw him last night."

"Say, but that boy Chess is happy," went on Jake, manifestly having shared Chess's joy. "He was worried some last night. I talked with him and encouraged him to keep secret that little trouble — you know — when Manerube first came. I like Chess. He's got a good heart. I'd sure like to meet his mother."

"Jake, what do you think of Chess's brother?" queried Sue, deliberately, yet the blood tingled in her cheeks. This kindly, just man was the only one in the camp of whom she could have asked that.

"I'll tell you when I make up my mind," replied Jake, seriously. "He's the finest-looking rider I ever saw. Too bad he's come to us with Manerube's —"

Captain Bunk, staggering under a load of firewood, jostled against Jake, interrupting what he meant to say.

"Heave to, Jake. You're always on the port side," said the sailor, pleasantly. "How are you, mate?"

"Couldn't be better, Cap," responded Jake, extending his broad hand. "Say, you're all scratched up. Why, man, have you been fighting wildcats?"

"Jake, yesterday I went to navigate a fleet of wild mules. They run me into the brush."

At that moment Chess swung up with his springy stride, bright, keen, all smiles, his eyes glad at the sight of Sue.

"Hello, sister! Where have you been all day? There's somebody here who wants to meet you."

"Yes? Oh, I suppose you mean your brother," said Sue, casually. But it was only outwardly that serenity abided with her. She seemed powerless to help her feelings. The sight of Chess simply made her heart beat unwontedly. He liked her so well. How plain that was! Not yet had the idea occurred to him that Sue might not care to meet this disgraced brother. Indeed, in Chess's mind no idea of disgrace could ever have been harbored. Sue wanted to resent the familiar word sister; she wanted to avoid meeting Chane

208

Weymer. But at that moment she did not have it in her to hurt this boy, who had promised to go straight for her sake. So, assuming an air of amiable indifference, which she was far from feeling, Sue permitted Chess to lead her away under the cottonwoods.

Chess was talking, as usual, only faster, and with elation — how he had moved Chane back in the grove, shaved him, and made him look presentable, and other things Sue did not catch. She was concerned with her own smothered emotions. Vaguely she seemed aware of other sensations — the sense of dragging footsteps over a long distance, the intensely vivid blue sky and gold of cottonwood, the fragrance of wood smoke that drifted across the way. Then Sue espied Chess's tent, and near it, in the shade of a full-foliaged tree, a bed in which a man was sitting upright. Sue did not see a disheveled head, a pallid face, a ragged beard, things she remembered. Could this person be Chess's brother? How stupid of her, as Chess was leading her straight to the tree! Sue dropped her eyes. It seemed as if she was being led to some sort of execution. Then a sudden fury of spirit dismissed this incomprehensible mood or perversity and left her as she used to be.

"Chane, here she is — Sue Melberne!" cried Chess, joyfully. His tone expressed a thousand times more than words.

"I'm sure glad to meet you," said Chane Weymer. His voice had the same ring that was notable in Chess's, only it was deeper.

"How do you do, Mr. Weymer!" responded Sue, lifting her eyes. "I hope you're better this morning."

Before he could reply to Sue they were accosted by her father, who, approaching from the other side, at once drew attention with his genial authoritative presence.

"Wal, heah you are, Weymer, entertained by the young folks," he said, in his loud voice. "Shore you look like a different man this mawnin'."

"You're Melberne, boss of the outfit, I reckon," replied Chane, extending his hand. "I'm much obliged to you. Yes, I do feel different. But I'm tired — and hungry. Your good wife said I must eat sparingly today."

"Shore. Go easy on grub. Reckon you've had some hard knocks lately?" rejoined Melberne, tentatively. He squatted down beside Weymer with manner curious, as if information was his due, yet wholly the kind and sympathetic host to an unfortunate guest.

Sue seated herself on one of the packs near by and proceeded to employ these few moments when her father's presence distracted interest from her.

Chane Weymer wore a clean corduroy shirt, too small for his wide shoulders. Sue had seen Chess wear that. This rider did not appear to be brawny of build, yet the muscles rippled under the tight sleeves whenever he moved his arms. His face, shorn of the ragged beard, was the most compelling Sue had ever gazed upon. It was brown and smooth, with a blue tinge under the skin. He did not resemble Chess, yet anyone could have told they were brothers. His dark hair appeared as if touched with frost.

"No, Melberne, I can't say I've had any particular hard knocks," he was saying. "I've been over in the Piute country. Bought a bunch of mustangs from Toddy Nokin. I'd had the bad luck to fall in with some horse thieves — Bud McPherson and his pals. They trailed us, stampeded the stock. I had to take to the river to save my life. McPherson had got hold of my rifle. They ran me up a box canyon, so I had to cross the San Juan. Lucky I had a grand horse. Both rivers were high . . . well, I missed the Hole in the Wall and had to climb out of the canyon country way round under Wild Horse Mesa. I had a little grub the Piutes gave me, but it didn't last long. Reckon that's about all."

"Hum! Lost your stock an' all your outfit?" replied Melberne, sympathetically.

"All I owned — no, I shouldn't say that. I've got Brutus left. Perhaps I'd never have known what a great horse he is if it hadn't been for my mishap."

"Brutus. That's the black bay you rode in on. Shore he's all horse. Wal, where were you headin' for?"

"Mormon country. I was goin' to borrow outfit from some of the Mormons, and then come back."

"What for?" demanded Melberne, with interest.

"I've several reasons," said Weymer, smiling. "One is I expect Toddy Nokin to come over with another string of mustangs. Then I'd like to look for Bud McPherson. And, well, Melberne, I've another reason I want to keep to myself for the present."

"I see. Wal, how'd you like to throw in with me? I need riders. We'll furnish what you want an' pay good wages. Chess will be glad to have you, I reckon."

"I should smile," replied Chess, for himself.

"Melberne, I'll take you up," replied Chane. "May I ask your plans? You're new to this wild-horse game, aren't you?"

"Reckon I am," returned Melberne, shortly. "That's why I want good riders. Wal, my plans are easy told. I'm aimin' to trap a thousand horses heah in Stark Valley, ship them out, an' then move west over there under Wild Horse Mesa, ketch an' break some good horses, an' then homestead a fine valley."

"A thousand wild horses! Reckon you are new to this game. If you do catch them how on earth will you ship them? Wild horses!"

"Wal, I reckon I don't know, but this rider Manerube knows, an' I'm leavin' that to him."

"Bent Manerube?" queried Weymer, sharply, his fine smooth brow wrinkling slightly between the eyes.

"Yes, he's the man," returned Melberne, and he gazed hard at his interrogator.

"Melberne! Do I understand you to mean you've hired Bent Manerube?" demanded the rider, in astonishment.

Sue felt Chess's hand gripping hers, and she returned the pressure, as if to reassure him. It might be a ticklish moment, but she had confidence in her father. He was wise, calm, and just. Sue's intensity of interest had to do with Chane Weymer. She gazed closely at him, as with piercing eyes he looked up into her father's face.

"Yes, I told you. Bent Manerube."

The rider laughed outright, and both incredulity, and something harder, sharper, vanished from his expression.

"Wal, reckon it may seem funny to you,"

213

said Melberne, gruffly.

"Yes it is," replied Weymer, frankly. "But if you don't know why, I'm sure not going to tell you."

"You had some trouble with Manerube across the river, didn't you?" queried Melberne.

The rider's head lifted, with the movement of an eagle. Then Sue saw fire added to the piercing quality of his eyes.

"No. I reckon I'd not call it trouble with Manerube," returned Weymer, in slow cool deliberation. "What did he say?"

Melberne seemed somewhat flustered, compared with his usual free directness. Chess sat as stiff as a statue, yet he was inwardly trembling, for Sue felt his hand quiver. The situation had grown bad for him. Sue bit her tongue to keep from bursting out. She wanted to kick her father to remind him of the issue at stake. But he was not close enough to her, and she did not know how to attract him. Besides, Chane Weymer's look, his laugh, and then the slow coolness of his last query had robbed her of the feeling Chess had inspired in her. Almost, it seemed, she wanted her father to blurt out Manerube's story.

"Wal, he didn't say much," replied Melberne, warily. "Just mentioned you an' he had a little scrap. Shore it's nothin' to fetch up heah. I'm runnin' this outfit. An' all I want to know is if you'll ride for me."

The frown deepened on Weymer's brow, and the sternness of his features, that had hidden behind his smile and glow of gladness, brought sharply to Sue the face she had seen in the moonlight. Certain it was he divined Melberne's swerving from the actual truth. Perhaps his penetrating gaze found all he wished to know. Then he turned to look at Chess, and as swiftly as a light or shadow could cross his face it changed, softened. He loved that boy. Nothing else mattered. He did not seem to remember Sue was there.

"Sure I'll ride for you, Melberne," he said. "If you want to know, I'm right glad of the chance. Here's Chess — and, well, I might be of other service to you. *Quien sabe?* as the Mexicans say."

Melberne shook hands with Chane, and with a curt word of thanks he got up and strode away. Sue was almost as powerfully impressed by the way her father had met this situation, how significantly he had betrayed a surprise, as she was by the effect Weymer had upon her. Face to face with him she could not remember the character Manerube had given him and that Loughbridge said was the estimate of him among desert men. There was more, too, that she could not divine at the moment.

"Boy, it seems I've taken a job to ride with you," said Chane to his brother.

"I should — smile," responded Chess, choking down some stubborn emotion. "And I'm sure glad. Aren't you, Sue?"

How the foolish lad always included her in his raptures! He could not see anything except that she must be glad.

"Why, yes, Chess, if it pleases you," she replied.

"Miss Melberne, my brother tells me you have been good to him," said Chane, directly, and fastened his eyes on Sue's face.

"Oh no, hardly that," murmured Sue.

"Don't believe her, Chane," spoke up Chess. "She's an angel. She calls me Little Boy Blue and I call her sister. Now what do you say to that?"

"I hardly know," replied Chane, gravely. "I'll reserve judgment till I see more of you together."

"Chane, listen," said Chess, with entire difference of tone. The boyishness vanished. His ruddy face paled slightly. He breathed quickly. "Sue has stopped my drinking."

"*No!*" exclaimed the elder brother.

"I swear to you she has," declared Chess, low and quick. "Chane, I fell in love with her.

She didn't know it, but I've never drank since . . . of course, Chane — you mustn't misunderstand. Sue doesn't love me — never can. I'm too much of a boy. Sue is twenty. But all the same she stopped me — and I'll promise you, too — I'll never drink again."

"Little Boy Blue!" replied Chane. "That's the best news I ever had in all my life."

Then Sue felt his eyes on her face, and though she dared not raise it, she had to.

"This boy's mother will love you, too, when she knows," said Chane. "As for me — I will do anything for you."

"I declare — you make so much of — of hardly anything," returned Sue, struggling with unfamiliar emotions. "Chess is the same way. You make mountains out of mole hills."

He smiled without replying, his dark eyes of fire steadily on her. Sue suddenly felt that if she had been an inspiration to Chess, wittingly or otherwise, it was a big thing. She must not seem to belittle it. And the reverence, or whatever it was she saw in Chane Weymer's eyes, went straight to her heart, unutterably sweet to the discord there. An incredible shyness was about to master her. In sheer self-preservation she turned to Chess.

"Boy Blue, I'd never make light of your fight against bad habits," she said. "I'm only amazed that I could help . . . but if it's true

— I'm very proud and very happy. I will indeed be your sister."

Sue left them, maintaining outwardly a semblance of the dignity she tried to preserve. She heard Chess say, triumphantly, "Chane, didn't I tell you . . . ?" That almost precipitated her retreat to a flight. What on earth had Chess told this brother? Sue walked faster and faster toward her tent.

Chapter 9

Days passed. The beautiful Indian summer weather held on, growing white with hoarfrost in the dawns, rich and thick with amber light at the still noons, smoky and purple at sunset. The cottonwoods now blazed in golden splendor, and the grove was carpeted with fallen leaves, like a bright reflection from the canopy above.

Melberne's riders labored early and late, part of them cutting and dragging fence posts, the others stretching barbed wire down in the valley.

But for Sue Melberne these days were unending, dragging by through hours of restless uncertainty, strange fleeting moments of indescribable joy, followed by quick fastening moods of vague unhappiness — all tormenting, verging on torture.

Then came the most perfect of autumn days, golden, fragrant, smoky, now with long, still, solemn, dreamy lulls, and again sweet and cool with gusts of wind that filled the air as by fluttering bright leaves like birds, and sent the carpet of gold rustling under the trees. Sue wandered about the grove and along the slope, believing she had fallen under a magic spell of Indian summer. For the most part she watched Chess and Chane at their labors up and down the hillside. She heard the sharp ring of Chess's axe, and sometimes she saw it glint in the sunlight. His mellow voice floated down, crude and strong, singing a cowboy song. The tall Chane gathered several trimmed saplings in his arms, and carrying them to a declivity, he threw them over, where they rolled and clattered down to a level. Here Jake and Bonny and Captain Bunk loaded them into wagons.

Sue watched all the riders, but her gaze went oftenest and lingered longest upon the lithe figure of Chane Weymer. She was not blind to it. She confessed it when moments of torment drove her to truth. But fair as she had been to others, she was stubborn, inconsistent, intolerant to herself. She would think only so far, then, shocked at the possibilities, she would defiantly dispel thought and live in her dreamful sensations.

But this golden day had dawned to strange purpose. Never had there been such a day in her life. All at once she faced her soul and knew her trouble.

She had perched in a favorite seat on a low branch of a gnarled and spreading cottonwood, quite remote from the camp, at the base of the slope where the canyon opened. Here she could see without being seen. Nothing unusual had happened. She had been free of torments for the hour, idling, watching, dreaming away the time. Indeed, the sweet strong spell of the golden and purple autumn lay upon her. Then came a moment when Chane Weymer passed out of sight on the timbered hillside and did not return. Revelation burst upon her quietly, inevitably, without the slightest shock.

"Chane Weymer . . . ! He's the man," she soliloquized, mournfully. "I felt something must happen out here in this desert. It's come . . . Chess was right. He said, 'You can't help but love Chane!' . . . I can't. I can't . . . Oh, I'm done for!"

At last she knew. That moment saw the end of her restless, unsatisfied, uncertain longings, her doubts and fears, her miserable moods and bitter railings at self. Her torments had suddenly given place to a great dawning of something immeasurable. Like a burst of sun in the darkness of her heart! Her spirit did not rise up to crush this betraying love. It could not be crushed. It was too new, too terribly sweet, for her to want to crush. It was herself, her fulfillment; and in a moment she had become a woman.

Long she sat there and time seemed to stand still. The golden day enveloped her. Shadow and sunlight played over her with the swaying of the branches above, the movement of the colored leaves. Before her eyes the red and brown hills sloped up to the black bulk of mountain; behind her rolled the purple valley, its horizon lost in haze. Solitude held the hills in its embrace. From the desert floated a still all-pervading atmosphere, like a fragrance from limitless space.

"When did it happen?" mused Sue, woman-like, trying to retrace the steps of her undoing. Having faced the fatal fact, she was more concerned with the when of it, the how and the why, than with its effect upon her future. The future could be put aside. In a flash of thought it looked appalling.

Sue recalled the night of Chane's arrival, when she sat beside him as he slept as one dead, his stern savage face blanched in the moonlight. Could love have come to her then? Surely it had been hidden in her heart, mounting unknown to her, waiting, waiting. She recalled the following morning, when the crudeness had gone with his unkempt beard and he had shown her in few words and single glance how forever he would be in her debt for her influence upon his brother. It could not have come to her then. Then, the following day — how utterly impossible to grasp by recollection of them one meeting, one exchange of look or speech more significant than another!

Still there were things she thought more of than others — little incidents that stood out, facts only unusual because of memory — the difference in Ora, the way Manerube avoided the camp fire, the splendid gayety of Chess, the piercing eyes of Chane, who watched her from afar, the wild joy which had come to her while riding Brutus.

"Ah! now I cannot ever ride Brutus again!" she murmured, in dismay.

That focused her thought upon the horse. Chess had brought Brutus up to her one day.

"Sue," he had said, "Chane says this horse saved his life. Brutus, he's called. Look at him! You wouldn't think he's the greatest horse Chane ever straddled. Chane has had a thousand fine horses. Look. Brutus will grow on you. But you'll have to take time to find him out, Chane says. Ride him — learn to know him — love him."

"Chess, the last won't be hard to learn," replied Sue, and after the manner she had acquired from riders she walked round him. Sue really knew but little about horses. She could ride because she had been accustomed to horses since childhood and because she was athletic and liked motion. She did not qualify in what the Westerners called horse sense, let alone the great fact of having been born on a horse. Nevertheless, she had it in her to love one.

"Sue, it'd never do for you to love Brutus and not his master," said Chess, very soberly, with a face as solemn as a judge's.

Had that been the moment? wondered Sue.

But she had laughed archly, taking him at jest.

"Why not? I don't see why I can't love a horse, any horse, independent of his master."

"Well, you see, in your case it would separate them. Any rider who loved you and found out you loved his horse would give him to you."

Brutus appeared to be a giant of a horse that somehow grew on her the more she looked. She liked the quick uplift of his head as she approached, and the soft dark eyes intent on her. He had an open honest face, one which on the instant inspired her with trust. She had not the least fear of him.

"How shiny his coat!" she exclaimed, smoothing the wide glossy neck. "He's black. No, not black. He seems to shine black through brown. Curious. Chess, his skin looks like water reflecting shadows of leaves."

Brutus took to Sue, not too quickly, not before he had eyed her and studied her and nosed her, but presently, when he had satisfied himself she was what he liked. Then he had acted in a way to delight Sue, to tickle her vanity, for Sue believed she had a winning way with animals.

Chess had put her saddle upon Brutus and insisted she ride him. So this was how it had come to pass that Chane, coming suddenly from under the cottonwoods, had surprised her astride his horse. Would she ever forget his look?

"You can ride?" he queried, earnestly.

"Oh yes. Don't worry. I'll ride him," she replied, loftily.

"Let him go, then," said the rider. "The faster he goes the easier his gait. Just stick on. Let him run and let him jump. He knows where he can go."

Brutus, free of rein, had taken Sue on the wings of the wind. After days of rest he wanted to run. Her weight was nothing. How surely she felt Chess and Chane watching her as Brutus raced over the green! She would ride him. Yet as he settled down to a speed she had never known, her audacity succumbed to thrilling fear. Her heart leaped to her throat as Brutus sailed over a deep wash she had not seen. Then wildness ran riot with pulse and thought. The blanket of wind, pressing harder and harder, lifted her out of her saddle, so that one hand had to grasp the pommel. She ran down wild horses that could not escape this fleet racer; and when she turned him in a curve back toward the camp, the wind blinded her, tore her hair loose and strung it in a long waved stream behind her. His hoof-beats clattered and beat faster, until they made a single dim sound in Sue's roaring ears. She cried out in the abandon of the ride. In her blurred sight the golden grove of cottonwoods seemed to grow and move toward her. Then the swift level sliding through the air broke to a harder gait. Brutus was easing out of his run. His change to a gallop threw Sue up and down like a feather before she could get his swing; and when she did he dropped to long lope, and from this to tremendous trot, so violent in stride that Sue just managed by dint of all her strength to stay upon him. When he pounded to a stop she could see only blurred images against the gold background of grove. She heard Chess's whoop.

Then, overcome by dizziness, she swayed in the saddle. Not Chess, but Chane had lifted her down, blinded, burning, thrilling. Yet she had felt his gentle hold, his strong arms on her. Had that been the moment?

"Say, Sue, I should smile you did ride him!" Chess was shouting in her muffled ear. "You sure looked good. Honest, I didn't think you'd dare let him run. And leap — say he went a mile high over the washes."

"Well, I reckon you rode him, when he was running, anyway," spoke up the cool, easy voice of that other. "But I'm advising you to break in easier next time."

And there had been a next time, other times, until Sue loved Brutus, the sight of him, the feel of him, his response to every word. She learned what a tremendous engine of speed and power he was, governed by a gentle and spirited mind, if a horse could have one. When she caressed his grand arched neck before a ride or rubbed down his wet quivering flanks after a race, she appreciated what the wonderful muscles were for. She grew to understand him. A horse took on new meaning to her. Brutus was a comrade, a friend, a sweetheart, and he could as well be a savior. Such a horse mastered the desert. Through her knowledge of Brutus and her love for him Sue no longer marveled at a rider's passion to capture Panquitch. She learned to know a desire to see that great wild stallion.

"Did Brutus ride me into this — this spell?" murmured Sue. But she was denied the satisfaction of understanding when or how or why she had come to fall in love with Chane Weymer. All might have contributed to it, nothing might have been particularly to blame.

Sue's inherent honesty of soul, as it had forced her to confess the naked truth of her dilemma, likewise in time forced other considerations, to which the dreams and wonderings had so far been subservient. They had been sweet, vague, dreamful, the questionings of awakened love. She next had to deal with sense, not sentiment. And shame flooded through her.

"What is he? A wandering rider, lover of wild horses and Indian girls! Squaw man!"

Clamoring voices from the unknown depths of her fought for hold in her conscience. But she silenced them. To realize that she had loved unsought, unwooed, made her untrue to the best in her, merciless to the man who had roused this tumult of her heart. She must hide it. She must avoid Chane Weymer; she must welcome anyone whose attention might help to divert suspicion of her humiliating secret.

That night Sue Melberne, with the fierce pride and strange egotism of a woman who must avenge herself upon the innocent cause of her pangs, was the life of the merry campfire circle. Chess, whom she blamed partly for

228

her woe, was as merry as anyone, until Sue sat down beside Manerube, flushed of face, bright of eye, and talked and laughed with him as she had with the others. Then Chess became suddenly sober. He backed away from the fire, watching her with big staring eyes.

Sue was aware of this. It helped her, somehow. But when Chane silently strode away into the shadows, her vivacity lost its inspiration. Still she kept amusing Manerube, who responded, expanded under her laughter and sallies. Her father gazed upon her with pleasure on his tired face. Ora, too, reacted characteristically to Sue's friendliness. She was not to be outdone. Between them Manerube became the center of repartee he manifestly took to his credit.

The evening wore on. One after another the members of Melberne's outfit went to bed, until only Manerube and the girls were left, with Chess sitting across the fire, his head on his hands.

Sue knew he was waiting for her to start for her tent — that he would wait no matter how she tarried. At last she could keep up the deception no longer, and rose to go, bidding them good night.

"Sue, let me walk with you to your tent?" asked Manerube.

"No, thanks. Take Ora. She's afraid of the

229

dark," replied Sue, tripping away. But once out in the shadow, her feet became as heavy as lead. Chess caught up with her, took hold of her arm, and turned her to face him.

"Sue Melberne, what's come over you?" he demanded.

"Over me? Why, nothing! Do you mean my — my cutting up a little?"

"Yes, I mean that — with Manerube."

"Oh! Chess, it's none of your business if I want to make merry — a little, is it, with him or anyone?"

"No, I reckon not," replied Chess, darkly, as he stared down at her. "But Manerube! You never were that way before. Didn't you see Chane walk away the minute you began flirting with Manerube?"

"I — I didn't flirt," declared Sue, hotly, and she was honest in her denial.

"Aw, you did. And it wasn't like you, Sue."

"How do you know what I'm like — really?" queried Sue. His pain, his reproach, stung her, drove her to say what she thought but did not mean to utter.

"Something's wrong with you, Sue Melberne. Tell me what it is. Please. Aw, Sue —"

"I've nothing to tell you," she replied, and turned away.

Chess followed her, and once again strode before her, just as she reached her tent. He was in the open, away from the trees. His head was bare, his face clear in the moonlight.

"Are you sure? You can't hurt us Weymers more than once."

"Yes, I'm sure. And I think you're rude."

"Rude!" he ejaculated. "What in damnation has come over you? You never called me that before. I'd do anything, though, to keep you from making eyes at Manerube, being sweet — like you were. Promise me you won't."

"Chess, have you any right to criticize my actions?" she demanded.

"I'm just asking you something. Will you promise not to flirt with Manerube again?"

"No! I deny I flirted, but if I'm wrong — I'll do it when I please," retorted Sue, passionately. The day's conflicting emotions had worn her out.

Chess stepped back from her as if she had struck him.

"Did you see Chane's face just before he left?" he asked, in different tone.

"No, I didn't. What's it to me how he looked?"

"Nothing, I reckon," replied Chess, with a dignity Sue had never noted in him. "I'm telling you, though. Chane looked terribly surprised, terribly hurt. He hates a flirt."

Sue heard a bitter little laugh issue from her lips.

"Oh, he draws the line at white color, does he? I hear he's not so righteous — or indifferent toward red-skinned flirts!"

"*Sue — Melberne!*" gasped Chess, starting as if he had been stabbed.

A sudden hot anger at herself, at Chess, at Chane had possessed Sue; and this, with a sudden tearing pang of jealousy, had given rise to a speech which left her shocked.

Certain it was that Chess turned white in the moonlight, and raised his hand as if to smite the lips which dishonored the brother he revered. Sue awaited that blow, invited it, wanted it, in the shame of the moment. But Chess's hand fell back, nerveless and shaking. Then with a wrench he drew himself up.

"I didn't know you, really," he said. "And I'll tell you one thing more. If I hadn't made that promise to Chane I'd sure get drunk tonight."

Wheeling with a bound, he plunged into the shade of the cottonwoods.

"Oh, Chess — I — I didn't mean that," cried Sue. But he did not hear. He was running over the rustling leaves. Sue went into her tent and fell on her bed. "What have I done? Oh, I'm a miserable little beast! I love that boy as much as any sister could. And I've hurt him. His eyes! He was horrified. He'll despise me now. He'll tell his brother I — I . . . oh, this day, this day! My heart will break!"

Sue rode every day, but no more on Brutus. She nursed the delusion that her pretended friendliness toward Manerube, by deceiving the brothers as to the true state of her heart, would assuage her pain during the process of her struggle. Therefore she adhered to the plan conceived in that hour of her abasement.

Where heretofore she had interested herself solely in the labors of Chess and Chane on the timbered hillside, now she rode far afield and watched the stretching of the barbed-wire fence. Its western flange zigzagged across the valley, cunningly broken at the deep washes, calculated to deceive wild horses. She carried warm food to her father, and otherwise served him during this long arduous task, growing farther and farther from the camp.

These rides kept her out in the open most of the day. Around the camp fire she encouraged Manerube's increasing attentions, though less and less did she give him opportunity to seek her alone. Ora had tossed her black head and said, tartly, "You can have Bent Manerube and welcome!" She had gone back to Chess, growing happier for the change. Sue sometimes found it impossible to avoid Chess's

233

scornful eyes. He seldom came near her. How she missed the little courtesies that now no one else had time or thought for! Manerube certainly never profited by kindly actions. Sue seldom saw Chane Weymer, except at a distance. Yet always her eyes roved in search of him. It was bitter to see him, yet more bitter when her search was unrewarded.

She happened to be present one night at the camp fire, after supper, when talk waxed warm about the proposed wild-horse drive very soon now to be started. The argument started by Melberne's query, "Wal, now our trap is aboot ready, how are we goin' to start the drive?"

Manerube, as usual, did all the replying, and Melberne had evidently learned by heart this rider's ideas. Most of Manerube's talk was devoted to his past performances; he had little to say about future accomplishments, except his brag as to results. This night Melberne, approaching the climax of his cherished enterprise, plainly showed dissatisfaction with Manerube.

"I've given you authority to handle this drive," declared Melberne, forcibly. "Reckon I want to know *how* you propose to go aboot it?"

"We'll just spread out and drive down the valley, toward the trap," replied Manerube, with impatient gesture of finality.

"Ahuh! So that's all?" returned Melberne, with more of sarcasm than Sue had ever heard on her father's lips. His eyes held a glint foreign to their natural kindly frankness. Then he addressed himself to his Mexican *vaquero*.

"Alonzo, what's your say aboot how to make this drive?"

"No savvy Señor Manerube," replied the half-breed, indicating the rider.

"What?" shouted Melberne, growing red in the face. "You mean you're not favorin' this barbed-wire trap Manerube's built?"

The *vaquero* had no more to say. His sloe-black eyes gazed steadily into Melberne's, meaningly it seemed to Sue, as if he was not the kind of a man to be made talk when he did not choose to. Melberne, taking the hint, repeated his query, without the violence. Alonzo spread his brown little hands, sinewy like an Indian's, to indicate that the matter was too much for him and he wanted no responsibility. Sue intuitively felt, as formerly, that the *vaquero* was antagonistic to Manerube.

"Wal, Utah, you know this heah wild-horse game," said Melberne, turning to the lean rider. "Will you tell me how you think we ought to make this drive?"

"Shore. I think we oughtn't make it a'tall," drawled Utah.

Melberne swore, and threw the stick he held into the fire, where it sent up a shower of sparks.

"I didn't ask that," he snapped. "You needn't get smart with me. I'm talkin' business."

"Wal, boss, I'm like my pard Tway Miller. Sometimes I cain't talk business or nothin'," returned Utah, with his easy, deliberate drawl. There was a smile on his lean bronzed face. Sue grew more and more convinced that her father, Texan though he was, did not understand these riders.

"Jim, look heah," said Melberne, turning to Loughbridge. "Come to think aboot it, you hired most of these close-mouthed gentlemen. Suppose you make them talk."

"Don't think thet's important, even if I wanted to make them, which I don't," replied Loughbridge. "Manerube's plan suits me to a T. An' I sure don't see why you're reflectin' on his judgment by naggin' these other riders."

"Wal, Jim, I reckon there's a lot you don't see," responded Melberne, with more sarcasm. "We're deep in this deal now an' we stand to lose or gain a lot."

"We don't stand to lose nothin'," rejoined

Loughbridge, "unless you make these riders so sore they'll quit us."

"Jake, please fetch Weymer heah quick," said Melberne. "Tell him it's important."

Sue gathered from this obstinacy on the part of her father that there was something preying on his mind. Quick to read the expressions of his mobile features, she detected more than the usual indecision characteristic of him in situations with which he was not familiar. His deliberate sending for Chane Weymer seemed flinging more than reasonable doubt in the faces of his partners, and especially Manerube. Sue slipped back into the shadow and waited. When presently she heard Weymer's well-known footstep, he was striding out of the gloom, in advance of Jake. The instant Sue saw the dark gleam of his eyes in the firelight, his forward action, guarded yet quick, the something commanding in his presence, she divined what had actuated her father in sending for him. He was a man to rely upon. The moment of Weymer's arrival held for Sue less of pain than other times lately, for she sensed that in some way he would become an ally of her father's.

"What's wrong, Melberne?" asked Chane, as he halted in the firelight. The absence of his coat showed his lithe powerful form to advantage, his small waist and round rider's hips.

It also disclosed the fact that he wore a gun belt, with gun hanging low on his right side. Sue had not seen him armed before. A slight cold shudder passed over her.

"Wal, Weymer, I cain't say there's anythin' wrong, exactly," responded Melberne, standing up to face the rider. "But I cain't swear it's right, either. Heah's the argument . . . we're aboot done fixin' this wild-horse trap I'm so keen aboot. Reckon the success or failure of this trick means a lot to me. Jim an' Manerube swear it cain't fail. Wal, now we're near ready to drive, I wanted to slow down. I asked Manerube what his plan was. An' he up an' says we'll just spread out an' drive the valley. That's all! — I asked Alonzo to tell how he'd do it, an' he says he doesn't savvy Manerube. I just don't get his hunch. Then I asked Utah, an' he drawls sarcastic like that he cain't talk no more'n Tway Miller. Mebbe these riders are just naturally jealous of Manerube an' won't support him. Mebbe it's somethin' else. I don't know much aboot Utah riders, but I reckon I know men. That's why I sent for you. I reckoned you'd never let personal grudges interfere with what was right. Now would you?"

"Why, certainly not!" declared Weymer. "And I'd like you to know I don't bear grudges."

238

"Ahuh! All right, then. I've a hunch you know this wild-horse-wranglin' game. Now I'd shore take it as a favor if you'd tell me what you think aboot this drive we're soon to make."

Without the slightest hesitation Chane responded with a swift, "Melberne, I hired out to ride, not talk."

Here Sue, in her mounting interest at this colloquy, expected her father to fall into a rage. Chane's reply had been distinctly aloof, even cold. But Melberne manifestly had himself now well in hand. He was on the track of something that even the bystanders began to feel. Manerube shifted uneasily from one position to another.

"Shore. That was our understandin'," went on Melberne, stepping closer to Chane. "Reckon you're not duty bound to express opinions to me, especially when they concern an enemy of yours. But on the other hand, I've befriended you. I fed you when you were starved, an' then I gave you a job. Now, as man to man, isn't it fair for you to tell me if you know anythin' for or against this wild-horse drive?"

"It'd be more than fair of me, Melberne," declared Chane, significantly. "It'd be more than you or any other man could expect."

Melberne took that as a man receiving a

239

deserved blow. Chane's retort had struck home to Sue as well. Chane Weymer was certainly not in duty or honor compelled to approve of or aid the plans of Manerube. Besides, there was a subtle pride in Chane's meaning, whatever that was.

"Ahuh! I get your hunch," returned Melberne, gruffly. "Mebbe you've somethin' to say for yourself. If so, I'll listen."

"No, Melberne, I don't have to talk for myself."

"Dammit, man, self-defense is only right," retorted Melberne, losing patience. "Even the law expects that."

"Talk is cheap out here on the desert," rejoined Chane, with cool disdain. "I'd never employ it in my defense. But you notice I pack a gun?"

"Ahuh! I shore didn't overlook it," said Melberne, and his tone lost impatience for menace. There was probability of imminent antagonism here. Sue held her breath. Chane's fearless disdain matched her father's fearless uncertainty. Chane showed the proud sense of right; Melberne seemed divided between his doubt of right or wrong. Sue divined that in both men's minds had risen the thought of the calumny which hung like a shadow over Chane. How scornful and reticent he was, considering what must be true!

"Melberne, any man who believes of me what you believe has got to know he can't *talk* it, unless he wants to hear my *gun* talk," declared Chane, bitterly.

Thus Weymer threw down the gauntlet between them.

"Weymer," began Melberne, in slow crisp utterance, "I asked you kindly to do me a favor. Now you're politely invitin' me to draw."

"Bah! Such talk from a Texan!" exclaimed Chane, quick as a flash. "You know I've respect and liking for you. The last thing on earth I'd want would be to fight you. The trouble with you, Melberne, is you've got your bridle twisted out here in Utah. Your two-bit partner Loughbridge and your skunk foreman Manerube are to blame for that. Why don't you use your own head?"

If Sue had not been in the cold clutch of deadly terror she would have thrilled to Chane's surprising arraignment of her father. But she could only stare open-mouthed and quake. Melberne shot a quick expectant glance at Manerube. That individual sat in the fire-lighted circle. At Chane's stinging remark his face turned livid. But he made no move to rise or speak. Then slowly Melberne shifted his gaze to Loughbridge, less expectant this time. He saw a stupid angry wonder on that worthy's features. It roused him to a laugh, gruff, not merry.

"Weymer, I reckon I feel like apologizin' to you for fetchin' you out heah," said Melberne, still with gruff, grim voice. The cold edge, however, had left it. His face, too, had lost its tightness. Then it was that Sue felt a sudden flooding warmth of relief, joy, admiration. Her father was indeed a man.

"You needn't apologize," returned Chane, visibly softening. "I'm glad you understand me."

These words from him, following her father's so wrought upon Sue that she answered to unconsidered emotional impulse.

"Chane," she called, rising to step into the light, "I think you ought to tell dad what he asked." Once spoken, she could not recall her thought, nor could she sink, as she longed to, back into the shadow that had concealed her. Brave it out she must, and so she gazed across the fire.

"Miss Melberne — you do — may I ask why?" he queried, courteously.

"I — I don't know just why, but I believe you will."

"*You* ask me to?" he went on, with an inflection that cut her.

"I beg you to," she returned. "I don't approve of this barbed-wire trap. If you know anything against it — please tell dad. If you

can make it easier for the poor horses —
please tell dad how."

"Do you realize you are asking me to go
against your friend Manerube?" went on
Chane, still so cool and courteous.

A hot blush burned up into Sue's neck and
cheeks. How glad she was for the cloak of
darkness!

"I am thinking of the wild horses, not of
Mr. Manerube's success or failure — or my
father's profit," returned Sue, in the spirit of
her rising temper. She became aware of someone close behind her. Chess! She had felt his
presence. He had been listening. As she half
turned, he took a step and encircled her with
his arm.

"Chane, old boy, she's got you figured
right," he spoke up, quite loudly. "Tell the
boss what you told me about this wild-horse
drive — what a bloody mess it'll be."

At this juncture Manerube rose to his feet,
sullen-faced, and unmistakably laboring under
stress.

"Melberne, am I a horse thief that I have
to listen to this gab?" he demanded.

"Wal, it's a little rough on you, I'll admit,"
declared Melberne, in perplexity. "But you
needn't indulge in crazy talk. If your wild-
horse deal is what you claim for it you needn't
fear heahin' what others think about it."

Chane had turned his back upon Manerube and was regarding Chess and Sue with something akin to ironical amusement.

"Melberne, the young couple there seem to endow me with great virtue," he said, smiling. "I'm supposed to concern myself about the good fortunes of your outfit when you all despise me."

"Wal, I've tried to keep this a confab on horses, not personal character," rejoined Melberne, testily.

"Melberne, you'll talk to *me* some day about personal character," retorted Chane. "Now, what do you want to know?"

"Your idea aboot drivin' wild horses into this barbed-wire trap," replied Melberne, eagerly.

"It's a cruel, bloody, cowardly method that originated in Nevada. It will catch twice as many wild horses as any other kind of a trap, and kill half of them, and maim many for life. It never ought to be done at all. If you must make this drive do it in the daytime, not by moonlight as Manerube wants."

"Why so?"

"Because more horses will cut themselves to pieces at night."

"Ahuh! I reckoned that myself. Now how many horses do you figure we can trap in one drive?"

"Somewhere round two thousand, if we work fast."

"*Two thousand!*" ejaculated Melberne. "Shore you're not serious?"

"I'm serious enough, Melberne. It's a serious matter — just how bad you don't realize."

"Wal, that knocks me flat. Two thousand wild horses in one drive! A whole trainload. Weymer, I could ship an' sell them all."

"Ah, there you are wrong. You might sell a trainload if you could ship them. But it's impossible. You'd be very lucky to get even a hundred head to the railroad in fit shape to ship."

"How's that?" queried Melberne, incredulously.

"Hasn't Manerube informed you how it's done?" queried Chane, just as incredulously.

"No. He says trap them an' drive them to the railroad, an' ship them," declared Melberne.

"Sounds easy. But it's the hardest, dirtiest, and meanest job ever tackled by horsemen," continued Chane, almost wrathfully. "Say you've got your horses trapped inside the first big wire corral. All right. We rustle down there at daylight. We open the gate from the big corral to the small one, and let in a few horses. Then we pitch into work. Five good men can handle a wild horse, but seven do it quicker and better. We rope a horse, throw him, jump on him, hold him down. Then one of us takes a short rope and doubles a front foot up under his knee and binds it tight. Round his knee tight! Then we let him up and go after another. The faster we work the more time we have to drive to the railroad. We've got to get the bunch of horses to the railroad the same day we tied them up. So we work like dogs say from daylight to noon. Then we start off with maybe a hundred or more horses. These three-legged wild horses take a lot of driving. They can run almost as well on three legs as on four. Some of them will get away from this small outfit. Others will kill themselves plunging and falling. The bound knees sometimes develop terrible swelling sores. Of course the knees have to be untied in the stockyard at the railroad. Then many horses that looked fit to ship develop gangrene and have to be shot. You don't get paid for them. Well, after the first shipment you ride thirty miles back to camp at night, get a couple of hours sleep, and at daylight tackle the same dirty job again. I'd say three days will be about your limit. The wild horses left in the corrals will cut themselves to pieces, if they don't break down the fence. Even if you had strong wooden corrals you couldn't keep so many horses long . . . there, Melberne, you have the barbed-wire game. It's a hell of a job."

At the conclusion of Chane's long statement there ensued a silence that testified to its effect. All eyes gravitated from Chane to Melberne. He did not appear in any hurry to speak. Sue imagined she detected a slight paling of her father's ruddy cheeks.

"Loughbridge," he said, at length, addressing his partner, "let's give up this barbed-wire drive."

"No, by dam!" shrieked Loughbridge, in a frenzy. "If you don't go through with it I'll demand half the outfit money back. I ain't takin' stock in this pretty talker. Besides, we cain't ketch wild horses without scratchin' them a bit. Sure it's tough on them, an' men, too. But we're out for cash, aren't we? What do we care if we kill a hoss or two?"

Melberne threw up his hands with a gesture of impotence. Disgust distorted his visage. "Turn in, everybody," he ordered, and taking Sue's arm he led her away from the camp fire toward her tent.

Sue felt so fatigued from the day's exertion and stress that she staggered along, leaning on her father. She was unnerved, too. That illuminating explanation of the barbed-wire capture of wild horses had been the last straw.

"Lass," began her father as they halted before her tent, "I'm shore glad you spoke up to Weymer. If you hadn't he'd never have told us. But he's sweet on you an' you fetched him . . . I'm bound to say, Sue, I'm worried. Not only by this horse deal we're in, but by this mix-up among the men. Loughbridge's a good friend an' bad enemy. This Manerube begins to look fishy to me. He doesn't ring true. Can you imagine a Texan swallerin' what Weymer called him, before us all? He's yellow, that's all. An' Weymer — he shore shot it into me . . . an' I deserved it. Sue, I was ashamed . . . mebbe this Weymer has been foolin' with Indian squaws, but he's straight with men. He has an eye on him, an' he's shore dangerous. I'm worried. There's been bad blood made, an' some of it'll get spilled."

"Don't worry, dad," replied Sue, coaxingly, and kissed his worn cheek. "It'll all come right. You've never been anything but fair and square. If the wild-horse drive turns out as we fear — why, you must never do it again. You got led into this. First Jim Loughbridge, and then Manerube . . . and, oh, dad, you must keep Chane Weymer from fighting!"

"Lass, I reckon it's got beyond me," replied her father. "But shore I'll do my best. Good night."

Sue went to bed fighting desperately to silence that insistent trenchant voice within, the voice which cried out in defense of Chane Weymer. What if her father had begun to rely upon this strong-spirited rider of the old school? Fearless he undoubtedly was, one to whom men and women would instinctively draw near in a moment of doubt or peril. He stood out in this company of riders. But for Sue all his fine qualities, that seemed to grow from his arrival in Stark Valley, had been poisoned at the roots. Lover of squaws! She hid her face at the shameful thought. But the still small voice bade her listen — to wait — to watch — to withhold judgment — to be tolerant — to give benefit of a doubt — to plead extenuating circumstances. A desert rider's loneliness, the need of woman's touch, kindliness of a big heart, the imperious desires of nature, the hard fierce life of that wasteland, the power of propinquity, even love — these one and all flashed through Sue's merciless mind, tried her, tested her, and before the flame of her pride and jealousy they perished. But forgiveness was one thing and love another. She could no more help loving Chane Weymer than she could forgive him. Yet as the struggle went on the balance shifted, to the slow corroding and wearing of her spirit.

Sue had been dissatisfied with all the horses

she had ridden of late. Brutus had spoiled her. When she passed him in camp, and he threw up his beautiful head with that quick look, to whinny at her, the desire to run to him was well-nigh irresistible. She rode this horse and that mustang, only to like each one less.

And on the last day before the drive, when the barbed-wire fence was completed, she went out to see it, riding another strange horse. He appeared tractable enough and soon she forgot any uneasiness she might have felt at first.

Away down in the valley bands of wild horses dotted the green, some moving, others grazing, ignorant of the plot against their freedom and of those miles of iron-toothed fence that stretched across their domain. Sue gazed upon them with pity, praying for something to scare them far away before it was too late.

In time she circled to the west, and eventually got into rough ground, which she desired to cross, so that she could climb to the valley rampart and ride the ridge top round to where it joined the mountain slope near the camp. Her horse stumbled over a shallow clay-banked wash, and, falling, threw her hard against the opposite bank.

The impact stunned Sue, though not to the point of total unconsciousness. She lay there, numb, for a few moments, slowly becoming conscious of pain in her right knee. After a while she recovered enough to sit up. And feeling of her injured knee she sustained such an excruciating pain that she had a moment of panic. She feared a broken leg. But, presently, despite the pain, she found she could bend her knee, and that relieved her dread.

As the pangs lessened to a considerable degree she stood up with great difficulty and looked for her horse. He did not appear to be in sight. This occasioned Sue genuine distress, and she was wringing her hands and crying out what in the world could she do, when she espied a horse and rider coming down the trail she had intended to climb. Surely he could not pass by without seeing her. Immensely relieved, Sue untied her scarf and waved it. The rider evidently had espied her even before her effort to attract him. And at that instant Sue recognized Brutus, then his rider.

"Chane Weymer!" gasped Sue, with swift change of emotion. "That it'd — have to be he! Of all the miserable luck!"

Clouds of dust puffed from under the great horse as he leaped the washes. Before Sue had time to think of composure he ploughed the clay and sand before her, sliding to a halt as the rider threw himself off.

"What's wrong?" he demanded, his searching eyes sweeping her from disheveled head to dusty boots.

To find herself tingling to the point of dwarfing her pain roused in Sue a very devil of perverseness.

"There's nothing wrong with *me*," replied Sue, flippantly. "I'm admiring the scenery."

"You've been crying," he said, coming close to her. "You've had a fall. Are you hurt?"

"Only my vanity," she said.

He looked doubtfully at her and inquired about her horse.

"He's gone, and I hope I never see him again."

"Did you let him wander off?" queried Chane.

"I reckon he just left without my letting him."

"Well, it's good you weren't hurt," he went on, severely. "But you shouldn't ride out alone this way . . . perhaps you meant to meet Manerube!"

"That's none of your business," she retorted, with a tilt of her chin. "But I didn't intend to meet him. I'd rather, though, it'd been he — than you."

"You can ride Brutus," he said, ignoring

her slighting speech. "I'll shorten the stirrups. Miss Melberne, I shall tell your father this is dead wrong of you — riding far from camp this way."

"I don't care what you tell. But ride back to camp. Send someone with a — a wagon."

She saw the brown flash out of his face, and as he whirled from beside Brutus she could not meet his piercing eyes.

"You are hurt!" he exclaimed.

"Yes. My knee. It's not broken, but it hurts terribly. It's getting stiff. I — I can't ride."

"I'll carry you," he said.

"No — no. Ride back to camp. Send someone with the wagon. Don't scare dad."

"But it'll be dark long before the wagon can get here. In fact, nothing on wheels could come within a mile of this place."

"Oh, what shall I do?" cried Sue.

"I am afraid you must submit to the humiliating necessity of my carrying you," he replied, with that slight scorn again in his grave voice.

"I'll not let you," declared Sue, hotly.

"Miss Melberne, I certainly don't want to carry you. But the afternoon is far gone. Your folks will be worried. I can't let you stay here alone. There's no other way."

"I — I don't care," cried Sue, succumbing to combined pain and mortification. "I'll —

I'll die before I let you — carry me."

"Well, what a sweet disposition you have!" he declared. "I wouldn't have guessed it."

Suddenly he placed a hand under each of her arms, and lifted her bodily, with a sweep, and set her feet gently down on the edge of the wash. It was done so adroitly and with such strength that Sue could only stare her amazement and resentment. He returned the resentment fourfold.

"I'm not a rattlesnake or a — a Mormon," he shot down at her, not without passion. "You stand still. If you make a fuss you're going to hurt yourself. So don't blame me."

Sue did not leave the spot where he had set her down, for the very good reason that her leg pained so badly she did not dare move it. Chane vaulted upon Brutus and rode him down into the wash and close to where Sue stood.

"I'll have to hold you free of the pommel," he said, as he leaned out of the saddle and reached for her. "I hope you show some sense. If you act the spoiled baby it'll hurt all the more."

Sue stood like a statue, with her head bent. But she could see his arms, one of which he slipped round her waist, and the other under her knees. Gently as he lifted her, the pressure and contact made her wince. Then she found herself resting in his arms, her head on his shoulder.

"Brutus, old boy, you can step out light," he said to the horse. "We've got rather a precious burden."

Sue closed her eyes, not so much from pain as from the stunning reality of her position. She felt him shift the hold of his right arm, so that it no longer came in contact with her injured knee. After that she began to feel easier. She was in a kind of swing, the light embrace of his arms, and felt only slightly the jar of the horse as he walked. Sue did not open her eyes. If she was detected looking at him she imagined her shameful secret would be known. How endless the moments! He spoke no word and she felt that he did not gaze down upon her.

She lay in his arms — Chane Weymer's arms — and could not help herself. Then flashed the monstrous truth. The secret emotion she despised reveled in the fact. It burned the truth over all her palpitating body, through veins of fire. It sent messages along her throbbing nerves. She lay in his arms glad, shamelessly glad, despicably glad. Vain to lie to herself! She had changed to a woman and had come to love him more every day. Her love had battened on her bitter, savage, perverse spirit, and now it mocked her.

Every time she swayed gently with the movement of the horse her cheek rolled against Chane's shoulder. She felt the vibration of muscle, the heat of blood. And her cheek flamed under the contact. She was undone. All the torments she had endured were as nothing to this storm that assailed her — deadly sweet, unconquerable, terrible, the staggering deeps of her betraying heart that had drowned her pride.

The time came when voices caused Sue to open her eyes. Dark had fallen. Brutus had come to a standstill.

"Melberne, it's all right. Don't be frightened," Chane was saying in a calm voice. "I found your daughter down by the west end of the fence. Her horse had thrown her and run off. I've packed her home . . . be careful, now. Handle her easy. She's not bad hurt. Lucky, though, for it was a mean place."

"Why, lass — is he tellin' the truth?" asked Melberne, hoarsely, as he received Sue in his arms.

"Oh, dad, I'm terribly hurt," cried Sue, "but it's only my — my feelings."

"Wal, you're shore pale, an' I reckon you're fibbin'. Wife, come heah. Our lass is hurt."

Then he glanced up from the girl in his arms to the rider.

"Ahuh! so, Weymer, you just happened along? Wal, now I wonder aboot you!"

The content of his words did not express thankfulness, but the tone trembled with an infinite gratitude.

Chapter 10

The first glimmer of dawn was lightening the east when Chane Weymer, with Chess and Alonzo, rode away from camp, down into the dark melancholy void of Stark Valley, to begin their part in Melberne's great wild-horse drive.

"Chane, I'll bet we owe it to Manerube that we got the hardest job today," complained Chess.

"I reckon. But what difference does it make?" returned Chane. "We'll have a day of tough riding. No worse than Utah's, though. Believe I'd rather have the wide level valley to cover, than that rough ground to the west. Anyway, the harder it is the better I'll like it, till we get the bloody business over."

"You think one drive will be enough for the boss, huh?" inquired Chess.

"Reckon I know it. Melberne's a white man, Chess. If he'd known about this barbed-wire game he'd never have gotten so far along."

"But if it's a success? The boss's keen to make money."

"If he made ten thousand dollars on this drive he'd never tackle another. I'm gambling on his daughter. She'd keep him from it."

"I'm not so sure of Sue, lately," returned Chess, thoughtfully. "One day she's this way and the next day that. But I was surprised when she spoke up to you the other night. Weren't you?"

"Boy, I told you twice," said Chane, trying to steer the conversation away from the charming topic Chess always led round to. It was not that Chane ever tired of eulogies to Sue, or the events of any day that included her, but Chess had an obsession. Some day Sue would be his sister! And when her name came up, which inevitably happened every time Chess came near enough to talk, he would dreamily or unconsciously or cunningly return to the shibboleth which had its pangs for Chane. But Chane never regretted Chess's beautiful and romantic love for Sue Melberne, for he believed it had been the turning point toward good in the boy's wild life. Chane's pangs were selfish. For it had been his misfortune to worship at first sight the dark-eyed Sue. Chane's dreams, if he had any at this fruitless time of his hard desert experience, never dared to verge on the extreme edge of Chess's enchanted visions.

"Horses, señor," said Alonzo, his lean hand pointing.

"Yes, there's the first bunch," returned Chane, peering through the opaque dawn at some horse shapes that moved like specters. "Reckon they'll run down valley for a while anyhow."

"Sí, señor," said the Mexican.

They trotted their horses on, keeping to the edge of the oval valley. The black mountain range loomed above, tipped with paling stars. The valley itself was losing its density of space at night, responding to the invisible influence that hid far under the gray widening mantle of the east. It was a frosty morning, nipping cold, and the iron-shod hoofs rang like silver bells on the stones.

Chess had lighted a cigarette, something he always did when Chane was not responsive to his favorite topic of conversation. His horse was mettlesome and wanted action. In fact, all their mounts showed the good of several days' rest. Chane saw the long ears of Brutus lifting now and then, as if he were waiting for the word to go. Brutus, however, never wasted energy unbidden. His gentle easy pace kept him abreast of the two trotting horses.

Chane's thoughts were not unhappy ones, despite the pangs of a passion he had never revealed, or the disgrace which had been laid upon his name by a liar and a coward. He knew, though no one had ever told him, what Melberne believed he was. He felt where he stood in Sue Melberne's estimation. The thing had happened before, though never in connection with persons whom he yearned to have know him truly and love him. But these Melbernes had steadied Chess, especially Sue, who had changed the boy. For that Chane would serve them with all he had in him. In this service he found something of happiness, the only happiness he had known in years. Yet so stern was he in his pride, so hurt by lack of instant faith in those to whom he had come in need, that he could never go unsolicited to Melberne and prove how Manerube was a snake in the grass. Could he say — Melberne, this outcast Mormon is what he has made you believe I am? How impossible for him to shame Sue Melberne with the facts! True, the genial father was wearing toward uncertainty and suspicion. Let him find out! But as for the daughter, who openly flaunted an incomprehensible regard for this Manerube, it could never matter what she believed. Chane was used to adversity. But this deep trouble of his heart was made supportable, even welcome, by Chess's mending of his wild ways.

As the riders rode on and down into the valley the dim gloom gave place to an opaque veil of gray, and that lightened with the gray of the eastern sky. A faint rosy glow appeared, gradually deepening. The gray mantle retreated, lifted, vanished. Dawn succeeded to day. The stark valley stretched clear, cold, steely from range to rampart, and far to the upflung level of Wild Horse Mesa. Droves of horses dotted the frosty floor, lending it a singular charm of wild life and beauty.

"Listen!" called Chane, suddenly.

They halted, faces turning sidewise and down. From the bold slope above the valley pealed down the piercing bugle of a bull elk.

"Blow elk, blow while you may!" exclaimed Chane. "The white man will chase your wild brothers off the desert. Then your turn will come."

"There he is — close — on the ridge end," said Chess. "Funny how much tamer elk are than wild horses."

"They don't know men, yet, in these parts," returned Chane. "Spread out now, boys, and begin the drive. Keep about a mile apart. Wave and yell and shoot as you drive. When a bunch breaks to run between us — ride!"

Chane was left alone. While waiting for his comrades to reach their stands he bent keen roving eyes on the valley below. Many bands of wild horses were in sight, more than he had entertained any idea would be so far away from toward the center of the valley. Perhaps during the erecting of the trap and fences many bands of horses had grazed north. Chane could see the dim shadow of ridges, far down, where the two flanges of the wire fence joined the corrals. They appeared ten miles distant, perhaps more. All of Melberne's force of riders were in the field, stretched across the valley; and the work of each and every one was to ride to and fro, and always down, driving the wild horses before them. It would not take hard riding until the horses had traveled miles. As this drive progressed down the valley, toward and into the trap, the lines of riders would converge, at last meeting at the apex of the long triangle of barbed wire.

"Devilish trick!" muttered Chane, grimly. "Wish I'd shot Manerube that day I caught him running off with Sosie."

The thought voiced so violently had flashed before through his mind, always to be subdued and cast aside. Yet he could not prevent its recurrence. As time went by he divined more and more that there was something wrong in regard to his status in the Melberne outfit. Nothing openly had been said, or even hinted; Chess had been noncommittal, too frankly so, in his brief remarks about Manerube's arrival at that camp. But Chane knew his reputation had suffered and that no other than Manerube could be accountable. Never before in any camp had there hovered a shadow over him. As he milled it over in his mind he felt that for Chess's sake he did not want to pry into the matter. What did he care for the gossip of a man like Manerube? This individual would soon enough hang himself. But the girl in the case had caused the situation to grow poignant.

Two terrible things had happened, Chane confessed — at first sight he had fallen in love with Sue Melberne, and secondly he had divined she had accepted some base estimate of him. The second made the first something to be vastly ashamed of, and as he had fought down many trials in his life, so he had struggled with this one. But the more he tried to forget the girl the more he loved her.

"Reckon I think of nothing but her," he soliloquized, aghast at the fact. "Well, it's only one more trouble . . . maybe I'll be the better for it. But she'll never know. I'll hang on with this outfit till she learns what Manerube is. Reckon that won't be long. Toddy Nokin will hit this camp sooner or later. It'll be funny. I rather like the situation. But I wouldn't want to be in Manerube's boots."

The time came when Chane saw Chess lined up with him a couple of miles distant, and Alonzo the same distance farther on. Likewise to the west, toward camp, Chane made out riders stationed far apart. Presently they began to move, as if by spoken order, and he turned his horse to the south.

Far below Chane espied wild horses, but there were none in his immediate vicinity. A scattered drove began to walk and trot half a mile in front of Chess, and a large number had headed away from Alonzo. The riders west of Chane would have considerable ground to cover before coming upon any wild horses.

Brutus did not want to go slow. He sensed a race with his wild brothers, and though he was good-natured in obeying Chane's word or touch, he repeatedly manifested his spirit. Moreover, he could see the wild horses very much better than Chane.

"Now I reckon you'd like to run wild with these mustangs," said Chane. "Brutus, I'm ashamed of you."

Chane kept his eye roving from west to east, to see how soon the action would begin. In perhaps a quarter of an hour, when he had covered a couple of miles, he saw Alonzo riding to head off a band of light-colored horses that were making a break. Chane halted Brutus and watched, and he espied Chess doing the same thing. Chane's opinion was that Chess would have to ride hard to help turn this band, and that he ought to be getting started pretty quickly. It turned out, however, that Chess's inaction must have been due to a better perspective than Chane's, for he sat on his horse watching, while Alonzo, riding like an Indian, intercepted the leaders of the band and turned them back down the valley.

Then Chane resumed his slow advance. If it had not been for the fact that this drive must develop into a brutal business, Chane would have found the prospect very thrilling. As it was, he watched the distant bands of horses with divided emotion — love for them in their freedom, pity for their inevitable doom.

He could tell when the leader of a band first lifted a wild head and espied him coming. Erect, motionless, like a statue he stood for a moment, then he ran toward his band, excited them, turned to look again, pranced and cavorted, and then drove them before him for a distance, only to halt and turn. Presently several hundred wild horses, in a dozen or more different bands, were moving to and fro across the valley before Chane, gradually working south. One huge stallion, bolder than his fellows, trotted toward Chane, stopped to gaze, and then trotted forward once more, until he satisfied himself that his archenemy man bestrode Brutus. His piercing whistle came faintly to Chane's ears. Wheeling as on a pivot, he ran back with the long, even wild stride that Chane so loved to watch, and with his band lifted a moving cloud of dust along the valley floor. In a few moments this particular band was out of sight.

"Wild boy, that fellow," mused Chane. "I'll bet he was born in captivity. He sure didn't like the looks of me and Brutus."

Chane rode on, and as he advanced, the interest of this drive began to increase. It was impossible to look in every direction at once, and as the bands of horses were now moving forward and back, to and fro, some trotting, others running, Chane was hard put to it to see everything. Dust clouds began to dot the green floor of the valley. They moved something like the smoke from a passing railroad train, seen at a distance. The valley floor was well carpeted with bleached grass and gray sage and green growths, though not over its whole area; and when a band of running horses struck a less fertile spot, the dust would puff in yellow clouds from under their hoofs.

Brutus whistled a blast and jerked under the saddle. Chane turned to see a string of wild horses racing for the wide open between his and Chess's position. At that moment Chess was making fast time in the opposite direction to head off another bunch.

At word and touch Brutus dashed into action. A short swift spurt of a quarter of a mile brought him so far in front of the escaping wild horses that they began to swerve. The leader, a lean white mustang, spotted black, wilder than a deer, let out a piercing blast of anger and fear. His mane and tail streamed in the wind. As he ran parallel with Brutus his followers, perhaps more fearful, swerved more to the right, and in half a mile there was considerable distance between them. Chane saw with great pride that Brutus, even carrying his weight, was faster than this spotted mustang. But then Brutus had twice the stride. Chane soon turned this leader toward the others, and presently they were running south as fast as they could go.

Whereupon Chane reined in the eager Brutus and trotted across the ground he had covered, so to regain as equal a position as possible between Chess on the east and the nearest rider on the west. A general survey of the valley straight across in both directions convinced Chane that it would have taken twice the number of riders to drive all these wild horses down into the apex of the barbed-wire fence. While Chane's back had been turned, a small band had raced across his regular position and were now sweeping north in close formation, dark bays and blacks, with their manes and tails tossing. How beautifully they ran! It seemed that nothing could be more smooth and free and fleet. Chane was glad that they had gotten by him.

For a while he had only to ride to and fro, working south enough to keep even with his comrade riders. Chess too was having it easy. But Alonzo, far to the east, evidently had a task cut out for him.

"He'll eat that job up!" declared Chane, in admiration of the *vaquero*.

Five thousand wild horses were in motion along a belt of valley three miles deep and perhaps three times as long. Farther than this Chane could not see clearly enough to make estimates. They appeared to be running in every direction, though the general trend was south. To Chane it was an inspiring sight. Horses of every color crossed his vision.

Suddenly Chane espied a big bay, at the front of a straggling bunch of mustangs, headed straight for him. The leader was as large as Brutus and he was a fierce-looking brute. There was nothing beautiful about him, unless it was his stride. Brutus manifestly wanted both to run and to fight, and plunged to meet this huge bay. Chane had been run down by wild horses more than once, and he did not intend to take chances of hurting Brutus. When the space narrowed to less than a hundred yards and the bay kept sweeping on straight as an arrow, Chane resorted to his gun to scare this gaunt leader. At the first shot the bay leaped into the air, seeming to turn in the action, and when he alighted on his feet his ugly head was pointed west. The shot, likewise, stampeded the band, and scattering to both sides, they passed at breakneck speed.

"I'd like to bet somebody that big stallion will never be caught by a wire fence," declared Chane as he halted to watch the bay run. "Didn't like him, did you, Brutus? Well, I was scared of him myself."

The bay quartering to the west was soon lost to view among the strings and patches of moving horses.

"Humph! I reckon this picnic for Chess and me is about over. We've got to ride some."

But Chane had another half hour of leisurely working to and fro across his beat before the strenuous riding he anticipated became necessary. For some reason or other the wild horses did not run his way as much as toward that of the other riders. He kept watch on Chess and was amused at that boy's undoubted troubles. Alonzo, however, had the widest stretch of valley, and by far the largest number of horses to contend with. In his daring dashes to turn back big droves he let many small bands pass across the line. Finally Chane saw a huge moving patch of black, many acres in extent, sweeping down upon the Mexican's position. There must have been a thousand wild horses in that drove. Dust rose in yellow clouds similar to the trailing smoke of a prairie fire. Chane did not expect the Mexican to turn back that stampede. The white puffs of Alonzo's gun showed against the green. Then as the horses swept on in a resistless tide Chane saw how Alonzo had to run for his life. He disappeared behind the moving level mass and showed no more.

That incident was the last Chane had time to watch. Straggling twos and threes of mustangs engaged his attention. And presently he had to get into the race in earnest. The first band of horses that eluded the fleet Brutus told Chane the futility of hoping to head all the horses which raced toward him. He gave up such object and did not attempt the impossible.

As Chane raced to and fro, firing his gun to frighten the horses that trooped toward him, the drive grew to be a rout toward the notch of the fence. Chane could not see it, but he appreciated the fact that it was now not many miles distant. Everywhere the valley floor appeared colorful and active with twinkling legs, bobbing heads, flying manes and tails. The air grew thick with dust, so that in some places a clear view could not be obtained. An intermittent trampling roar of hoofs mostly drowned the gunshots of the riders. From time to time Chane heard faint shots, like spats, on both sides of him. But he never saw a rider.

Brutus grew hot and wet, and a dusty lather collected on his chest and neck. Whenever a stallion passed near, Brutus would answer the wild whistling challenge. Bands of horses grew numerous and thick, making Chane's task more difficult and dangerous. He might have turned more horses back if he had been more free with the use of his gun, but Chane had a grim excuse for saving ammunition. He knew presently it would be merciful to shoot with deadly intent.

The drive approached the flanges of the fence. Thousands of wild horses were being driven into a triangular space of comparatively small size. The roar of hoofs, the whistling and snorting, became incessant. A gray dusty haze made fast riding perilous. Chane had to peer through the gloom to protect Brutus. That drive indeed brought out the many and incomparable qualities of this horse. Many times Brutus equaled the keenness and caution of his rider.

At length Chane found himself in a *mêlée* of running, plunging, maddened wild horses, criss-crossing the space in every direction. There came to be as many horses behind him as in front or on either side. They streaked by like specters. Then, despite dust-clogged nostrils, Chane caught the odor of blood. From this he concluded that he had reached the vicinity of the wire fence.

Wheeling Brutus and slowing to a trot, Chane headed to the left, away from the increasingly thickening streams of horses. As far as he could tell, the riders had driven thousands of horses down into the notch of the trap. Pandemonium certainly reigned down in that pall of dust. Soon Chane rode out into clearer atmosphere where he could see, and found that his deductions were not far short of the mark. All the riders evidently had worked down into the triangle he had left. Still, wild horses were numerous, running both ways. They were mad with terror.

Chane at last came upon the left flange of the fence. It presented a gruesome spectacle, that part of it which was still standing. Bits of flesh and tufts of hair showed on the sagging wires, and many places red with blood. The top wire was gone entirely. Sections of the fence had been laid flat or carried out of sight; posts were broken and leaning. Farther east along this flange the fence was intact, and here Chane began to encounter crippled and dying horses. Promptly he shot them. Brutus reacted strangely to this work: he did not balk or show unwillingness to go on, but he grew exceedingly nervous.

Most of these wounded horses had been cut across the chest, great deep gaps from which the blood poured. It sickened Chane, yet relentlessly he rode on, until no more horses appeared along that flange of the fence. Upon riding back he saw the dust lifting, rolling away on the wind, and through the cloud a blood-red westering sun shone with weird sinister effect. Strings of horses were running north and west, away from that fatal notch. In the huge corral a dark mass of horses, acres in area, moved in close contact; the whistling, snorting, squealing din was terrific.

Chane heard a spatting of gunshots, out along the western flange of the fence, and as he neared the center of the notch he espied Utah riding in, manifestly from the merciful task of ending the misery of crippled mustangs. Chane's heart was heavy and sore and there had risen in him a temper that boded ill.

At length he reached the spot where Melberne and his riders formed a singular group. Some were still sitting on their wet heaving horses. Chess hunched on the ground with his face in his hands, Captain Bunk was trying to walk, Alonzo was so pasted with froth from his horse as to be unrecognizable in feature, Miller was a dust-begrimed rider who would never have been taken for a white man. Utah came riding up, his gun in his hand, a black sternness on his lean face. Loughbridge was jabbering like a wild man, beside himself, evidently, with the extraordinary success of the drive.

"Seventeen hundred! More mebbe! Near two thousand horses trapped! We've struck a gold mine!" he shouted.

Manerube received this acclaim as one his just due, but as he encountered Chane's gaze his pompous air suffered a blight.

Chane last bent a curious look upon Melberne. This was where the Texan must be judged. The leader of the outfit showed nothing of the feeling that characterized Loughbridge. He was weary, and heavy on his feet.

"Well, Melberne, what do you think of your barbed-wire drive?" demanded Chane, in a voice full of scorn and curiosity.

Melberne turned to disclose a gray face and gleaming eyes. He seemed another man. Savagely he cursed, and gave Chane no intelligible reply. But his profanity was expressive enough. It took the edge off Chane's bitterness, as he replied:

"Man, the worst is yet to come."

Chapter 11

Dusk found the weary riders approaching camp. Chane led the cavalcade, finding Brutus, as always, light of foot and eager to get home. The flickering camp fire shone like a pinpoint through the gathering darkness, growing larger and brighter as he rode on. At last Chane, announced by a shrill neigh from Brutus, entered the circle of firelight.

The womenfolk, excited and anxious at his arrival, inquired as one voice the whereabouts of the men and if all was well.

"They'll be in soon. It's been a tough day, and I reckon Brutus is the only horse not dead beat," replied Chane as he wearily swung out of the saddle.

"Good!" ejaculated Mrs. Melberne. "Hungry as bears you'll all be. We'll have supper ready right off."

Sue Melberne limped out of the shadow into the firelight. She was bareheaded and her eyes seemed unnaturally large and dark in her pale face.

"Tell me — was it successful — the drive?" she asked, intensely.

"Successful? Yes, if you mean a big bunch of horses captured," replied Chane, slowly.

"I don't mean numbers. Were they caught without crippling and torturing many?"

"No. I'm sorry to say it was the bloodiest mess I ever saw," returned Chane, grimly. "I wouldn't tell you how many horses I shot — how they looked. We can never tell the number that broke through the barbed wire — to die lingering deaths down in the desert."

"Oh! I feared that!" said Sue, in distress. "How — how did dad take it?"

"I'd rather not say what I think," returned Chane, and led Brutus away into the grove to have a care for him.

A little later, when Chane went back to the camp fire, all the riders were in and more than ready for the bountiful supper spread by the women. Mostly they ate in silence and like famished wolves. Chane was as hungry as any of them, but he did not miss word or look that passed. He was curious to see the reaction of this day.

Loughbridge, somewhat rested and with appetite satisfied, reverted again to the manner and expression which had so disgusted Chane at the end of the drive. Naturally, after supper, the talk waged vigorously, and opinions, deductions, forecasts were as many and varied as the personalities of the riders. Loughbridge was already raking in big profits from the drive. Manerube had taken upon himself the honors of a hero, and swaggered before the listening women. Chess sat hollow-eyed and raging, his voice lifted high. Melberne presented a queer contrast. He had not spoken a word, but he no longer seemed stultified and thick. Presently Manerube detached himself from the half-circle of men on one side of the camp fire and crossed to where the women sat listening. Ora obviously gave him the cold shoulder. Sue, however, began to question him eagerly.

"You women go to bed," spoke up Melberne, gruffly.

His wife obediently left the group, but Mrs. Loughbridge and Ora paid no attention to him, and if Sue heard she gave no sign. She stood looking up at Manerube with an interest which could very easily be misunderstood.

"Sue, I told you to go to bed," called Melberne, sharply.

"But I'm not sleepy," protested Sue. "I want to hear all about —"

"Go to bed!" interrupted her father, in a voice that Chane had never before heard him use, and he swore at her.

"Why — dad!" faltered Sue, shocked out

of her usual independent spirit.

"You seem to take it for granted there's only one man heah," replied Melberne, sarcastically. "The rest of us were aboot when it happened, I reckon."

Sue's pale face flamed, and turning away without another word she limped into the shadow.

Chane felt sorry for her, that she should be so pointedly reprimanded by her father before them all, but the significance of the incident made his heart beat quickly. The situation grew more to his liking. Sooner or later he would find himself vindicated.

"Loughbridge, listen heah," said Melberne, deliberately. "You remember our deal. I lent you the money for this outfit an' you were to pay me half out of your share of the proceeds of our wild-horse huntin'."

"Yes, I reckon thet was the deal," replied the other, somewhat wonderingly.

"Wal, on condition I boss this outfit I'll consider your debt paid right heah. How about it?"

"Suits me fine, Mel," returned Loughbridge, with his greedy smile.

"Ahuh! All right, it's settled," went on Melberne, and then turned to Manerube. "You said we'd divide the outfit into two squads for this ropin' an' hawg-tyin' stunt tomorrow.

Now I'm tellin' you to pick your men."

"All I need is some help," said Manerube. "I'll do the roping and tying. My men will be Loughbridge, Miller, Alonzo, and Utah."

"Nope, you're wrong, Mister Manerube," retorted Utah, coolly. "I wouldn't be on your side."

"Utah, you'll take orders," said Melberne, testily.

"Shore, but not from him. An' if you say for me to go on his side, I quit."

"Manerube, pick another man," returned the leader.

"Bonny," said Manerube, shortly.

"Wal, that leaves me, Utah, Captain Bunk, an' the Weymers. Jake can stay in camp," said Melberne, reflectively. After a moment he addressed Chane. "I reckon you ought to take charge of our squad?"

There seemed to be a good deal more in Melberne's mind than he saw fit to speak.

"If you think so I'll do it," replied Chane, slowly.

"I'm thankin' you," said Melberne. "Now, men, you'd better turn in, as I'll call you aboot three o'clock."

Whereupon he left the fire. Chane followed him. Melberne did not walk like a man with hopeful prospects. Chane caught up with him and strode beside him into the grove until they

280

reached a point where Chane's way led to the left.

"Melberne," said Chane as they both halted, "I know how you feel. This drive looks bad. It *is* bad. And I told you, the worst is yet to come. But I reckoned you'd put too much store on the success of catching large numbers of wild horses for the market. You've just followed wrong hunches. This deal will likely lose you money. It'll do worse than that. It'll hurt you, because you're a man with human feelings. But it's nothing to discourage you as to the future. You'll do well in Utah. The country has great possibilities that men such as you will develop. So don't worry. This barbed-wire mess will be over in a few days. You'll soon get things straight."

"Say, Weymer, are you giving me a good hunch?" inquired Melberne.

"Hardly. I see you're a little down tonight, and I just wanted you to know I understood."

"Ahuh! Wal, mebbe you do," responded Melberne heavily, and went his way under the cottonwoods.

It was one thing for Melberne to say he would rout everybody out at three o'clock next morning and another to accomplish it. As the matter transpired, Chane was the early riser who called the men and built the fire

281

and went out after the horses. All these except Brutus had been left in the corral at the far end of the grove. In the darkness Chane had difficulty locating Brutus. Instead of being found, he answered Chane's whistles and made it easy for Chane, though he did not come in of his own accord. Chane led Brutus back through the grove and gave him a double handful of grain.

"Chess, wake up. You're late," called Chane.

"I'm — asleep," mumbled Chess.

"Roll out and get your horse. Breakfast's 'most ready."

"I'm dead. Aw, Chane, do I have to help murder those poor ponies?"

"Boy, you've got to help me make it as easy as possible for them. Melberne has made me boss of our squad."

"I forgot. Sure that's different," returned Chess as he rolled out of his blankets, dressed except for his boots.

Chane found a bustle round the camp fire. Jake was cook, with several assistants. Melberne had a quick, serious manner.

"What'll we need?" he asked Chane.

"Lots of soft rope. Saddlebags for grub and water bags for water. It'll be a twenty-hour day. And don't let any fellow forget his gloves!"

Chane's squad of five rode out of camp into the dark hour before dawn while Manerube's men were getting ready. The air was cold, the ground gray with frost, the sky steely blue lighted by white stars. The silent grim men might have been bent on a deadly scouting mission. Chane led at a brisk lope, and when the first streaks of morning brightened the east, he drew rein before the huge trap corrals. A whistling and trampling roar attested to the fact that the wild horses had not broken the fence.

"We'll wait for the other gang," said Chane. "Reckon we'd better throw off our saddles. It'll be noon before we get ready to ride."

The men unsaddled, haltered their horses, uncoiled and recoiled their lassoes, and lastly cut the short lengths of soft rope designated as necessary by Chane. When this was done the other squad rode up.

"You fellars get a hustle on," said Melberne.

"No rush," replied Manerube. "Are any of you fellows betting we don't tie up two horses to your one?"

"Manerube, this is a gambling matter for me, but not for you," retorted Melberne, significantly.

"Now, boys," said Chane, "crawl under the wires. We'll go round to the empty corral."

Two corrals had been constructed, one a quarter of a mile in diameter, which now contained the seventeen hundred wild horses, the other smaller in size, and with a fifty-foot gate of poles and wires.

"Boys, here's our system," said Chane, when his men gathered round him inside the empty corral. "We'll open the gate and let in ten or a dozen or twenty horses. They won't need to be driven in yet a while. Keep out of their road. Some wild horses are bad. I'll do the roping. When I throw a horse you all make a dive to hold him down. Melberne, you're the heaviest. You sit on his head. Chess, you hold one front foot while I tie up the other. Utah, you know the game. I'm asking you to look out for Cap till he gets the hang of it."

Manerube's squad now appeared in the gray gloom of the morning, and all approached the wide gate. When it had been released at the fastening it was swung open wide. Horses were thick in the gray obscurity of the larger corral, but evidently the dim light did not prevent them from seeing well. Soon a wild leader shot through like an arrow from a bow, to be followed by several passing swift as flashes, and then by a string of them, whistling and plunging.

"Enough. Shut the gate!" yelled Chane.

They were just in time to stop a stampede. "Now follow me round," added Chane, and broke into a run toward the dim shapes of the wild horses. Chane swung his lasso as he ran. Its use was an old story to him. As a boy he could rope the sombrero off a cowboy's head as dexterously as it might have been snatched by hand.

"Chase them past me," yelled Chane. "Chess, you stick by me to lend a hand. If a horse gets the jerk on me instead of me getting it on him, I'm liable to be yanked out of my boots."

A group of wild horses broke up and scattered, running everywhere. Chane ran forward, to one side, swinging a wide loop round his head. In the dim gray he had to guess at distance. But this roping was as much a feeling with Chane as an action. Several horses raced past. At the fourth, a lean wild bay, clearly outlined against the gray, Chane cast his lasso. He did not need to see the horse run into the loop. Bracing himself, Chane gave a sudden powerful jerk just as the noose went taut round the forelegs of this horse. It was in the middle of his leap, and he went down heavily.

"Quick!" yelled Chane to his comrades as hand over hand he closed in on his quarry. Melberne plunged down on the head of the prostrate horse. Utah was almost as quick at his flanks. Captain Bunk fell on the middle of the horse. "Good! Hold hard," shouted Chane. "I got both his legs."

Chane loosened the noose and slipped it off one leg, which he drew back from the other. "Grab that leg, Chess. Hang on."

The groaning, quivering horse lay helpless. He could kick with his two free legs, but to no purpose. Chane hauled the foreleg back, then let go his rope to grasp the leg in his hands. Chess, by dint of strength and weight was holding down the other leg. Chane pulled one of the short lengths of soft rope from the bundle hanging in his belt. He had to expend considerable force to draw the leg up, bending it back. The horse squealed his fury and terror. Then Chane's swift hard hands bound that bent leg above the knee. It gave the leg an appearance of having been cut off. The foreleg and hoof were tied fast against the inside of the upper part of the leg. Chane slipped off the noose of his lasso, and jumped up.

"Get away and let him up," ordered Chane. All the men leaped aside with alacrity.

The wild horse got up as nimbly as if he had still the use of four legs. He snorted his wild judgment of this indignity. His first move was a quick plunge, which took him to his knees. But he bounded up and away with amazing action and balance. His speed, however, had been limited to half.

Chane heard the rival squad yelling and squabbling over a horse they had down. The gray gloom was lifting. Chane coiled his lasso, spread the loop to his satisfaction, and ran to intercept another passing horse. His aim went true, but it was good luck that he caught one foreleg instead of two. This horse was heavier. As he went down he dragged Chane, boots ploughing the ground. Chane's helpers piled upon the straining, kicking horse and forced him flat. Thus the strenuous day began.

Chane tied up fifty-six horses before he was compelled to ask Melberne for a little rest.

"My — Gawd!" panted Melberne, as he flopped down against a fence post. "I'm daid — on my feet . . . Weymer — you're shore — a cyclone — for work."

The sun shone bright and hot. A fine dust sifted down through the air. All of Chane's squad were as wet as if they had fallen into a pond. Melberne's face ran with dirty streaks of black sweat; his heavy chest heaved with his panting breaths. Chess was the least exhausted of the squad, as his labors had been least. Captain Bunk was utterly played out for the moment.

"Blast me!" he gasped. "I could — drink

— the ocean — dry."

"Cap, don't let the boys guy you any more," said Chane. "You're awkward, but you're game, and you haven't shirked."

They passed the water bag from one to another, and passed it round again. Then Melberne, beginning to recover somewhat, began to take active interest in the operations of Manerube's squad. On the moment they were dragging a mustang down.

"Weymer, that man cain't throw a horse," declared Melberne, testily.

"Wal, boss, how long are you goin' to be findin' out he cain't throw anythin' but a bluff?" drawled Utah.

Manerube, with the help of Bonny and Miller, downed the mustang. Loughbridge tried to hold down its head, but did not succeed until Alonzo came to his assistance. They were a considerable time tying the knee.

"How many horses have they tied?" inquired Melberne, shifting his gaze to the far side of the corral, where the bound animals stood, already pathetic and dispirited.

"Sixteen or seventeen at most," replied Chane. "I counted them twice."

Melberne cursed his amazement and disgust.

"Weymer, let's go over an' watch them," he said.

"Not me. You're boss of the outfit. You go," replied Chane.

Whereupon Melberne got up and strode toward the other squad. Perhaps his approach caused them to speed up in action, but it did not add to their efficiency. Chane had needed only one glance to see that Manerube was only ordinary in the use of a lasso. Alonzo could have done better blindfolded. Manerube cast his noose to circle the neck, and this hold, when accomplished, was not a good one for the throwing of a horse. It took three men to haul the horse over on his side, and then he was half choked to death. Melberne lent a hand in holding down this particular horse. Manerube did quicker work this time, but as the horse staggered up Chane saw that the job of tying had not been cleverly done, and certainly not as humanely as it was possible to do. Manifestly Melberne saw this, for he pointed at the flopping shortened leg as the horse hobbled away.

The only unbound horse left in the corral now was a chestnut sorrel, a stallion that had several times taken Chane's eyes. He was a beauty, big, smooth, graceful, and wild as a hawk. Alonzo and Miller, both clever at herding horses, finally drove him within reach of Manerube's rope. But Manerube missed, and the lasso, crackling on the head of the stallion, scared him so that he seemed to have wings. In half a dozen magnificent bounds he got stretched out. Then headed for the fence he gave such exhibition of speed that some of the riders voiced their feelings.

"Oh — look at him!" yelled Chess.

"Boys — he's going to jump the fence," declared Chane, excitedly.

"He's got a bone in his teeth," called out the sailor, admiringly.

"Shure now — he's gr-rrand!" said the Irishman.

The sorrel meant freedom or death. His action showed more than mere brute wildness of terror. He had less fear of that terrible barbed fence than of the man enemies with their ropes. Like a greyhound he rose to the leap, having the foresight to leave the ground far enough from the fence to allow for the height. Up he shot, a beautiful wild sight, his head level and pointed, his mane streaming back. His forehoofs cleared the top wire, but his hind ones caught it. With a ringing twang the wire snapped. The stallion fell on head and shoulder, rolled over, and regaining his feet, he raced away, evidently none the worse for the accident.

Chane let out a short exultant shout. Melberne, who had come back, gave sharp orders for the men to let in more horses from the big corral. As they ran to do his bidding Chane took a bundle of short ropes from the fence and tucked one end of them under his belt.

"Manerube hasn't the knack," declared Melberne, fuming.

"Who said he had?" retorted Chane.

"He did."

"Well, if you were damn fool enough to believe him, take your medicine," rejoined Chane, grimly.

Then, as another band of snorting, shrieking wild horses thundered from the big corral, both Chane and Melberne had to take to the fence to save their lives. The frightened beasts trooped by; the men closed the gate and hurried up.

"Come on, you wranglers," shouted Chane. "See if you can stay with me."

It was a boast, but not made in the cheerful rival spirit characteristic of riders of the open. Chane's heart was sore, his blood was hot, his temper fierce; and his expression was a taunt, a grim banter. He meant to lay Melberne and the others of his squad flat on their backs, as if he had knocked them there. But they, likewise inflamed, answered violently to his challenge. Chane ran out into the corral, swinging his lasso.

The glaring sun stood straight overhead and

dusty heat veils rose from the trodden floor of the corral.

"Sixty-eight," said Chane, huskily, as with cramped and stinging hands he slipped his noose from the leg of the last horse tied. "Let — him — up."

Utah rolled off the head of the horse and lay where he rolled. The struggling beast rose and plunged away.

"Shall we — make it — sixty-nine?" asked Chane, gazing down upon the spent and be-grimed rider.

"I — pass," whispered Utah.

Chane and Utah had been working alone for some time. Chess had given out, then Melberne had succumbed, and finally Captain Bunk, after a wonderful exhibition of endurance, had fallen in his tracks. He had to be carried to the fence. Manerube's squad had quit an hour ago.

Approaching the spot where Melberne sat against the fence, Chane slowly drew in his dragging lasso.

"Melberne — we made it — sixty-eight. And that — finished Utah."

"Damn you, Weymer!" declared Melberne, with deliberation.

Chane could only stare a query as to the reason he was being damned, when he had worked like a galley slave for eight hours.

Melberne was rested. He had wiped the sweaty, dusty lather from his face, so that his expression could be noted. It seemed enigmatical to Chane.

"Sixty-eight an' fifty-six make one hundred twenty-four," said Melberne. "That with the forty-nine Manerube has accounted for sums up one hundred seventy-three."

"For ten men — some of them — green hands — that's a mighty — good showing," panted Chane as he wearily seated himself and began to wipe his dripping face.

"Hell!" ejaculated Melberne, throwing up his hands.

"Sure. I told you — it'd be hell," replied Chane.

"I don't mean what you mean," grunted Melberne.

"Well — boss, the worst — is yet to come," replied Chane, with as much of maliciousness as he could muster.

"Ahuh! Reckon you said that before. Weymer, have you heard me squeal?"

"No, Melberne," returned Chane, quietly. "I've only respect — for you."

"Wal, let's eat an' make the drive to the railroad. I'm shore curious aboot that. Chess, fetch the saddlebags of grub, an' call the men over."

All the riders, except two, were mounted

and ranged on each side of the gate, which, being opened by the riders on foot, left an avenue of apparent escape to the disabled wild horses. They did not need to be driven out. Before the gate was half open some of them broke for the desert, and soon they were all plunging to crowd through.

Chane, closing the gate and leaping astride Brutus, was the last rider to get into action. A long line of bobbing horses stretched before him across the valley, and on each side rode the riders. These three-legged wild horses would take a good deal of driving. Brutus had to run to keep up with them. It was necessary, therefore, to keep them at as uniform a gait as was possible, for if some traveled fast and others slow, the line would spread so wide that ten riders could not prevent escape of many. Drives like these were nightmares to Chane. He had never taken one that was not a race. Indeed, the crippled wild horses were racing for freedom. But if any did escape, it was only to meet a lingering death. Chane had Alonzo and Utah with him in the rear of the moving line, and they, moved by compassion, would ride their best to keep all the wild horses in.

The first spurt led up out of the valley, over the ridge, and into the level country that stretched north. The three-legged horses had been deprived of their fleetness, but not of their endurance. Still, not until the rough rocky country had been reached did they slow their gait or begin to show an unnatural strain. Chane knew what to expect and hated to look for it. He rode hard, and the chasing and heading and driving of these wild horses occupied his thoughts to the exclusion of all else.

Toward the middle of the afternoon, what was left of Melberne's first assignment of captured wild horses was driven into the corrals at Wund, a hamlet at the terminus of the railroad. Here help was available, as wild-horse shipping had become quite a business in that section of Utah. Melberne's drove were on the verge of collapse. Thirty-seven had been lost or killed on the drive in. Some were in a condition necessitating prompt shooting; others had great raw sores already fly-blown. Many had legs swollen to twice their original size.

The ropes that bound the bent forelegs had at once to be removed. This meant roping and throwing the horses, and holding them down until the bonds could be cut. The suffering of these wild horses was something that worked more deeply upon Chane's emotions than any cruelty to beasts had ever done before. If he had not known how his skill and speed had saved them much more agony he could never have completed the job.

Out of one hundred and seventy-three bound at Stark Valley a total of one hundred and twenty were available for shipping, from which Melberne received a little more than fifteen hundred dollars.

"Wal, that's twice what my outfit cost me," he muttered.

Chane, who heard this remark, turned it over in his mind, pondering at its significance. From Melberne's tone he gathered that it would have been pleasure to throw the money into the sage. Neither disappointment nor bitterness showed in Melberne's tensity. He labored under a stronger emotion than either. He was no longer his genial self, and showed scant courtesy to his former partner, Loughbridge, who evidently regretted his hasty relinquishing of joint authority in the deal. Most thought impelling of all Melberne's reactions was the obvious fact that he seemed to want to get out of hearing of the loudmouthed Manerube.

During supper, which was eaten in a tavern kept for cattlemen and horse-wranglers, much talk was indulged in regarding the remainder of the captured wild horses back in Stark Valley. Melberne took no part in it. Manerube, backed by Loughbridge, was loudly in favor of taking a large force of men to help tie up the rest of the wild horses.

"I was handicapped," protested Manerube. "I had to do it all alone. Alonzo lay down on the job. He could, but he wouldn't. Same with Miller. If I had men, now —"

"Y-y-y-y-you — you —" stuttered the accused rider, fiercely.

"Manerube," interrupted Melberne, coldly, "I reckon Miller is tryin' to call you a liar."

"Is that so?" shouted Manerube, rising from the table and glaring at the little rider. "If you can't talk, make signs, you stuttering idiot. Do you call me a liar?"

Miller had never been an aggressive fellow, and now, dominated perhaps by Manerube's swaggering assurance before all the men, he did not attempt an answer. He dropped his head and resumed eating his supper. Chane observed that Miller was not the only one who bent his face over his plate. Melberne and Utah both seemed absorbed in the food before them, which on the moment they were not eating. Again Chane sensed the passing of a crisis to which Manerube was as ignorant as if he were deaf and blind.

Sunset found Chane leading Melberne's outfit out on the trail for Stark Valley. Brutus at last was satisfied to accommodate his gait to the trot and walk of the other horses. Chess rode beside Chane, too weary to talk. And Chane, steeped in the gloom of that sordid day, had nothing to say, nor any thought of what usually abided with him on a ride through the dark, lonely, melancholy desert night.

Chapter 12

Sue Melberne realized fully what she was doing when she hid in the cedars on the west ridge of Stark Valley and watched the riders drive the crippled wild horses northward toward Wund. Her intention was to see them pass out of sight, leaving her safe to carry out a desperate plan. But she had not prepared herself for the actual spectacle of seeing a long line of beautiful wild mustangs hobbling by on three legs, some of them lame, many of them dripping red, all showing an unnatural and terrible stress.

Chane Weymer was the last of those riders. Something in the earnestness of his maneuvers to save the mustangs useless action, the fact that he did not spare Brutus, and once, when a mustang fell, a sharp gesture expressing poignant impotence to do what he would like to — these roused in Sue impressions that not only warmed her heart toward Chane, but strengthened her spirit for the deed she had in mind.

"If dad ever finds me out he'll half kill me," soliloquized Sue as she watched the last of the captured wild horses and their drivers disappear. She would have had the nerve to carry out her design even if she had not just been an eyewitness to the brutality of this business. Nothing now could have deterred her. "How can dad do it?" she muttered. "It will be a failure. Those poor mustangs are ruined. Oh, I'd like to tie up that Manerube and drive *him* — horsewhip *him!*"

Sue went back to where she had hidden her pony in the cedars, and mounting with difficulty, for she still had a stiff knee, she rode down the ridge over the ground that the wild horses had just covered. In the distance she could see a dark patch on the valley floor and knew it to be the captured wild horses trapped in the corral. The sight sent a little quiver over her and spurred her to ride at a lope, even though she suffered twinges when her horse broke his stride for the differing lay of the ground.

This ride of Sue's was not for pleasure. She did not watch the distant purple ranges, or gaze in rapture at the wonderful walls of Wild Horse Mesa. Rabbits, coyotes, lizards caught her quick eye, but did not incite her interest. She was bent on the most independent and reckless deed of her life. She felt driven. The pangs of a consuming and increasing love had played havoc with Sue's temper. The days since her injury had been dark ones.

At last the wide trail made by the mustangs led to the level of the valley and on to the high barricade of posts and barbed wire. She reached the first corral. It was the smaller one and empty. The gate had been dragged back in place, but left unfastened. Sue got off her horse and, by tugging hard, opened the gate to its limit. This done, she deliberated a moment. Across this corral she saw another and larger gate. Behind it moved a mass of pounding, snorting, whistling mustangs. Dust rose in a pall over them. The sun poured down hot. How thirsty those poor creatures must be!

"Shall I tie my horse here or over there?" queried Sue, in perplexity. Finally she decided it would be best to keep him near her. Owing to her stiff knee, she preferred to walk across the intervening corral, so she led her horse, and every step of the way felt a rising tumult in her breast. No easy thing was this to do! Had she a right to defeat her father's labors? When she reached the far side of the corral fear and conscience were in conflict with her love of wild horses. She was panting for breath. Excitement and effort were fatiguing her. Then her pony neighed shrilly. From the huge corral came a trampling roar. The dust flew up in sheets.

She gazed at the wide gate.

"Oh, can I open it? I *will!*" she cried.

She had intended to tie her horse and then open the gate. But she saw that it would be necessary to use him. Going close to the barbed-wire fence, she peered through at the horses. Her approach had caused them to move away some rods back from the fence. All heads were pointed toward her. Lean, wild, beautiful heads! She saw hundreds of dark, fierce, terrible eyes, it seemed, fixed accusingly upon her. As she stood and gazed, so the wild horses stood, motionless, quivering. What an enormous drove of horses! There must be hundreds, thousands. Sue trembled under the weight of her emotions. Impossible to draw back!

Then she became aware of an incessant buzzing. It had not been in evidence when the horses were moving. Flies! A swarm of flies buzzed around and over her. Flies as thick as bees — a black cloud of them — horseflies, the abominable pests that made life miserable for all horseflesh. Next Sue's sharp eyes caught sight of red cuts and scratches on the legs and breasts of the horses. Thus she had a second actual sight of the work of the barbed wire. Bleeding sores and horseflies! There could be no more horrible combination, to one who loved horses.

It took all Sue's strength to unwind the wires that held the gate shut. The gate itself she could not budge. Taking her rope from the saddle, she tied one end to the gate, and then pondered whether or not she should ride the horse while he pulled open the gate, or walk and lead him. She decided the latter would be safer, even though she risked losing her horse. So she wound the other end of the rope around the pommel, and urged the horse. He pulled the gate open wide. Hurriedly Sue untied the rope, fearfully listening for the expected stampede. But she had plenty of time to lead her horse away from the gate. Then she peered through the fence.

The foremost wild horses of that dense mass saw the break in the fence which had hemmed them in. They were fascinated. A piercing blast from a stallion seemed signal for a whistling, snorting chorus. Next came a restless pound of hoofs. A leader appeared — a stallion, the wildest creature Sue had ever beheld, black as coal, instinct with fire. He trotted warily forward, neared the gate, gazed with fierce bloodshot eyes. Then he bolted. Like a black flash he passed through the opening. A white horse, a bay, a buckskin leaped to follow and, fleet as their leader, sped out to freedom.

"Run! Oh, run!" screamed Sue, her heart bursting in the joy and terror of the moment.

The restless pound stirred, quickened, closed into a roar of trampling hoofs, smiting the hard ground as one horse. The gate emitted a stream of moving horses, heads up, manes and tails tossing. Sue saw the stream lengthen and widen across the corral until it connected both gates. Then dust obscured clear vision. The ground shook under her feet. The din was terrific. It swelled until she could not hear more. What endless time it seemed until the roar of hoofs, the thud of bodies, the shrill blasts passed by her position, sped on, lessened, and died away.

Sue found herself sagging against a post, holding the halter of her horse, weak from tumultuous emotions. Near her the dust clouds floated away. Far out on the valley floor a yellow mantle moved toward the west, and with it a wonderful diminishing sound. Sue sank down on the ground.

"Gone! Free! Oh, Heaven, what have I done?" she gasped.

It dawned on her then, the wrong she had done her father in being true to something as deep and wild in her as the instinct the horses had shown — for love of life and freedom. For a long time Sue sat there, overcome by the consciousness of the accomplished deed. At length she saw how imperative it was to get back to camp. It was a long ride, and already the sun had gone far on its slant to the west.

Twilight had fallen when Sue rode into the eastern end of the cottonwood grove and on to the encampment. Jake was not in sight. The women were busy at their tasks. Sue unsaddled and freed her horse, and reached the security of her tent without being seen. There she fell upon her bed in a state of exhaustion and agitation unparalleled in her experience. Her body burned and ached. The injury to her knee seemed renewed. And her thoughts and emotions were mostly in harmony with her physical ills. A few moments of utter relaxation and then a little rest enabled her to find composure, so that when she was called to supper she felt she could safely go out. Mrs. Melberne had evidently no idea when Sue returned to camp, and her chief concern was because she had been late in cooking supper. In the shadow round the camp fire neither sharp-eyed Ora nor kindly, attentive Jake saw anything unusual about Sue. The truth was, however, that Sue could just drag herself back to bed.

During the night she was roused out of heavy slumber. She heard horses, then the deep voices of men. The riders had returned. Recognition of Chane Weymer's voice seemed to lift her heart. Soft thud of hoofs and rustle of leaves passed her tent.

"Brutus, old pard, the day's done. I wish there was no tomorrow."

His voice sounded low and sad, full of weariness of effort and of life, yet strong in love for that noble horse. Sue felt a tide of feeling wave over her. What would she not have given to hear that note in Chane Weymer's voice for her? In the pitch blackness of her tent she could speak to her lonely and aching heart. The day made her false.

Sue fell asleep, and did not awaken again until morning, and then she lay for hours, it seemed, before she rose. What would this day bring forth? When she went out she was politely informed by Mrs. Loughbridge that she could get her own breakfast. This eminently pleased Sue, for she wanted to be round the camp fire, yet with some task to cloak her intense curiosity. While she was eating, the different members of Melberne's outfit rode singly and in groups into camp. Sight of them roused Sue's audacity. She had outwitted them. Yet, presently, when her father rode up, Sue could not find it in her to face him.

"Wal, lass, is it breakfast or lunch?" he asked, cheerfully, and bent to kiss her cheek.

It flashed over Sue that he was like his old self this morning. That delighted while it pained her.

"Why, dad — back so soon?" she replied, raising her eyes.

"Shore. An' I'm a tired dad," he said.

"I — I thought you were to drive horses to Wund today," she managed to say, despising her deceit.

"Haw! Haw! Were is good. Yes, I were! But, Sue, the horses broke out of the corral gates or somebody let them out. They're gone! An' the only hide an' hair of 'em is left on the barbed wire."

"Oh!" cried Sue. It was an outburst of emotion. That it seemed relief to Sue instead of a natural exclamation of wonder or amazement or regret was something assuredly beyond her father's ken.

He bent down to her ear and whispered, hoarsely, "Never was so damn glad aboot anythin' in my life!"

"Dad!" cried Sue, springing up so suddenly as to spill what remained of her breakfast. The joy in this word was not feigned. She kissed him. She felt on the verge of tears. "You — you won't use barbed wire again — ever?"

"Huh! I shore won't. Sue, there ain't a cowman in this heah West who hates barbed wire more than me. An' I'll tell you real cowmen, the old Texas school where cowmen came from, all hate wire fences."

"Dad, I — I'm very — happy," faltered Sue. "I hope you haven't lost money."

"Broke just even, Sue. An' I'm square with Loughbridge an' the riders. But listen, don't you let on I'm glad aboot this busted deal."

"Dad, dear, I've secrets of my own," replied Sue, with a laugh. Someday she would dare to tell him one of them, at least.

Loughbridge roughly called Melberne to join the group beyond the camp fire. Manerube was there, with two strange riders that no doubt had come from Wund. Sue did not like their looks. The rest of Melberne's outfit stood back in a half-circle. Excitement attended that gathering, emanating from the Loughbridge group. Sue, in response to a wave of her father's hand, moved back some steps to the big cottonwood stump, where she halted. Unless absolutely forbidden to stay, she meant to hear and see what the issue was.

"Melberne, somebody in this camp let out them wild horses," declared Loughbridge, forcefully.

"You still harpin' on that? Wal, Jim, I'm a tired man an' your voice ain't soothin'."

"All the same, you gotta hear me," replied Loughbridge, hotly. "Manerube swears he can prove it."

"Huh! Prove what?" snorted Melberne, his manner changing.

"Thet somebody from this camp opened them corral gates an' let loose our horses."

"Say, talk sense. Nobody but Jake an' our women were heah," retorted Melberne.

"Some of your outfit rode into camp before eleven last night," went on Loughbridge. "Between then and daylight there was plenty of time for a *rider* to do the trick."

"Wal, I reckon that might be so," drawled Melberne. "Is Manerube accusin' any rider who got heah early last night?"

"No, he ain't. Not yet."

"Ahuh! All right. I shore hope you tell me before he begins his accusin', because I'm too dog tired to go dodgin' round. I want somethin' to get behind."

Loughbridge fumed over this slow, sarcastic speech, and he regarded his former partner with some doubt and much disfavor. Then he burst out with redoubled vehemence.

"If Manerube does prove it, you'll have to pay me half the money we'd earned for two more days' drive."

"Loughbridge, you're plumb locoed," rejoined Melberne, in a voice that had gathered might. "You're as crazy as I was when I made a partnership with you or when I listened to Manerube."

"Crazy, am I?" shouted the other, hoarsely. "But you'll pay me just the same."

"Crazy, shore. An' as for Manerube provin' that, why I'm tellin' you he couldn't prove anythin' under this heah sun to me."

"Hell! I'm not carin' what you think or what you tell. I'm talking business. Money!"

"Wal, you've shore got your last dollar from me, Jim Loughbridge. An' if you think so little of my talk — mebbe you'd listen to bullets!"

The sharp, quick, cold voice ceased and there was a silence that proved the effect of the sudden contrast in Melberne's tone and manner.

"What!" bellowed Loughbridge, his red face turning ashen.

"Reckon I've learned patience from Mormons. But I was born in Texas," replied Melberne, with more dignity than passion. Still, the menace of his voice and eye had not disappeared.

"Melberne, here we split," said Loughbridge. "I want half this outfit."

"Wal, you're welcome — when you pay me for it. Not before," rejoined the leader, and with a gesture of finality he strode toward the tents.

Loughbridge drew Manerube and the two strange riders aside, where they took up a low and earnest conversation.

Sue, nervously recovering from the shock of the encounter between her father and Loughbridge, was about to move away when Chane Weymer confronted her. The smile in his dark eyes disarmed Sue for the moment. Certain it was that her heart turned traitor to her will.

"Sue, you're a dandy brave girl," said Chane, very low. Never before had he addressed her by her first name, let alone paid her a compliment.

"Indeed?" returned Sue, impertinently. But she knew she was going to blush unless fury or something rushed to her rescue.

"You have such dainty little feet. Your riding boots make such pretty tracks," went on Chane, still low voiced, still smiling down into her eyes. But now his words held strange significance. Sue felt a cold shiver run over her.

"You — think so," she faltered.

Chane glanced round, apparently with casual manner, but Sue saw the piercing keenness of his eyes. He was deep. He was kind. She trembled as she realized that somehow again he was helping her. Suddenly he bent lower.

"Manerube must have seen your boot tracks down by the corral gates," he said, swiftly. "But he can't prove it. I found them later, and I stepped them out in the dust. They're gone."

"Ah!" breathed Sue, lifting her hands to her breast.

"You did a fine thing. You've courage, girl. I wanted to free those wild horses."

Sue could not answer, not because she did not want to thank him for both service and compliment, but for the reason that the look in his eyes, the depths she had never seen before, rendered her mute. He was gazing down at her wonderingly, as if she presented a new character, one that stirred admiration, and he was going to speak again when something interrupted. Sue heard voices and the patter of light hoofs on the leaves. Chane straightened up to look. His dark face lighted with gladness.

"Piutes! By golly! My friend Toddy Nokin has come with my mustangs," he ejaculated, and he ran toward an Indian rider just entering camp.

Sue saw a small squat figure astride a shaggy pony. Chane rushed to greet him. The Piute's face, like a mask of bronze, suddenly wreathed and wrinkled into a beautiful smile. He extended a lean sinewy hand which Chane grasped and wrung. Sue could not distinguish the words of their greeting, but it was one between friends.

A drove of clean-limbed long-maned mustangs had entered the grove, surrounded by

Indian riders, picturesque with their high-crowned sombreros, their beads and silver. How supple and lithe their figures! With what ease and grace they rode!

When Sue's gaze reverted to Chane and the Piute she was amazed to see an Indian girl ride up to them. She was bareheaded. Her raven-black hair glinted in the sunlight. She was young. Her small piquant face, her slight, graceful form, the white band of beads she wore round her head, the silver buttons and ornaments bright against her velveteen blouse — these facts of sight flashed swiftly on Sue, just a second ahead of a strange dammed-up force, vague, powerful, yet ready to burst.

Chane shouted something in Indian to this girl — perhaps her name — for she smiled as had the old Piute, and that smile gave a flashing beauty to the dusky face. It broke the barrier to Sue's strange emotion. Her blood left her heart to confound pulse and vein. The might of that blood was stinging, searing jealousy. Pride and scorn and shame, bitter as they were, could not equal the other. Sue tortured herself one moment longer, with a woman's perversity, and in it she saw Chane greet the Indian girl. That sufficed for her. Averting her gaze, Sue walked slowly toward her tent and upheld herself with apparent in-attention. But when she had once closed and tied the flaps behind her the pretense vanished, and she sank to her knees in misery and shame.

Sue did not answer the call to the midday meal. She remained in her tent, fighting for the fortitude she would need to carry her through the inevitable worst to come. She welcomed the fact that it appeared she had been forgotten. The camp was much livelier than ever before, and Sue's ears were continually assailed by low voices passing her tent, by loud laughter of the riders, by the movement of horses. Anxious as she was over the break between her father and Loughbridge, she did not long dwell upon it. Her personal trouble was paramount.

A heavy clinking step outside her tent brought Sue up, excited and thrilling.

"Sue, are you home?" asked her father.

"Always to you, dad. Come in," she replied, untying the tent flaps.

He entered and closed the flaps after him. Then throwing his sombrero on the bed, with the gesture of a man come to stay awhile, he faced Sue with an unusual expression, which to her meant sympathy, perplexity, remorse, and something beyond her at the moment.

"Lass, if you want to see a locoed daddy, just look at me," he said.

"I'm looking — and, well, you don't seem quite so bad as you say," replied Sue, with a nervous little laugh. "What is the matter?"

"Wal, a lot of things, but mostly I'm a damn fool."

"Have you had more words with Loughbridge?" queried Sue, anxiously.

"He's all words. He's been houndin' me again aboot money. But I'll settle him shortly. It's not Loughbridge who's botherin' me now."

"Who, then?"

Her father sat down on the bed, and Sue, with heart beginning to misbehave, dropped to her knees before him. If he had not seemed so kind, and somehow protective, Sue would have been frightened.

"Who's bothering you, dad?" she went on.

Then he met her eyes. Behind the smile in his there was sadness.

"This heah Chane Weymer," he said.

"Oh, — dad, don't say you've quarreled with him!" she exclaimed wildly.

He studied Sue closely, peering deep into her eyes. "Wal, what'd you do if I said me an' Weymer was goin' to fight?"

"Fight? Oh, my Heaven! no — no! Dad, I'd never let you fight him," she cried, suddenly clinging to him.

"Ahuh! I had a hunch you wouldn't, my lass," he returned, shrewdly. "Wal, I was just

315

tryin' to scare you. Fact is there's no quarrel."

Sue sank against his shoulder and hid her telltale face, while the awful panic that had threatened slowly subsided in her breast. She grew aware of her father's arm round her, tenderly and closely holding her.

"Lass, you an' me are in a devil of a hole."

"You mean about the horses?"

"No. Aboot Chane."

"Chane!" she echoed, blankly.

"Yes, Chane. You're not bright this mawnin'. Wal, I don't wonder. But haven't you a hunch what the trouble is?"

"Your trouble with Ch— with him? No, dad."

"Wal, I shore hate to tell you. Yet, I'm more glad than sorry. Lass, we've done Chane Weymer wrong. I felt it days ago. Now I know. He's the finest man I ever met in all my life. Manerube is a dirty liar. He's what Chess called him that night. He's just exactly what he made out to us Chane was."

Sue felt as if she had been stabbed. Then joy welled up out of her agony. She sank into her father's arms, blinded with tears.

"Lass, you love Chane?" he whispered.

The query, the simple spoken words, the tremendous meaning of them in another's voice, made Sue shake like a leaf. She could speak no answer. She had betrayed herself.

Yet it was not the revealing of her secret that held her mute.

"Wal, you needn't give yourself away," continued her father, gently. "But I reckon I know. I seen you look at Chane once — the way your mother use to look at me."

After that he held her in silence for a long while, until Sue recovered in sufficient measure to sit up and wipe her eyes and face the situation.

"Dad, you can't guess how glad I was to hear you say that about Chane. Never mind now why. Just tell me — how you know."

"I shore will," replied her father, earnestly. "These heah Piutes an' Navajos are friends of Chane's. They have a bunch of mustangs for Chane to sell, an' I've bought them. Wal, when the old Indian — Toddy Nokin — saw Manerube he just grabbed for his rifle. He shore was goin' to do for that rider. But Chane got hold of the gun, took it away from him, an' talked. Toddy Nokin was shore a mad Indian. He couldn't understand Chane. Neither did I then. But you can bet I was keen to find out. It seems this Piute is a chief an' a man of dignity an' intelligence. He speaks some English. He says he thinks Manerube is a horse thief, in with Bud McPherson, but he can't prove that. But he an' Chane caught Manerube carryin' off the little Indian girl,

317

Sosie. You remember how Manerube's face was all black an' blue when he came to us? How he bragged we ought to see the other fellow! Wal, Chane beat Manerube soundly an' drove him off. You remember, Sue, how Manerube said he did just that to Chane?"

"Remember! Can I ever forget I *believed* it?" cried Sue, shrinking.

"Wal, Manerube is the one with the bad name among the Indians. Not Chane! We talked with the Navajo, too. He said Chane was never a squaw man. Then I got hold of the girl Sosie. Shore I had the surprise of my life. Sue, she's educated. Talks as well as you! An' what she said aboot Manerube was aplenty. I'll gamble the Piutes kill that rider. Wal, Sosie said Chane was the kind of man among the Indians the missionaries ought to be but wasn't."

"Oh, I *knew* it, in my heart," wailed Sue. "But I was a jealous cat."

"Wal, lass, Chane said as much aboot me," went on her father, breathing heavily. "I went to him an' I up like a man an' told him I'd wronged him an' was sorry. An' the darned fellow asked me what aboot. I told him I'd believed Manerube's gossip. An', Sue, what do you think he said?"

"I've no idea," murmured Sue.

"He said, 'Melberne, you're a damn liar.

318

You *knew* that wasn't true. Now shut up aboot it an' let's be friends.' Wal, Chane has stumped me more than once. But that was the last straw. Funny, too, because he was right. I knew he was a man. But this horse-wranglin' had upset me, sort of locoed me."

"So he forgave you?" queried Sue, dreamily. "Will he ever forgive me?"

"Shore. Why, that fellow's heart is as tender as your mother's."

"Dad, it's different in my case . . . I shall go straight to him, presently, and confess I wronged him. I can tell him I'm — I'm little, miserable, but I couldn't ask his forgiveness."

"Huh! You won't need to. The fellow's crazy about you. He —"

"Dad, please don't," whispered Sue, dropping her head.

"Lass, never mind my bluntness. I'm rough an' thick. Don't fret over the turn of affairs. It's sort of tough, but I'm glad, an' shore you'll be glad, too."

"I'm glad *now*. But it's terribly worse for me."

"Wal, lass, fight it out your own way," he responded, with a sigh. "I know things will work out right. They always do."

"What'll you do about Loughbridge and Manerube?" inquired Sue, remembering other issues at stake.

"Get rid of them," her father replied, tersely. "Then we'll strike for Wild Horse Mesa."

"To catch more wild horses?"

"Yes, but in an honest way. Mebbe I'll have the luck to catch Panquitch. If I do he's yours. But Chane says the man doesn't live who can beat him to that stallion."

"Then — Chane is going with us?" asked Sue, veiling her eyes.

"Shore. An' he's goin' to take us to Night-watch Spring, which he swears is the most beautiful place for a ranch in Utah."

Later Sue sat on the cottonwood log with Chess and Ora, assuredly the most absorbingly interested one in the Piute girl, Sosie. Sue had bravely sauntered forth on what seemed a severe ordeal for her, yet so curious was she to see and hear this Indian maiden that she would have endured anything to satisfy herself. Besides curiosity, disgust had been her most prominent feeling.

Sue found herself in line to be as surprised as was her father. At first she regarded Sosie as an alien creature, unsexed, a wild little savage. Her impressions having been formed long before, had become fixed.

Sosie evidently liked the opportunity to be with young white people. Chess soon overcame what little shyness she had felt and inspired her to tell them about herself. Never in her life had Sue listened to so fascinating and tragic a story. Sosie told about her childhood, tending goats and sheep on the desert, how she had been forced to go to the government school, and later to a school in California, how she had learned the language and the habits of white people. The religion of the Indians had been schooled and missionaried out of her. Then when she had advanced as far as possible, she was given a choice of becoming a servant or returning to her own people. She chose the latter, hoping her education would enable her to teach her family better ways of living. But her efforts resulted in failure and misunderstanding. Her people believed the white education had made her think she was above them. She could no longer accept the religion of the Indian tribe and she would not believe in the white man's. She had to abandon her habits of cleanliness, of comfort, of eating, and return to the crude ways of her people. Lastly, she had been importuned to marry. Her father, her mother, every relative nagged her to marry one of her own color. Finally she had yielded and had married one of the braves of her tribe, a young chief who had also received an education at the government schools. He and she had this much in common, that they understood each other and the fatality of the situation. The future held nothing for them, except life in the open, which, somehow, seemed best for the Indian.

An hour after this Indian girl had begun to talk, Sue had shifted from disgust and intolerance to amazement and sorrow. Sosie was not what she had expected. The girl was a little beauty. Her small proud head, her shining black hair, like night, her piquant face lighted by great dusky eyes, her red lips and white teeth, her slender form adorned in faded velveteen and ornamented with silver and beads, her little moccasined feet — all these features fascinated and captivated Sue. A white man might have been excused, certainly forgiven, for being attracted to this girl. It was hard for Sue to believe she was an Indian.

At length Ora coaxed Chess to go with her on some errand, and this circumstance left Sue alone with Sosie, which was the opportunity she craved. Sue felt it in her heart to be kind and good to this unfortunate girl. How Sue despised her hasty judgments! The white people, the civilization to which she belonged, had made this Indian girl what she was. But first of all, Sue strangely and passionately longed to hear Sosie speak of Manerube as he had spoken of Chane.

"My dad says you knew Manerube — over there across the rivers?" began Sue, driven to this issue.

"Yes, I knew Bent Manerube," replied Sosie, frankly, but without rancor. "He made love to me. You know Indian girls like white men to do that. Manerube got me to run off with him. But my father and Chane Weymer caught us."

"Then — then what — happened?" questioned Sue, faltering in her eagerness.

Sosie laughed, showing her little white teeth. "Chane ordered me off the horse. Then he made Manerube confess he didn't mean to marry me. They fought, and Chane whipped Manerube. I enjoyed that. I wanted to see him kill the liar."

"Did you — love Manerube?" continued Sue, desperately. How almost impossible it was to ask these questions! Only Sosie's simplicity, her lack of sophistication, the something about her that was not white, strengthened Sue to go on with this interrogation.

"I suppose so. But I didn't after Chane made him tell. And certainly not after my father beat me."

"Oh, did your father do that?" cried Sue, aghast.

"He did. And he said he'd kill me if I ever ran off with another white man. My tribe once upon a time tore a girl limb from limb for infidelity."

"How terrible!" exclaimed Sue.

"My education says that was wrong, but my Indian conscience says it was right."

"Did you know that Manerube came over here and told us he had beaten Chane Weymer for — for mistreating you?" demanded Sue, at last coming to the climax of her importunity.

"Yes. My father took me to your father," replied Sosie. "And I told just what a dirty lie that was. Manerube is bad. Chane Weymer is good. My father will tell you. Few white men who come among Indians are as good as Chane. I never met one. What's more, while I was at school I never met a white man like Chane. If I had listened to him I'd never have fallen in love with Manerube. But Chane scolded, advised, talked, almost preached to me when what I wanted was to be made love to. Chane wouldn't do it. He said he couldn't love me because he couldn't marry me."

"Oh, it's all wrong — this that the white people have made you suffer," cried Sue, in distress.

Eventually Sue ended her long talk with Sosie, and, stirred to her depths by the revelations of this day, she made her way toward

324

the tent of the Weymers. Her full heart cried out to make amends. That was all she could do. She would hurry to abase herself now while she had this tremendous false courage, this accusing conscience, this scornful pity for herself and mounting joy for Chane and Chess. How truly Chess had known his beloved brother!

Sue found them together, Chess at work on a quirt he was braiding for Ora, Chane watching her approach with sad dark eyes. She vowed she would meet their gaze even if they penetrated to her shameful secret love. She vowed she would be her true self if it were the last time in all her life. She walked straight up to him.

"Chane, I have wronged you."

His bronzed face lost something of its still calm, and it paled.

"You have? How so?" he returned.

"I believed what Manerube said about you."

"Well. That was unfortunate for me, wasn't it?" he rejoined.

"I was stupid and shallow," added Sue, in a ringing bitter voice. "Then — afterward — I was too slight and miserable to listen to my weak little conscience."

"Sue Melberne, this is what you say to me?" he demanded, incredulously.

"Nothing I can say matters to you now. But I wanted you to know what I think of myself."

"No, it doesn't matter now what I think of you — or you think of — yourself," he said.

"But you must hear what I think of myself," cried Sue, beginning to break under the strain. "You must hear that I'm a silly, mindless, soulless girl. Why, even when Chess denounced Manerube as a liar I couldn't see through it! Worse, when Chess spoke so nobly of you I didn't believe. Most shameful of all, after they fought, when I saw Manerube's horrid face after he'd beat Chess down —"

"What!" cried Chane, in piercing interruption. He sprang erect, and the look of him made Sue quake. "Beat Chess down!" he repeated, menacingly. "Say, boy, come here."

"Sue, you darned little fool! Now you've played hell!" wailed Chess.

Chane fastened a powerful hand in the boy's blouse and with one pull drew him close.

"Boy, you've kept it from me," he said, deliberately. "You've double-crossed me. Because I asked you."

"Yes, Chane — I lied," choked Chess.

"What for?"

"I was afraid of what you'd do to Manerube."

"Then he beat you? For defending me? Out with it!"

"Sue's told you, Chane. But, honest, she's made it worse than it was . . . what's a few punches to me? It was only a fight and he didn't get so awful much the best of it."

Chane let go of the boy's blouse and shoved him back.

"I knew there was something," he muttered, darkly, to himself; and then abruptly he dove into the tent.

"Sue, you've played hell, I tell you," said Chess.

"Oh, I didn't mean to tell. It slipped out. What can I do?"

"You can't stop Chane now."

"Yes I can," cried Sue. She recognized she must do something desperate, but she had no idea what it should be. Her mind seemed clogged. Then, when Chane emerged from the tent, she quailed before the lightning of his eyes. He held a rawhide whip in his left hand. And on his right side a heavy gun swung from his belt.

"Sue Melberne, I'll use either gun or whip on your lover. But I suspect it must be the whip."

"Lover! Bent Manerube? How dare you?" burst out Sue, suddenly infuriated beyond endurance. She gave him a swift hard slap in the face.

A bright red spot stained his pale cheek. He lifted a hand to feel the place, while his gaze blazed down on her.

"Thanks. I like that. It was human and womanly, something you've never been to me. Did I wrong you with my insinuation?"

"You insulted me. I despised Manerube. I *never* liked him. I — I flirted with him — to my shame — because — well, I don't choose to tell."

"So. You are indeed clearing up much this day," returned Chane. "I apologize. I reckon that was temper. I didn't really mean it. All the same, I'll use my gun or whip on Manerube."

Chess did not even attempt to stop Chane, but Sue cried out some incoherent entreaty and tried to hold him back. Not gently did he thrust her aside, and without another word strode toward the group of men plainly discernible round the camp fire.

"Come to your tent, Sue," begged Chess.

"I guess not. I'll not quit — like that," panted Sue. "I'll tell dad. He'll stop them."

"Sue, it's too late. Anybody getting in front of Chane now will be hurt."

"But, Chess — he — he might be killed!" whispered Sue.

"Who? Manerube, you mean? Well, it'll be darn good riddance," rejoined Chess, hotly.

"Oh, I mean Chane — Chane. Listen, if you tell I'll hate you forever. Forever! I — I love Chane. It's killing me. Now do you understand?"

"You poor girl!" replied Chess, in wonder and pity, and he put his arm round her. "Sue, don't be scared. Manerube is a coward. He'll never face Chane with a gun. All he'll get will be a horsewhipping. Come on — let's see him get it."

Sue was unsteady and weak on her feet and needed Chess's support, yet slow as they were they got out to the edge of the grove in time to see Chane confront the staring half-circle of men, among whom Manerube stood out prominently.

"What's up?" demanded Melberne, loudly.

"Manerube's game," retorted Chane, curtly.

Certain and significant it was that Melberne hurriedly moved out of line, and every man on either side of Manerube backed away, leaving him standing alone.

"Manerube, the jig's up," said Chane. "I don't care a damn about the lies you told. But you laid your dirty hands on my brother for defending me . . . you beat him! Are you packing a gun?"

"I reckon," replied Manerube, white to the lips.

Sue swayed to a resistless upsurging spirit.

Tearing herself free of Chess, she ran swiftly to confront Chane, to grasp him with hands strong as steel. But her voice failed her.

"Sue, you're mad," he protested, with the first show of softening. "We've got to fight. Why not now?"

Melberne stepped swiftly up to Chane, calling to his men. Utah and Miller ran in. Jake followed.

"Grab him, boys," ordered Melberne. "Chess, get Sue out of this." Then he strode toward the men opposite. "I won't have my womenfolk runnin' risks round heah. Manerube, you're shore gettin' away lucky. Take your two rider pards from Wund an' get out of my camp. An' Jim Loughbridge, you can go along with him. I'll make you a present of wagon, team, grub."

"All right, Melberne," returned Loughbridge, harshly. "I'll take you up. But you haven't seen the last of this deal."

Chapter 13

Far west of Stark Valley the reconstructed Melberne outfit had halted on a lofty rim to gaze down into a gray-carpeted, green-dotted, golden-walled canyon, wide and long, running close under the grand bulk of Wild Horse Mesa.

"Nightwatch Spring is there, up in the rocky notch where you see the bright green," Chane Weymer had said, directing Melberne's gaze. "It's so big it makes a brook right where it comes out from under the cliff."

Melberne had never been a man to rave. Here he gazed as if spellbound, at last to burst out, "Beats any place in Texas!" From him that was not unlikely the most extravagant praise possible. Then he continued, with a singular richness and depth in his voice: "Wife, daughter, heah we shall make our home. A rancher down there will shore be rich in all that makes life worth livin'. I'll send for my brothers, who are waitin' for word of good country to settle in. We've relatives an' friends, too, who'll take my word. We'll homestead this place, an' right heah I pick the haid of this canyon, takin' in the spring. One hundred sixty acres for mine, with all them miles of range land to control. Weymer, I reckon my debt to you grows. I wonder now — won't you an' Chess throw in with us heah?"

"*Quien sabe?*" replied the rider, musingly. "Chess surely will. It's good for him. But I — well, I'm a wandering wild-horse hunter."

One dim rough trail led down into this gold-enrimmed abyss. Neither Chane nor Toddy Nokin knew where the bands of wild horses dotting the gray had descended from the uplands above, if indeed they had gone that way. This league-wide rent in the rocky earth zigzagged away westward, under the tremendous benched wall of Wild Horse Mesa, and the western end could not be seen. Toddy Nokin said it ended in a split in the stone that no Indian had explored.

Sue was entranced. She had been prepared for something rugged, beautiful, in accordance with Chane's simple statement, but no words could have done adequate justice to this marvelous place. Not paradise or fairyland was it to her, but sublime in its vastness, unreal in its isolation, gorgeous in color, wild as the sky-towering mesa that bulged stupendously above.

The notch toward which Chane had pointed proved to be a labyrinth of indentations in the wall, all narrow, lined by green borders of spruce and cedar, floored by rich thick bleached grass, turning and twisting, full of golden shadows reflected from the looming walls, lonely, silent, sweetly fragrant with the dry canyon tang, and purple with sage.

Melberne pitched camp on the site he chose for the ranch house he would erect eventually. It was a low bench, sloping with sage toward the open, backed by a belt of timber, and canopied by a leaning golden wall. Nightwatch Spring burst from under this cliff, a thick rushing volume of pure water, and made music down the slope, to meander between willow-bordered banks far as the eye could see. Wild horses, deer, rabbits, and many birds proved the fertility and lonesomeness of this spot.

Through the thin belt of spruce trees, higher up on the last swell of sage slope under the wall, Sue espied a place that she determined must be her camp. It looked down upon the bench; it was sheltered by the curve of the wall; and seemed dreamily and drowsily permeated by the song of the stream. It was indeed a throne from which perhaps some barbarian queen of ages past had ruled her subjects. Purple sage bloomed there, and the scarlet of Indian paintbrush, the vermilion of cactus, lavender daisies, and an exquisite flower unknown to Sue, a delicate nodding three-petaled blossom of white with violet heart.

She enlisted Chess and Jake in her service, with the result that sunset and supper time found her task completed — a camp which must surely become a home, comfortable, safe, secluded, and open to a view beautiful close at hand, and in the distance one of exceeding grandeur.

Camp that night had for Melberne's outfit the best of all virtues for the tired traveler — permanence. It did not disturb Melberne or any of his party that Loughbridge and Manerube had followed on their trail.

"Reckon we'll have six more weeks of this heah fine weather," remarked Melberne, as he stood with his back to the fire.

"Hope so. But winter is mild down in these protected canyons," said Chane. "The snow seldom lays long."

"Good. Wal, that'll give me time to throw up a log house heah. Will my wagons be safe where we left them?"

"They're well hidden. Only an Indian would run across them, and he wouldn't steal."

"We cain't ever drive a wagon down in heah," observed Melberne.

"That's the beauty of it. Build a corral and barn up on the rim, and down here also."

"Chane, you shore have idees. Wal, in a day or two I'll send Utah an' Miller back to Wund to mail letters an' fetch back a wagonload of supplies. Mebbe my brothers will be so keen aboot this place they'll come before the snow flies. If not, then by spring, shore . . . wal, wal, I reckon I'm happier than I've been for long."

Sue wondered what her father meant by that. It brought back to her the subtle intimation of an enemy he had always been expecting to meet. Here in this out-of-the-way corner of the world perhaps he felt secure at last from the fear he must kill a man. So Sue interpreted that strange observance of her father's.

Without the disturbing element of Manerube and the Loughbridges, camp life had indeed taken on a happier order. Chess confessed that he missed Ora, and hinted he might go after her some day. Sue also missed a girl companion, but the rest of that disorganizing contingent did not occasion regret.

"Say, Chane, I reckon I can make a big pond heah, judgin' by the lay of the land an' the rocky ground," observed Melberne, whose mind obviously was active on possibilities.

"Sure you can," replied the ever-optimistic and enthusiastic Chane.

Captain Bunk removed his pipe, manifestly to deliver a remark of importance.

"Shiver my timbers if I wouldn't dam up the other end of this hole in the rocks and fill her up with water to the gunwale."

"W-w-w-wh-wh-what'n hell for would you do t-t-t-t-th— that?" stuttered Miller.

"Why, mate, I'd have a bit of a lake, and run boats on it, and start a fish ranch," replied Bunk, impressively.

"Haw! Haw!" roared Melberne. "Shore that's a new one on me. Fish ranch! — Wal, a fish pond ain't a bad idee. Cap, you're shore helpin' me to establish a home. Sue, we haven't heard from you aboot this heah homestead of mine. Reckon I'd like somethin' good from my girl."

"Dad, it's wonderful!" replied Sue. "But I can't think of anything to tell you — except I'll stay. It'll be my home, too."

"Wal, listen to that, wife," ejaculated Melberne, his broad face beaming in the firelight. "Sue will not go back to the cities to teach. She'll stay with us — to teach kiddies when they come heah, as shore they will. Mebbe some of her own! These boys will be gettin' themselves wives before long. An' that'll be good."

Night down in this deep-bottomed, high-walled solitude kept Sue awake for hours. It was so strange, so different from any other night she could recall. It had a haunting melancholy, a perfect peace, a glory of starlit loneliness. The insects might not have belonged to species she knew, so clear-toned and high-pitched were they. A lonesome owl far back in the notched fastnesses bemoaned his watch. The murmuring stream made music like all fast-flowing streams, yet somehow more mellow, the same because it was swift water tumbling over rocks down the mound to a level, yet differing because of innumerable imagined melodies.

Dawn came gray, cool, rich in its dark clearness, taking long to grow lighter. Sue wondered what was the cause. She had never before awakened to a dawn like this. Daylight came, yet all seemed shadowed.

Where was the sun? Where was the east? At last she realized she was down in the very bowels of the earth. The mighty wall of Wild Horse Mesa loomed above her, shutting out the sunrise.

At last a clear wonderful deep-blue light shone over the eastern rim. Low clouds, faintly rose, floated above a strange live effulgence that centered the horizon line. Here was the effect of the sun. Beneath Sue the wide canyon slept, still dark, except over the gray levels, and they were vague. Far to the west the faces of the great escarpments that lifted high above the rim began to brighten, to turn purple. Sue watched the changes, sure of them, though they seemed imperceptible. Under the wandering wall of Wild Horse Mesa showed only a soft dark freshness of dawn.

Sue rose to begin the day, aware of the whistle of the riders below, of the ring of an ax, the smell and blue of a column of smoke, the hearty voice of her father. She felt light, quick, buoyant. She wanted to run, to sing, to ride, to go wild with it all. She was happy, yet there was that break, that wound in her heart. But her sorrow and her shame were not as they had been. Some incalculable difference had followed her avowal of injustice to Chane Weymer, her abasement of self. She had told him. That had not mitigated her blunder, but it had eliminated her vanity. The absence of Manerube had much to do with her mounting pleasure in the present. He was not there with his swaggering figure, his hateful handsome face, to mar every scene for her. How wrong she had been to encourage his attention just to sting the man she loved! She had never forgiven herself for that blindness; she was always uneasily conscious that the end of her blunder was not yet come. Nevertheless, happiness encroached more and more on her trouble. She stifled the whispering voices of dreams; she would not listen to the woman temptress strong in her depths, the feminine that would bid her use charm, coquetry, sex, love to win Chane Weymer. In his heart he must despise her, and though at times this conviction roused a flashing fiery rage in her, she always reverted to the justice of it and accepted it as her punishment for unworthiness. Even sight of Chane had grown bearable, and then a joy, provided he was not close enough to see her watching him. Seldom he spoke to her or noticed her, never unless politeness or the kindness of service made that imperative to a man of his character. Sue had welcomed this aloofness, but as the days passed it had begun to gall her — a fact about which she did not like to conjecture.

Chess had been loyal; he had kept her secret, but always, womanlike, she feared he would betray her to Chane. More and more the lovableness of the boy manifested itself to her. He was a friend, a comrade, a brother. Yet at times he exasperated her so exceedingly that she could scarcely keep from flying at him to slap and scratch. Chess never let her forget that she loved Chane.

Melberne began the second day in this place

he had chosen to labor and end his years with an energy and heartiness that augured well for his ultimate achievements.

After breakfast he dictated letters which Sue wrote for him, sitting on the ground beside the camp fire, with her writing case on her lap. Then he dispatched Utah and Miller on the long wagon trip back to Wund.

"Pack your guns an' don't be slow in usin' them," was his last instruction.

Next he set to work with all the men available to fence the mouths of two verdant prongs at the head of the canyon, where he turned loose all his horses. He now had over fifty head, counting the mustangs he had bought from Chane. Toddy Nokin had promised to return in the spring with another band to sell. Melberne had conceived the idea of raising horses as well as cattle. He had vision. He saw into the future when horses would not be running wild over every range, when well-bred stock would be valuable. It took half the day to erect those cedar and spruce fences.

"Wal, now we can breathe easy an' look around," he said. "Shore was afraid one of them stallions down there would come up heah an' stampede us."

"Melberne, you'll want this canyon free of wild horses," said Chane, thoughtfully. "Because your stock will never be safe where wild stallions are ranging. You know tame horses, once they get away, make the wildest of wild horses."

"Wal, what're you foreman of this heah Melberne outfit for?" rejoined Melberne, jovially.

Chane laughed pleasantly. That pleased him. "We'll get busy and catch the best of the wild stock in here, then drive the rest out. It's a big country down here. You can't tell what we'll run into."

"Mebbe Panquitch, huh? Forgot that stallion, didn't you?"

"Forgot Panquitch? I guess not. I'll bet I've thought of him a thousand times since I saw him. There's his range, Melberne."

Chane swept a slow hand aloft toward the yellow rampart, so high and far away that the black fringe of cedars and piñons looked like a thin low line of brush.

"On top, hey? Wild Horse Mesa!" ejaculated Melberne, craning his neck. "Chane, I reckon if Panquitch ranges up there he's no longer a horse. He's an eagle."

In the afternoon Sue accompanied her father and the riders out upon a venture that promised thrilling excitement. Alonzo, the Mexican *vaquero*, was to give an exhibition of his ability to run down and rope wild horses. Sue heard Chane tell her father that Alonzo was the only rider he had ever known who could accomplish this. It seemed a fair and honest matching of speed and endurance against the wild horse, with the advantage all his. Sue imagined it would be worth a good deal to see the *vaquero* at work.

Melberne had abandoned any further idea of cruel practices in the capturing of wild horses.

Creasing with a rifle bullet, a method considerably used in Nevada and Utah, was to his mind as obnoxious as barbed wire. A skilled marksman could shoot a wild horse through the outer edge of the nape of the neck and so stun him that capture was easy. The fault with this method of creasing, as it was called, was that if the bullet did a little more than crease, which happened more times than not, it killed the horse.

Water-hole trapping was a humane and easy and exciting way to catch wild horses, but seldom or never did it yield the best results — that is, the fastest and finest horses, especially the stallions, would refuse to enter the trap, or if they did they broke out or leaped the fence or killed themselves. Wild-horse wranglers, however, liked this method, and often employed it. First they located a spring or water hole much frequented by wild horses, and round it they constructed a large corral of poles or logs, and mostly cedar trees which they cut whole and dragged into close formation, leaving space for a wide gate. This gate had to be one that could be shut quickly. When the trap was completed the hunters watched by night for the wild horses to come in to drink. It was always necessary to hide on the side against which the wind blew from the horses. Otherwise their keen noses would soon detect the scent of man. Not always on the first or the second night did the horses enter the trap. But usually their thirst conquered their suspicions. When a number had gone in to drink the hunters rushed out to close the gate.

Chane Weymer's favorite method, so he told Melberne, was to find a favorable location where wild horses grazed, and one preferably with natural obstructions to flight, such as a wall of rock, or a canyon rim on one side. Then cedar trees were cut and dragged to make a long fence, a wing that stretched as far as needed, perhaps a mile in extreme instances. At the point where this fence joined the wall, or, if there was a canyon rim, at the apex of the triangle, a large corral was built. The wild horses would be chased and driven toward this fence and down into the corral.

"I've often tried a method that I got on to

by accident," said Chane as they were riding along. "It takes a mighty fast horse, though. I'm keen now to try it with Brutus. But this particular place wouldn't suit. The idea is for a rider on the fast horse to get *in front* of a bunch of wild horses and ride away from them. Other riders must be on both sides and behind the wild horses, driving them. Now the strange fact is this. If the rider in front can keep ahead of the wild horses, they will follow him clear to a trap corral. Such drives begin with a small bunch. But as they run along they draw in other wild horses, and at the end of a fifteen-mile drive upward of a hundred and fifty might be in the band."

"Huh! There'd shore be fun in that," replied Melberne. "But I reckon none of them stunts would work with your stallion Panquitch."

"Hardly," declared Chane, with a short laugh. "If he's ever caught it'll be by an accident or trick."

The riders kept close to the western wall, under cover of the cedars that lined the gentle slope of the wide gray grassy canyon. Thus they avoided frightening the several scattered bands of wild horses that dotted the meadowlike expanse.

To Sue the ride was a continually growing delight. What a perfectly beautiful and amazing place! The deer trotted away into the spruce, scarcely showing fear. Small game was abundant. Birds in flocks fluttered up at the approach of the horses. The high wall was notched like a saw, and each indentation appeared to be a deep fissure, red-walled, thick with green spruce and russet oak and golden cottonwood. Winding gray aisles of sage led back mysteriously, huge blocks of cliff choked some passages, caverns yawned. Along the outside of the main wall the scattered groups of oak, the lines of spruce, the dots of cedar, looked as if they had been planted on the gray grassy level to insure the effect of stateliness, of park-like beauty. Though it was crisp October weather above, down here the sun shone warm and wild flowers bloomed everywhere, nodding in the soft breeze.

Three or four miles from camp Chane led the riders out into the open, stationing them wide apart across the canyon, for the purpose of keeping the wild horses at that end so Alonzo could have favorable opportunity to chase them.

Sue stayed with her father, who had a central stand. The lithe, sinewy *vaquero* resembled an Indian jockey. He wore neither coat, hat, nor boots. Sue inquired how could he manage to race without spurs?

"Shore, I'm blessed if I know," replied her

father. "But he shore looks good to me. All muscle. No bones. Reckon he doesn't weigh more'n a feather."

Sue thought Alonzo made a picturesque figure as he sat on his black racer, scanning the level grassland. His horse was not a beauty, but he had every other qualification of greatness. He was lean, long, slim, powerful of chest, ragged and wiry, with a challenging look. He quivered under the bare heels of the *vaquero*. Around his middle was belted a broad surcingle. This appeared no less than a band with a ring in the right side, and to this ring was fastened the end of the thin, greasy, snake-like lasso Alonzo carried in loops. Alonzo rode bareback. His horse did not have even a bridle.

"Wal, Sue, I reckon this will be as good as a show," said Melberne.

Presently Alonzo gave his horse a gentle kick. No spur could have brought better response. The horse sprung from one leap into a long easy lope. How lightly he moved! He did not even raise the dust. And the dark-skinned rider seemed a part of him. Sue had learned that the Mexican *vaqueros* were the great horsemen of the Southwest, from whom all the cattle-driving and bronco-busting cowboys had learned their trade. It had been a heritage from Texas, and Texas had learned it from Mexico. Sue did not see how it was possible for a rider to sit his horse so perfectly.

Alonzo headed to go round the closest band of wild horses, so to place them between him and the riders on the stands across the canyon. The wild horses saw him, stood erect and motionless, watching for a moment, then began to move restlessly. When he had approached to within a quarter of a mile they broke and ran eastward. Sue uttered a little cry of delight at the beauty and wildness of their appearance and action. The leader, evidently not a stallion, was red in color, and there were whites, blacks, tans, and bays, all actuated as by one instinct. Like the wind they raced, long tails and manes streaming behind them. Then suddenly it appeared that in one bound they had halted and wheeled at once, to gaze back at this lone rider. Presently it developed that the red mustang had espied enemies to the east. Chane and Chess were riding in to turn them back toward Alonzo.

But first the wild horses trotted this way and that, fiery in motion, proud and wild, intolerant of this intrusion upon their lonely precincts. Alonzo kept a little to the north of their position, no doubt fearing a break in that unprotected direction. But manifestly the wild horses knew the unobstructed open distance lay in the opposite direction. Sue espied other bands farther off, gathering together, trotting to and fro, evincing the same curiosity that had at first affected the band upon whom Alonzo had concentrated.

Sue enjoyed this watching experience to the full. The surroundings were such as to exalt her. Calm acceptance of this place of rugged grandeur and isolation was not possible to Sue. The dry sweet air, unbreathed, the blue sky above the great walls, the gray meadow with its waving grass, the borders of green, and then the wild horses and the riders, and the surety that this was to be a clean fine race devoid of deceit or brutality — all this appealed powerfully to Sue, waking again that something which the Utah upland had discovered in her.

The moment came when the *vaquero* launched his black into the race. Sue, who had seen racehorses leave the post, could not but recognize the superiority of Alonzo's black. All in a second he seemed wild, too. The band of horses broke and ran, in a way to make their former running seem slow. They stretched out to the east, and the fleetest forged to the front. The red leader had two rivals for supremacy, and these three drew away from the others, though not far.

Alonzo did not appear to gain. He kept to the north of his quarry. His reason for this was obvious. For perhaps half a mile eastward this position was maintained, then shots from Chane's gun acted like a wall upon the running wild horses. They sheered in abrupt curve toward the open, and were turned by Chess back toward the west. Here the wonderful race began.

The *vaquero* had now only to head directly toward them to gain the distance that he had been behind. If the fleetness of those wild horses was something thrillingly incredible, that of Alonzo's black was even more so, because he carried weight. No doubt the *vaquero* meant this particular race to be short, or perhaps this was his method. At any rate he closed in on the rear of that band, and began to pass mustang after mustang. He wanted to rope one of the best and fleetest.

Wild horses and pursuer were now racing back toward where Sue and her father waited, and the line on which they would pass, if they kept straight, was scarcely two hundred yards.

"Oh, dad, they'll come close," cried Sue.

"You bet. Reckon I'll shoot to scare them if they head closer . . . say, Sue, look at that half-breed ride!"

The stretched-out band did head closer toward Melberne's stand, and probably would have broken through the line had he not fired his gun. That made the leaders swerve a little north. It also enabled Sue to get a perfect view of the race. The rhythmic thud of flying hoofs thrilled her ears. Thin puffs of dust shot up. The lean, swift, wild mustangs rushed on apace. The very action of them suggested wildness, fleetness, untamableness — spirits in harmony with their wonderful flight. But to Sue they did not seem frightened.

As they came on the Mexican gained foot by foot upon the leaders. He could have roped his pick of those behind. But plain it was he wanted one of the three. Sue had only admiration for Alonzo, and something greater for his horse, yet her heart was with the wild mustangs.

"Run! Oh, you beauties, run!" she cried, wildly. "He can't keep up long."

"Go it, Alonzo," roared her father, in stentorian voice. "Ketch me that red mare."

But Melberne's ambition was not to be, and Sue's hopes were only half fulfilled. The black racer was running so terribly that soon he must fall or break his stride. Yet he could only hold the place he had gained. He could not run down the fleet leaders; and as they passed, a wild and beautiful sight to a lover of horses, Sue saw them begin to draw a little away from Alonzo. He saw it, too. The long looped lasso began to swing round his head and he closed in on the horses behind the leaders. Then, at this full speed, he cast the rope. It shone in the sunlight; it streaked out, and fell.

"He's got one. Whoop!" yelled Melberne.

Sue was not so sure. Presently, however, she saw Alonzo's horse break his stride, sway and sag, catch himself to go on slower and slower. The band of wild horses swept on and beyond, to disclose one of their number madly plunging and fighting Alonzo's rope. Then it ran wild, dragging the black. Alonzo appeared to be running with this mustang, yet at the same time holding back. They went a mile or more north, turned to the west, and then faced back again.

Meanwhile Sue and Melberne watched. "Oh, I'm glad, but I'm sorry, too," said Sue.

"Haw! Haw! You'll shore make a fine horse-wrangler's wife."

"Dad!" expostulated Sue.

"Wal, there's no cowboy to marry, or schoolteacher or preacher out heah," declared her father. "You shore gotta marry somebody someday."

The subject did not appeal to Sue and she rode a little way to meet Alonzo, who appeared to have gained some control over the lassoed mustang. She saw the original band of wild horses halt far to the west, and turn about to see if they were still being chased. Chane galloped up to join Melberne, and

Chess appeared to be coming.

In a few moments more Sue saw a captured mustang at close quarters, and one that she could gaze at in pleasure, without seeing any evidence of the things that had alienated her.

The mustang was a beautiful animal, a gray-blue in color, with extremely long mane and tail, black as a raven. Alonzo's rope had gone over its head and one foreleg, so that the noose had come taut around its shoulders and between its forelegs at the breast.

"Wal, he couldn't have done better with his hands," declared Melberne. "No chokin' round the neck, no breakin' legs."

"He's a wonder," replied Chane. "By golly! I thought once he'd get in reach of the red mare. Say, there's a horse."

"What'll we do now with this heah one?" inquired Melberne.

"We'll throw him, tie his feet, and let him lay a little while. Alonzo is good for another race on his black. Then I'd like him to ride Brutus. I'll be darned if I don't believe he can rope that red mare off Brutus."

That evening at sunset Melberne's outfit were a happy, merry party. The environment perhaps had something to do with satisfaction, and then the day had been gratifying. Alonzo had roped three wild mustangs, and one of them was the red mare, which had fallen prey to the *vaquero*'s unerring lasso and to the fleetness of Brutus.

This occasion was the first time Sue had ever seen Chane Weymer happy. He was more of a boy than Chess. The victory of his horse over the wild mustang must have been the very keenest of joys. His dark face, clean-shaven and bronzed, shone in the sunset glow, and his eyes sparkled. He even had a bright look and nod for Sue.

There was one thing forced home to Sue, perhaps, she reflected at the moment when Chane condescended to observe that she was still on the earth. This was, that after the wonderful day, and now facing in mute rapture a sunset of extraordinary glory of gold and rose and purple, seeing for the first time the phenomenon told by Chane about the lilac and lavender haze on Wild Horse Mesa, she could not call herself unhappy.

"Melberne, I reckon I see two of Toddy Nokin's Piutes riding down the trail," observed Chane, shading his eyes from the last golden glare of the sun.

"Ahuh! I see them," replied Melberne. "Ridin' in for supper, hey?"

Chane looked thoughtful, and, watching the Indians, he shook his head ponderingly, as if he could not just quite understand their coming. Presently two little mustangs, with the wild-appearing riders unmistakably Indian, rode out of the cedars and came across the level in a long swinging lope.

"One of them is Sosie's brother," said Chane, peering hard down the bench. "And, by golly! the other one is her husband."

With that Chane strode down to meet them, and at the foot of the bench he detained them in conversation for some minutes. Presently they dismounted and, slipping the saddles and bridles, they let the mustangs go, and accompanied Chane up to the camp fire.

Sue had seen Sosie's brother, but not her husband. He was a slender Indian, with a lean, dark, handsome face and somber eyes. He did not smile or talk, as did his comrade. He carried a shiny carbine which he rested on the instep of his moccasined foot.

"Jake, rustle some grub," called Chane, and then he turned to Melberne. "Some news, Melberne. Though I'm not surprised. Loughbridge and Manerube, with *five* men and no women, are camped back on the rim about five miles."

"Five men now, an' no womenfolk!" ejaculated Melberne. "Huh! that's kind of funny. How'd they get rid of Ora and her mother?"

"They're packing their outfit. They haven't

354

the wagon you gave Loughbridge. Reckon that's gone to Wund with the girl and Mrs. Loughbridge."

"Wal, that's where Jim Loughbridge ought to be, I'm thinkin'. But shore I'm not carin' where he is."

"Would you mind if he packed down here?" inquired Chane.

"Huh! I shore would," declared the other, bluntly. "I just wouldn't let him. This is my range."

Chane threw up his hands as if he had understood before he asked. "That talk is as old as the West, Melberne. You can hold the water rights of Nightwatch Spring. But that's all."

"I reckon it's enough. What's your idee aboot it?"

"Water is power here. We might be in for trouble if Manerube has control. I'm just wondering if those extra men could be Bud Mc-Pherson and his cronies."

"Wal, I don't know, that's shore," declared Melberne. "But your wonderin' aboot it makes me think."

Chane bent lower toward Melberne, so that none but he and Sue who sat with him, could hear.

"It's got a funny look. Both ways," whispered Chane. "Especially Sosie's brother and husband trailing along when I supposed them over the rivers. Do you get my hunch?"

"Ahuh!" ejaculated Melberne, seriously.

Chapter 14

October ended, but Indian summer still lingered down under the zigzag walls of Wild Horse Mesa.

Melberne, along with wild-horse chasing, had thrown up a two-room log cabin of peeled spruce. Utah and Miller had returned with two wagonloads of supplies, not the least of which was a plough Melberne regarded with the pride of a pioneer. In the spring he meant to drive in cows for domestic use, and cattle to range the grassy reaches.

Loughbridge's threat that Melberne had not seen the last of their deal was far from being forgotten. Nevertheless, as the days passed without any sign of him or the riders with whom he had chosen to consort, gradually expectation dwindled. Perhaps in the swift rush of the full days, if it had not been for the two Piute Indians riding into camp now and then, without any apparent reason for remaining in the vicinity of Wild Horse Mesa, Melberne and Chane would not have felt any further concern. But the presence of the brother and husband of Sosie Nokin was proof to Chane at least that Manerube still hovered on the trail of the Melberne outfit. Whatever anxiety Chane betrayed, however, appeared to be in the interest of the Indians. Often he was seen in earnest conversation with the Piutes, particularly Sosie's husband, but he did not divulge what transpired between them.

In the two weeks of their stay there Alonzo had roped close to fifty wild horses, which was about as many as Melberne felt he could handle that fall. The Mexican was now at the harder and longer task of breaking them. Sometimes the Piutes would help him, to Chane's satisfaction, for they were skilled in that regard. It had been decided a better plan to build a fence of cedar posts and spruce poles all the way across the canyon instead of attempting to drive the wild horses out. More and more horses showed up down in the canyon as the days went by. As yet Chane had not been able to find where they entered. This elongated and walled box was called canyon only for want of a better name. A month of hard riding would be needed to explore the nooks and crannies of the western wall, and thus far Chane had devoted his efforts only to the Wild Horse Mesa side.

He would return at sunset, sometimes on

foot, at others riding Brutus, with stories of his vain attempts to find a way up over the wall to the first escarpment of the great mesa.

"I'm sure one of these cracks in the wall can be climbed," he said. "But I've not hit it yet. It'd take days to go up our trail and under the Henry Mountains and round west through the canyons. I want to get up right at this end and save seventy-five miles' travel."

"Wal, keep huntin'," replied Melberne. "I shore want to know all aboot Wild Horse Mesa. Reckon I'll run cattle up there some day."

November ushered in days as still and mellow and golden as had been those of October. The only difference Sue could see was a gradual increase in the nipping morning air, a deepening of the autumn purple and gold and red, and an almost imperceptible southward trend of the setting sun.

One afternoon Chane came back to camp ragged and dusty of garb, beaming of face, and bursting with news.

"By golly! I've found a way out on top," he ejaculated, happily. "Funny how easy, after I found it. Took me right under the sharp bluff of the mesa. Grandest view in all the world! Now I can explore the great wall all along this side. And on the other I'll be right on the bare rock benches that slope down into the canyon country. Fact is, I was close to the place where I worked up from the rivers."

Sue, watching Chane and listening to him, was inclined to believe Chess's whisper — that Chane had something up his sleeve. "Sue, the son-of-a-gun is on the track of Panquitch," added Chess, in her ear. Anything concerning Chane had power to interest and excite Sue, and this time she was fascinated. Under his physical weariness and the contrasting enthusiasm of his talk there seemed a deep suppressed emotion. Could Chane care so much about the capture of a wild horse? It was just the intensity of his nature.

"Wal, I'll tell you what," interposed Melberne. "I'll go with you. We'll take a packhorse an' explore for a few days."

Chane did not exhibit his usual happy acceptance of any plan by which he could serve.

"Dad, I want to go and I'm going," declared Sue, with sudden positiveness.

"You couldn't keep me from going if you hawgtied me," spoke up Chess.

"Say, is this a picnic I'm to be scout for?" queried Chane.

"Shore it's a picnic," replied Melberne. "We'll take the kids, Chane. They can look after themselves. I'll do the same. That'll leave you free to carry out your own explorations.

360

But we'll have a camp we'll all come back to."

Sue suddenly realized that she was staring at Chane, caught off her guard. The guilty blood warmed her cheek. What did he mean by his penetrating, almost stern gaze? The days had passed by until the Stark Valley episode seemed dim and far away, yet Chane had not changed. She was nothing to him.

"All — right," drawled Chane, with returning good nature, "if you can keep up with me."

"Huh! Thought you said it was an easy climb," retorted Melberne.

"Boss, the talk of this brother of mine is a delusion and a snare," averred Chess. "But we don't care what his easy means. Hey, Sue?"

"We don't care in the least what Chane — thinks," rejoined Sue, demurely, with eyes cast down.

Chess let out a merry peal of laughter, Melberne looked wise, and Chane retreated within himself.

Next morning in the cold dark clearness of dawn, Sue rode out of camp with Chess, following her father and Chane, who were driving two packhorses. The adventure to Sue had an alluringly bright face.

"Well, sister dear," began Chess, "this little trip will be Chane's finish. The big stiff of an iceberg!"

"Chess, I declare, if you begin to tease me about — about him — I — I'll not go," replied Sue.

"Not go? You're crazy. This'll be the chance we want. But I know you're bluffing. You just couldn't keep from going."

How well he knew her! Indeed, Sue could not have imagined on the moment anything that could have kept her back. Chess seemed unusually happy, brotherly, protective, and yet more devilish than ever. He absolutely could not be trusted, so far as his verbosity to her was concerned. Sue no longer had control over Chess. Since that moment of anguish when she had confessed her love for Chane — that it was killing her — Chess had made her completely his own, in a boyish, masterly, brotherly way. She could do nothing with him. He had closed her protesting lips with a kiss. When she slapped him, with no slight hand, he had offered the other cheek. She was afraid to be alone with him, because of this propensity to torture her; yet, strange paradox, his presence, his laughing eyes, his never-ending habit of yoking her name with Chane's, her future with Chane's, caused her as much ecstasy as torment.

362

Sue followed Chess into one of the many mouths of the cracked wall, finding it identical with others she had visited. Presently they passed the zone of fertility, to go into a narrowing gulch where riding soon became impossible. Climbing on foot, however, had one relieving virtue — Chess had to save his breath and so could not tantalize her.

The fissure in the wall narrowed, zigzagged, grew steeper and more choked with rock and shale, until Sue gladly welcomed those intervals when Chane and her father worked to make a trail, cracking with sledge hammer, heaving the stones. There were places where the packhorses had to squeeze through. It was slow, hot, laborsome work, and Sue felt so confined and restricted by the winding upward passage that she had no pleasure in this part of the day's adventure.

An hour was consumed on the last devious steep ascent of the split in the wall.

"Ea—sy! That — son-of-a-gun said — easy," panted Chess, as he surmounted the rim. "Come on — Sue."

Sue's leaden boots could barely be lifted; they seemed riveted to the trail. At length she made it, and raising her eyes was almost staggered by a colossal red corner of wall, cracked, seamed, stained, sheering up so high that she had almost to unjoint her neck to bend back her head to see the top.

"What's — that?" she asked, huskily.

"Reckon it's Wild Horse Mesa. Isn't Chane an awful liar? Easy to get on top, he said. Why, we've only climbed one step of a stairway to the sky."

The bulging red corner hid whatever lay to the east and south. In the other direction, the view showed the country back upon which Sue had so often gazed — desert upland, sweeping away, grass and ridge and range, to the distant black mountains. Suddenly she gazed down. The gray canyon yawned at her feet, not unlike when she had first seen it from the other rim. Her father's labors seemed lost in the vastness of gray and green. Only the column of blue smoke proved that the homestead was a reality.

"Get on and ride," called Chane.

The bare red rock sloped up gently in the direction Chane and her father were leading. Sue trotted her horse to catch up with them. To her left the stone slanted gradually, growing broken, and at length merged in the deceiving irregularity of the desert. She felt a mounting curiosity to see what lay beyond the close horizon. As for the wall of the mesa to her right, that somehow staggered her.

Chane and her father halted with the packhorses just as Sue reached them. Then for Sue, the very world of stone upon which she stood seemed to have dropped away before her transfixed gaze.

The southwest country, the canyon country, lay beneath her, as if by some incredible magic, within the grasp of her vision. Waving gently, bare and red, the rock beneath her sloped down and down, until it seemed to be lost in the gleaming abyss.

Sue did not need to be told that the first terrible gap in the terraced stone was the Grand Canyon. She saw the granite walls, almost black, and under them the swirling red river. Dark and menacing, this canyon wound in rugged sweeps through the leagues of bare stone, meeting lines of cleavage that were other canyons, emptying into it. Between and beyond rolled the endless waves, knolls, ridges, domes of red and yellow rock; and dark clefts, thin, wandering, showed deep in every rounded surface. It was a grand and stunning spectacle. Dimly, across this waste of canyon-cut stone rose a flatland, purple in color, over-topped by a round black mountain. The west seemed all closed by the bulk of Wild Horse Mesa. It ranged away, an unscalable wall, for many miles, regular and clear-cut at single glance, but discovering to long study a mountain of seamed and creviced stone, with millions of irregularities, sheering down to the base of bare stone that appeared to be its foundation. This mesa rose from a tableland that in itself towered above the canyon country. The far end of Wild Horse Mesa stood up in supreme isolation and grandeur, bright-walled in the morning sun.

If Chane expected those whom he had brought here to exclaim with rapture their impressions of this spectacle, he had reckoned falsely. Chess was the only one to speak, and his exclamations proved the natural tendency of some persons to be funny when they mean to be impressive. Sue wanted intensely to get off by herself; she gazed no more because her faculties seemed to have become dwarfed.

Chane rode down over the waving stone, to enter a curving-walled break, that soon became a canyon in itself and swallowed them up. It opened at length into a loftier walled canyon, where clear water ran, and the richest of green grass and most exquisite of flowers, white, yellow, lavender, made verdure on the narrow benches. Cottonwood trees showed foliage just beginning to turn gold.

"Here's a good place to camp," said Chane. "Grass, water, and wood. And we can explore in four directions."

"Wal, I reckon we'd better hang up right heah," declared Melberne. "Because, I'll be darned, if you show me any more pretty places

I'll get discontented with my homestead."

"Melberne, did you see any tracks on the way across the bench above?" asked Chane as he swung out of his saddle.

"Tracks! On that bare rock? I shore didn't," replied Melberne.

"Well, I did, and some of them were fresh, made by shod horses. They were headed west along the bench. The Piute boys rode up this way yesterday, but their ponies were not shod. I'm inclined to believe Manerube and his outfit made those tracks."

"Ahuh! Wal, what if they did?" demanded the other.

"No matter, I reckon. They're leaving us alone," rejoined Chane, thoughtfully. "But it bothers me — the idea that they may be trying to climb Wild Horse Mesa. They're on the wrong track down that bench, for about ten or twelve miles down there's an impassable break which runs square up to the wall. That'll turn them back."

"How far have we come down heah?"

"Two or three miles, I should say."

"Wal, I'll take it afoot an' go back, keepin' an eye peeled for them. Shore I'd just as lief do that as go further into these canyons. I want to climb where I can see. What'll you do?"

"Melberne, I don't mind telling you I think

I can get on top of the mesa."

"Good! You make shore," he replied, with satisfaction. "An', Chess, you an' Sue prowl around to please yourselves, only don't work back up the way we come. Now let's make camp quick, have a bite to eat, an' then be free till dark."

Sue and Chess, more in the spirit of fun than for any other reason, had trailed Chane down the canyon until they lost his tracks.

"Doggone him! Has he turned into a bird?" complained Chess.

"He's an angel," said Sue, who had responded strangely to this growing adventure.

The canyon had grown to be a remarkable one, narrow, lofty-walled, full of golden gleams and hollow echoes. It drew Sue on and on. Chess gathered flowers, caught frogs and butterflies for her, helped her over the boulders.

"Do you suppose he climbed out?" inquired Sue.

"Who?"

"Chane, of course, silly."

"So-ho! You're just toddling along with me because of *him*. Sue Melberne, I'd be ashamed."

"I am," confessed Sue, boldly. "But then you're nice at times. And when you are I like to be with you."

"I don't see how we could have missed any

place where Chane could have gone up with Brutus. It sure is queer. But, Sue, we've come mostly over bare wet rock and granite boulders. I'm not so bad following tracks. Still, with a distractingly sweet girl like you, I couldn't track an elephant in the mud."

"Chess, you can shore spout," replied Sue, merrily.

Presently the canyon narrowed until all the space was covered with water. It ran swift in places, and appeared shallow.

"Looks like we're stumped," observed Sue, ruefully.

"Us stumped? Never. I'll carry you," said Chess, gayly, and without more ado he gathered her up, as easily as Chane had once, and splashed into the stream. The water began to rise above his knees. Chess slipped, then caught his balance. Sue cried out:

"Don't you dare fall with me, Chess Weymer."

Suddenly he halted in the middle of the canyon, with roguish eyes on hers. Sue recognized the gleam of deviltry.

"That gives me a wonderful idea," he said.

"Does it? All right. But hurry and get me out of this."

"Not at all. That isn't the idea. I suddenly thought just how much love Chane and I have wasted on you."

"Oh! Have you? Well, you needn't waste any more. Hurry, I tell you."

Chess hugged her a little and laughed down at her.

"Sue, you kiss me or I'll be sure to slip and fall."

"I will not. Chess, this isn't fun," she said, hurriedly.

"It's great. I never had such a chance. I'm sure Chane won't miss one little kiss. Come —"

"Shut up!" interrupted Sue. "I declare you are no — no gentleman."

"You don't appreciate me. I'm fighting *you* for your happiness and for Chane's. You love each other and you're a couple of fools."

"*I* am, yes. But not he . . . Chess, don't hold me here — jibbering that way — like an idiot."

"Kiss me, then, and call me brother," he went on, shaking her gently.

"You — you —" began Sue, and ended abruptly. There did not appear to be any other way out of the dilemma. Chess seemed just a little different today. Yet the look of him was the same as always when he teased her, only now it held something sweet, possessive. "Very well, Little Boy Blue," she went on, and raised her face to his, to kiss his cheek. "Brother!"

Not the kiss, which she really meant, but the word, which she felt was untrue, sent the blood surging to her temples. Chess gave her a radiant smile, and ploughing through the water, soon reached the dry rocks, where he set her upon her feet. She had meant to upbraid him severely, once she was safe on terra firma, but his happiness disarmed her.

"If Chane only knew! Wouldn't he just die? Come, sis, we're having a jolly adventure," he babbled, and taking her hand he led her on down the canyon.

"Chess, it's getting fearful," murmured Sue, gazing up the dark, almost perpendicular walls to the narrow flowing stream of blue sky overhead.

"What? Roaming round with me this way?"

"No. I mean the canyon. Isn't it just wonderful? Look! I see golden sunlight far ahead."

"Sure is a place for sweethearts," replied Chess, knowingly.

"Chess, you've got girls and sweethearts and — love on the brain."

"Sure have. But it's stopped my drinking and fighting."

He could always turn her flippancy into thoughtful silence. She thought she would try not answering him at all. So they walked and waded on down the canyon, inspired now by its alluring mystery and beauty. Presently they

371

entered an enlargement of the canyon, so remarkably and abruptly a contrast that they halted in their tracks, hands locked and eyes roving everywhere. It was a great red-wall oval, open on the right, with a most stupendous waving slope that apparently lifted to the clouds. One side of the huge oval was bathed in golden sunlight and the other was deep shadowed in shade. Sand bars gleamed in the sun like gold. Gravelly beds shone white. Here the stream had disappeared underground. Grassy benches were colorful flower gardens. Cottonwood trees straggled along, growing more numerous, until they bunched in a beautiful grove, with fluttering leaves half yellow and half green. The hollow murmur of swift water down the canyon made dreamy music. Canyon swifts glinted gold in the sun, blue in the shade, and their wild twitterings were in harmony with the place. Yet silence brooded there, and the strange fragrance of deep canyons permeated the air.

Like two children Sue and Chess explored the benches, the grove, and the caverns under the wall. Then, upon going across toward the waved slope, Chess discovered horse tracks in the sand.

"I'm a son-of-a-gun! Wild-horse tracks!" he exclaimed, in amazement. "Sue, can you beat that? Here, way down in this canyon!

Look at that slope. Wild horses could climb it . . . oh, Sue, I believe Chane knew there were wild horses down in here. He wasn't like himself. But I haven't seen any sign of Brutus's tracks. I'll look."

He went all over the sand and gravel bars, to return to Sue with a puzzled shake of his head.

"Got me buffaloed," he said. "We trailed Chane so far down this very canyon. Then we lost his tracks. We must have missed some place he went up. But I'll gamble on one thing sure. He's got some big idea."

"Panquitch!" cried Sue, thrillingly.

Chess cracked his fist in his palm.

"It might be. He raved about this side of Wild Horse Mesa. Then, when we wanted to come, all of a sudden he was mum. Sue, it's early yet. Let's climb up this slope. We can't get lost. All we've got to be careful about is to get down and past that deep water before dark."

"Come on, brother," cried Sue, carried away by the thrill of his words.

"You mean that, don't you?"

"Now, Chess, the moment I — I try to be nice you spoil everything."

He took her hand again and led her toward where the yellow sand met the red slant of the rock.

"Be honest, Sue dear," he went on, suddenly tender and deep-voiced, in an earnestness that drew Sue against her will. "I mean — you do love Chane? You haven't gone back on him? Tell me."

They reached the slope and began to climb, Sue hanging her head, and Chess leaning to see her face.

"You've kept my secret?" she asked.

"I cross my heart, yes. And it's been hard," he replied.

"You'll still keep it? Remember, Chess, if you betray me I'll hate you forever."

"I'll never tell what you say to me," he answered. "But don't think I'll not move heaven and earth to fetch you two to your senses."

"Then — once more — the last time — I'll tell you," she said, very low and solemnly, and she looked up at him. "I love your brother with my whole heart and soul."

Chess took her avowal differently from the way she expected. Instead of breaking out into robust gladness he took it in poignant silence; his face worked, his eyes filled, and he squeezed her hand so hard it hurt her. Then he drew her on up the slope.

The rock was soft brown sandstone which crumbled under the nails of Chess's boots. The tracks of wild horses could be followed by slow and careful scrutiny. Climbing was easy, compared with the steep trail Sue had essayed that early morning. Moreover, it was exhilarating. Sue and Chess played a game of picking out direction, safe ascents, easy inclines, detours, not yet paying any particular attention to the lofty summit above.

As they ascended, however, they found that difficulties began to face them, and to increase. It grew to be perilous and strenuous work, and therefore the more thrilling. Something drew them onward and upward. They climbed to and fro much farther than straight up. The red stone gave way to a zone of yellow, and then to light green, almost as soft as chalk. At their backs, the wall appeared higher than the one they were ascending, and it obstructed their view in that quarter. In other directions, knobs and domes of bare stone loomed up, growing larger as Sue and Chess climbed higher.

There came a time when Sue could look round over a remarkably large area of slopes, mounds, pits, bowls, slants, and curves, as naked and bare as tombstones. Gradually they worked to the base of lofty lemon-colored crags, and to the right of them, keeping always to the easiest travel. This sometimes drew them off a straight course to the height they could see, and were surely attaining.

What little talk Sue and Chess indulged in

was devoted to the exigencies of their task. Sue's emotion grew to be an exultation. This climb was strange. Not only physical! Not only was it an adventure of sport and achievement. A voice seemed to call from the heights.

Blue sky only showed above the wavy horizon line so long unattainable. But as they had almost reached it, suddenly the grand black-fringed, gold-walled level of Wild Horse Mesa rose above the horizon into the blue. It seemed so close as to be overpowering. Then the last few rods of that climb turned the backs of Sue and Chess to the mesa, so when they finally gained their objective point, and stood on the height of the slope, they found themselves gazing down into a tremendous enlargement of the canyon, a valley of marvelous shapes and hues, clear and open in the sunlight, seemingly close, yet far below. Like that of a colossal octopus, the dark green body and arms seemed to float on a sea of opal. There were no clouds or sunset to confuse the eye. Nevertheless, there was an impression of many colors, all pale, imperceptibly shading into one another.

Beautiful as Sue found that valley, the instant she turned she forgot it. Awe possessed her. Chess drew a deep hard breath. Wild Horse Mesa loomed before and above them, its great western cape a magnificent promontory, running toward the westering sun. Its inaccessibility seemed more paramount than ever, yet from this height Sue conceived a haunting sense that it was indeed the abode of wild horses.

"Sue, sit down and rest," said Chess. "I've got something to tell you — soon as I can breathe — and talk. This is the place."

Absorbed in her own feelings, Sue did not want particularly to hear Chess, but gazed and watched and felt with an intense delight. Presently Chess gripped her hand.

"Sue — my brother loves you," he said.

The absence of his old teasing tone or any semblance of fun, the direct simplicity of his assertion, robbed Sue of power to ridicule, or retreat in anger. She could only look at Chess.

"He loves you terribly," went on Chess, with swift eloquence. "He dreams of you. He talks of you in his sleep. He keeps me awake."

Sue covered her burning face with her hands, and bent over, shot through and through with a tumultuous bliss that all her morbid and hateful doubts could not quell. There was truth in Chess's voice. It had lain at the root of all his teasing.

"But you've got to do some big thing to square yourself for believing Manerube's lies," went on Chess. "That hurt Chane. He's never been the same, not even to me. But

I've watched him close. I know he worships you. But he'll never tell you unless you break him down. He'll never forgive you unless you make him."

"Chess, if you force me to believe he — he loves me — when he doesn't — I could never stand it," she whispered.

"No fear. I know."

"Then what on earth can I do?"

"I've no idea, unless you've the nerve to do something desperate. Telling him wouldn't be enough. You've got to *do* something. And, Sue, you must do it quick. Only last night he told me he reckoned he'd be on the go soon."

"Oh — he means to leave us?"

"Sure he does. I'm afraid he can't stand it longer. But you mustn't let him go. His happiness, yours, and mine, too, all depend on you, little girl."

"Oh — what — what —" choked Sue, overcome by the sudden onslaught of amazement, joy, love, and fear, all in rapid succession.

"Find him alone," whispered Chess, tensely. "On this trip, before we get back. Throw your arms round his neck!"

"I — I could not," cried Sue, starting up wildly. "Are you mad, Chess? Have you no — no —"

"It's a desperate case, Sue," he interrupted,

hurriedly, in the persuasive tones of the tempter. "He adores you. If you can only make him see you love him — quick — throw him off his balance! Chane's the proudest of all the Weymers I ever knew. He'd freeze you to death if you tried any ordinary way to make up with him. Storm him, Sue, storm him!"

Suddenly, before Sue's whirling mind could meet that last insidious speech, Chess grasped her arm so violently as to jerk her upright.

"Look! Look!" he shouted, in a frenzy of excitement, pointing down and across the waving hollow bowl. "Wild horses! A whole string of them!"

Sue leaped erect with excitement thrilling out her agitation. Wildly she gazed down, trying to follow where Chess pointed.

"Oh, I can't see them. Where?"

"Far across and down," he replied, swiftly. "On the *other* side of this ridge. Not the slope we climbed. Over the yellow, down on the red, among the cedars . . . Sue, sure as we're alive they've come down from Wild Horse Mesa and are working round to go down into the canyon we came up. Maybe for water."

At last Sue espied them, a file of horses, long-maned and long-tailed, unmistakably wild, passing through some dwarf scattered cedars. Looking toward the head of that file Sue saw a horse the sight of which made her start. Even at that distance he seemed to embody extraordinary beauty and wildness. He was tawny in color, with mane like a black flame, and tail as black that swept the stones. How proudly he stepped! How he moved his wild head to right and left!

"Chess. Look at the leader," called Sue, in delight.

Then Chess burst out, "PANQUITCH! Sue, we're looking at the greatest wild stallion Utah and Nevada ever knew. Oh, the color of him! Look at that mane! I told you Chane had something up his sleeve. Sue, he's after Panquitch. But, oh, where is he now?"

Chapter 15

Chane rode Brutus down the dark-walled portal into the rocky maze of the canyon country.

This he meant to be the first of an exhaustive exploration of every possible place that could be an exit or egress of the wild horses to and from Wild Horse Mesa; yet, as it was by no means uncertain that he might not meet Panquitch at any time, he was prepared for such a momentous event. He carried two lassoes on his saddle. Presently he dismounted, and taking several burlap sacks he had brought with him, he cut them up, and folded them thick, and tied them securely round the big hoofs of Brutus. Chane did not want to make noise going down the canyon, or leave any tracks. Brutus looked on rather impatiently while this was being done, as if he would like to know what was wrong with his hoofs. Then Chane mounted again and rode on.

It was still early in the day, for now and then the white sun shone above in the narrow gap between the lofty rims. Chane felt that he would have leisure today and the following days to explore every nook and cranny under the mysterious wall of the great mesa. Brutus walked noiselessly over the rocks and left no trace. Chane avoided the sand bars. If the wild horses were out on top and should come down to see horse tracks in the sand of their secret passageway to and from the mesa, they might, under the leadership of Panquitch, at once turn back. Chane remembered wonderful instances of the intelligence, almost reasoning power, of wild stallions. The longer a stallion was hunted the keener and wilder he became. Panquitch had outwitted a hundred wild-horse wranglers. But that had been in open country. Here, deep in these narrow canyons, with their abrupt turns and deep waterways, he would be decidedly at a disadvantage. Chane had not in the least been tempted to bring Alonzo to help him, though he acknowledged the superiority of the *vaquero*. Chane had the wild-horse hunter's strange ambition, so far as a great stallion was concerned: he would corner and rope Panquitch unaided.

As Chane progressed down the canyon he paid strict attention only to those places where a crack in the wall, a branch canyon, or a wide enlargement might hide a possible means of exit to the rim above. It was astonishing what careful investigation brought to light.

Chane found places where he might have climbed out on foot, but where Brutus, agile as he was, could not follow.

At length he reached the big park-like oval, the expansion of the canyon, where in his memorable flight across the rivers and out of this labyrinth he had encountered Panquitch with his band. Near the upper end of this huge oval Chane dismounted to walk along the stones at the edge of the sandy bars, and worked back to where the water disappeared. He found horse tracks, made, he was sure, the day before. They came to the water and went back toward the low rise of red slope. This point was not where he had encountered Panquitch. That, Chane remembered, was a beautiful constriction of this enlargement of the canyon, a bowl-like place, full of cottonwoods and willows, and characterized by a more wonderful slope than this one.

Chane studied the whole opposite wall, as far as he could see. He could see perhaps a mile of this oval. Just opposite where he stood, a wide break in the wall came down to the sand. It was smooth and worn rock, widening like a fan toward the wavy summit of yellow ridges. These he knew were the round knolls so marked when one gazed down upon the canyon country from the rims. Beyond and above, of course, rose Wild Horse Mesa, but Chane could not get a glimpse of it. He noted how the wavy red rock spread beyond and behind bulges of the wall, that to the left and right of him sheered down perpendicularly to his level.

That one to the right of him held his studious attention because he believed it hid much from his gaze. This huge frowning section of canyon wall lay between the slope opposite him and the one below where he had watched Panquitch climb. It looked to Chane as if the wild horses could come down one slope and go up the other. Then he remembered the narrow gleaming walls and the long deep pools of water. Surely the wild horses could not swim these except when on the way out to the upland country above, or when they were returning to their mysterious abode. Chane decided that it would take days to get a clear map in his mind of this maze.

Returning to Brutus, he rode on down the oval, keeping to the curve of the wall, far from the center. As he rode he got higher, and farther back, so that his view of the slope opposite was better. Soon, however, the bulge of the intervening wall shut out his view entirely of that slope. Then he attended more keenly to what lay ahead.

The oval park ended in a constriction like the neck of a bottle. The sunlight came down from a marvelous slope of red rock, waved and billowed, resembling a sea on end. This slope he recalled so well that he felt a thrill. Here was where he had watched Panquitch climb out. A dark cleft, V-shaped, split the ponderous bulk of the cliff at the end of the oval. It was still far off, but Chane recognized it. Down in there was where he hoped some-day to meet Panquitch. His hope was merely a dream, he knew, for the chances were a thousand to one that he never would have such luck.

"Reckon I'll leave Brutus and climb that slope," soliloquized Chane.

Whereupon he rode on down past the break in the wall toward the grove of cottonwoods. Here, there were shade and patches of green grass. As Chane dismounted Brutus lifted his head and shot up his ears, in the action that was characteristic of him when he heard some-thing unusual.

"Hey! What'd you hear, old boy?" queried Chane, suddenly tense.

A distant hollow sound seemed to be filling Chane's ears. But it might have been just the strangeness of the canyon wind, like the roar of the sea in a cave. Chane waited, slowly los-ing his tensity. But he observed that Brutus lost nothing of attentiveness. Chane trusted the horse, and desiring to get under cover he drew Brutus in among the cottonwoods, and selected a place where he could see in all directions without being seen, and have at least one hidden exit, that down into the V-shaped cleft. Chane remembered Manerube and Bud McPherson.

Brutus turned so that he could head up the canyon, and only Chane's hand and low voice kept him still. The keener ears or nose of the horse had reacted to something Chane could not yet detect.

All at once a weird, horrid blast pealed out, not far from Chane, and higher than where he stood. The echoes bellowed from wall to wall. Chane, seeing that Brutus was about to neigh, clasped his muzzle with strong pressure.

"Keep still," whispered Chane, fiercely.

He had never heard a sound so uncanny and fearful. It made his blood creep, and for a second he sustained a shock. Then his quick mind solved the realization that in this country nothing but a horse could peal out such a cry. Therefore, when it was followed by a light quick clatter of hoofs, Chane was not at all surprised.

"Brutus, we've heard that before," he whispered, patting the horse.

Chane was several hundred yards from where the slope merged into the level canyon floor, and the lower part of it, owing to the cottonwoods, was hidden from his sight. But wild horses were surely coming down, and they might turn to enter the V-shaped cleft instead of up the canyon. Something had frightened them.

"By golly!" he muttered. "This's a queer deal." He wanted much to linger there and see the wild horses, but instead of staying he leaped on Brutus and, riding close to the wall, under protection of the cottonwoods, he made quick time to the end of the grove. Here lay sections of wall that had broken from above. At the mouth of the cleft Chane rode Brutus behind a huge boulder, and dismounting there, he peeped out.

This point of vantage, owing to the curve of the wall taking him out and away from the restricted view in the cottonwoods, gave him command of the canyon.

He was just in time to get a glimpse of red and black and bay mustangs entering the cottonwoods from the slope.

Far up that wavy incline he espied a slight figure, moving down. He could scarcely credit his eyes. Did it belong to an Indian? Yet the quick lithe step stirred his pulse! He had seen it before, somewhere. Dark hair streamed in the breeze.

"*Sue!*" whispered Chane, in utter astonishment. "Well, I'll be — She and Chess have wandered up there. They're having fun chasing wild horses. But where's he?"

Chane could not see that part of the slope to his right, for a projection of overhanging wall hid it from sight.

Then a band of wild horses burst from the cottonwoods, out into the open sandy space of several acres. They were trotting, bunched close, frightened but not yet in panic. Presently, far out on the sand bar they halted, heads up, uncertain which way to go.

From the far side of them Panquitch appeared, trotting with long strides, something in his leonine beauty and wildness, his tawny black-maned beauty, striking Chane as half horse and half lion.

Certain it was that sight of him sent a gush of hot blood racing over Chane. His mind seemed to be trying to overcome mere tense and vibrating sensation, to grasp at some strange fatality in the moment. Here he hid. Panquitch was there, not a quarter of a mile away. If Chess should happen to be on the other side of that band of wild horses they would run pell-mell down toward the V-shaped cleft. Chane's hand shook as he pressed it close on the nose of the quivering Brutus.

Panquitch trotted in front of his band, to one side and then the other, looking in every direction. He did not whistle. To Chane he had the appearance of a stallion uncertain of his ground. He looked up the slope, at the girl coming down, choosing the easiest travel from her position, now walking, now running, and working toward a bulge of cliff. Then Panquitch gave no further heed to Sue. He was sure of danger in that direction. He trotted out to the edge of the sand bar and faced down, his head high, eager, strained, wild.

"By golly! I'm afraid he's got a whiff of me and Brutus!" whispered Chane. "What a nose he has! The wind favors us. Now, I want to know why he doesn't make a break up the canyon."

Panquitch wheeled from his survey down the canyon to one in the opposite direction. His action now showed that his suspicions were strong in this quarter. His great strides, his nervous halting, his erect tail and mane, his bobbing head, proved to Chane that he wanted to lead his band up the canyon, but feared something yet unseen.

A sweet, wild, gay cry pealed down from the slope.

Chane espied Sue standing on the bulging cliff, high above the canyon floor, and she was flinging her arms and crying out in the exultance of the moment. Chane saw the sunlight on her face. He strained his ears to distinguish what she was voicing to the wildness of the place and the beautiful horses that called it home.

"Fly! Oh, Panquitch fly!" she was singing to the wind, in the joy of her adventure, in the love of freedom she shared with Panquitch.

Chane understood her. This was girlish fun she was having, yet her sweet wild cry held the dominant note of her deeper meaning. She loved Panquitch, and all wild horses, and yearned for them to be free.

"Girl, little do you dream you may drive Panquitch straight into my rope," muttered Chane, grimly.

The stallion suddenly froze in his tracks, making a magnificent statue typifying fear. A whistling blast escaped him. The nature of the hollow walls must have given it tremendous volume. It pealed from cliff to cliff, and then, augmented by united whistles from the other horses, it swelled into a deafening concatenation.

Chane's keen eye detected Chess up the canyon, bounding into view. At the same instant, Panquitch wheeled as if on a pivot and leaped into headlong stride down the canyon, with his band falling in behind him.

Like a flash Chane vaulted into the saddle. He sent Brutus flying over stones and through water into the cool shadow of the cleft. Any narrow place to hide, from behind which he could rope the stallion! All Chane's force went into the idea. A jutting corner tempted him, as did another huge rock, but the gleam of water drew him on. One of the deep long pools lay just ahead. Brutus padded on at tremendous gait. The canyon narrowed, darkened, and more than once Chane's stirrup rasped on the wall.

Full speed Brutus charged into the pool, and plunged through shallow water. To his knees, to his flanks he floundered on — then souse, he went into deep water, going under all but his head. How icy the water to Chane's heated blood! He gazed back. Not yet could he see any movement of wild horses.

Fifty yards ahead the straight wall heaved into a corner, round which the stream turned in a curve. If Chane could find footing for Brutus behind that corner, Panquitch would have no chance. What a trap! Chane reveled in the moment. The wildest dream of his boyhood was being enacted.

He did not spare Brutus, but urged him, spurred him, beat him into tremendous action. The swelling wave made by the horse splashed on the walls. Brutus reached the corner — turned it. Chane reined him into the wall. There was a narrow bench, just level with the water. But that would be of no help unless

Brutus could touch bottom. He did. Chane stifled a yell of exultation. Fate was indeed against Panquitch. Brutus waded his full length before he reached the ledge. He was still in five feet of water, and on slippery rocks. Chane had no time to waste. The cracking of hoofs up the canyon rang like shots in his ears. Panquitch and his band were coming. Chane needed room to swing his lasso. Should he get out on the ledge or stay astride Brutus? Both plans had features to recommend them. But it would be best to stay on Brutus.

Chane turned the horse round. Brutus accomplished this without slipping off the rocks into deep water.

"Brutus, what do I want with Panquitch when I have you?" Chane heard himself whisper. He did not need Panquitch. It was his hunting instinct and long habit.

Then Chane had burst upon him the last singular fact in the string of fatalities which now bade fair to doom Panquitch. The important thing at the climax here was to have room to cast the lasso. Chane had felt the nearness of the corner of wall. He had planned to urge Brutus into the water the instant Panquitch appeared. But this need not be risked. There was no necessity to get beyond the corner of wall.

Chane was left-handed. He threw a noose

with his left hand, and in the position now assumed he was as free to swing his rope as if he had been out in the open.

The trap and the trick were ready. Chane's agitation settled to a keen, tight, grim exultation. Nothing could save Panquitch if he ever entered that deep pool. Chane listened so intensely he heard his heartbeats. Yes! He heard them coming. Their hard hoofs rang with bell-like clearness upon the boulders. Then the hollow muffled sound of hoofs on rock under the water — then the splashing swish!

Soon the narrow canyon resounded to a melodious din. Suddenly it ceased. Chane realized the wild horses had reached the pool. His heart ceased to beat. Would the keen Panquitch, victor over a hundred clever tricks to capture him, shy at this treacherous pool? — Clip — clop! He had stepped out into the water. Chane heard his wild snort. He feared something, but was not certain. The enemies behind were realities. *Clip — clop!* He stepped again. *Clip — clop!* Into deeper water he had ventured. Then a crashing plunge!

It was followed by a renewed din of pounding hollow hoof-cracks, snorts, and splashes. They were all taking to the pool.

Chane swung the noose of his lasso round his head, tilting it to evade the corner of wall.

It began to whiz. His eyes were riveted piercingly upon the water where it swirled gently in sight from behind the gray stone. Brutus was quivering under him. The plunging crashes ceased. All the wild horses were swimming. The din fell to sharp snuffing breaths and gentle swash of water. A wave preceded the swimming band.

A lean beautiful head slid from behind the wall, with a long black mane floating from it. Panquitch held his head high.

At that short distance Chane could have roped one of his ears. Even in the tremendous strain Chane could wait a second longer. Panquitch was his.

The stallion saw Brutus and his rider — the swinging rope. Into the dark wild eyes came a terror that distended them. A sound like a horrid scream escaped him. He plunged to turn. His head came out.

Then Chane cast the lasso. It hissed and spread, and the loop, like a snake, cracked over Panquitch, under his chin and behind his ears. One powerful sweep of Chane's arm tightened that noose.

"Whoopee!" yelled Chane, with all the power of his lungs. "He's roped! He's roped! *Panquitch!* — Oh — ho! ho! He's ours, Brutus, old boy. After him, old boy!"

Panquitch plunged back, pounding the

water, and as Chane held hard on the lasso the stallion went under. Chane clacked the rope, and urged Brutus off the rocks. Pandemonium had begun round that corner of the wall. As Brutus soused in, and lunged to the middle of the stream, Chane saw a sight he could never forget.

Upwards of a score of wild horses were frantically beating and crashing the water to escape back in the direction they had come. Some were trying to climb the shelving wall, only to slip, and souse under. They bobbed up more frantic than before, screaming their terror. Some were trying to climb over the backs of those to the fore. All were in violent commotion, and uttering some variation of horse sounds.

Panquitch, hampered by the lasso, was falling behind. Chane pulled him under water, then let him come up. Brutus had to be guided, for he tried to swim straight to the stallion. Chane did not want that kind of a fight. It was his purpose to hold Panquitch in the pool until he was exhausted. With that noose round his neck he must tire sooner than Brutus. This unequal struggle could not last long. Chane had no power to contain his madness of delight, the emotion roused by the feel of Panquitch on the other end of his lasso. Panquitch, the despair of Nevada wranglers long before he had shown his clear heels to those of Utah! Panquitch roped! It was incredible good fortune. It was the great moment of Chane's wild life.

"Aha there, old lion-mane," he called, true even in that moment to his old habit of talking to horses. "You made one run too many! You run into a rope! Swim now! Heave hard! Dive, you rascal! You're a fish. Ho! Ho! Ho!"

But when Panquitch plunged round to make for his adversaries the tables were turned. Chane's yell of exultation changed to one of alarm, both to frighten Panquitch, if possible, and to hold Brutus back. Both, however, seemed impossible. Brutus would not turn his back to the stallion. His battle cry pealed out. Chane hauled on the lasso, but he could not again pull Panquitch under.

Despite all Chane could do, the stallion and Brutus met in a head-on collision. A terrific *mêlée* ensued. Chane was thrown off Brutus as from a catapult. But he was swift to take advantage of this accident. A few powerful strokes brought him round to Panquitch, and by dint of supreme effort astride the back of the wild stallion.

Chane fastened his grip on the ears of the stallion, to lurch forward with all his weight and strength. He got the head of Panquitch under the water.

"BACK! BACK!" yelled Chane to Brutus.

It was a terrible moment. Chane preferred to let Panquitch free rather than drown him. But if Brutus kept fighting on, crowding the stallion, Chane saw no other issue. Under him Panquitch was shaking in convulsions. Chane let go of his head. The stallion bobbed up, choking, snorting. But if terror was still with him it was one of fury to kill. He bent his head back to bite at Chane. His eyes were black fire, his open mouth red and dripping, his teeth bared. Chane all but failed to keep out of his reach.

In his cowboy days Chane had been noted for his ability to ride broncos, mean mustangs, bucking horses, mules, and even wild steers. The old temper to ride and conquer awoke in him. Fighting the stallion, beating Brutus off, keeping his seat, Chane performed perhaps the greatest riding feat of his career. He had, however, almost to drown the stallion.

At length Panquitch, suddenly showing signs of choking, headed for the shallow water. His swimming was laborious. Chane loosed the tight rope, then plunging off, he swam back to Brutus and got in the saddle. He urged Brutus faster and faster, to pass the sinking Panquitch. Not a moment too soon did Brutus touch bottom, and plunging shoreward, he dragged Panquitch after him. The stallion could no longer breathe, yet he staggered out of the shallow water, to the sand, where he fell.

Chane leaped off Brutus to fall on Panquitch and loosen the lasso. The stallion gave a heave. He had been nearly choked to death; perhaps the noose had kept water out of his lungs. His breast labored with a great intake of air. Then he began to shake with short quick pants.

"Aw, but I'm glad!" ejaculated Chane, who for a moment had feared a calamity. But Panquitch would revive. Chane ran back to the heaving Brutus, and procuring a second lasso from the saddle, he rushed again to the stallion and slipped a noose round his fore-legs.

"Reckon that's about all," he said, rising to survey his captive.

Panquitch was the noblest specimen of horseflesh Chane had ever seen in all his wandering over the rangelands of the west. But in these flaming black eyes there was a spirit incompatible with the rule of man. Panquitch might be broken, but his heart would ever be wild. He could never love his master. Chane felt pity for the fallen monarch, and a remorse. He was killing something, the like of which dwelt in his own heart.

"Panquitch, it wasn't a square deal," declared Chane. "I played you a dirty trick. I'm not proud of it. And so help me God, I've a mind to let you go."

So the wild-horse-hunting instinct in Chane found itself in conflict with an emotion compelled into existence by the defeat and prostration of the great stallion. Chane missed that crowning joy of the wild-horse wrangler — to exhibit to the gaze of rival hunters a captive horse that had been their passion to catch and break and ride.

"Wo—hoo! Oh—h, Chane, I'm coming!" called a girlish high-pitched voice, pealing along the narrow walls.

Sue appeared at the mouth of the cleft, standing upon a boulder, with her hair shining in the sun. She had espied him and Brutus from afar, and perhaps had guessed the issue. Then Chess's voice rang down the canyon.

"What you-all doing, Chane Weymer?"

He caught up with Sue, and lending her a hand, came striding with her over the rock benches. He had lost his hat.

Chane heard them talking excitedly, out of breath, wondering, tense and expectant. Brutus whistled. Then Chess and Sue came out of the shadow, into the strip of sunlit canyon. They saw Panquitch lying full length on the sand. Chess broke from Sue and came rushing up. One glance showed him Panquitch was alive.

"Good Lord!" he screeched, beside himself with excitement, running to grasp Chane and embrace him. He was sweating, panting, flushed of face, wild of eye. "*Panquitch!* And you got him hawg-tied!"

He ran back to the stallion, gazed down upon him, moved round him, gloated over him. "Hurry, Sue! Come! Look! Will you — ever believe it? — We chased — Panquitch right — into Chane's trap! Of all the luck! Hurry to see him! Oh, there never was such a horse!"

Then he strode back to Chane, waving his hands.

"We climbed that slope — back there," he went on. "Just for fun. Wanted to see. Then from up on top — I spied the wild horses. Sue saw Panquitch first. We ran down — having fun — seeing how close we could get. Then Sue said: 'Run down ahead, Chess. I'll stay here. Turn them — chase them by me — so I'll get to see Panquitch close.' So I ran like mad. Queer place up there. I headed them. They ran back — up over that hollow — behind the big knob of wall. Right by Sue! I saw her run down the slope — this way. But I made for the canyon. Just wanted to see them run by. Couldn't see them. I ran some more. Then the whole bunch trotted out of the cottonwoods. Panquitch lorded it round. He was prancing. He didn't know which way to run. I heard Sue screaming at him. Then Panquitch bolted this way — and his bunch followed. Just think! You were here. You saw them. You must have hid . . . you roped Panquitch! Chane, you owe it all to Sue. She drove Panquitch to you."

"I reckon," replied Chane, conscious of unfamiliar riot in his breast. "Where'd the bunch go — when they ran back?"

"Passed me — like the wind," panted Chess. "Straight up the canyon!"

"You don't say!" exclaimed Chane, in surprise. "I thought they'd take to one of the slopes. Chess, these wild horses have more than one outlet to their burrow."

Sue had held back, and was standing some rods off, staring from the prostrate Panquitch to Chane. Her hands were pressed over a heaving bosom. Her eyes seemed wide and dark. There was something about her that made Chane catch his breath. This was not Sue Melberne as he knew her.

"Come on, Sue," called Chess. "Nothing to fear. Panquitch has ropes on him."

"Oh, it's all my fault — my fault," cried Sue, pantingly, as again she hurried toward them, keeping away from the fallen stallion. "Is he hurt? He breathes so — so hard."

"Reckon Panquitch's only choked a little,"

replied Chane. "You see, I roped him in the water. Brutus and I had to follow. Panquitch got mad and charged up. I couldn't manage Brutus. He wanted to fight. So they had it hot and heavy. I was knocked off Brutus. But I swam to Panquitch, straddled him, and had to hold his head under water to keep him from drowning us both."

"You're all bloody! You're hurt," replied Sue, coming to him.

Chane had not noted the blood on his hands and his face. Evidently he had been scratched or barked in the struggle.

"Guess I'm not hurt," he said, with a laugh, as he drew out his wet scarf. "Here, Chess, hold the rope while I tie my cuts. If Panquitch tries to get up just keep the rope tight."

Chess received the lasso and drew it taut. "Hyar, you king of stallions," he called out. "You've sure got tied up in the wrong family. We're bad *hombres*, me and Chane. Just you lay still."

Chane became aware that Sue had come quite close to him.

"Let me do it," she said, taking the scarf. And without looking up she began to bind his injured hand. She was earnest about it, but not at all deft. Her fingers trembled. Chane, gazing down upon her, saw more signs of agitation. Under the gold brown of her skin

402

showed a pearly pallor; the veins were swelling on her round neck. Her nearness, and the unmistakable evidences of her distress and excitement, shifted the current of Chane's mind. How momentous this day! What was the vague portent that beat for entrance to his consciousness?

Sue finished binding his hand, and then she looked up into his face, not, it seemed, without effort. She was strained with the exertion and excitement of this adventure. But would that have accounted for a subtle difference in her?

"There's a cut on your temple," she said, and untying her own scarf, she began to fold it into a narrow band. Her blouse was unbuttoned at the neck, now exposing the line where the gold tan met the white of her swelling bosom. "Bend your head," she added.

Chane did as he was bidden, conscious of mounting sensations. The soft gentle touch of her hands suddenly inflamed him with a desire to seize them, to kiss them, to press them against his aching heart. Stern repression did not, however, on this occasion, bring victory. He had no time to think. It was like being leaped upon in the dark — this attack of incomprehensible emotion.

"There — if you put your sombrero on carefully — it will stay," she said.

"Thanks. You're very good. Reckon I'm

not used to being doctored by tender hands," he replied, somewhat awkwardly, as he drew back from her. That was what made him unsure of himself — her nearness. Strange to him, then, and growing more undeniable, was the fact that as he retreated she followed, keeping close to him. When she took hold of the lapel of his vest and seemed fighting either for command of herself or strength to look up again, then he realized something was about to happen.

"I'm all wet," he protested, trying to be natural. But he failed. It was not a natural moment or situation or position for them.

"So you are. I — I hadn't noticed it," she said, and instead of drawing away she came so close that her garments touched him. Even this slight contact caused Chane to tremble. "Chane, come a little away — so Chess won't hear," she concluded, in a whisper.

Chane felt as helpless in her slight hand as Panquitch now was in his. She led him back a few paces, in the lee of a slab of rock that leaned down from the wall.

"What's — all this?" he demanded, incredulously, as she pushed his back against the rock.

"It's something very important," she replied, and then she fastened her other hand in the other lapel of his vest. She leaned against

404

him. The fact was so tremendous that Chane could scarcely force his faculties to adequate comprehension of it. Yet there came to his aid an instinct natural to him through all the strenuous and perilous situations of his desert life, and it was a kind of cool anger of self-preservation.

"Yes?" he queried, doubtfully.

She was quite pale now and the pupils of her dark eyes were dilating over deep wonderful shadows and lights. He felt her quiver. His response was instantaneous and irresistible, but it was a response of his heart, not his will. He would never let her know what havoc this contact played with him.

"Would you do something great for me?" she whispered, her husky voice betraying a dry mouth.

"Great!" he ejaculated. What little control he had when one word could throw him off his balance! "Why, Sue Melberne, I reckon I would — for you — or any girl, if I could."

"Not for any other girl," she returned, swiftly. "For *me!*"

"I'll make no rash promises. What do you want?"

"Let Panquitch go free."

Chane could only stare at her. So that was it! Sudden relief flooded over him. What might she not have asked? How powerless he was to refuse her most trivial wish! But she did not know that. This longing of hers to see Panquitch freed was natural and he respected her, liked her, loved her the more for it. Easy now to understand her white face, her soulful eyes, her quivering lips and clinging hands! She loved wild horses. So did he, and he could see her point of view. Alas for the strange vague rapture that her close presence had roused! But he could prolong this delicious moment of torment.

"Are you crazy, girl?" he demanded.

"Not quite," she replied, with a wistful smile that made him wince. "I want you to let Panquitch go. It was my fault. I was his undoing. I longed to see him close — to scream at him — to watch him run. So I drove him into your trap."

"Quite true. I'd never have caught him save for you. But what's that? I don't care. Once in my life I had a wrangler's luck."

"Something tells me it'll be bad luck, unless you give in."

"Bad luck? Ha! I reckon I've had all due one poor rider," he replied. "And the worst of it, Sue Melberne, was on your account."

"You mean — about Manerube?" she whispered.

"Yes, and what went before," he returned, darkly.

"Chane, did something happen before that?" she asked, softly.

"I reckon it did," he answered, bitterly.

"Tell me," she importuned.

Chane felt as if about to fall from a height. What was this all about? His wounded heart probed! Yet did it matter?

"You know," he said, almost violently. "Chess gave me away."

"Then, what Chess said was — is true?"

"Yes, God help me, it *is* . . . but enough of talk about me. You wanted me to free Panquitch?"

She did not reply. He had a glimpse of her eyes filming over, glazed, humid, before she closed them. Her head, that had been tilted back, drooped a little toward him, and her slender body now lent its weight against his. Chane had no strength to tear himself away from her, nor could he bear this close contact longer. The poor girl was overwrought, all because of sentiment about a horse.

"Sue, what ails you?" he demanded, sharply, and he shook her.

His voice, his rudeness, apparently jarred her out of her weakness. It seemed he watched a transformation pass over her, a change that most of all nonplused him. A blush rose and burned out of her face, leaving a radiant glow. She let go of his vest, drew back. And suddenly

407

she seemed a woman, formidable, incredible, strong as she had been weak, eloquent of eye.

"Something did ail me, Chane, but I'm quite recovered now," she replied, with a wonderful light on her face.

"You talk in riddles, Sue Melberne."

"If you weren't so stupid you'd not think so."

"Reckon I am stupid. But we've got off the trail. You asked me to let Panquitch go."

"Yes, I beg of you."

"You're awful set on seeing him walk off up that slope, aren't you?" he inquired, trying to find words to prolong the conversation. He despised himself for longing to have her come close again, to appeal to him. Presently he must tell her that her slightest wish could never be ignored, that Panquitch was hers to free.

"Chane, I'll do anything for you if only you'll let him go."

He laughed, almost with bitter note. "How careless you are with words! No wonder Manerube got a wrong hunch."

She flushed at that, and lost for a second the smile, the poise that so baffled him. But swiftly they returned.

"I was a silly girl with Manerube," she replied. "I'm an honest woman now . . . I said I'll do anything for you, Chane Weymer — *anything*."

"Reckon I hear you, unless I'm locoed," he said, thickly. "I'm not asking anything of you. But I'm powerful curious. If you're honest now, suppose you tell me a few of the things you'd do for me."

"Shall I begin with a lot of small things — or with something big?" she inquired, in so sweet and tantalizing a voice that Chane felt the blood go back to his heart. She was beyond him. How useless to match wits with any woman, let alone one whom a man adored madly and hopelessly! Chane felt he must get out of this. One more moment, then she could have Panquitch!

"Well, suppose you save time by beginning with something big," he suggested, in a scorn for himself and for her. It was a farce, this talk, all except her earnest appeal and her sweetness. He could not argue with her, nor follow her subtleties.

She stepped close to him again. And then Chane shook with a sense of impending catastrophe. She seemed cool, brave, and honest as she claimed to be. But her dark eyes held a strange fire.

"Very well. The biggest thing a woman can do is to be a man's wife."

Stupefaction held Chane in thrall. It took a moment to recover from the shock of that blow. He had heard her speak. He was not out on the lonely desert, listening to the voices of the cedars. All about Sue Melberne belied that slow, sweet, cool speech. Suddenly a fury of bewilderment, of uncertainty, assailed Chane. Laying powerful hands on her shoulders he shook her as he might have a child.

"You'd marry me to save that horse?" he demanded, incredulously.

"Yes."

"You'd throw yourself away for Panquitch?" he went on, sternly.

"Yes. But — I'd hardly call it that."

"Sue Melberne, you'd be my — my *wife!*" The very idea of such fortune made Chane mad. He released her. He wrestled with himself. Thick and heavy his heart beat. It mattered not why or how he might possess this girl, but the fact that he might was maddening. Still he fought for the right. What a sentimental inexplicable girl!

"Yes, I will, Chane," she said.

"You love Panquitch so well. I remember you risked much to free the wild horses in the trap corral. But this is beyond belief. Yet you say so. You don't look daft, though your talk seems so. I can't understand you. To sacrifice yourself for a horse, even though it's Panquitch!"

"I wouldn't regard it as — sacrifice," she whispered.

"But it is. It'd be wrong. It'd be a crime against your womanhood. I couldn't accept it. Besides, you're doing wrong to tempt me. I'm only a poor lonely rider. I've always been hungry for a woman. And I've never had one . . . It's doubly wrong, I tell you."

Chane stamped up and down the narrow place behind the rock. Hard violent action in the open had been his life: he brought it to bear on the conflict in his breast. With a black, hot, tearing wrench he got rid of the spell.

"Sue, I brought this — on myself," he said, gentle of tone, though his voice broke. "I wanted to hear you beg for Panquitch. I wanted you to be close to me. It was madness. All the time I was lying. For the moment you asked me to free Panquitch I meant to do it. You helped me catch him. You can free him."

Sue walked straight to him, closer than before, almost into his arms. The poise of head, the radiance of face, the eloquence of eye — these had vanished and she seemed stranger than before, a pale thing reaching for him.

"That will make me happy, but only — if I can pay — my debt," she faltered.

"What *do* you mean?" demanded Chane, harshly.

"If you free Panquitch you must make me — your wife."

"Are you out of your head or lying to me?"

"Both," she whispered, and fell against him.

Chane clasped her in his arms, and held her closer and closer, sure in his bewilderment of only one thing, that if she persisted she would break him down. But now she was in his arms. Her head drooped so that he could not see her face, but she was stirring, turning to him, sinking on his breast. Never could he let her go now! It was all so astounding. His mind and body now seemed to leap to the sweetness of possession. The golden amber sunlight of the canyon moved about him like a glory of lightning and it was certain that thunder filled his ears. He was realizing what he could not believe. The stunning truth was that Sue Melberne lay in his arms, strangely willing. That was enough for his hungry heart, but his conscience stormed at him. Then, last of all, he felt as in a dream Sue's arms go up round his neck and fasten there.

"My God!" . . . he gasped. "Sue, this can't be for Panquitch."

Her face came up, white like a flower, wet with tears. But strain and strife were gone.

"If you had any sense you'd have known I — I loved you!"

"SUE MELBERNE!"

"Now, my wild-horse hunter, take your rope off Panquitch — and put it on me," she replied, and raised her lips to his.

A little later Chane took the rope out of Chess's hands and held it to Sue. Then he knelt to slip off the noose of the other lasso, the one that was tied to the saddle on Brutus. Swiftly Chane stripped this from the stallion.

"Hey! What you doing?" yelled Chess, in amazement. "He's come to. The son-of-a-gun will be on his feet in a jiffy."

Chane apparently took no note of Chess's concern. This moment was full of unutterable joy in that he was making Sue happy and slipping his rope off Panquitch — freeing the last wild horse he would ever capture. Bending over the stallion he loosed the knot round the forelegs.

"Pull it — easy," he called to Sue.

Chess actually leaped up in the air, to come down with cracking boots.

"What — the — hell!" he cried, piercingly.

Sue drew the lasso taut, and slid it gently from the stallion. He gave a fierce snort. Then he raised his head. Actually he looked at his legs, and then with muscles knotting all over his body he heaved hard and got up. He was free and he knew it. Hate and fear flamed in his bloodshot eyes. Chane thrilled when he met that look and knew in his soul what he was giving up. Panquitch stood for a moment, with his breaths audible. Thus Chane saw him

413

close, standing unfettered, in all his magnificent and matchless beauty. Indeed, he was a lion of wild horses. Perfect in build, perfect in color, the rarest combination and the only one Chane had ever seen in a tawny shade of yellow, with flowing mane and tail black as night. He had not a scar, not a blemish, not a fault. He represented the supreme handiwork of nature — a creature too beautiful, too proud, too noble, too wild for the yoke of man.

Panquitch shook himself and moved away. He was still weak, but his spirit showed in his prance. He snorted fiercely at Brutus. And Brutus returned the challenge.

"Run — oh, Panquitch, run!" cried Sue, with a rich and mellow sweetness in her voice.

But the stallion did not run. His slow action was that of a spent horse. Keeping to the middle of the canyon, he trotted on, by the sand patch where lately he had pranced so proudly, by the cottonwood grove and the wavy slope of rock, and on, out of sight.

Then Chess exploded. He cursed, he raved, he glared, not for a full moment becoming intelligible.

"You let him go! Panquitch, the greatest wild horse in the world. You had him. You could have given him to me. I've no great horse, like Brutus. I always wanted one . . .

let him go for Manerube to rope! Or some damned lucky rider who'll happen on him before he recovers . . . oh, you're locoed. The two of you. Sue, you're a sentimental fool. Chane, you're a damn fool. I could cry. Chane, whatever has come over you?"

"Chess, I reckon I'm no longer boss of the Weymer outfit," replied Chane, striving to keep undue pride and joy out of his words, but failing utterly.

"Hey?" ejaculated Chess, as if he had been struck. His mouth opened wide, likewise his eyes, and he made a picture of stupidity and incredulity.

"Little Boy Blue, I'm sure going to be your sister," said Sue, with all of gladness.

Suddenly transfigured with rapture, Chess made at them.

Chapter 16

Chane strode up the canyon as one in a dream, leading Brutus, with Sue in the saddle. From time to time he looked back to see if she were a reality. Her dark eyes shone, her lips were parted. There was a smile on her face, an exquisite light, a spirit that must be the love she had confessed. Life had become immeasurably full and sweet for him.

Chess had passed from every manner of congratulation, boastfulness as to his bringing about this match, delight in Chane's good fortune, back to his former despair at the loss of Panquitch.

"Now you two have each other, you don't care for nothing," he growled, with finality and forged on ahead to leave them alone.

It appeared to be about the middle of the afternoon when the amber light of the canyon began to tinge with purple. The breeze had ceased and the air was warm. Less tremendous grew the looming walls, wider the stream of blue sky overhead, lower the rims, and therefore the oppressiveness began to wane, and the sense of overpowering weight and silence.

In many places showed the fresh tracks of the wild horses, last of which were those of Panquitch. He was following his band, on the way to the uplands. Chane would have preferred that they had turned off at the wavy slope below and were now safe under the lee of Wild Horse Mesa. Panquitch, in his spent condition, would hardly be able to escape a fast rider. Still, Chane's exalted mind could not harbor misgiving, or doubt, or anxiety, not on this day in which he had been lifted to the kingdom of happiness.

Chess strode on with his head bent, his gaze on the tracks of Panquitch, and he passed out of sight round a bend in the canyon.

Many times Chane halted to let Brutus come abreast of him, so that he could look up at Sue or touch her. And all at once something which had been forming in his mind coalesced into an insupportable query.

"Sue, when will you marry me?"

She laughed happily. "Why, we've only just become engaged," she replied, roguishly.

"Darling, this is the wild canyon country of Utah," he protested. "People only stay engaged in cities or settlements."

"We'll really be pioneers, won't we?"

"Yes. But I shall always see that you go into civilization every summer, for a visit. Tell me, how long must I wait?"

A rosy glow vied with the gold of Sue's warm cheek.

"Surely until Uncle Jim comes," she said, shyly.

"Your uncle! I remember now — he's a preacher. And he may come yet this fall, certain in the spring?"

"I wish I could fib to you," returned Sue, "and say spring. But dad is sure Uncle Jim will come by Thanksgiving."

He pressed her hand, unable to utter his profound joy and gratitude. Then he took up the bridle and strode on, leading Brutus. He saw the widening canyon, the sand bars cut up by many hoofs, the lowering rims, the shallow brook, yet he was not conscious of them, for he walked as one in a trance.

The time came when ahead the canyon made a curve into brighter light. Beyond this point was the junction of the four canyons where camp had been made. As Chane turned the corner Brutus shied so violently that he tore the bridle from Chane's grasp.

"Hands up, Weymer," called a rough, husky voice.

Chane's dream was rudely shattered. More than once he had heard the ominous note which rang now in his ears. He was unarmed. He raised his hands, and at the same instant he saw a dark-bearded man, with leveled gun, stride from behind the cliff.

"Up they are," he said, and ground his teeth in sudden impotent anger. Then he recognized the man. "Howdy, Slack."

"Same to you, Weymer," replied the other, sidling round in front of Chane toward Brutus.

"Reckon you see I'm not packing a gun."

"Yep, I shore was glad you wasn't wearin' any hardware. But just keep your hands up an' a respectable distance. I'm a distrustful fellar," replied Slack, and presently, getting within reach of Brutus, he secured the bridle.

Chane's line of vision, as he stood rigidly, did not include Sue, until Slack led Brutus forward. Then she appeared, white of face and mute in her fear. Manifestly she had no thought of herself, but of the gun Slack held leveled at Chane.

"Mosey on in front, Weymer," ordered the outlaw.

Chane had no choice but to comply. He had been in such situations before, and this one would not have greatly perturbed him if Sue had not been there. He lowered his hands and strode on towards the camp, intensely curious to see if what he found there would be identical with what he expected.

The triangular space of intersecting canyons presently came unobstructed to his view. A camp fire was burning, and several men surrounded it, one of them sitting. Even at considerable distance Chane recognized the hard lean face of Bud McPherson.

Chess sat on a stone to one side, with his hands tied behind his back. Melberne did not appear to be present.

"Oh, there's Panquitch!" burst out Sue, in shrill distress.

Chane, shocked at Sue's exclamation, saw a number of horses, all saddled, standing bridles down, to the left of the camp-fire group.

"Look! Look!" cried Sue, as if choking.

As Chane did not know where she was looking and did not care to take too many risks with Slack, he shifted his gaze in search of the stallion.

"Chane! Look!" screamed Sue, this time with fury and horror.

"*Manerube! Manerube!* He's got a rope on Panquitch!"

The content of her words flashed on Chane just as he espied Manerube hanging on to two lassoes that were fast on Panquitch. The great stallion was holding back with a spirit vastly in excess of his strength.

Many as had been the bitter moments of

Chane's life, that was the bitterest. Sue's cry of anguish rang in his ears. The wild horse which she had loved and freed was now in the power of a hated rider. It was a blow that to Chane struck home acutely. Panquitch, spent from his fight in the canyon pool, and expending what little strength he had left to catch up with his band, had fallen easily into Manerube's clutches. The cheap and arrogant rider probably had not even credited his capture to the weakened condition of the stallion. He was crowing like a gamecock over his prize, with his braggart's and bully's air more pronounced than ever. He whipped the ropes that secured Panquitch, making the horse flinch. The effect of this on Chane was to distort his vision with passion and hate, so that it seemed for a moment he was gazing through a blood-red haze.

"OH-H!" cried Sue, now deep and poignantly. "He's hurting Panquitch. I won't stand it."

"Sue, keep still," ordered Chane, sharply. "We can do nothing."

"Hyar, you squallin' bobcat," growled Slack, "stop walkin' your hoss on my heels."

They reached the camp fire, with Chane a little in the lead. One of the other men, whose face was familiar but whose name Chane could not recall, drew a gun and pointed it at him.

"Bill, he ain't got no gun, but your idee is correct," drawled Slack, and turning to Sue he laid a rough and meaning hand upon her, which she repulsed in anger. Then Slack swore at her and pulled her out of the saddle.

"Say, wench, if you know when you're well off, you'll be sweet instead of catty," he declared.

On the moment, when the other men were haw-hawing at Slack's sally, Chane happened to catch Sue's eye and conveyed to her in one glance the peril of the situation.

"Howdy, Weymer," said Bud McPherson, coolly. "I'm savin' some of your good grub."

"Howdy, Bud. It's a habit of yours to help yourself to other people's property," rejoined Chane. This outlaw was the most dangerous of the group, Chane decided, though he knew little of the two strangers who had followed Manerube from Wund. But McPherson, though a horse thief and a bad man, had elements that Manerube and the others did not show. He was not little.

Back of the camp fire, near where Chess sat bowed and disconsolate, crouched another man, also tied, and he appeared a pretty worn and miserable object. Chane at last recognized the unshaven and haggard face.

"Loughbridge!" he ejaculated, in both amazement and satisfaction. "Well, what're you hawg-tied for? Reckoned you'd thrown in with this outfit."

"Weymer, I was fooled worse'n Melberne," said Loughbridge. "I took Manerube at his brag. I had no idea he was a hoss thief —"

"Stop your gab!" yelled Manerube, stridently. "You're a white-livered liar. I'm not a horse thief."

"Bud, give it to me straight," said Chane. "What's the deal with Loughbridge?"

"Wal, it ain't so clear to me," replied McPherson, wiping his mouth and scant beard and rising to his feet. "Somebody gimme a smoke. Fact is, Weymer, I wasn't keen on havin' this man thrown in with us. Wal, when he found out our plan to appropriate Melberne's stock — which shore come out at this camp — he hedged an' began to bluster. You know I never argue. So we just put a halter on him."

"Where's Melberne?" added Chane.

"Shore you ought to know. We're waitin' fer him."

"Then what?" demanded Chane.

"Weymer, you allus was a hell-bent-pronto *hombre*," declared McPherson, with good humor. "Reckon you want to know bad what the deal is. Wal, I'll tell you. We've been loafin' in camp waitin' for you-all to ketch the last bunch of hosses before fall set in cold. Then we seen them two Piutes prowlin' around, an' we figgered they'd fetched you another bunch of mustangs. Wal, the deal is hyar. When Melberne comes we'll rustle back to his homestead an' relieve you-all of considerable hoss wranglin' an' feedin' this winter."

"Then, next summer, you'll look us up again," asserted Chane, with sarcasm.

"Haw! haw! You shore hit it plumb center," rejoined the ruffian.

"Bud, you're no fool," said Chane, seriously. "You can't keep up this sort of thing. Somebody will kill you. Why don't you cut loose from these two-bit wranglers you've been riding with? I've known horse thieves to go back to honest ranching. It paid."

McPherson had no guffaw or badinage for this speech of Chane's. It went home. His frankness relieved Chane. McPherson would hardly resort to blood-spilling unless thwarted or cornered. Chane felt greatest anxiety on behalf of Sue. The outlaw leader, however, had never struck Chane as being a man to mistreat women, white or red. Slack was vicious, but under control of McPherson. It narrowed down to Manerube.

This individual swaggered into the camp circle. He had stretched two ropes on Panquitch, in opposite directions, and for the time being the great stallion was tractable. Manerube's blond face showed heat, not all of excitement. He shot a malignant glance at Chane, and leered. The true nature of the man came out when he was on the side in control. As he turned to look Sue up and down, Chane saw the surge of blood ridge his neck. Chane also saw a whisky flask in his hip pocket and a gun in his belt.

"Bud, I heard you weren't boss of your outfit," said Chane, whose wits were active.

"Huh! The hell you did. When an' whar did you hear thet?"

"Reckon it was in Wund, when we drove Melberne's horses in."

"Wal, you heerd wrong," replied McPherson, gruffly, and his glance fell on Manerube with a glint that surely fanned a flame of cunning in Chane's mind.

"Bud, I trapped Panquitch in a deep hole down in the canyon," went on Chane. "It was a dirty trick to play on such a horse. I roped him. We had an awful time. He nearly drowned Brutus and me. But we got him out. And then — what do you think?"

"I've no idee, Weymer," returned the outlaw, eagerly. He had the true rider's love for a horse, the true wrangler's ambition and pride. Only adverse circumstances had made him a thief. Chane knew how to work on his feelings.

"Bud, I let Panquitch go free!" declared Chane, impressively.

"Aw now, Weymer, you can't expect me to believe thet," said McPherson, with a broad smile.

"I swear it's true."

"But you're a wild-hoss wrangler. I've heerd of you for years," declared the outlaw, incredulously.

"I was. But no more. Bud, I'm giving it to you straight. Panquitch was the last wild horse I'll ever rope. I let him go free."

"But what fer? You darned locoed liar!" shouted McPherson, getting red in the face.

"Ask Sue Melberne," replied Chane, recognizing the moment to impress the outlaw. He was intensely interested, curious, doubtful, yet fascinated. He turned to Sue. She was pale, yet composed, and aside from the heaving of her bosom, showed no agitation.

"Girl, what's he givin' me? Guff?"

"No, it's perfectly true. He let Panquitch go. I watched him do it."

"So did I," spoke up Chess, in a loud voice. "He and Sue were out of their heads. They let Panquitch go!"

"Wal, I'll be damned!" ejaculated McPherson. "Shore, girl, I don't see any reason for you to lie about a hoss, even Panquitch. But

426

I gotta know why, if you want me to believe."

"It was my fault," replied Sue, deliberately. "I told Chane — if he'd free Panquitch — I'd be his wife."

"An' he took you up," shouted McPherson, in gleeful wonder.

"Yes. He let me pull the lasso free."

"Wal, I've seen the day I could have done the same, even if it had been Panquitch," boomed McPherson. From the rough, hardened outlaw that speech was a subtle compliment to both Sue and Chane. It hinted, also, of a time when McPherson had not been what he was now. Suddenly he lost that shadow of memory, and wheeled to Manerube, who stood derisive and rancorous, glaring at Chane.

"Didn't I tell you that hoss was tuckered out? Didn't I say he was all wet?"

"Yes, you said so, but I don't have to believe you. And Weymer's a liar," retorted Manerube.

"Sure I'm a liar — when you've got a gun and I haven't," interposed Chane, stingingly.

"Huh! You wouldn't call the little lady a liar, too, would you?" demanded McPherson.

"She would lie and he would swear to it," snapped Manerube.

"Wal, that's no matter, except where I come

from men didn't call girls names. But what I gotta beat into your thick head is this, that Panquitch was a spent horse. An' you never seen it. You thought you roped him when he was good as ever. You never *seen* it!"

"Suppose I didn't," returned Manerube, furiously. "I roped him, spent or not. And he's mine."

"Hell! You're a fine wild-hoss wrangler!" exclaimed McPherson, in disgust. "You don't even get my hunch. Let me say it slow an' plain. In this heah Utah there's a code, the same among hoss thieves as among wranglers. It's love of a grand hoss. An' I'm tellin' you it's a damn shame Panquitch fell into your rope."

"Say, Bud, are you going to let Manerube keep that horse?" demanded Chane, ringingly, sure now of his game. He could play upon this outlaw's feelings as upon an instrument.

"Wha-at?" queried McPherson, as if staggered. The idea Chane launched had struck like a thunderbolt.

"If it's your outfit — if you're the boss, Panquitch is yours," asserted Chane, positively. "That's the law of the range. But even if it wasn't would you let Manerube keep that grand stallion? He'll ruin the horse. He couldn't break him. He couldn't ride him. For this man is not the real thing as a rider. He never was a wrangler. Now, McPherson, listen. You may be a horse thief, but you're a real rider. You have a rider's love for a grand stallion like Panquitch. You have a wrangler's pride in him. You'd never beat Panquitch, now would you?"

"Hell no! I never beat any hoss," shouted the outlaw, hoarsely.

"There you are," announced Chane, with finality, and he threw up his hands. How well he knew the state into which he had thrown McPherson! Chane actually thrilled in the suspense of the issue at stake. His argument had been sound, his persuasion hard for a rider to resist; but he staked most on McPherson's dislike of Manerube. Any honest rider would despise Manerube, but McPherson, hard, strong, matured outlaw, who, bad as he was, would have died for a horse, would hate him.

"Reckon you're talkin' fine, Weymer, but ain't a little of it fer your hoss Brutus," queried McPherson, shrewdly.

"No. I never thought of my horse. But now you mention him, I'll say this. You stole my last bunch of mustangs. Brutus is all I have left. A horse and a saddle! That's the extent of my riches. You'd not be so mean as to rob me of them?"

"Wal, Weymer, I reckon I wouldn't now," he replied, significantly. "Brutus ain't so bad.

But what'd I do with him now? Haw! Haw!"

Chane drew a quick breath of relief, yet the suspense of that argument was in no wise diminished.

Manerube grew black with rage. His light eyes gleamed balefully.

"Bud McPherson, you mean you'll take Panquitch?" he rasped out.

"Wal, you heerd Weymer's idee of the code of the range," replied the outlaw, calmly. With all his acumen and experience he had no fear of Manerube. Rather contempt!

"Code be damned!" yelled Manerube, fiercely. "Panquitch is mine. I roped him."

"Shore. But you're in my outfit, an' what you ketch is mine, if I want it. An' I want Panquitch. Savvy?"

Chane, watching so piercingly, saw a break in Manerube's quivering rage. His body grew rigid before the blackness left his face. If Chane had been in McPherson's boots he would have reacted with subtle keenness to those peculiar changes.

"You're a — horse — thief," panted Manerube, suddenly crouching.

"Wal, wal, wal!" guffawed McPherson, and he bent double with the mirth of the joke. When he straightened up it was to meet the red flame, the blue spurt of Manerube's gun. He uttered a gasp and fell limply, as if his

430

legs had been chopped from under him.

Manerube did not lower the leveled gun. Smoke issued from the dark hole in the barrel. All the men seemed paralyzed, except Chane, who stepped aside, with eyes roving for a weapon in the belts near him. But none showed. Chane read Manerube's ferocious face. It was now gray and set with murderous intent.

"Jump aside, Slack, or I'll kill you," he hissed. "I want Weymer."

Slack frantically leaped aside, leaving Chane exposed. But Manerube did not fire. The smoking gun shook in his nerveless hand, and fell. At that instant, perhaps a fraction of a second before, Chane heard a tiny spat. He knew what it was. A lead bullet striking flesh!

Chane's gaze shot over Manerube's outstretched hand to his face. It was the same, but fixed. Then from the ragged brushy cliff above rang out the crack of a rifle. The echoes clapped back and forth. Over Manerube's glazed blank eyes, in his forehead, appeared a little round hole, first blue, then red. He swayed and fell, full length, face down.

This action was incredibly swift. Before Chane could make a move to rush to Sue he heard another spat. The bullet spanged off bone. Slack was knocked flat. Again the sharp crack of a rifle rang out. It broke the rigidity of that group. Frantically the three left of McPherson's band rushed for their horses. Slack leaped up, bloody of face, wild of mien, and he bellowed:

"It's them hell-hound Piutes! Bud swore they was trailin' us. Get on an' ride!"

Not far behind was he in a leap to the saddle. The horses plunged madly and broke up the canyon. Another shot sounded from the cliff, deadened by the trampling hoofs. Then the swiftly moving dark blot of riders disappeared.

Chane's first thought was for Sue. He ran to her, took her in his arms. She seemed stiff, but her hands suddenly clutched him. Her cheek, which was all he could see as he grasped her, was ashen in hue.

"Come away, Sue dear," he said, gently, half carrying her. "Over here where Chess is . . . you're safe. I'm all right. We're all saved. They went up a different canyon from the one your father took. They won't meet him."

Sue hid her face against his breast while a long shudder went through her.

"How — terrible!" she whispered, hoarsely. "All so — so sudden! Let me sit down. I'm weak and sick. But I won't faint."

"Sure you won't. Just keep your eyes away — from over there," replied Chane, and releasing her he ran to untie Chess's bonds.

"My Gawd! What blew in here?" queried Chess, in decidedly weak voice.

"Kinda stormy and smoky, wasn't it, boy," replied Chane. "I've seen some of that sort of thing. Been in it, too . . . you go to Sue and talk. Get her mind off it."

Chane's next move was to release Lough-bridge, who sat up with popping eyes and incoherent speech. From him Chane ran to the dead men, who had fallen close to each other. He covered them with a canvas. After that Chane gazed up at the cliff whence had come the rifle shots. Thin clouds of blue smoke were floating on the still air, gradually thinning. The cliff was broken and ragged, green with brush, and marked by a wildness of ledge up to the rim. It was not far to the top. Full well Chane knew who had fired that shot fatal to Manerube. But he would never tell, and no one else would ever know. The depths of the canyons hid many mysteries.

He hurried back to Sue, finding her recovered, though she was leaning on Chess's shoulder. Chane promptly relieved him of the burden.

"Humph! I thought she was in the family now," protested Chess.

"Boy, you wander in mind," returned Chane, softly.

"If only dad would come!" exclaimed Sue,

in anxious dread.

"Well, he's coming," said Chane, gladly. "Look up the canyon. Did you ever see your dad run like that? He's scared, Sue, either for himself or us."

Sue gave vent to a smothered sob of relief and then broke down.

Chapter 17

Melberne amused Chane, and appeared to be a fascinating object to Chess. The leader of the outfit had returned out of breath, and if Chane was any judge of men, both frightened and furious. When he caught his breath he blurted out many queries, but vouchsafed no information about himself. Chane's observant eye, however, noted Melberne's skinned and bruised wrists, and how conscious he was of them, a circumstance undoubtedly due to pain.

Bud McPherson had lied to Chane. The outlaws had happened to run into Melberne and had tied him up. Chane grew more convinced of this as the moments passed. Besides Melberne's telltale wrists, which he had probably skinned by working free of a tight rope, he had come back minus his gun. Moreover, his relief at the sight of Sue safe and well, though pale, was so great as to approach collapse. Lastly, when Chane had pulled aside the canvas to expose Manerube and McPherson, lying so ghastly and suggestive, he had cursed them under his breath.

But the amusing part of this sequence was the argument between Melberne and Lough-bridge, and Chess's deep concern.

"I'm sorry, Jim, you shore have queered yourself with me," declared Melberne for at least the tenth time. His demeanor, however, was not in harmony with his hard words. He strode to and fro nervously, as was his wont when perturbed.

"But, Mel, this here Manerube made a damn fool of you, same as me," persisted Loughbridge.

"Shore I acknowledge that. But he didn't make me double-cross you."

"I didn't. You ain't fair. We couldn't agree, about money mostly, an' you fired me out of your outfit. I leave it to Chess, here. You ain't jest fair."

"Boss, if you'll excuse me, I think it was more temper with you than justice," replied Chess, with immense gravity.

"Huh! Wal, I'll be darned!" quoth Melberne, surveying the boy in great disfavor. "I reckon you'd like to see Loughbridge homestead with us over there at Nightwatch Spring."

"That'd be fair and square of you," returned Chess, losing his dignity of a judge.

436

"An' fetch Ora along to live with him, huh?" went on Melberne, ironically.

"I should smile," answered Chess, with an anticlimax of weakness.

"See heah, young man, you've got good stuff, but you talk too much. I've a mind to fire you."

"Aw now — boss," appealed Chess, abjectly.

"Wal, if you don't marry Ora before spring I will fire you," growled Melberne.

Then he turned to his former partner. "Jim, I reckon I've no call to crow over you. I've had my lesson. An' if you've had yours, mebbe we'll both profit by it. My fault is temper, an' yours is a little too much fondness for money. Let's begin over again, each for himself. It's a new country. You're welcome to homestead in my canyon. There's room for another rancher. Some day before long there'll be a settlement west of Wund. An' that'll make our problem easier."

Panquitch startled Chane, and all the others, with one of his ringing neighs; and with head, ears, and mane erect he faced up the canyon.

Shrill whistles answered him. Chane espied a troop of wild horses coming out of the shadow.

"By golly! There's Panquitch's band," said

Chane, pointing. "They're looking for him. They'll pass us . . . everybody lie low."

Chane crouched behind a rock with Sue, who whispered that Panquitch should be free to go with them. It did seem to Chane that the straining stallion would free himself from Manerube's ropes. For some moments the wild horses could not be seen, owing to the fact that Chane and Sue were low down. At last, however, they came in sight, trotting cautiously, wary as always, but not yet having caught scent of the camp. Only a faint breeze stirred and that came down the canyon. The whistling of Panquitch must have been a factor in their cautious approach. At the junction of the canyons the space was fully a hundred yards wide, and owing to the stream bed, somewhat lower on the side opposite the camp. The wild horse band worked down this side, trotting, with heads erect, until they caught scent of the camp, then burst into headlong flight, and in a dusty cloud, with a clattering roar they sped by, and down the canyon to disappear.

"Sue, wasn't it great?" queried Chane, as he got up.

But Sue had not been looking at the fleet band of wild horses; her startled gaze was fixed on Panquitch.

"Oh, Chane, look! He's broken one of the

ropes!" cried Sue.

Chane wheeled in time to see the remnant of broken lasso fall off the superb tawny shoulder. The other lasso was round the noble arched neck of the stallion and had now become taut. Panquitch reared and lunged back with all his weight. As luck would have it, the rope broke at the noose. The stallion fell heavily, then raised on his forefeet, with mouth open. The broken noose hung loose. He was not yet sure of freedom.

Chess broke the silence with a wailing: "Oh, the ropes were rotten. They broke. He'll get away . . . gimme a rope. A rope! A rope!"

"Boy, keep still," shouted Chane, sternly. "Can't you see Panquitch was never born to be roped?"

The stallion painfully got to his feet. As the broken noose slipped from his neck he jumped as if stung. Then he walked through camp. He shied at the canvas covering the dead men, and breaking into a trot, he headed down the canyon.

"Wal, I cain't pretend to savvy you, Chane," observed Melberne, scratching his head in his perplexity. "But shore I will say this. Somehow I'm glad you let him go."

"Damn it! So'm I!" yelled Chess, suddenly red of face, as if he had been unjustly accused.

"But I — I was so crazy to keep him!"

Chane turned to Sue with a smile.

"He's gone, my dear. Suppose we ride down to the slope where he'll climb up to the mesa. There's work to do here that I'd rather you didn't see."

Melberne approved of that idea for Sue. "An' when you come back we'll be packed to change camp."

Not until Sue had ridden at quite a brisk trot, keeping up with Brutus, all the way down to the oval break in the canyon, did her blood warm and beat out the dark blot of horror in her mind.

But at the foot of the beautiful slope of wavy rock all that turgid emotion fell away from her, as if it had never been. She had grown weak, but now she was strong. The purple heights above, gold-rimmed under the sun, inspired her as before, only now with something added to the wild joy of freedom.

"Follow me close, sweetheart," called Chane. "I see Panquitch far above. If we hurry we can reach the top and watch him climb the mesa."

"Ah, Chane, you'll never lose me now, on any kind of trails," called Sue, in reply, and urged her horse close to Brutus.

To and fro, across and around, up and

down, far to this side, and back to the other, onward and upward they rode over the smooth waves and hollows of red sandstone. As they climbed, the purple and amber lights grew brighter, and the shadows of the canyons below grew deeper. They reached the zone of cream and yellow rock, crumbling like baked clay under the hoofs of the horses. Out of the dark depths they rose to the sunset-flushed heights.

"Oh, where is Panquitch?" Sue kept calling. But he had always just gone over a wave of rock.

All above the corrugated world of wind-worn stone streamed fan-shaped bars and bands of light, centering toward and disappearing over the height of ridge they had almost attained. Broken massed clouds floated in the west, dark-purple, silver-rimmed, golden-edged, in a sea of azure blue. The lights of sunset were intensifying. Sue felt that she rode up the last curved wave of an opal sea. She saw Chane shade his eyes from the fires of the sun. Like a god of the riders he seemed to her, bareheaded, his face alight, his sharp profile against the background of gold. Then she mounted to Chane's side, and it was as if in one step she had surmounted a peak.

All the forces of nature seemed to have united in one grand spectacle — the rugged canyon country of colored rock waved level with the setting sun, and above it, from west to north, loomed the cloud-piercing bulk of Wild Horse Mesa.

"Panquitch! I see him, Sue," said Chane, his voice ringing deep. "He's all alone. His band has gone up . . . look! The fold in the wall! It could never be seen except when the sun shines as now. What a trail! Even the Piutes do not know it. Hard smooth rock over the bench, and then the zigzag up that crack . . . see, he shines gold and black in the sun!"

At last Sue's straining gaze was rewarded by clear sight of Panquitch climbing, apparently the very wall of the mesa. With abated breath Sue watched him, conscious of more in the moment than just the climbing freedom of a wild horse. But it was beyond her. It led her thoughts beyond emotions, deep into the dim past of her inheritance. But she had loved Panquitch or some creature like him in a world before this.

The intense flare of gold changed as the sun began to sink behind cloud and rim. It yielded to the wondrous lilac haze. Sue cried out in a transport. Panquitch, too, seemed less a wild horse, more of an unreal creature, giving life to the grandeur and desolation of the naked rock ribs of the earth.

"He's almost on top," said Chane, joyfully.

He clung to the physical thing — to the flesh and blood Panquitch, to his pursuit and capture and release, to his recapture and escape, to the long, winding, mysterious and hidden trail in and out of the canyons, to the wonderful wall of Wild Horse Mesa.

Sue felt all these, deeply, poignantly, but beyond them, inexplicable and vague, was the spiritual thing Panquitch typified. She endowed him with soul. She had gazed at him, recognizing in him something within herself.

Panquitch came out on top of the rim, sharply silhouetted against the blue sky, and stood a moment looking down, with his long mane and tail streaming in the wind. The lilac haze lent him unreality, but the uplift of his head gave him life. Wild and grand he seemed to Sue, fitting that last stand of wild horses. He moved against the sky; he was gone.

"Oh, Panquitch, stay up there always!" called Sue.

Chane smiled upon her. "Sweetheart, I'd stake my life he'll never feel another rope."

"We alone know his trail to the heights. And we never will tell?"

"Never, Sue."

"You will not show dad how to get on top of Wild Horse Mesa?" she begged. "So he could run sheep and cattle up there?"

"I promise, Sue. Why, do you imagine I could ever become that much of a rancher? It may be long before another rider, or an Indian, happens on this secret. Maybe never. Some distant day airships might land on Wild Horse Mesa. But what if they do? An hour of curiosity, an achievement to boast of — then gone! Wild Horse Mesa rises even above this world of rock. It was meant for eagles, wild horses — and for lonely souls like mine."

Slowly the transformation of sunset worked its miracles of evanescent change and exquisite color. Gold and silver fire faded, died away. The sun sank below the verge. Then from out of the depths where it had gone, rose the afterglow, deepening the lilac haze to purple.

"Chane, you have made Wild Horse Mesa yours," said Sue. "Millions of men can never take it from you. As for me — Panquitch seems mine. He's like my heart or something in my blood."

"Yes, I think I understand you," he replied, dreamily. "We must labor — we must live as people have lived before. But these thoughts are beautiful . . . you are Panquitch and I am Wild Horse Mesa."